December 2014

To Robin

Becoming Sand

LG Pomerleau

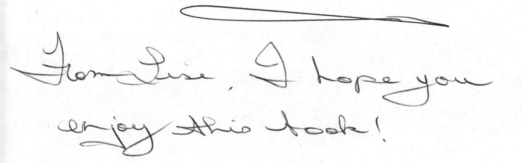

From Lise, I hope you enjoy this book!

4th Floor Press, Inc.
www.4thfloorpress.com

Library and Archives Canada Cataloguing in Publication

Pomerleau, L. G., 1957-
Becoming sand / LG Pomerleau.

Also issued in electronic format.
ISBN 978-1-897530-33-7

I. Title.

PS8631.O474B43 2012   C813'.6   C2012-906634-6

Published by 4th Floor Press, Inc.
www.4thfloorpress.com
1st Printing 2012
Printed in Canada
Cover Art and Interior Art by Jeremy Mayne
www.3degreestudio.com

Dedication

To the pioneers, on both sides of our family, whose dreams turned to sand, but whose fortitude lives on, in their descendants.

Pour Jessica

Author's Note

This book is a thirty-year labour of love. It represents my past, my ancestors' past, and the history of settlement in Québec and Alberta. As a child, I felt powerless and trapped. Books and writing saved me. Thank you to two teachers, Mrs. Kassian, Grade 4 and Mrs. Wold, Grade 7, who encouraged me in my dreams of becoming a writer, and inspired my desire to pursue teaching as a career. Thank you to my dear soulmate, Jeremy, whose love has sustained me through the years and whose beautiful art, most appropriately, graces this, my first published book. Thank you to my agents, Johanna Bates and Anne Bougie-Johnson, who believed in the strength of this story, and guided me through to its publication.

Becoming Sand

River in constant motion – racing
   Onward, away
Rock – stable, quiet, still, solid,
   Tumbled, heated, cooled, erupted
   expelled, dropped…to arrive
At this spot on the bank – and remain
Silent testament
To some mysterious process
We cannot grasp.
How did you come to be here, at this place? This time?
How many millennia have you
Journeyed alone. Free of your
Mother, Stone.
At what point did you
Break?
Then, what forces shaped you,
Altered your form?
How did you become
your Self?
Your colour, shape, texture, bruises,
imperfect perfection,
unique.
A rock like no other
abandoned on the gravel bed.

Seemingly unimportant, like so many others

Discarded by the river, in one place and time.

Then, you endure more:

Driving rain, numbing ice, blasting wind, cracking heat...

Even now, at rest – you are becoming.

Yet the more your inner beauty is revealed,

The closer you are

to sand.

But I come upon you,

Stumble, stop and stare

Marvel at your face, your skin,

Your body, the designs of your secret heart.

Enraptured, in love,

I draw you near

And bring you home.

You warm to my touch

Brighten under my gaze

Rubbed clean in my cold, wet fingers,

you sing to me

Without words.

There - rest you safe upon my mantle

Huddled with the other darlings of your kind.

Rescued from the vagaries of the river and the weather

That could take you far away.

A selected miracle.

Held in slow motion

but not arrested.

A chunk of time displayed.

Halted for a moment

In a still-frame

To be admired, yet all the while,

Becoming sand.

The very air I breathe will erase your curves, your lines, your

jagged face,

as together we turn

to sand.

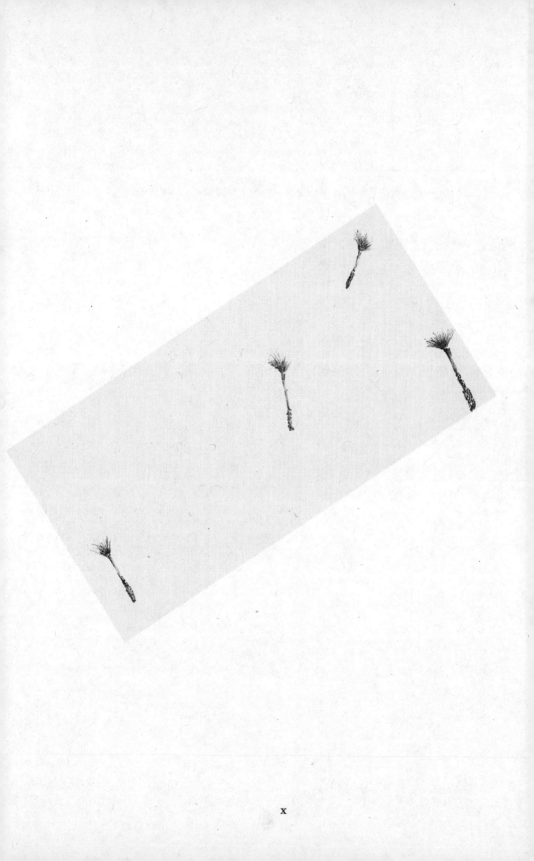

Prologue

Vinland, New World, 1009 A.D.

"Freya! Come!"

"Bran, come! Hurry, my husband is calling!"

"Freya! Where is that infernal woman? We depart on the ebb-tide! Freya!"

"Bran, oh, oh, I feel it. There, come, come. Faster, faster, that's it," she cried between gritted teeth, riding hard aboard the man's bare hips. As soon as he sighed, she rolled off into the leaves, her skirts falling back down around her.

"Quick now, move! You head back first. I will follow shortly behind you so he doesn't suspect," she urged, helping her lover up with an extended hand, then practically pushing him back toward the shore where the ship awaited.

Obediently, he scurried off, while she searched the foliage for dock leaves to clean the traces of her encounter from between her legs. Silently, she cursed the unfamiliar landscape, as she had to tear out some unknown leafy plant by the roots and simply hope it was not poisonous. The last thing she needed was a rash to contend with on the journey back up the river and across the sea to Greenland.

She had to bunch three layers of thick garments into her lap, her smock, gown and apron dress, while squatting next to a tree to relieve herself. Leaning one shoulder against its trunk for support, she struggled to wipe away the evidence of her encounter as best she could without toppling over. Her muscular legs trembled with the effort of maintaining the awkward pose and sweat trickled into her eyes. From his perch on one of the lower branches, a bird observed her movements with sparkling black eyes, cocking its head from side to side and chirping as if to say, "What are you up to, you silly girl?"

The bird's bright red breast charmed her. "Your breast is the same colour as my caftan. I just love red, don't you, sweetling?" she cooed. She wished to feel its soft grey back under her hand. She rose slowly to approach it without frightening it away, when another shout nearby made her gasp and create a flurry of wings just above her head. A tiny grey feather drifted toward her upraised face. She caught it and tucked it in the belt of her apron dress, as a memento. Then she quickly retrieved her caftan from the ground where she and Bran had made their temporary bed. As she turned toward the harsh voice, she whirled the wide strip of fabric in the air, inadvertently catching it on a thorny branch. She had to wrench it free before she could rush down the hill to meet her husband on his way up. She had just finished re-coiling her red-gold hair, awkwardly twisting it against the nape of her damp neck as she stumbled ahead, when she ran straight into Thorfinn's broad, hairy chest.

"Curse you, woman, we were about to leave without you. Where have you been and why didn't you answer my call? I thought the Skraelings had got you, for sure! Now I don't know whether to hug you or smack you!" He started a laugh, which was cut short by the flash of his wife's green eyes and the lash of her sharp tongue.

"Smack me and you'll regret it, husband. Can't a woman have some time to herself? There are women's matters that need attending to, things that can't be done in the close confines of the boat, with all you men in the way. I'll come when I am bloody good and ready, and not before. Just you mind your own business. I can look after myself well enough," she said, patting the dagger in the belt at her waist. Noticing that her cap was tucked into her waistband, she casually tugged it out and began arranging it over her hair.

Clearing her throat, she added, "Besides, there's not a Skraeling in sight. Even they wouldn't want to live in this miserable land. Where are the open pasturelands Bjorn spoke of? He probably lied, puffing himself up for glory. Here there is nothing, but rocks and trees and unknown bugs, especially these wretched flies that bite and suck blood. Ugh! Take that! Ha, won't bite me again now, will you? Ouch, slapped myself too hard. Well, I for one am glad to be going. But at least we know of another source of lumber to build our ships, if need be. The fishing's good, but it's no better than on the sea coast, where it's way less trouble than down river. And besides, we need pasture land for our livestock, not more salmon, though they are delicious. Anyway, just because we haven't seen any inhabitants, doesn't mean there aren't any, and since they think we tried to poison them last winter, with milk of all things, they no longer welcome us with open arms. Here we are, trading in good faith with fresh, sweet milk, they puke it up and shit themselves and then blame us! Savage brutes, I will never understand..." her voice trailed off as she noticed that her husband was staring at her, probably in surprise at her unusual verbosity. Worried that she had aroused his suspicion, she turned her head and pretended to cough, then stepped around Thor's massive frame, making for the shore.

"Well, come on then, let's get going, if you're all in such a lather to go. I'm ready now. Are all the water barrels full? We might as well head for home, I guess. This voyage was a lost cause."

Standing on the deck of the longship as the men rowed backwards against the current to retreat from the land, Freydis allowed the breeze to free her loosely braided hair. She shook the wild curls all about her head, and ran her fingers through the locks of hair which had been compared to the color of wild strawberries. Letting her hair down broke the rules of Norse decorum for a married woman. She didn't care. She revelled in the stares of the crewmen standing nearby and the slaves hauling on the oars. Deliberately thrusting out her chest, she drew biting draughts of air into her lungs, allowing herself to become almost dizzy with the sensation of deep breathing. But not quite. The motion of the ship, the sun in her face, the strength of her arms supporting her on the wooden rail, everything felt exquisite.

Leaning into the wind, her heart surged with joy. Her restless spirit had been invigorated by her recent adventures, both on land and at sea. As a female, she knew how lucky she was to be allowed on an exploratory voyage at all. Of course, her renowned beauty, sailing skills and winning personality didn't hurt either, she thought, grinning inwardly. Anyway, luck ran in her family. Weren't they calling her half-brother Leifur, "Leif the Lucky?" Just because he had found his way out of a storm when the others didn't! That wasn't luck, but ability, passed on to all three of her siblings and herself, from their famous father, who had taught them well. Why should the gods get credit for it? But it was a good moniker anyway and added to the prestige of her family.

Still, shouldn't they be giving her a nickname and singing her praises also? She had lived in an uncharted settlement for three years, establishing trade with the wild men who lived there. Shouldn't she be renowned for singlehandedly fighting off the Skraelings, when they had turned on her people and chased them to their boats, by facing them down, screaming, baring her breast and brandishing a sword in front of her swollen, pregnant belly! Her brave escort of warriors, including her husband, had abandoned her on the beach! Running for their lives to the ship, leaving her to her fate! They had had the gall to congratulate her afterwards for her quick reflexes and courage. Bah! She had scorned them for their shrivelled balls. She would have dispatched some of the Skraelings, she was sure, before she was through, if they too hadn't run off in terror! Terrified of her! Worthless men! That tale should be told around campfires for time immemorial, and would be, as long as she had breath to tell the stories of her travels.

Well, she wouldn't quite tell everything, she smiled to herself, tugging her woollen cloak closely about her chest and catching her lover's scent. Her fingers frantically searched the fabric for her talisman, the metal pin that not only held the garment firmly around her throat, but also, she believed, protected her from evil. A first sign of ill fortune—the woven edge of her caftan was now tattered and frayed. How had that happened? Then she remembered the bramble that had caught it in her hurried flight back to the path.

Gone: the piece that had been passed to her from her father, Eirik. Perhaps the brooch had belonged to his father before him, for it was obviously very old, a simple but beautifully worked metal brooch whose whorled face had been worn smooth by her constant rubbing. Even though he could not acknowledge her as his legitimate heir, he had given her his name, Eiriksdottir, and the brooch as a gift. That was all she had left of him, since he had died of the gods only knew what. A lump rose in her throat. Her admiration for him was boundless. He had killed the sons of that cheating bastard Thorgest and been exiled from Iceland for it. But if he had not, Greenland might never have become a settlement, where Eirik had lived better than a king! As his daughter, his status as "The Red" had allowed her to come on this trip and prove her mettle as an explorer and trader.

"Shit," she cursed aloud, drawing a look from a crewman, who received a scowl in return.

"Stupid, stupid, stupid!" she admonished herself, stamping her leather-clad foot on the planks of the deck. How could she have left it pinned to her cloak when she had gone ashore? She had known the catch was loose! Now it had fallen off in a strange land to which she would probably never return! Why hadn't she noticed it missing before now, when there might still have been time to go back and search for it?

This boded ill. Her face flushed with anger, at herself for her uncharacteristic carelessness, at Bran for, for being a man, and at the wasted voyage that had cost her a prized possession without yielding any personal profits. With her source of luck gone, she would have to be more careful. Upon their return to the village, Bran must be called off, passed on to her younger sister or cousin, and sworn to secrecy, upon his life. She regretted that this tryst had been their last, as she smoothed the downy feather against her bodice, brought it to her lips for a kiss, and then released it to the wind. Bran amused her and deceiving her husband added to her pleasure. She wondered if this lover would be wise enough to hold his tongue. If not, she might have to resort to other measures. She could always accuse him of rape and demand that her husband avenge her honour. She could easily shame Thor into killing Bran, as custom demanded. He was no match for her, never had been. Yes, that is how she would manage the problem, if it arose.

In the meantime, she would have to concoct an excuse for returning to this place, next summer at the latest, in order to search for the brooch. She would tell the Greenlanders about the fine timber and surely one of her brothers would see the profit in making the journey, equipped with enough men and an extra ship to bring back timber. But how would she find this spot again? As the ship headed for deeper waters, she frantically searched the receding shore for a landmark. Nothing faced her but an unbroken line of rocks, trees, and drifting clouds. Only by luck would she ever recognize the precise landing place, the next time.

No, there, just along the shoreline, an outcrop of rock in the shape of a dragon's head! Just like the dragon carved on the prow of this very drakkar, which would bring her safely home to Greenland. Perfect, she thought to herself, a sign she could not miss. The dragon lord of this strange land would be waiting right here, when she returned to find her treasure.

Part I

The Farm: Central Alberta, 1962

Chapter One

"Wehui, weuuhui, wehuiwhi, whui, whui, whuiii, wehui ..."
- a lilting birdsong spiralled in the open window with the breeze,
awakening the child. Turning her head on the pillow, she gazed
sleepily at the dust fairies whirling in the shafts of light. She pushed
up on one elbow to look outside. The spring air tingled in her nose
as she drew a breath deep into her tiny chest.

She revelled in this bed, and was reluctant to leave it. Here, chez
Grandmère, she always slept soundly. Best of all was the coverlet,
awash with faded brown images of cowboys and horses. She often rode
those same horses in her dreams. This had been her father's bed, his
room. Snuggling into the sunken mattress, she pulled the sheets up
closer to her nose to take in their scent, running her legs back and
forth under the blankets to feel the rough cotton against her skin.
Dear Grandmère believed that sunshine was the only way to brighten
sheets, so if it was sunny on washday, she spread them on the lawn
and placed rocks along the edges to hold them down. The child loved
helping to anchor the giant, white squares and then spending the
afternoon running along the green alleyways in between. Just another
of the exotic delights she enjoyed while staying with her grandmother.

Pushing downward with palms at her sides, she slid her back
up against the wooden headboard and smiled, delighting in the
awareness that she had spent one more night in Papa's old bedroom.
She gazed around at the magazine pictures of antique planes and
cars tacked to the walls. From the dresser the model plane that her
father had built when he was a boy begged her to touch it, but she
knew better, and just shook her head in admiration and wonder.
How had Papa done it, and when? Sitting up straighter, she smelled
the musty mothballs in the open wardrobe from across the room,
and unconsciously pinched her nostrils shut. Deliberately, she kept

her eyes on the sunny window, but she didn't have to turn around to see Jesus behind her, above the bed. She always avoided looking at the thin, naked body nailed to the cross, wherever it happened to appear in the house. Crucifixes were hung in every room, above every bed and every doorway, for protection, Grandmère said, though she never explained what against. The bleeding hands and feet and the downcast eyes made her feel sad. She much preferred the guardian angel in the picture above the dresser: a beautiful lady wearing a golden halo who pointed toward heaven, as her fluffy wings held her atop pink, billowing clouds. Grandmère had shown her the picture and said emphatically, "Voici ton ange gardien. Here is your angel, who will protect you, all your life. All you mus' do is pray to her, an' she will 'ear you."

"I wonder if you were Daddy's angel too?" she mused aloud. She imagined her father waking up in this tiny bed, swinging his long, hairy legs out to put his giant feet down on the icy floor. The birdsong filled the room once more, persuading her to kick free of the covers. Silently daring herself, she touched her naked feet to the wooden floor. She giggled, for it was surprisingly warm in the morning sun. She raced across the room to the open window, aching to find out what could fill the air with such a piercing, glorious sound. She caught only a flash of yellow as her movements startled the bird from its perch on the telephone wire. Momentarily disappointed, she resolved to ask Grandmère the name of the bird, as she thrust more than half her small body across the sash to inhale the farmy smells outdoors. She balanced on her narrow hips, grasping the ledge with both hands, and luxuriated in leaning as far over the edge of the wooden sill as she dared.

Grandmère believed in keeping the windows wide open all night: "Bes' for to sleep an' much bet'ter to stay 'ealty an' strong," resulting in a silent battle of wills between her grandmother and her mother.

"Not even a screen for heaven's sake!" her mother would complain.

"What if a bat flies in at night? Not to mention all the mosquitos! The draft can't be good for the child! That woman and her old-fashioned ideas! I get so tired...!" and the window would be slammed

4

shut. But never in Grandmère's presence.

The young mother would have screamed with fright if she had seen her daughter at this moment, tipped half out of the second-floor window. The child might indeed have fallen to the cement sidewalk below. As it was... Deep breath—ahh! First the spicy scent of rock roses in the flowerbed beneath the window, then the steam rising from the damp cement. Slowly, layer after layer of smell: grass, pine trees, gravel road, then, ever-present and bitter, the pig barn. Lifting her body still higher, she let her feet lift off the floor to launch herself into the ice blue sky, just for an instant. Then, with the breath squeezed out of her body, she dropped and landed backwards, whisking ahead of her the smell of breakfast from the kitchen below. Such a buzzy, dizzy feeling—never mind the bump on the back of her head! It was worth it! Mmmm, breakfast! She performed a clumsy somersault before scrambling to her feet, leaned down quickly to grab her rumpled clothes from the wicker chair next to the door and headed into the hallway.

Here the light was sombre, admitted by small panes of frosted glass in the gables at either end of the roof, and through one open bedroom door. Even so, the hardwood floor and oak banister gleamed. It was like walking on toffee in bare feet, a delight to slide on in socks. She zigzagged towards the bathroom, strumming the rungs of the banister, fondling the glass door handles of the two closed, empty bedrooms, stopping to sail the lace curtains above the bookcase at the end of the hall. She ran a stubby finger along the top row of leather spines with the shiny gold letters, before she tiptoed past her parents' room and into the stark, white cubicle.

This room always felt cold as a cave. The black and white tiled floor next to the tub was covered by a smelly sheepskin rug. Convinced it was the skin of one of the farm dogs, she hopped off instantly every time her mother lifted her onto it from the dreaded bathtub, which she hated even more than the mat. That giant stood on its stubby legs clutching glass balls in its claws, waiting to invite her into its stained, noisy nightmare. The pedestal sink stood high above the child, but her grandmother had placed an old milk stool by the window for her use. She was just able to turn the shiny, four-pronged tap enough to dip her fingers under cold running water. She didn't bother to turn it off again but ran her hands across her face and through her short hair. Then she yanked her nightgown over her head and let it fall at her feet, before stepping into her cord pants. Without zipping them up, she sat on the stool to pull on one black sock, then one blue sock before hoisting herself onto the cold toilet seat. As her feet dangled above the asymmetric black and white chequerboard below, she awkwardly tried to button her plaid shirt while peeing into the bowl. Warm urine trickled against her leg as she made a desperate reach for the toilet paper, which slipped from her fingers to continue spinning on the wooden roller and then pool on the floor. Her greatest fear was that she would fall off the toilet with her pants down and someone would have to rescue her. Added to that, the toilet's flush terrified her, echoing from the upper water cabinet to the monster beneath the tub, so she had begun to avoid it. Hopping down from the high seat, she quickly zipped her pants, flung open the heavy door, smashing it against the toilet seat, as she had been warned not to, and escaped.

"I wonder if I can help feed the pigs today?" she thought, as she skated down the hall, delighting in the tingle in the soles of her feet. She grabbed the carved top of the square banister and swung to a stop in front of her aunt's open door at the head of the stairs.

"Bonjour, Chantale," she offered timidly.

"Ma'll skin you if you keep whalin' on that banister like that, ya know. And quit slammin' that goddamn bathroom door, I've told you a million times," came the sullen reply. Jocelyne merely shrugged her shoulders, and then sat on her bottom to descend the stairs one at a time, headlong into the clouds of steaming coffee, cigarette smoke, and frying bacon.

"Morning, Grandmère."

"Bonjour, chérie. Must you go tumping down dose stairs comme ça chaque matin? It 'tis so lout and it will spoil de car-pet, tu sais. 'Ow many time I tell you, come down on your feet, pas sur ta derriere! Where is Maman? I start de egg any minoute. An' Chantale? I swear dose girl don' know how to get out of bed in da mor-ning. In my time, why we..."

"I heard Maman, Gram. She'll be down right away. Do we have beans this morning?"

"Oui, oui. Such a one for bean, I never saw. I tink it tis de sirop d'érable, de sweet maple syrup from Québec dat makes dem taste si délicieux, n'est-ce pas? Look in da pot at de back of da stove. I will show your Maman how to make it for you, since you like it so well. You're a real French Canadienne girl, eh, ma Jocelyne, born wit' a taste for de bean in 'er mout. Move back now, I put da grease in for de egg."

Though her broken English was heavily salted with French, the child understood her grandmother perfectly. She watched her closely, mirrored her movements and mimicked her language. Eager to see her white and gold teeth flash in a ready smile, the child never stopped chattering in her grandmother's presence. She especially loved the way her name was pronounced in French—not Josie, or Joss or Josseleen, as most people said it, but Joss - lyne. The right way. The way her grandmother had named her.

The old woman moved efficiently about the large bright kitchen, preparing breakfast for eight people. Her white apron was spotless, over an equally clean and pressed flowered dress. Her small, powerful hands seemed to move by themselves as she stood at the counter, slicing bread, turning bacon, pouring coffee. All in easy, relaxed gestures, never hurried or out of control, making everything happen with no apparent effort at all. Her old-fashioned high-topped black shoes moved lightly across the floor, never leaving a mark or making a sound. She wore the high-heeled boots like slippers, both inside and outside the house. Beneath her skirt, the dark seam of her beige stockings was just visible, tracing a perfect line up each thin leg. Wispy grey bangs curled neatly above green eyes framed by wire-rimmed spectacles.

Jocelyne glowed with pride as she exclaimed, "A real French-Canadian girl! Tu penses, Grandmaman, really? Hey, if breakfast is ready, can I ring the bell for Richard? Please, please!"

Ringing the old dinner bell suspended in the yard, a relic from the days of the threshing crews, was a ritual she loved. Ding, ding, ding, ding! The louder, the better! Imagine-toi, Grandmère had told her, when the bell used to bring twenty men in from the fields at harvest time, all hungry and waiting to be fed. So many people to sit down, they had to put boards over the table, and have lunch in two shifts. Grandmère and her daughters were duty-bound to feed and serve them all a huge lunch and supper in exchange for their labour. A long time ago, when Grandpère was still alive. She and Grandpère were pioneers, the first to homestead this section of Alberta prairie. When Jocelyne rang the dinner bell, she imagined the sound calling all those people back to the house, maybe even Grandpère, whom she would have loved to meet. Instead, it just summoned Uncle Richard from the pig barn.

"Non, pas maintenant. It will wak'en your brodder. I 'aven't 'eard 'im cry dis mor'ning'. En tout cas, I imag'ine Richard is on 'is way. 'Is stomach 'as a good nose. 'E been at chore since six o'clock, of course. Ah, tu vois?" The screen door squawked as a man entered the kitchen, slapping white dust from his clothes with one hand as he removed his hat with the other.

"You see, like I tol' you, 'e must 'ave smelt da bean aussi, hein? Now, dose girl. Where are 'dey? Jocelyne, fetch Chantale an' tell 'er I want 'er at dis ta-ble toute de suite. Et ben, Richard, ça ben était à matin..."

The girl tuned out their French as she headed back toward the staircase, and bumped headfirst into her younger sister. Behind Pauline was her mother and baby Nicolas.

"Jocelyne, watch where you're going! What are you going upstairs for now? Grandma will be ready with breakfast. And we mustn't keep her waiting." Her mother's voice struck sharply. She bounced Nicolas almost violently on her hip at the top of the stairs. Jocelyne smiled at her brother's bobbing head.

"She is. She told me to fetch Chantale."

"Well, good luck with that, if she's anything like her usual cheery self. Hurry and call her then and come right back down," she whispered harshly.

Jocelyne slid past her mother's distended stomach to mount the stairs. The door was closed now. She tapped with a fat, round knuckle and called, "Chantale, Grandmaman says hurry."

"Yeah, yeah, I'm comin' for Chris' sake."

To avoid her aunt's angry morning glare, Jocelyne turned around and slid back down the stairs on her bum, rising just before the last few steps so as not to be caught doing that again. Beneath the swinging, half-sized door separating the stairway from the kitchen, she glimpsed Richard's enormous misshapen woollen socks trailing straw across the linoleum floor. She heard her mother's cooing voice, trying to calm her baby brother screaming above the lilt of the adult discussion. Her mother's feet and thin legs were shaking violently against one of the chrome chair legs.

Suddenly, her Grandmother's tone changed and, much louder than the crying baby, she said in English, "Dat child is suffer from too much gas, like I tol' you, Suzanne. 'Tis too bad you didn' nurse him, den you wouldn' 'ave all dis problème. I will never understan' you girl nowadays not wanting to nurse your bébé. It seem selfish, à mon avis, I tink. But de doctor today don' advise it, je sais. Me, I nurse all six, an' I never 'ad a child scream like dat alla da time. What will you feed 'im dis mor-ning? 'E trew up ever'ting you give 'im yesta-day. Maybe 'e cutting 'im some teet already, hein? C'est possible, even if 'e 'as only two mont' now. We rub brandy on 'is gum, dat usually 'elp a lot."

"He's kinda young to be cutting teeth, don't you think? But maybe you're right. I think he's just really hungry, though. He slept all through the night at least," the younger woman softly replied. Jocelyne hardly recognized her mother when she spoke to her grandmother. She was like another person, so quiet and shy, a stranger.

As her mind absently registered her mother's subdued tone, she heard Chantale slam her door at the top of the stairs. The swinging doors were flung aside, and Chantale flopped down into her place at the table, next to the highchair. Across the table, her mother was again bouncing Nicolas on her knee and spooning cereal into his mouth. He sucked it up greedily, his face a gaping hole. On her high stool, Pauline, Jocelyne's younger sister tapped her arm with a spoon to get attention. Jocelyne ignored her sister completely, turning to her uncle.

"Hi, Richard! How are the pigs this morning? I can't wait to see if there are any new babies. Did that old sow sit on any more of hers? I think that is so mean! What a stupid, fat pig not to see her own babies and crush them to death! By the way, remember you said we were going to bury those kittens today? 'Member, you promised, and they're still underneath that pine tree by the road. I went and looked yesterday to set up my doll's picnic, and I still can't because, um, they're still there. I want to have a fruneral, frun, fooneral, anyways I want to say prayers and stuff when we bury them. I think we better do it right away because they look awful and they stink so bad. They have flies all over them. Those mean dogs! I hate those dogs! Next time that cat has kittens I'm going to find them and put them in a box so they…"

"Oh, this is really nice conversation to eat breakfast to. Dead pigs and stinking cats. Oh, this really gives me an appetite for my greasy eggs." Chantale's voice was vicious. She slumped further down on the red vinyl seat and lit a cigarette. Her small, slanted eyes darted angrily from Jocelyne's to Suzanna's face.

"Can't you teach this brat that we don't talk about guts and gore at the table? And when is she going to learn to flush that damn toilet? I'm sick of going into the bathroom after her mess, piss all over the seat, worse than havin' a goddamn baby … "

"Chantale, ça suffit! Dat's e-nough. Sit down nicely at de ta-ble an' eat now. Jocelyne, 'elp me put de bread an' de bean on. 'Ere, now we sit an' eat an' 'ave nice con-vers-a-tion." Grandmère's voice was even, but stern.

No one spoke. Chantale hung her head over her plate and between puffs, shoved pieces of torn bread into her mouth. She looked up from time to time through strands of long, greasy brown hair. Richard, arm around his plate as though fearful someone might steal his breakfast, proceeded to devour forkfuls of food. Jocelyne was reminded of the way the dogs growled over their dinner bowls, fending each other off. The old woman sat upright in her chair and dipped bread daintily into her beans with her left hand, pinky raised, shaking her head at Chantale from time to time.

Sitting on her knees, head lowered to hide her red face, Jocelyne swallowed her much-loved homemade beans with difficulty. Her mind reeled with the knowledge that she had again done something wrong, unsure what exactly it had been. Nicolas gurgled and spat as he was fed. Her mother ate nothing. Pauline wiggled on in her highchair and continued to tap her spoon against her sister's arm between mouthfuls of egg and beans. Jocelyne pushed her sister's hand back over her plate and suddenly remembered that she wanted to ask her grandmother about the bird. She inhaled sharply and looked up, her ears still aflame, her eyes seeking her mother's, and then her grandmother's face. Her mother smiled at her, a slight sad smile that was just a little encouraging, for all its weakness. The old woman stared out the window, smoothing her white apron with her right hand, while the other deftly cut her egg with a fork. The child's voice interrupted the fork's journey to her mouth.

"Grandmaman, I had a question I wanted to ask you."

"Oui, Jocelyne. Qu'est-ce que c'est?"

"Well, I heard this bird outside my window this morning and it had the most beautifulest sound. I never heard a bird sing like that before. It was like … hui ou, hui, ou, hui iii, something like that. What bird would it be, Grandmaman?"

Jocelyne heard her mother sigh and saw her turn Nicolas to her shoulder and pat his back gently, rocking slightly in her chair.

"Well now, 'ard to say. We 'ave so many bird. A robin may'be?"

"No, Gran, I know what a robin looks like and sounds like. You've shown me and this was different. It wasn't red at all. I saw a bit of yellow, but that's all I could see before he flew away. And he went like… hui iii."

Richard pushed his chair back from the table, scraping the rubber-tipped legs and marking the polished floor to bring his chair nearer the screen door. He bent over for his workboots and shoved them on his feet, then rose, leaving imprints of mud under the chair. Leaning across the table for a toothpick, he slapped Chantale roughly on the shoulder.

"What a bitch you are, Chantale. It's always so nice to have breakfast with you in the morning. I look forward to it. C'mon,

Squirt, we have chores to do. Meet me at the barn in two minutes."
He laughed tonelessly, then turned to retrieve his cowboy hat from
the rack and pushed aside the screen door, whistling for the dogs as he
left. Chantale writhed away, sticking out her tongue at her brother's
back. Pushing up noisily from her seat, she crushed her cigarette
into the egg yolk on her plate and whirled from the room, setting the
swinging doors banging behind her. She pounded up the stairs two at
a time, and then slammed her bedroom door so loudly the swinging
doors shook.

Again there was silence for a few minutes. Jocelyne waited with
what seemed like great patience to her. Then, just as her Grandmother
moved to scrape the plates, she began again.

"Anyways, this bird, Grandmaman, it was sort of brown and
yellow I think and it went like this." Her voice cracked like a breaking
dish. Her throat tightened as tears rose in her eyes and began to spill
down her chubby, freckled cheeks. She tried the yellow birdsong
again. She was almost desperate to know the name of the bird. She
didn't know why. She went on imitating the song she remembered as
best she could, gasping for breath between each attempt.

"Jocelyne, that's enough now. Go on outside," her mother
demanded. Pauline overturned her cup of milk and her mother
sighed. As she rose to retrieve a cloth from the counter, she made a
shooing motion toward Jocelyne, as though batting away an annoying
fly. Milk dribbled to the floor as she mopped the table, still balancing
Nicolas on her hip.

"Grandmaman, what bird do you think it was? It was brownish-
yellowish and it was on the wire just outside my window this morning.
Have you heard a bird like that before?"

"Jocelyne, pleeease, go on outside now, find Richard and help
him with the chores." Her mother pleaded, as she stooped to wipe the
floor with her one free hand as Pauline tugged at the loose front of
her top, whining about her wet clothes.

"I tink, Jocelyne, dat it would be a meadowlark. I'm not sure but
dey like to sit on wires de bes an' you 'ave to be up very ear-ly to 'ear
dem. Dey do 'ave a beautiful song, too. Dey 'ave a special morning

song for de prairie. A meadowlark, I'm preddy shoure dat's what it tis. 'Ere now, Pauline, Grandmaman va tout nettoyer. We clean dis up now. No need to fuss. Why in de olden time, when we 'ad de cow, we polish de floor wid milk, make it shine like a new penny."

Meadowlark. Meadowlark. A little chant sounded in her head as she skipped from the house into the morning sun shimmering outside. Behind her the huge white house threw shadows across the yard, spread out wide on its haunches like a brooding cat. The incident at breakfast had confused and unsettled her. She looked over to where the dead kittens were sprawled, rotting, under the trees, where the dogs had abandoned them after mauling them to death. She shuddered and decided she wouldn't mention it again. She would just avoid the place, even though it was one of her favourite spots to play. The huge soft branches of the pine trees had swept a perfect place to play house. Oh well, maybe Richard would remember to bury them, even if they wouldn't get a proper funeral. She would check in a few days. Anyway, her father would be home soon and he would help, for sure.

"That's it, when Daddy comes I'll talk to him about the dead cats and he'll know what to do. I wonder if there are any more dead pigs. They look so horrible, with their eyes wide open. Maybe Richard will let me give them a frooneral, too. They need one!"

She had seen them yesterday, crammed against the fence where their mother had unknowingly crushed them to death. The dead pigs were bigger than kittens and wouldn't fit into a shoebox. Who would help her? Not Chantale, not Mom, not Grandmaman. Richard would probably just laugh at her. What did he do with those baby pigs when they died, anyway? She would have to remember to ask him.

Chapter Two

The sun glinted on the gravel path that led from the house to the farmyard. The six-bedroom home had been built on a rise sheltered by giant pine trees, well away from the chicken coop and pig barn, in hopes of catching northerly winds. Near the outbuildings, the sour aroma of pig manure strangled the fresh air.

"Richard must be shovelling," Jocelyne muttered aloud, knowingly nodding her head as she skipped towards the long red building at the bottom of the hill. She scuffed the toes of her frayed canvas sneakers as she hopped deliberately into the puffs of dust she kicked up. But she slowed her pace as she approached the bunkhouse. The oldest and meanest black and white collie was usually tied there, guarding the door to Richard's sleeping quarters. Butch was old and mean and as ugly as his name. Pink and black lips curled back to reveal his sharp yellow teeth. He hobbled around on a twisted back leg that had been run over by Richard driving the farm truck, years before. No matter. Butch was fiercely loyal to his master. One glazed eye stared straight ahead, dripping a sour-smelling fluid, but the other gleamed clear and menacing, watchful for anyone who approached his territory.

Jocelyne scanned the bunkhouse steps cautiously before continuing down the path. If Butch was there, she would have to take the shortcut through the weeds to avoid a terrifying chase. But then she would get in trouble for all the burrs and brambles caught on her socks, as she had yesterday. It had taken hours for her to pull them off, one by one. Her fingers still ached from the chore.

"Whew, he's sleeping somewhere," she sighed with relief, as she tiptoed past the bunkhouse. Just a few more steps ... "Ouah, ouah ouahouhouah Ouah!" She broke into a run down the hill beside the machine shed, breathing hard but knowing she was safe, as the dog's tether ran out just past the dilapidated cabin.

Laughing at her triumph, she crossed the path and hopped up to the wooden platform surrounding the water pump. This fascinating contraption was so much fun! She wildly rattled the iron pump handle up and then yanked it down with both hands, lifting herself off the platform, trying to achieve the delightful pull of pressure which would mean the beginning of the water's flow. She never seemed to succeed on her own, but one of these days… She let go of the handle as it descended, then rushed to open her mouth below the water spout. A few drops of rusty-tasting water dripped in, just enough to make her realize she was really thirsty. Mmm, salty bacon had left her parched. She smacked her lips together. Oh well, she would have to ask Richard to pump for her, after the chores. She slid across the rough wooden surface of the pump platform, unaware that her corduroy seat had caught a few slivers of wood and peeled paint, and swung her feet over the edge, ready to drop down into the damp weeds and head back to the path. She glimpsed her mismatched socks below her bare legs, and groaned.

"Stupid, stupid burrs! How do they get there? I didn't even see them in the bushes! Well, I'll get them off later, before Mom sees."

She arrived at the barn out of breath from a solitary race, rubber-soled feet slapping the cement pad at the entrance. Hurling her small body as hard as she could into the white door jamb, she giggled to herself at the sheer exhilaration of halting her burst of speed so abruptly. She waited for her pounding heart to slow a bit before entering the barn. Experience had taught her that the first whiff would almost knock her back, unless she prepared for it by pinching her nose and breathing in through her mouth. She waited, propped against the frame of the open door, basking in the sun's warmth on her shoulders.

Slowly, she let go of her nose. Breathing through her mouth, but more accustomed to the smell, she left the sunlight for the cool, dark, dusty, musty, wriggling, squealing, meowing, scraping, scratching, snorting world of cats and pigs. There were windows in the barn, but they were so caked with dirt that they admitted very little light, just enough to see the stalls on the sunniest days. Otherwise, and always in the early morning and evening, the electric lights were on. In the bright silver light the pig smell seemed even more potent. When the barn was fully lit, or too hot, Jocelyne never stayed inside for long. But when it was cool and the pigs were rooting softly in the shadows, it welcomed her as a cozy refuge.

Jocelyne immediately noticed that fresh bedding had been strewn in the stalls nearest her, and already the smaller pigs were burrowing their snouts into the straw, pushing each other out of the way to claim their own space in the pen. The sows stared indifferently, blinking their small, watery blue eyes, adjusting their position only slightly and grunting when their flabby teats were accosted by first one pig, then the whole litter. She climbed up the gate of a stall to watch the noisy competition and managed to catch a glimpse of one of the mangy barn cats, prowling for mice right below her. Even though it swung its tail and hissed fiercely to warn her off, the child called "Kitty, kitty," and put out her hand to coax it to her.

Suddenly, her uncle Richard came in at the side door, loaded down with a bucket in each hand.

"I've told you not to bother with them damn cats, Joss. They'll only scratch you if you get near anyways. They're barn cats."

"I know, but I thought I could tame one. I don't get it why they have to be so mean. Nobody ever bothers them."

"They're only here to work. Gotta keep the mice down. They're wild and don't take to coddlin'. There are no pets on a farm. Sooner you learn that, the better off you'll be. Everything has a job to do, just like you do now. Here, you can help fill the feeders with chop."

Placing a full bucket near her feet, he turned to empty the remaining one into the feeder of the closest stall. Jocelyne scrambled up the boards of the stall next to the door to retrieve her own scoop from its nail. She had to lean well over the edge of each stall to ladle the chop into the wooden feeder on the inside of the gate, pour it down in a musty cloud and continually climb up and down to refill the scoop from the bucket. It was slow, heavy work, but she didn't mind. She watched the pigs at each stall scramble over one another, shrieking, grunting and diving into the food with their pink snouts. They smacked their jowls as they ate and raised puffs of oat dust around their blocky heads. She laughed at their grunts of pleasure, "Like baby Nicolas, when he eats!"

Richard had finished all the other stalls in the long barn by the time she had only half-emptied her bucket. She looked up from her position balanced on a stall gate and watched him coming toward her, his tall lanky frame outlined against the square of light at the end of the barn. His approaching figure left only the round hill of the manure pile silhouetted there, as he moved further down the dark length of the building. He banged his bucket against a few of the stalls, cursing at the pigs in French. Jocelyne knew how much he hated them—he had told her so many times, swearing at "les maudits cochons" even as he fed them. To him, they meant only one thing. Once, when she had complained of their stink, he had laughed and replied, "Ahh, that's not pig shit you smell. That's the smell of money. Just you remember that."

And she had. On the next family visit to the village store, she had asked her mother if she could see the money, just as she handed it across the counter to the clerk. Her mother had looked puzzled, but shrugged and handed her the bill. Three sets of eyebrows went up, as the child put the money to her nose, sniffed, and exclaimed, "Yup, sure enough—smells just like pig shit!" only to have the money instantly torn from her hand and a smart smack to her bottom, right in front of the laughing eyes of the old grocer. She still didn't understand why her mother's face had been so red. She tried to explain, "But Uncle Richard said…" and was cut off with, "Don't you repeat what Uncle Richard says, ever again!"

It was not until he was within two stalls of where she now stood that Jocelyne could clearly see his familiar face, so similar to her father's: same high cheekbones, ruddy complexion, thick black hair and blue-green eyes, yet different, younger, yes, but more narrow featured, the nose very pointed, the eyes deeper-set, hooded beneath thicker brows. His thin lips rarely formed a smile, and she had never heard him laugh out loud, as her father did so often, so readily. But she liked Richard's company, here in his private domain where no one else ever intruded. She somehow felt that she was not in the way, maybe even wanted. Richard always gave her a chore and trusted her to do it, never even bothering to check up on her. She had come to the barn to help Richard every day since they had been at Grandmaman's farm, every day for the whole summer. He never seemed annoyed by her chatter, never told her to be quiet. He rarely spoke but when he did, he talked to her as if she were a "grownup." Instead of just five years old and a "baby" as Chantale always said.

"That Chantale is so mean," she thought suddenly, leaning over as far into the stall as she dared, then pulling herself upright at the last moment. It wouldn't do to fall in with the pigs, though it might be funny!

"Oink, oink," she snorted at the old sow.

She hadn't noticed that Richard was right behind her. He grabbed her around the knees and swung her to his shoulder. With a lilt in her chest, she ducked her head as they walked out of the barn. It felt good to be back in the sun.

"Richard, could you take me over to the pump? I can never make it work, and I need a drink."

"Oh, so you want a drink, do you?" His arm encircled her knees as he skipped down the slight incline of the gravel path leading to the pump. Just where he should have turned toward the platform, he let go of Jocelyne's knees, dropped her into both arms, turned and ran back to the open trough in front of the outdoor pigpen.

"You're thirsty are you? How--about--a---nice---cool---driiiiink?" he chanted, balancing her around the hips and shoulders and swinging her over the trough. Jocelyne tried to laugh, but a choking sound escaped her throat. She couldn't understand what he was doing.

"He wouldn't drop me in, would he?" she wondered frantically as she hovered above the trough. She suddenly felt as though he were a stranger. Her sense of easy companionship evaporated. Her glance kept catching sight of the black water and the things floating in it, bugs, straw, pig drool, bugs ...

"He wouldn't drop me?" Her mind raced ahead to what it might feel like to be dunked in the yucky water in the trough.

"Ri... Rich... Richard... dooooon't." She made a laughing, crying plea, like when she was tickled too much. She hated being tickled by her father, but she could never say, except to cry breathlessly, "Dooooon't!" until her mother would stop him. Now she felt Richard's hot hands on her bare back under her shirt. She could smell the pig smell, on his clothes, on his breath, wafting up from the pigsty. Her skin shivered where her loose shirt, wet now and streaming through the water, left it exposed to the waist of her pants. She couldn't breathe. The blue sky looked so high as her body flailed toward it. She closed her eyes and felt herself rolled over in Richard's powerful arms.

"Richard, put her down. Right now! Now, I said, tout de suite, or I'm telling. I mean it," Chantale's voice came from somewhere, sharp, demanding. Jocelyne squeezed her eyes more tightly, her stomach turning, still swinging back and forth over the trough, the front of her wet shirt slapping against her pants with each upswing.

"You're telling. Oh oui, la maudite vache, what will you tell?"

Richard's deep voice echoed in the cold depths of the metal water trough.

"Quel est ton problème, bitch? She wanted a drink, so... we're just horsin' around, right, Jocelyne?" Richard laughed as he swung her high up in the air once more.

Jocelyne opened her eyes and saw, within the swoop of the arc, the puffy white clouds in the sky, the house, the tall pine trees, then closer, Chantale clasping Pauline's chubby hand, then the murky water swirling in the gaping mouth of the trough, Richard's belt buckle and, finally, jammed against the fence of the pigsty, a wide-eyed dead baby pig. She screamed.

... .And was swung up over the trough and planted roughly on her feet. She stumbled, dizzy, and lost her balance. She reached for the rim of the trough to catch herself, but instead plunged her hand into the filthy cold water. Her stomach rolled as she wiped her clammy hands on her pants. From far away she could hear her mother's voice.

"Bastard. That wasn't funny." Chantale's voice, compressed between her thin lips, rasped out between her teeth.

"Me wants swing. Mon oncke Richard give Pawine swing."

Pauline whined as she tottered toward Richard on her chubby legs.

"Ah shut up, bitch. It's just for fun. Jocelyne knows it's just for fun, don't you, Joss? See, see, Pauline gets a swing now from mon oncle Richard. Whee…" he swooped the little girl around in circles by her arms. Pauline chortled in utter delight.

"Jocelyne! Jocelyne?!!"

"It's okay, Suzanna. She's over here with us. I'm taking her and Pauline for a walk," Chantale called over her shoulder to Suzanna, looking out anxiously from the back door. Then she turned back to Richard with an unblinking, cold glare.

"Give me that kid right now. Put that kid down. I mean it. And leave Jocelyne alone. I'm serious, Richard."

"Oh, you're serious, are you?" he said with a sneer, but set the child on her feet. Pauline waddled unnoticed toward the shiny metal trough.

"Well, we'll just see about that. Come on, Josie, I'll pump you some water."

"No, I don't want any. I'm not thirsty anymore," Jocelyne croaked hoarsely, as she twisted the wet front of her shirt into a knot. Her whole body shook. The slight breeze felt cold, though the morning sun beamed. Her throat burned. The back of her head buzzed with a sound like the flies on the dead kittens. What about kittens? She couldn't remember. Then Pauline was beside her, stretching up on her toes, about to reach into the water.

"No, Pauline!" Jocelyne shouted. Grabbing her sister's fist, she whirled her around, and found herself nose to belt buckle with her uncle. He leaned down and looked straight into her eyes.

"It was just in fun, Jocelyne. 'Course you know I was just foolin' around. I wasn't really going to drop you into that dirty old trough, now was I? Would I do that to my best girl? Come on, let's get that ol' pump to workin'," he cajoled, brushing a dirty index finger to her cheek and encircling a loose brown curl in front of her eyes. Jocelyne stared at him, her mouth open, unable to move or speak. The smell of the pig barn wafted from his hands straight into her nostrils.

"C'mon, Jocelyne. We'll go for a walk down to see the horse. You'd like that, wouldn't you? C'mon, let's go," insisted Chantale, grabbing her shoulder.

Still clutching her sister, Jocelyne moved one foot away from her uncle. He moved aside, and she took another step to follow her aunt. Suddenly, she felt a stinging slap on her bum. Her wet seat stung where he had hit her with the flat of his hand.

"It was just a joke. C'mon, Josie, I was only kiddin'. I'll get you some fresh water now."

She looked back, but not toward her uncle. She turned her head the other way and looked around the side of the trough. Yup, it was still there. All she could see was a withered pinkish-white body, curled in the muck against the fence. The rump of another pig was forcing it deeper into the straw. Suddenly, she was retching and spewing vomit all over her feet. She was trembling and about to fall over when Chantale caught her.

"See what you've done now, you sick son-of-a-bitch? You never know when enough is enough, do you? She's probably gonna puke all day now. Christ, what a mess. I hope you're happy," Chantale spat at him viciously as she tugged on her niece's icy arm, pulling her away from Richard's outstretched hand. Chantale lifted Pauline to one hip and then yanked Jocelyne beside her.

Jocelyne had no choice but to shuffle next to her aunt. She stumbled as if in a dream, past the machine sheds, the old farm truck, off the path, through the wire gate, and under the wire fence, until at last she collapsed face first, into the meadow.

Chapter Three

With only one horse grazing the pasture, the grass grew wild and thick enough to break Jocelyne's fall. She lay where she had fallen, wrapped in a blanket of sun, soothed by the drone of bees in the clover. Chantale didn't disturb her, but kept Pauline occupied by tickling her cheek with strands of grass. After a while, Chantale came over to Jocelyne, raised her up gently by her shoulders and handed her a blade of bearded grass.

"Here, suck on the white part. It's juicy and sweet. It'll help your tummy." Obediently, Jocelyne stuck the tip of the grass strand into her mouth and squeezed it between her teeth. A cool, thin juice slid down her throat. Jocelyne's colour finally returned to normal. Suddenly, Chantale grabbed each child by the hand, and led them in one direction, then the other, in search of the old mare. Buzzing dung pies dotting the field were the one sign that she was somewhere grazing the pasture. As the girls stumbled along, the long grass brushed their bare arms, making their skin itch and tingle. Their heads seemed to melt in the sun. Jocelyne's sensitive nostrils detected the oily scent of Chantale's hair and the baby powder smell of Pauline's. Jocelyne didn't understand why, but their smell somehow bound the three of them together in their quest for the horse. She could sense it. So too, it seemed, could the flies, which began to annoy them all, buzzing about their ears. As if on signal, the older girls broke into a run, Chantale launching Pauline onto her hip without stopping. Gophers scampered out of their way, peeping an angry warning and flagging their stubby tails as they dove into their holes.

The field rose to a hillside, shorn bare by the horse, except for clumps of sage weed left to ripen in the sun. On a previous visit, Chantale had told Jocelyne that the pungent weed burnt Blackie's sensitive nose. Here, where the grass was mown by the horse's voracious appetite, flowers bloomed in wild abandon: golden dandelions, orange tiger lilies, sapphire bluebells, white daisies and brown-eyed "suzies"; Jocelyne had learned to name them on her walks with her grandmother.

Chantale puffed and gasped, winded from the sudden exertion. She dropped Jocelyne's hand, plumped Pauline down beside her and flopped herself on the ground. Leaning back, her face to the sky, she sighed.

"Wouldn't it be nice just to fall in there, into that deep blue sky? I love coming here, just to lie all alone where nobody can find me, and stare at the clouds. Look, see the horses' tails? That's what you call those kinds of clouds. Don't they look like horses' tails flying in the wind? Hey look, one has broken up and turned into a zipper! And see, there's a rabbit and oh, a dragon. Those are the best! Can you see it? Right there, there's the eye, the nose...see?"

Jocelyne could not answer. Speechless, she stared at her aunt in wonder. She couldn't recognize her voice: so soft, dreamy, so... different. Could she really see pictures in the sky?

Pauline began tearing at the dusty grass, pulling up handfuls, then throwing it toward Jocelyne.

"Stop it, stupid! You'll get dirt in my eyes ... " she shouted and reached out to smack her sister's hand. Before she could reach her, Chantale sat up and gently pulled the three year-old to her chest, encircling her with her legs. She began humming, and the gophers, becoming brave now, peeked their heads out of their holes and seemed to whistle along. She noticed a ladybug in the grass and extended a finger for it to climb upon, to cross the mountains and valleys of her hand. She showed Pauline, who squealed with delight.

"I gets bug too. Me too! Gimme!" In answer, Chantale held out the little girl's chubby hand and let the orange, spotted bug walk onto her palm.

"Funny tickles," the toddler chortled.

Chantale began to sing very softly, "Ladybug, ladybug fly away home. Your house is on fire and your children are alone. Fly away, fly away, fly away home."

With the last word, she leaned over and blew on the bug. It instantly cracked apart, sprouted wings and rose into the air. Pauline screamed.

"Me wants buggy! Come back. Come back," she whined.

"She can't come back, Pauline. She needs to go look after her children. They are all alone. You don't want them to burn up, do you? Didn't you hear, their house is on fire! They need their maman, just like you do."

Chantale's voice was soothing, crooning to settle the child. She wrapped her arms about her, rocking her and singing until the sweaty, impatient Pauline wiggled free. Chantale let her crawl nearby. She leaned across her backside and picked one of the lanky dandelions that had turned from a yellow flower to a cottony cluster of seeds.

"Do you know how to make wishes with these clocks?"

"Clocks," what did she mean, "clocks?" Still amazed at the change in her aunt, whose voice, actions, and smile had become so unfamiliar, Jocelyne didn't dare to ask. She silently shook her head "no."

"You close your eyes and make a wish. A secret wish. And you can't tell anybody. And then you blow as hard as you can, keeping your eyes shut. If all the parachutes are gone when you open your eyes, your wish will come true."

Chantale squeezed her eyes to make two lines above her chubby cheeks. A long moment passed while she concentrated on her private wish. Then, suddenly, she blew, hard, almost wheezing, spit flying from her mouth, and the fluff from the dandelion broke free, whirling about in the slight breeze. Chantale's eyes flew open.

"Damn."

Two seedlings held on tenaciously to the brown, bulbous head of the flower.

"Oh well, sometimes it works, sometimes it doesn't. C'est la vie, as Ma would say," she sighed as she squeezed milk from the stem into her hand and rubbed it in her palm.

"Patty cake!" Pauline chortled as she waddled toward them,

clapping her hands together between something brown and smelly.

"Shit! Oh, merde, Pauline, you little brat. Why'd you get into that? Et Chris..." Chantale swore, her voice back to its normal tone, the family cuss words such a familiar sound that Jocelyne almost relaxed. Now she recognized her aunt. Chantale grabbed the child by the waist and roughly rubbed her hands into the grass and weeds, to clean them as best she could.

"Come on. We'd better go back. I think there's more than one patty cake to deal with now. Great, just great."

Carrying the child by the waist, legs out behind and face downward, Chantale stumbled awkwardly back down the hill. Jocelyne skipped along beside her. As they crossed through the deeper grass, Jocelyne caught sight of Blackie, trotting towards them.

"There she is!" she shouted, pointing straight ahead.

Chantale hoisted the baby to her hip with a grunt, trying to balance her without resting the toddler's smelly bottom against her body. With her free hand, she reached into her jean pocket and withdrew a lint-covered sugar lump.

Jocelyne took up a position behind her aunt's wide backside. The five-year-old was attracted to the horse, yet at the same time, terrified of its giant legs that might kick outward at any moment. Jocelyne knew that the thin white scar on Chantale's chin was from a horse's hoof, when she had been bucked off while learning to ride. Instinctively, she covered her face with crossed arms as the horse approached.

Blackie came right up to Chantale's open hand and nuzzled it with pink, spotted lips, searching for the sugar lump. Jocelyne glimpsed its yellow teeth. The loud crunching on the sugar seemed to resonate in her spine. Its smoky scent filled the air.

Carelessly, Chantale dropped Pauline to her feet and leaned forward to pet the horse's head and neck. Pauline screamed with fear and clung to her knees, but Chantale ignored her, totally absorbed in the horse.

"You crafty old girl! You just bide your time and then come over here to see if we have a treat, don't you..." she cooed.

Jocelyne stood perfectly still as the horse kicked at a huge fly under its belly, tail swishing at all the insects swarming around its behind. It lowered its head toward Pauline, who began howling at Chantale's feet. Chantale swatted Pauline as she hissed at her to "shut up, for Chrissake!" Then she turned to find Jocelyne and ordered her to pull some long grass.

"Here, I'll show you how to feed her," she whispered softly.

Jocelyne succeeded in tearing the tips off a few long shoots of grass and held them out, clenched in her tiny fist.

"No, not like that, dummy. Here, open your hand flat. It's alright. She won't bite you. Lay them across your hand, like this."

She forced Jocelyne's hand open and laid more grass in her palm. Holding her niece's wrist, she pulled her forward to make the offering to Blackie. Chantale held on firmly as the horse nibbled Jocelyne's palm with her pink lips and puffed warm, sweet breath across her wrist, searching for more food. The child held stock still, cringing inwardly in terror.

"There, you see. She won't eat you. She doesn't like the way you smell. That's why you have to make sure horses smell you. And I'm sure she doesn't like the way YOU smell, you stinky little brat," she grunted, turning around and lifting Pauline up by the waistband of her pants. She held her high, sniffing.

"Euch, poopy pants for sure! Come on. I can't deal with you. Anyways, we'd better get back before your mom has a fit and thinks the horse ate you or something."

She headed for the fence, carrying Pauline by the waist. Jocelyne stayed close on her aunt's heels, keeping well ahead of Blackie, who was following them, head lowered, swinging her tail. Maybe the mare would knock them down if she didn't get more sugar lumps. Jocelyne was not sure, but she didn't want to find out.

For an instant, she glanced up at the sky to look for the white horses' tails whisking along above them, but the sun was higher now, so they had disappeared. She trotted closer behind Chantale until they reached the barbed wire fence. Chantale separated the two middle wires, holding the top strand with her left hand and the bottom one down with the sole of her shoe as she hoisted Pauline through by her backside. She then climbed through herself, barely missing scraping her exposed back on the top wire, and turned back to hold the opening for Jocelyne. By this time the horse was sniffing Jocelyne's pant cuffs in search of more treats.

Jocelyne's heart pounded as she scrambled through the fence to escape the horse, scratching her bare ankle on a barb. Suddenly, she felt warmth rush across her bottom. Her face flushed with shame as she realized that she had wet herself.

Lagging behind Chantale, praying her aunt wouldn't notice the accident, she pretended to be absorbed by the wildflowers, and tried again to pluck a few. In vain. The bluebells held fast to the earth. She either pulled them out by the roots, or ended up with a crushed mass of petals and leaves in her sweaty hand. Frustration brought her to tears, and she threw everything to the ground except one straggly bluebell, which she had wrested from the ground by the roots. At a cost: her hand burned from pulling at the wiry stem. Far ahead, Chantale was calling. She ran to catch up, her wet pants rubbing uncomfortably against her inner thighs.

She arrived breathless and sobbing next to her aunt and little sister. Chantale's blue eyes narrowed even more in her round face as she looked at Jocelyne, but just for a moment. Then she turned her attention casually to the bluebells.

"Those are hard to pick 'cause they want to stay here. They have to be tough to stay on this dry old hill. Why anything wants to live on this stupid ol' prairie is beyond me, but I call them fairies' dinner bells. You know, like the big ol' bell in the yard? Well, these are the ones the fairy mothers ring, to call their children to supper. Isn't that neat?"

As Jocelyne guiltily opened her hand to drop the flower, Chantale reached out to stop her.

"No, let's take it home and put it in water. You have the roots, so it might grow again. Look, I want to show you a magic trick with these flowers." She snapped the head off one of the dandelions abundant at their feet. She pulled the tail of her plaid cotton shirt out of her pants and leaned forward to wipe the younger girl's face.

"Now to make this work, you have to hold your chin up to the sun, and the other person holds the dandelion under it. If your chin turns yellow, it means you like butter. Here, let's see. No, turn your head up more. There. Yup, you like butter. It's really yellow."

Jocelyne hated butter. But the warmth on her chin combined with the gentleness of her aunt convinced her that she should change her mind. The sun of the flower glowed inside her body.

"Here, let's try it on Pauline," she suggested with a smile.

Chantale steadied the youngster against her side, while Jocelyne tested her chin with the flower. Pauline squirmed.

"Tickles. Yuck. Me want down, Aunty," she complained.

"No, you see, she doesn't like it," Jocelyne said with a superior tone. The magic had not shown up in her. Ha!

"Let's try it on you, now, Chantale. I bet you like butter."

"No, it doesn't work on me. Anyway, we'd better get back. Listen, that's the dinner bell. Better get a move on or the old bag will have a shit fit."

Jocelyne's stomach turned to ice at Chantale's open disrespect for her beloved Grandmère. Hastily, she plucked a handful of dandelions, pinching them off by the stems. Her hand dripping in sweat and dandelion milk, she clutched the flowers tightly. Then, following her aunt at a skip, she soon found they had arrived at the huge pine trees lining the gravel driveway. They only needed to cross the road and the lawn to reach the back door, and they would be home for lunch. Heading up the gravel path, the girls purposely avoided the shortcut through the pines on the opposite side, where they knew the dead cats were still rotting in the heat. They raced to land on the cement patio, where shade created by the wooden awning cooled the entrance to the kitchen. Two panting border collies rose to greet them, lazily wagging their shaggy black and white tails, not bothering to bark as they recognized Chantale.

Jocelyne was about to throw open the screen door and run to her mother with the flowers, when Chantale murmured, "Here, give me those and I'll go in first with Pauline. You sneak in behind me and head upstairs."

The child's face reddened to her ears. She followed her aunt's instructions, though, slipping in unnoticed, kicking her dirty sneakers off onto the mat. She then scuttled under the swinging kitchen doors and climbed on hands and knees up the dimly-lit stairs. No one would know her shame, but Chantale. Oh yeah, and her mom, when she found the wet pants on the floor.

"Oh well. At least Richard won't see, and be able to tease me."

At the thought of her uncle, she relived the moment of almost falling into the trough, and shivered. The wet pants stuck to her skin as she furiously peeled them off, panties and socks coming off together. The smell made her retch. She kicked the bundle under her bed, and then dug in her drawer for fresh clothing, deciding on a pair of shorts. Not bothering with panties or socks, she struggled to tug them up her cold, damp legs. Then, closing the door softly behind her, she started down the stairs on her bottom. She had bounced down three steps before she caught sight of her filthy hands, and stood, knowing she might as well go up to the bathroom and wash, before her mother had to scold her in front of everyone. For the first time in her life, she found herself planning to avoid attention. She hoped she could join the lunch table without being noticed at all.

Chapter Four

When she arrived in the kitchen, the family had already started eating. Jocelyne took her customary seat, then adjusted her position to sit on her knees and began to greedily and noisily slurp the cabbage soup. Every hot lunch at Grandmaman's always started with a thin carrot and cabbage soup, which she loved. She remained immersed in sucking up as much as possible, until she spied the fresh buns across the table. Unaware that she was interrupting, she asked, "Please pass a bun, Grandmaman. Oh, and the butter, too. Chantale showed me a magic way that you can tell if you like butter and I do, even though I never knew it before. Mom, did you know about ... hey, did you see the flowers I brang you. Where are they?"

"Hush, Jocelyne. Eat your soup quietly. And don't waste that bun like you usually do. Dip it in your soup and that way you'll finish it." Her mother passed her a bun and the hard pat of butter while her grandmother and her uncle continued their conversation in French. Just as she had finished struggling to cut a wad of icy butter from the pat in the dish and scoop it onto her bread, Jocelyne felt Chantale's cold eyes on her.

"You are to be seen and not heard at the table, in case you didn't know. You're always making such a racket."

Where had that voice come from? Chantale with the golden flowers, so sweet and kind, where had she gone? The morsel of buttered bun stuck in Jocelyne's throat. Unable to swallow, she tasted the butter as it melted on her tongue. The sour-milk taste reminded her that butter made her feel sick.

"Ahhh, leave her alone, you sow." Richard halted his conversation in French to interject.

"No, YOU leave her alone," Chantale screeched back, "and you

31

know damn well what I mean, you bastard!"

Their mother cried out, "Chantale, Richard, qu'est-ce qu'il y a, à parler comme ça à table? Mon doux, vous me donnez mal à la tête, vous autres! C'est bien assez! Enough!"

Glaring at her mother and brother, Chantale pushed herself away from the table. Her chair crashed to the floor as she flew from the room, belting the swinging doors on her way out with a fist and then stomping up the stairs.

Jocelyne reached for her milk, swirled it in her full mouth and finally succeeded in swallowing the bread. Hungrily, she devoured the next course, pink baked beans smothered in mustard, mashed potatoes and fat, juicy homemade pork sausages. But she didn't speak again, keeping her head down, eyes focused on her plate, glimpsing from time to time Chantale's empty, clean plate next to hers. The adults continued to talk as though nothing had happened, Richard and her grandmother in French, her mother muttering to Pauline and the baby. Jocelyne resolved to take a dish of leftovers up to Chantale after lunch. There must be some way to get back the Chantale from this morning. She munched on silently, not noticing that the adults had long since finished and Richard had left the table.

"Jocelyne, help Grandma clear the table now. I've got to put the baby down, then I'll come and do the dishes."

Grandmaman passed the dishes down to Jocelyne. She clumsily scraped the leftovers to one plate and stacked them, piling the silverware into the empty salad bowl. Few scraps remained, only a bit of lettuce for the pigs and the sausage tails, which she and her mother hadn't eaten. These could go into the slop bucket for the dogs. Richard had again butted his cigarette into his empty plate, so it couldn't be stacked with the others. She would have to scrape it into the garbage. The smell of the cigarette butt and ashes mixed with the cold sausage grease on the plate made her gag, but she had learned to breathe through her mouth for the task. She took the plate and a fork toward the garbage can next to the door and raised the lid of the white metal can by pressing her small foot on the pedal at its base.

The bluebell stem had been folded and sprang up crazily with the lid like a jack-in-the-box, at the top of the full can of garbage. The dandelions wilted over the stinking mass.

Numbly, she pushed the cigarette butt and ashes with the fork, onto the droopy flower heads. Then she let the lid fall with a bang.

"Jocelyne, fais pas ça. It's too lout." Her grandmother reprimanded her as usual for banging the garbage can lid.

The old woman hated unnecessary noise—it got on her last nerve, she always said.

"Viens ici, tu vas m'aider à faire la vaisselle. Ta maman, she is busy wid' de liddle one an' all so, she need 'er res'."

Planting a chair against the cupboard under the sink, she snapped a clean towel in the air and tied it around Jocelyne's waist. Richard, toothpick jutting from between his teeth, came back into the kitchen from the living room. He came up and ruffled her hair, whistling tunelessly, then patted her bottom and strode out of the room, deliberately banging the screen door behind him.

Jocelyne raised a hand to her head and smoothed her fine brown curls, as she climbed onto the padded kitchen chair. Hot tears burned her eyes, rolled down her face and spilled into the soapy water. Hiding her face from her grandmother, she plunged her arms up to her elbows into the sink.

As usual, she had forgotten to roll up her sleeves. Gently her grandmother undid the buttons at her wrists, rolled up the wet sleeves and adjusted the chair again as she looked quizzically at her but said nothing about the tears. Jocelyne breathed deeply of her spicy scent as the old woman leaned over her to place the glasses gently in the sink. Suddenly, she hiccupped. She held her breath as long as she could, until her sobs subsided. She didn't even know exactly why she was crying. Her head ached and her body was tired, but she would never admit it, or she would be put down for a nap, just like the babies, Nicolas and Pauline!

"Sur le pont, D'avignon, On y danse, on y danse…" Grandmaman sang in French as she wiped the dishes. Jocelyne lifted her nose toward her, so she could wipe it with the dishtowel, in their usual ritual.

"Why is it, Grandmaman, that your nose always gets itchy when you do the dishes?" she asked for the hundredth time. Her grandmother just shrugged as she turned to place a glass in the cupboard.

"Grandmaman, comment dit-on 'spoon' en français?" she ventured, using the phrase she had been taught by her father.

"C'est une cuillière, chérie. C'est bien que tu voudrais apprendre le français! I should speak in French to you all de time, den you would learn more fas'. Mais, it 'tis 'ard when your mudder, she speak only Ing-glish. But she is not force to learn, tu vois, as I was. Comink 'ere, I 'ad to learn, firs' from my 'usband, your Grandpapa, an' den, when dey go to school, from da chil-dren. I use to sit an' work on der book right beside dem, to learn along wid dem. Dey was not allow to speak French at school at tall, so we, Papa et moi, we 'ad to 'elp dem as much as we could, an' soon, dey could teach me an' correc' mes erreurs. But I insis' dat, odder dan school works, we speak in French in de 'ome, to keep da language. Dat is up to de mudder; de fadder, 'e too busy to min' an' 'e tink it more important to learn good Ing- glish. But my chil-dren, now dey 'ave bot lang-wage." She flashed the gold sliver between her front teeth.

"You need to learn French al-so, ma belle, an' beside, French make so much more sense dan Ing-glish. Everythink 'as her hown word, much more precize. I could not believe it at firs' when I start to learn, 'ow difficult it could be. Par exemple, take da word 'trew.' I remember da kid tryink to explain dat one word to me. Lissen: 'I 'trew' da balle 'trew' da win-dow, an' when I was 'trew,' I was in trouble, 'trew and trew!'' Now you tell me, does dat make any sense at tall?" she looked so perplexed that Jocelyne started to giggle. That prompted the old woman to laugh, and soon they were both in stitches. Jocelyne slipped from her perch on the chair, and had to be righted by her grandmother's strong, bony arm.

The child sensed that her tongue had been released from an uncomfortable bond, and so she continued to chat, telling her grandmother about the horse, how she had learned to feed Blackie and...how scary it was to have her follow you across the field and she might run over you if you were in her field and didn't have a sugar lump, and next time we go to the store, Grandmaman, we have to remember to buy more sugar lumps because I think we don't have very many left and....

A short while later, Jocelyne waited in the hall in front of her aunt's closed door, shakily holding a tray with a dish of warmed-over food. Finally, her knocking was answered. Chantale, swollen faced and dishevelled, hid behind the door but opened it a crack to let her in. Jocelyne had to turn sideways with the tray to enter.

The breathtaking beauty of the room startled Jocelyne so much she almost dropped the tray. She had expected Chantale's room to be a mess. Instead, she was awestruck by beauty and order, and the delight of finally being allowed to see what was behind the perpetually closed door, after so many weeks of staying at her grandmother's house.

The room smelled fresh and clean. The hardwood floor gleamed. The dresser top, covered with lace doilies, displayed a shiny, silver hairbrush and comb set. The mirrored lid of an elegant jewellery box reflected a tiny ballerina. The bed had four carved wooden posts holding aloft a transparent pink canopy. A white lace bedspread floated to the floor. Three pink velvet cushions were propped in a neat row against the curved headboard. The white and gold trimmed furniture gleamed in the light filtering in through a huge, open window covered with lacy curtains. Even though it was midday, a shapely, lace-shaded lamp lit up the objects on a desk by the door. Jocelyne hesitantly set the tray down on it and waited expectantly. After the disastrous meal, she was sure Chantale would yell at her to "get out, you little brat!" On her brow was written the question, "Why are you so mad at me, after you were so nice this morning?" But she didn't dare say it aloud.

Chantale sprawled on her stomach on her bed and stared at the child for a moment. Then she nonchalantly lifted from the bedspread a cardboard square covered with what appeared to be bits of coloured glass.

"Wanna see?" she asked, holding it out on the flat of her hand.

Jocelyne approached the bed, hesitantly, to take a look.

"I'm making a mosaic. It's going to be a picture of the Virgin

Mary. You glue these bits of coloured rock on this white board with the numbers, like so," she demonstrated, using her dirty fingernail to pick out a bit of blue glass from a box next to her on the bed.

"And when you're done you have a beautiful picture. You can't tell close-up, but when you're done, it looks really neat. I did those ones, too. See those clowns on the wall above the desk? You like them?"

Jocelyne turned around to look at the pictures more closely, which at first glance had seemed to be paintings, and found that they were indeed covered with tiny stones.

"They don't look much like clowns, though. They're crying," Jocelyne remarked softly.

"They're supposed to be like that, dummy," Chantale sighed and rolled her eyes.

"Jeez, don't you know anything? They're French clowns, called mimes. Boy, were they ever hard to do, just black and white pieces to work with. This one is lots easier, 'cause there's more colours. Here, want to do some? I'll tell you what colour to look for, you find it and I'll glue it on. Okay?"

Jocelyne joyfully climbed up to sit cross-legged on the bed.

"Careful, don't knock the box or we'll have the stones all over the bedspread to pick up, and it's murder getting them out of the lace!" Her voice came across as a bit harsh, but Chantale twisted over on the bed to give Jocelyne more room.

After a while, the child's back ached from leaning over and she started to fidget. Chantale didn't reprimand her again. She simply swept up the tiles that hadn't been glued down, emptied them into the divided box in the appropriate colour groups, placed the unfinished picture on top and popped on the lid. She then rolled off the bed, landing on all fours, and proceeded to drag another, bigger box from underneath.

"Look here. I want you to see something. This is all my best stuff. I keep it hidden under here so no one can find it."

She raised the cardboard lid, and one by one, proudly showed her treasures to Jocelyne: a black velvet ribbon, a perfect blue marble, an assortment of tiny coloured bottles, a set of plastic red doll shoes with "diamond" bows, and some postcards.

"Neat, huh? But this is the best thing ever," she exclaimed, unwrapping something from a handkerchief that seemed to be nothing more than a stiff sheet of paper. She held up a shiny photograph of a young blue-eyed blond girl, smiling angelically. The child in the picture wore a green velvet dress and held a fluffy, golden puppy in her arms. She was holding her head tilted to one side to show off long, shiny hair curling over her shoulder.

Jocelyne thought it was the most beautiful girl she had ever seen. She took the picture gingerly by the edges as Chantale had done, and gasped when it caught the light as she moved it back and forth. Slivers etched in the photograph seem to trace perfect circles. Her curious fingers reached out from the edge of the picture to feel the even ridges across the little girl's face. Suddenly, Chantale slapped her hand and snatched the picture away from her by one corner.

"No, don't touch it. It's a record, dummy. If you get your fingerprints on it, it'll get scratched and then it'll skip."

The child had no idea what a "record" was. She wondered how a piece of cardboard could skip. Skipping was what she always did outside in the yard or with a rope, on the sidewalk. How could the little girl in the picture start to skip? Did that mean she would come alive?

"Wh... What is it?" she asked, mesmerized, holding her breath in anticipation of the answer. Chantale's eyes dramatically searched the ceiling for patience, once more.

"You put it on a record player, and the girl in the picture sings a song. Look, it tells which one here on the back, *White Christmas*. Neat, hey? My friend gave it to me for my birthday last year, because it's right at Christmas. But we don't even have a record player so I can't play it yet. Maybe I'll get a record player of my own, and then I'll play it for you. So, what do you think?"

Jocelyne shook her head, speechless. She was still not convinced that this piece of cardboard could actually sing a song, and even

37

"skip!" Like in skipping a rope? How could that be? She would have to ask Mom.

But as Chantale put everything carefully back into the box, she forced Jocelyne to make a promise. "You can't tell anybody this stuff is here. Cross your heart and hope to die. Swear it right now." She drew an X with her fingernail across Jocelyne's chest, so hard that she felt it etch the skin under her thin cotton blouse.

Groaning inwardly, she made the oath. Chantale nodded in satisfaction, then re-rolled the velvet ribbon, stood the little red shoes in one corner of the box and finally wrapped the cardboard "record" in its handkerchief and placed it face up on the top.

Hoisting herself up from the floor, she moved to the window, drew aside the light curtain and stared out. Jocelyne could see that Chantale had an open view of the sky from this high, north-facing window. The farmyard was on the other side of the house, far away.

"Holy cow, is she ever lucky! She has the nicest room in the whole house," Jocelyne thought.

Lifting her bare feet up and down on the smooth floor, she continued to look around the room, drinking in its pure air. She jumped when her aunt suddenly spoke, though her voice was barely a whisper.

"Did Richard ever... you know, scare you before today?"

"Well, no, not really. I don't know why I puked today. Musta' been that dead pig. See, we have this game where we do the chores, and then he swings me up on to his shoulders and takes me for a 'horsey-ride.' That's lots of fun. I have to hold on really tight around his neck with my legs because he can run... Fast! We run all the way up the hill and back again. Sometimes it's scary, when I think I might fall off, but he always catches me."

"Oh he does, eh? Well, I'm going to make sure you get out of here, Jocelyne. It's nothing against you. You'll understand someday. Tonight, when your dad gets back, I'm going to make sure you get the hell away. You've been here too long already. God, look what nearly happened today. Lucky I came when I did. Your father was a fool to bring you here. But what do you expect; he's so stupid, anyways.

They're all so bloody, goddamned…"

The curse caught in her throat and she seemed about to choke. Coughing, she whirled around, glared at Jocelyne and from her mouth came once again the voice of the "downstairs" aunt. The face had changed back, the eyes squeezed almost shut, the lips drawn down in a thin sneer.

"Now go outside and play and just leave me the hell alone. And take that slop down to the pigs. I don't want it. If I smell another bean in my life it'll be too soon. I hate the damn things. Go on. Now!" She pointed to the door, folded her arms across her ample chest and tapped her foot.

Jocelyne shakily picked up the tray from the desk and tried to leave, but the door was closed. She stood facing it, unable to figure out how to open the door without dropping the tray. Tears started to well in her eyes and her back shook in a sob.

From the window came a heavy sigh. Chantale thumped over to the door, turned the glass knob and held the door ajar. She stepped back only slightly as Jocelyne sidled past her. The tray brushed against Chantale's protruding belly, setting the dishes a-rattle

Jocelyne heard her mutter, "Don't worry, sweetie. Everything'll be all right. I know what to do," as she quietly closed the door.

Chapter Five

Jocelyne hadn't understood much of what Chantale had said, except that her father was coming home that night. Hooray! But why hadn't Mom told her before? She probably wanted it to be a surprise. Trust Chantale to spoil it. And not to like Grandmère's beans! She was definitely strange, Chantale. And had she said Papa was stupid?

"Stupid! What was she talking about? He's a lot smarter than she is, that's a for shore. She's just crazy and mean, just like those barn cats, and that's that," she muttered to herself as she descended the steps sideways, one at a time, holding the banister for support with one hand, so as not to trip and spill the tray. Then she pushed her narrow shoulders against the swinging doors, barely grazing the bottom edges, and scurried through to avoid being hit from behind.

Her mother stood at an ironing board, next to a pile of clothes in a basket on the floor, where Pauline sat banging on pots and pans with a wooden spoon. Baby Nicolas dozed in his wicker bassinet on the corner of the chrome table, relieving his mother at last from his constant crying. Jocelyne placed the tray down carefully on the kitchen counter. She picked up the slippery glass of milk with both hands and gulped down all that remained. She set the glass back into the thin soup of milk on the tray. Then she leaned over and spooned in a mouthful of beans, cold now, but still delicious to her.

"Mom, what's a record?" she asked through the mushy mass she hadn't yet swallowed.

"What kind of record do you mean?"

"A record for music. Chantale said that records play music. But I don't see how."

"Well, that's true. You know how you hear music on the car radio? Well, they play the music from records. They are black, shiny things that look like plates, only perfectly flat, and they have music recorded on them. That's why they're called records. It's very nice to be able to play your own music. Maybe when we have the new house, we can have a record player. Wouldn't that be nice? They are very expensive though. We'll have to see."

"Is Daddy coming home today?"

"Yes, he's supposed to. How do you know?"

"Yeeahh! I can't wait to see him. I wonder if he'll bring me a present? You think he will, like always? One thing for sure is, I'm going to get him to help me bury those kittens, so then I can play in my house under the trees again. I bet he'll help me for sure."

"Su-zanne, come 'elp me 'ere for a minoute. I can't seem to fine de 'ook on de back of 'dis blouse."

The old woman strode into the room, wearing only a blouse half-buttoned in back, her slip and high-heeled boots. Jocelyne was always amazed at her grandmother's openness. She thought nothing of coming into the kitchen in her underwear, in front of any family member, even Richard! Her own mother would never dream of doing that! The little girl couldn't help staring at the elaborate corset peeking out beneath the blouse. Her mother set her iron upright on the blankets padding the ironing board, moved Pauline away from near her feet, and then hurried across the room to help the older woman. They began a conversation about shopping, so Jocelyne turned and headed back through the swinging doors.

Upstairs? No. Better not. She could hear water running in the bathroom. Might bump into Chantale. She threw herself lightly onto the faded green sofa in the room at the bottom of the stairs. This was the dining room. Fancy dishes and sparkly glasses filled the mirrored shelves in a cabinet covering one full wall. A solid wood table squatted in front of the picture window, covered with a lace cloth and encircled with carved chairs, with leather seats and feet of claws. The table seemed just heavy enough to support all the books and papers stacked on it. In the corner, a plant stand overflowed with an abundant fern tumbling to the floor, its clawed toes covered in dry, curled leaves. Light filtered in the paned glass windows through thick lace curtains, but the room remained in shadow. Past the dining room, a parlour extended the length of the house facing the veranda. But the glass doors separating it from the dining room were kept closed and no one ever went inside. Grandmère wanted it kept clean for "special" company. Jocelyne had never been in the parlour.

Jocelyne couldn't remember the family eating at the dining table, either. The sofa was pushed up tight against the backs of the dining room chairs, another armchair leaned in close by, and both faced the television console, standing on tall, wooden legs next to the fireplace. The fireplace was as dark as the empty television screen. When Jocelyne had asked to see it lit one Sunday evening while the whole family was watching *The Ed Sullivan Show* on television, Grandmother had explained:

"In de olden day we 'ad to 'ave a fire alla da time. We use gas now, an' de fire too messy to clean up. I much pre'fer gas, ana way. But we will 'ave a fire for shure when toute la famille come 'ome, pour Noël." A fire was reserved for Christmas, only. Christmas was a long way away, but maybe she would still be here by then. She hoped so!

Even without a fire, the room gave the child a cozy feeling, especially on Sunday nights, Jocelyne's favourite night of the week. After their bath, the two girls were allowed to curl up on the couch in their pajamas and watch television with the adults, just until Ed Sullivan was over at 9:00 o'clock, way past their usual bedtime of 8:00 o'clock. Jocelyne usually sat cuddled up next to Richard. Mom was often upstairs, busy with the baby, and Grandmère sat in her own chair where she could knit, "in peace." She needed room to work her needles, and would push all comers off her lap, even the dog. Chantale never joined them, even when Grandmère called her down to see the puppets or an amazing acrobatic performance.

When the music started for *Bonanza*, Richard would pick her up over his shoulder, smack her bum lightly if she whined to stay up, and race her up the stairs, catapulting her into the air and onto the bed from as far away as the door. What fun! Then he would bounce her up and down on the bed by pushing down on the mattress with his strong arms (which she loved), or tickle her ribs (which she hated), until Grandmère's annoyed voice would call him from downstairs to tell him his show was on.

Thinking of him, Jocelyne worked her arm into the spaces between the back and the seat, in search of treasure. Her fingers retrieved nothing but crumbs. Persistently, she lifted each seat cushion one by one and... ah ha! She knew she'd find some: two quarters and a dime! Hers to keep, according to their secret rules: If Richard left loose change in his pockets and lay down on the couch, where it would slip out into the cushions, oh well. Too bad for him. "Finders keepers, losers weepers," was their agreement. Once she had even found a dollar bill. Her mother had wanted her to give it back, but no, "mon onc" was true to his word. A whole dollar!

He used to be so nice, but today, he was so mean! Why'd he have to go and swing her like that? The thought still made her head spin. And Chantale, how could she be so nice, like a big sister, and then so mean, exactly like those cats in the barn, spitting and clawing? At least with the cats, they were always the same—not nice, then mean, then nice again. If that's how they acted, they might let you pet them and then cover you in scratches! Better not to pet them at all, like Richard said.

She heard the kitchen door slam. Her grandmother was headed for town with Richard. Whew, he was gone and she wouldn't have to see him until suppertime. Her face started to burn at the memory of her morning ordeal. She jingled the money in her pocket. Her mother would stay in the kitchen, she was sure. She made up her mind to venture through the beautiful glass "French" doors. Of course, Grandmère would have "French" doors in her house! Only "de bes" for the Gérards, as she always said.

On the other side of the doors, the space was dark. Sunlight was kept out by thick, red velvet drapes that were always drawn across the broad windows. At night, the lights in the dining room made the unknown room seem like a cave at the front of the house. Distorted reflections of strange objects behind the glass intrigued yet frightened her. When there was a storm, the windows rattled, buffeted by the wind trapped in the veranda. So creepy. What was in there?

The doors opened out easily and didn't make a sound. Her bare feet sank into deep, floral-patterned carpet. She looked guiltily down at her dirty bare feet. Scrunching her toes tightly to make her feet as small as possible, she moved further into the room. The couch and chairs were covered in rich red velvet traced with raised patterns of ferns and flowers. Their wooden arms curved down to become thin legs, ending in claws clutching glass balls for support. The balls looked like giant crystals. How did the couch stand on those? she wondered. Shrugging, she tiptoed further into the room.

In the corner, a tall glass cabinet displayed delicate white statues of people wearing fancy clothes. Against the wall, a spinning wheel waited for a princess to spin the wool in the basket next to it. She knew how it worked from a fairy tale her mother had read to her. She approached with caution, touching it timidly. The wheel moved and she leapt back as a spindle of wool twirled to the floor. She checked her finger for a telltale spot of blood, like in the fairy tale. Whew— must have let go just in time! Whirling around to leave, she saw that the room she was in opened out into an even larger one. Here, another velvet couch crouched against one wall on its clawed paws. Facing it stood a high, strangely shaped wooden box, also supported by wooden cat feet.

She could not have given the instrument its name. Stealthily, she moved to stroke the fine wood, noticing that the rounded narrow top was slit straight across like the lid of a toy box. Just above the centre was a keyhole. Maybe it was locked. She slipped her small fingers under the lip and pulled. The top slid up with a bang, resonating within the depths of the box. Her heart pounded as she gingerly pressed one of the white bars. She caught her breath as sound pounced into the room. Fascinated, she ran her fingertips all along the smooth, cool surface of the white bars in the centre, and then hit one of the shorter black ones. Different in both texture and tone—strange.

"Jocelyne, you know you're not supposed to be in here. We mustn't snoop through Grandma's house. We're guests and it's not polite. Ah... what have you found?"

Startled, she jumped at her mother's voice, almost wetting her pants again. She caught herself in time, squeezed her legs together and turned around with a guilty expression on her pale, freckled face.

Hoping to keep out of trouble, she used her most innocent tone to ask, "I don't know, Mom. What is it?"

Her mother approached and stretched her right hand outward. Keeping her eyes on the white and black pattern before her, she reached down and slid a long bench from underneath, which Jocelyne hadn't even noticed. Sitting down, she placed both hands on the black and white bars. Instantly, her fingertips flew up and down the board and beautiful sounds filled the room. Jocelyne stood next to the bench, staring in amazement as her mother's back swayed while her hands dashed up and down the length of the board. Her shoes clicked against golden pedals, which had also magically appeared when Jocelyne knelt down to look. Standing up again, she sensed that her mother's slender arms needed all the space next to her, so she backed up into one of the velvet armchairs. Still gaping in awe at her mother's transformation, she started to absentmindedly rub the incisions carved into the arms of the chair. The music continued, loud, then soft, then loud again. After a few moments, she sank happily back into the corner of the cushion. Dreamily, she stuck her thumb in her mouth,

Something hard poked into her back. She turned around and discovered that a doll had been propped in the chair. Its head was made of something white and solid, barely covered by straggly bits of reddish hair. The painted face wore a toothy, vacant grin below faded pink cheeks. Naked blue eyes made of glass blinked open, then closed with a click, as Jocelyne rocked the doll up and down, up and down. Though its head was hard, its body was soft. Stiff little hands dangled below the sleeves of its ragged dress, and its tiny booted feet seemed to dance to the music as she held it in the air.

"She's so old and ugly. I feel sorry for her, in here all by herself. Here, you sit with me and listen. What's your name? Isn't it nice, Mummy's music?" Jocelyne plopped the doll into her lap and started to nod sleepily, contentedly sucking her thumb while tracing the china face with a stubby finger. Nose, eyes, cheeks, ears, even, hmmm. Mmmm.

"That was wonderful, Suzanna. I didn't know you could play the piano. I was upstairs and I couldn't believe what I was hearing. I just had to come down and see." Jocelyne jerked her head up to see

Chantale's figure outlined in the bright passage between the rooms, and immediately plucked her thumb out of her mouth.

Chantale's voice was thick and she seemed barely able to whisper. "I don't think anyone has played that old piano since I quit. I wasn't any good at it anyway, but Ma insisted. There were only a few pieces I could play... Please, don't stop."

"Alright, just one more ... then I'd better get supper on before your mother gets home from town, or she'll think I haven't done anything all day."

Chantale's wide backside perched on the arm of Jocelyne's chair, waking her from her dreamy state as she squished her into the corner. Suzanna started playing a bouncy tune that had none of the sweetness of the last one. Jocelyne sat up straight, guiltily hiding her wet thumb in her fist as she held the doll stiffly in front of her. Suzanna finished the song, then pulled the cover hastily over the keys and stood up, her distended front brushing the rounded and polished wooden cover.

"Come, Jocelyne, you can set the table. And you won't come in here anymore without permission, right?" Suzanna admonished, wagging a finger.

"Well, the main thing is, don't let the old bag catch you with that stupid doll," Chantale warned. "It's over a hundred years old, don't you know, and nobody is allowed to touch it. The head, hands and feet are made of porcelain—it's a kind of glass that's supposedly very breakable. God knows why anyone would want the horrible thing anyway. Look at that face. Yikes! Gives me the heebie-jeebies!" She grimaced and shuddered.

"But you know Ma and her precious antiques. What the hell good they are, I'd really like to know. Sit in here collecting dust is all they do, and yours truly gets the fun of dusting them! What a bunch of useless junk," she exclaimed, flinging the spinning wheel into motion as they passed by.

Back in the kitchen, Chantale offered to help, surprisingly for Jocelyne. The young women chatted and worked together to prepare the meal, peeling potatoes, cutting carrots, rolling out pastry. Jocelyne felt content to listen to the soothing rhythm of their voices.

She hummed to herself as she set the table.

"How did you learn to play the piano, Suzanna?" Jocelyne perked up her ears at this. She also wanted to know.

"Oh, well, my dad taught me the basics. He's amazing, can play anything, the piano, the fiddle, the banjo. Totally self-taught. Even had me playing the harp for a while. I can't read music, only play by ear, like him."

"I wish I could play even half as well as you do! I wanted to learn too, but Ma had me taught by the nuns and they smacked you with a ruler every time you made a mistake. And I made lots, of course. Too lazy to practice. So I had to quit, or lose my fingers altogether!" Chantale laughed.

Jocelyne was stunned. She had never heard her aunt laugh, in all the time they had been there. Again, she noticed how different her aunt was with just her mother and herself in the room. Suzanna was more at ease, too. Jocelyne enjoyed the sense of calm their mood created. She finished her chore and skipped out into the sunshine, gleefully letting the screen door fly and slam with a bang behind her, because Grandmère wasn't home to scold her.

She flopped down on the front lawn and gazed at the clouds creating animal shapes in the sky. As her eyes explored the cloud farm above, she wondered about what Chantale had said in her room. Why shouldn't she be here? She loved being at the farm. She was almost glad their house in the village had burned down, though the image of the flames lighting up the night sky still woke her with nightmares from time to time. When that happened, she would do as Grandmère had suggested and sit up, turn around in bed on her knees, and thank her guardian angel, watching over her from the picture above the bed. Grandmère said she had done the very same, when she learned the family was safe. As bad as it was, the fire had brought Jocelyne here, to this wonderful farm. The best place in the world! She could roam freely down by the barn, the machine sheds, even into Blackie's meadow if she were brave enough. It smelled here: smell was everywhere! She loved the way her grandmother smelled, a combination of scents of cinnamon from the pies she made and the horse liniment she rubbed on her arthritic hands, very pungent, earthy and strong. Just now, taking in a deep breath, she could sniff fresh newly mown grass, rich earth, pig manure, pine trees, dead kittens under them (shudder), dinner cooking in the house... everything. The outdoors exhaled rich aromas and she sucked them in greedily. It also thrummed with sound: insects, birds, voices, engines, the wind...

She thought too of the wonders of the house that she continued to discover, even today. Luxurious things the likes of which she had never seen: ornaments on beautifully carved wooden shelves, a piano and records—two new things in one day, books bound in leather, artwork on the walls in golden frames and a spinning wheel, just like in her storybook! Everything so captivating and magical she could hardly believe it was real.

Chez Grandmère was so different from her former, sparsely furnished home: a chrome table and four blue vinyl-covered chairs in the kitchen, a worn out sofa, Mom's rocking chair and one standing lamp with a ragged shade in the living room. Remembering the house brought back the fearful images of that horrible night. Awaking to loud voices. Stumbling into the kitchen to ask for a glass of water, blinded by bright light. Her father, singing at the top of his lungs, with three or four other men, scooping her up into his arms and asking blearily, "Why are you up? Sing us a song, sweetheart!" Mother screaming, yanking her away from her father and rushing with her in her arms back to her room. Then more noise filtering through the paper-thin walls: yelling, banging, breaking glass, while she cried and cried in the dark. What had she done to make Mommy so angry? She had been half asleep and wasn't sure now whether the memory was real or a bad dream. But since they had moved to Grandmère's, Daddy was always in a good mood when he came home, and brought her lots of presents.

"Good thing that fire burnt up that house. Like Grandmère said, it was a bad place, not fit for a pig!" she thought smugly. Now they were living here at the farm and it was so much better, with Grandmaman to look after them, and the pigs and the cats and Blackie, and well, Richard, yes, when he acted nice and even Chantale to play with, sometimes. She barely remembered watching their house turn to ashes, as the firemen doused it with streams of water. All that remained for her were body memories: the chill of standing outside clad only in pyjamas, in the early hours of that morning, the stench of wet wood, the sound of the fire alarms. Someone had left a cigarette burning overnight, or maybe dropped it in the couch, her mother had explained later. Maybe one of those men, or Papa... No, don't think about that.

"We're safe now, and that's all that matters, as Grandmère always says. And now, Daddy's coming home and he'll bring me a present for sure, like always!"

Chapter Six

"Well 'ere 'e is, big as life!" her grandmother exclaimed, as her father's huge outline filled the doorway into the kitchen. He was over six feet and taller still in his cowboy boots and cowboy hat. Jocelyne shrieked with joy, clapping her hands.

"Salut, Ma! Comment ça va? Ça va tout ben, icitte? Where's my gals? Ah, there you is! Ha, can't even surprise you, can I? Well, we'll just see about that!" and from his large coat pocket, he produced a handful of sparkling jewels.

"Oh Daddy, I just can't believe it, well I can *believe* it because I knew you'd bring something but I just love this. I love it, love it, love it!" Jocelyne rejoiced, parading around the kitchen with her arm extended to show off her new beaded bracelet. She snapped the elastic to set the beads dancing on her wrist.

"Careful now. I got it in elastic so's to be sure it'd fit, but it can break. And for you, mon petit chou—what did Daddy bring to his little girl? Ta da—a new dolly. And for Mommy? What's Mommy got here?" Smiling, the man wriggled a small box from the bottomless pocket. His thick, dirty thumb popped the lid with a click. On a bed of blue velvet sat a ring set with pearls and diamonds, a cluster of gems the size of a quarter.

"Oh my God, Paul, you shouldn't have. I mean it, you *shouldn't* have. What with the new house, and another baby on the way. What do I need this for?"

"To light up your life, you silly woman! Just put it on and see what it does for you, for Cripe's sake! S'ppos'd to make you feel like a million bucks, or so the fella said who sold it to me! Anyways, I liked it! It'll make you look like a movie star, by God! Now c'mon over here, let's see what she looks like."

Paul took the ring from the box and placed on the fourth finger of her right hand, then held it out for all to see.

"There ya go, now ain't that just the prettiest thing you ever seen? Everybody in the whole town will be jealous when Suzanna Gérard flashes this at the old grocery store!"

"Well, I sure won't be wearing it when I go to the grocery store in the village, for heaven's sake. This is the kind of thing you only bring out for weddings and funerals, or to go out for a night on the town, and I won't be dancing for a while. It's very… sparkly. Thanks, Paul, but I still say you should take it back. We could do with the money for…"

"Oh damn it, woman, just forget about money for once and enjoy it. Money comes and goes, tabarnak, look at what happened to the house! Sometimes, you just have to live for today and damn tomorrow. Anyways, I have one more gift to give, for my baby boy. Look here what I got on the Indian reserve!" And out of the same deep pocket slipped a tiny pair of leather moccasins with rabbit fur trim.

"Now that's something! I've never seen baby moccasins. Aren't they cute?" exclaimed Suzanna, as she quickly tucked them over her son's chubby naked feet, maneuvering him deftly in her arms, then lifting him up to show his grandmother.

"Oui, ils sont très mignons. Tu dis qu'ils sont fabriqués à la main? Par les femmes indiennes? Sur quelle réserve?"

"I got them from the Sarcee, down south where we're buildin' the road. They make lots of stuff to sell to tourists in the shops in Calgary, but these are ones they make for their own babies. All hand sewn and beaded. Now you look just like a little papoose! And his mother is my Indian princess, with the jewellery to prove it!" he guffawed, with a smart slap to his wife's backside.

"Cut it out, Paul!" Suzanna whirled out of his reach, blushing to the roots of her dark hair.

Oblivious, Paul went on. "I might get myself a pair next time, but they're awful expensive, even at the rate they was askin' me. What I'd really like is a buckskin coat. You should just see the coats the squaws make to sell to the tourists. But they said they'd make me one, tailor-made. Imagine, now wouldn't that be something, eh, Richard?" Paul addressed his brother, just coming in from the yard. A dog tried to nose his way into the kitchen and Richard booted it in the muzzle. The yelping and the slam of the screen door caused him to miss his brother's question.

"Qu'est-ce qu't'as dit? Somethin' about buckskin?"

The conversation turned to French among Richard, Paul and their mother, while Suzanna put the baby in his highchair and then she and Jocelyne finished setting cutlery, glasses and steaming bowls of vegetables on the table. Suzanna motioned to Jocelyne to go upstairs to get her aunt. Jocelyne felt relieved when she saw Chantale coming into the kitchen without the need to be roused from her room, which always seemed to make her grumpier than usual.

"So, the mighty Paul has returned, bearing gifts I see. What'cha brung me, brother? Don't I deserve something for putting up with your brats all this time? Hey, what's in this fancy box, I wonder? Jesus, Mary and Joseph, look at the size of this thing! Fit for Elizabeth Taylor! He can't even afford to get his own house, and look what he's splurging on for his little wifey. Feeling guilty about something are we, perhaps? Hmmmm?"

"Take that off and put it back in the box, right now. Just sit down and shut up for once, can't you? Why do you have to come in here and ruin everything? What'd I ever do to you? I have just as much right to live here as you do, you know. I was lookin' after this place long before you was born, I wiped your snotty nose when you was a baby, and I did a hell of a lot more to help on the farm than you ever do! Is it my fault my goddamn house burned down? What do you want me to do, put my family into the street?"

"No, not into the street. Suzanna doesn't deserve that! Although what she did to deserve you is beyond me! Why don't you get off your cheap, sorry ass and rent them a house in town? This is crazy, having a house full of your brood and you not even here to help out. Ma isn't getting any younger, you know, and I sure ain't about to do all the cookin' and cleanin' after 'em all."

"Oh no, that might be too much to ask. You're so busy, with all your boyfriends sniffin' around, yes I can just imagine!"

"Bon, ça suffit! Chantale, assieds-toi et tais-toi, mon doux! Paul, viens m'aider avec le rôti de boeuf."

"Yeah, let's eat. Just don't expect table manners from these brats. Then you really will be askin' somethin'. Worse than those pigs down there, eatin' slop from the trough."

"Chantale, please," Suzanna interrupted. "We don't mean to be a burden. And the kids are just little, what do you expect? It's hard enough feeling like I'm squatting here, and with everybody speaking French, God knows what you're saying about me. None of you even took the trouble to even try to pronounce my name right, but I haven't minded. I've just put up with it. I can't wait to have our new house too, and move out, but it doesn't help to have you constantly harping about it. I just can't stand it anymore," Suzanna wailed, throwing down the dishtowel she had been using to bring a hot dish to the table. She spun out of the room, throwing the swinging doors aside before struggling up the stairs. Her sobs carried to the kitchen until she reached the upper hallway.

"Chantale, regarde ce que tu as fait! Va dans ta chambre et reste-y, sans souper! Mais avant, va faire tes excuses à Suzanne. C'est insupportable, ton comportement à soir. Mon doux, je sais pas ce qui te prends, mais j'en ai assez. You never know when e-nough is e-nough!"

Jocelyne sat open-mouthed, shocked by her grandmother's tone toward Chantale. She had never heard Grandmère raise her voice to anyone before, or even come close to swearing as she had by saying "mon doux." Even though she couldn't understand everything she had said, Grandmère was obviously very angry.

Chantale stomped from the room, while Richard calmly began dishing a mound of potatoes onto his plate. The rest of the family joined him at the table. Grandmère said a perfunctory grace, not bothering to involve the little girls, as she usually did. Paul served a plate for Pauline while his mother mixed a bowl of potatoes and milk and began spoon-feeding the baby. Jocelyne helped herself to slices of roast beef, potatoes and gravy, avoiding the carrots and peas. Though she loved potatoes and her grandmother's gravy, she could barely eat. Her throat felt like it was swollen shut. She kept her head down, focusing her gaze on her wrist, turning her hand this way and that to admire her sparkling bracelet, between mouthfuls.

The meal was unusually quiet. Paul made a few subdued comments to his mother and helped Pauline with her dinner. Richard, his head bent over his plate, remained silent, concentrating on his fork. Grandmother unconsciously fed herself and the baby at the same time, cooing to him as she spooned in his food and constantly wiped his mouth with the bottom of her apron.

When the girls had finished, Paul reached over to the counter, grabbed a dishcloth and wiped their faces, then sent them to the parlour to play.

"I'll make up a plate for Suze' and take it up, Ma. Would you change Nicolas and get his bottle ready? I'll take him up after she's had something to eat. She needs some time to rest."

A short time later, Paul came back downstairs with an untouched plate. He hoisted his clean, freshly powdered son from the highchair, tipping him forward to ease his legs out of the plastic straps holding him in. Encircling the baby with one hairy arm, he turned to lift the bottle from the pot of boiling water on the stove.

"Ouch, ouch, maudit, c'est chaud." His mother tut-tutted with her tongue, appalled at her son's swearing. She wrapped the glass bottle in a dishtowel, tested the milk on her wrist, and shooed him into the dining room. The clatter of dishes accompanied singing from the easy chair, where Paul found himself bottle-feeding his son.

"Hush, little baby, don't say a word, Papa's gonna buy you a mocking bird. And if that mocking bird don't sing, Papa's gonna buy you a diamond ring..." Jocelyne perched on the arm of the chair and nuzzled against her father's shoulder, revelling in the sound of his voice, his smoky smell, his gentle song. Pauline, curled on the floor at his feet, clung to his leg, trying to climb up to his knee. Paul adjusted his arm awkwardly to insert the bottle's nipple into the baby's searching mouth.

"Jocelyne, va aider ta grandmaman. She's stuck doing all the dishes by herself."

"Non, non, Paul. Laisse-faire. Elle t'a pas vu depuis des semaines. Reste-y là, Jocelyne, avec Papa. Just relax and enjoy. Grandmaman will see to it tall, don' worry," Grandmère called from the kitchen. She, too, seemed to want some time alone.

"What's been going on in this house while I been gone, Jocelyne? Why are all the women in such a temper? Fightin' like cats in a bag! Man, oh man, what a homecoming! A fella'd just as soon stay on the road. So, what you gonna name your dolly, Pauline? You made any better friends with them ol' cats, Jocelyne? What was this about some dead cats, anyway?"

The evening passed quietly. Nicolas was soon asleep in the crook of his father's arm, and Paul dozed off with Pauline curled on his lap and Jocelyne tucked under his shoulder, sucking her thumb. It seemed only a moment had passed when Grandmère shook them awake and herded them upstairs to bed.

Grandmère kneeled beside Jocelyne while she recited her bedtime prayers and when she had finished the list of everyone for God to bless, reminded her, "Don' forget your new brudder or sister, hein. Make shore to say a blessing for 'im or 'er every night as well, so 'e come safely into dis worl'. Now tuck up an' sleep tight," she whispered gently, as she anchored the blankets securely under the mattress. Jocelyne could hardly move or breathe, but she didn't complain.

"Dere you go, snug as a bug in a rug. 'Ere, we open de window jus' a crack to let in some fresh air, but de win' 'e preddy cool tonight. Dat's one ting I appreciate about Alberta compare to Québec—I love de cool evening breeze, me. At 'ome, in de summertime, it was so 'ot at night an' sticky, it was 'ard to get any sleep at tall! Fais de beaux rêves, chérie. Sweet dreams an' we 'ave your favourite—crêpes et sirop d'érable—in de mornin' time. Bonne nuit." The spicy scent of her grandmother wafted over Jocelyne when she bent down to kiss her forehead and placed her wrinkled hand there in blessing. Her grandmother's smell reminded her of apple pie baking in the oven, another of the special treats to be enjoyed regularly at meal times on the farm. Shuddering with pleasure, Chantale wriggled her thumb up from beneath the blankets as soon as the door was softly closed. The day's events seemed like a far-off dream. Everything was peaceful and maybe, if she woke up early enough, she would hear that bird again and get a better look at it. What was it called, oh yeah, a meadowlark. How did it sound again? Oh so pretty, so...

Suddenly, noise and movement broke into her sleep. The furniture downstairs was moving around the rooms, stomping around on huge clawed feet, bumping into walls, knocking over the cabinets, smashing the spinning wheel, breaking through the glass doors! Somehow, she had woken them all up by going into the rooms in the dark and now their cat paws were tearing up the sofa, climbing the stairs, ripping the carpets, knocking down the banister, breaking down the bedroom doors! The wooden cat feet hurled glass balls everywhere, shattering the dining room windows and all the ornaments on the china cabinet. Grandmère, Grandmère, come quick, I didn't mean to, really, they were awake when I got there, and they started chasing me! Help! Help!

Her heart was pounding. Her face and pillow were wet with drool. Her sticky hair clung to the pillow, soaking in sweat. She struggled to hear, despite the blood roaring in her ears. The heavy blankets suffocated her. Kicking to free herself, she swam to the surface of consciousness and immediately reassured herself.

"Oh, I get it. Whew! It was just a nightmeer. Holy cow! I hate, hate, hate nightmeers! Now I'll never get back to sleep! I wonder if I made a noise. I wonder if anyone heard me. Why is it so hot in here? Mom must have come in and shut the window. I'm soaken wet! Oh no, don't tell me, don't tell me..."

Certain she had wet the bed, she fearfully felt under her blankets to check. Whew! No, but she'd woken up just in time. Her belly felt hard and swollen; she really had to go. She burned with urgency. She didn't think she'd make it, but she had to try. She would die of embarrassment if she peed the bed! Wouldn't Chantale just love to tease her and call her a baby then?

It was very dark, but the yard light brightened her room enough to see the door clearly. Glancing up at the invisible, protective spirit on her wall, she hopped out of bed and sped across the icy floor, pushed the slightly ajar door open wide and put a foot into the hallway. Tiptoeing toward the bathroom with her legs held tightly together, she heard voices coming from her parents' room: angry tones, muffled by the door. She couldn't make out the words, and anyway, didn't have time to think about anything but hurrying to the toilet, when suddenly the bedroom door opened and her mother stood before her, in a white nightgown, sobbing. She stumbled into her, just in front of the bathroom door.

"Jocelyne! Oh dear Lord, you scared me half to death! What in God's name are you…"

"Mom, I really, really, have to go. Can you help me? Otherwise I might pee on the seat and then Chantale will be so mad at me again." Jocelyne's voice was almost strangled with fear and she felt near to bursting into tears.

"Yes, yes, come on then, let's hurry up about it," her mother hissed under her breath. Suzanna steered Jocelyne by the shoulders into the bathroom, heaved her onto the cold white toilet seat, and knelt down in front of her, waiting. Jocelyne saw that her mother's cheeks were wet and her face was red and swollen.

"Did you have a bad dream, Mommy? Were you crying? I had a nightmeer and it woke me up and I was so scared! I thought I'd peed the bed and…"

"Shhshh, now. Hush up and hurry up and go. Everyone is trying to sleep!" The whisper was harsh, urgent.

She couldn't go. Even when she strained, nothing would come out. On the cold toilet seat, wearing only her light pyjamas, she started to shiver. Her mother didn't notice. She just stared straight ahead. Then she started at a noise in the adjacent room, where Paul waited, and she stood up. She moved to the sink in the dim light coming through the window from another yard light, turned on the tap and let it run. Returning, she dripped warm water from her hands onto the child's naked thighs. Then she held her daughter's head, petted her hair and hummed the gentle tune she had played on the piano. Finally, Jocelyne relaxed enough to let go. When at last the tinkling had ended, her mother lifted her off the toilet, wiped her bottom and closed the heavy lid without making a sound.

"Shouldn't we flush, Mommy? You know what Chantale will say in the morning. That I'm a baby or something," Jocelyne whispered.

"I don't give a damn what Chantale says," her mother responded at full volume. "We are not going to wake up the whole house just to please her. We don't flush at night in my book, and that's final."

Then she dropped her voice and her tone suddenly sounded tired.

"Quickly now, let's get your hands washed and I'll tuck you back in bed. And we'll say your prayers one more time together, so you won't have any more nightmares, okay?"

Her voice caught in her throat as she whispered, "We've both had enough nightmares for one day."

Chapter Seven

The following day was Saturday, the women's "town day." Children never went to town. Only grownups got to go. Still, Jocelyne loved the bustle in the house in the morning: the smell of steam and starch and the hiss of the iron, the prickly hair curlers discarded on the table for the girls to roll back and forth, back and forth, and stick with their plastic pink and blue pins against the smooth, grey arborite surface, the click of Mom's high heels on the kitchen floor as she rushed around to get ready. Jocelyne had learned to stay out of the way. She would find a quiet spot to observe every detail of the performance, as her mother and grandmother transformed themselves into a princess and a queen. When they finally left, the afternoon would be either wonderful or miserable, depending on Chantale's mood.

But today would be different. She was going to town, too! Mom had shaken her awake early, dragged her into the bathroom, given her a dreaded "sponge bath," scrubbed her ears and elbows until she felt like they were bleeding, brushed her teeth as if they were covered in glue, and yanked a comb hastily through her fine, knotted hair. All this torture—why, she wondered? Then, she hauled her by the arm back to her room and dressed her in her best Sunday outfit. What in the heck was going on? It wasn't church today, was it?

"Grandma wants to take you to town with us today, so you have to be extra good. I want you to sit quietly, don't speak unless you are spoken to, not a word, you understand, and do exactly what you're told. And whatever you do, don't touch anything in the stores. Here, wear your white gloves, that way you'll remember to keep your hands by your sides and to yourself, just like in church. Now, don't get dirty while I get dressed. Just sit in the kitchen. Take your gloves off when you eat your cereal, and put a towel over your front in case you spill on your dress. But DON'T spill on your dress—it's all you've got to wear and I won't have time to clean it if you mess it up!"

Downstairs, her grandmother was ready to go. In her hat and crisp, striped dress she had changed from a plain farm woman to a fine lady, wearing her white-laced boots, white gloves, a white overcoat and carrying a white purse. Under the hat, a brown, curly wig covered her thin, grey hair. Jocelyne loved Grandmère's soft, downy hair, and thought the wig made her look like a clown in the circus. She wouldn't dare to say so, though.

And she was wearing lipstick! "Only to town, never in church, of course!" she exclaimed when Jocelyne made a remark about it. Her mother, on the other hand, came down with her "face on" as usual. Such a strange thing to say: where was her face the rest of the time? It was true, she looked different. But which was her "real" face—her everyday one, or the one with the makeup? Watching her mother "put her face on" was mesmerizing. She would remove coloured paints and creams in little pots from inside a tiny suitcase with a mirrored lid, use many different brushes, and make funny expressions in the mirror as she drew lines on her eyebrows and eyelids, powdered her cheeks and darkened her lashes with a wand. Some things looked like they hurt, like when she plucked her eyebrows with tweezers or curled her lashes with a strange looking instrument. But Mom always seemed to enjoy it, smiling at herself in the mirror when she was finished. Anyway, today, Jocelyne had missed the magic show. Mom was already made up, looking a little flustered and rumpled in her loose-fitting blue suit.

"I'll do my lipstick in the car. I think I'm ready. Now, did I forget anything? Chantale, there are bottles in the fridge and make sure Pauline has her nap, otherwise she'll be on the tear all night. We shouldn't be late. We'll pick up fried chicken for supper, so don't worry about that," Suzanna said in an artificially bright tone.

"Yeah, sure, no I won't worry about supper," came a dark voice from under a cloud of cigarette smoke at the kitchen table.

"Boy, it looks like Chantale is her old self today. Good thing I get to go to town," thought Jocelyne, resisting the urge to stick her tongue out at her sister, clinging to her mom's knee. She thought herself too big to tease her sister today. That was for babies, and she was going to town. She ignored her sister's whining as her mother unfastened her from her leg, and simply said, "Bye, Pauline. See you when I get back." She smiled to herself as she pulled on her short white gloves and spun around to follow her grandmother out of the house. Pauline's screaming voice trailed behind them, "Me come too. Me wants to come. Yeeeeesss. Aaaaahhhh, Moooommmmy..."

Jocelyne had to pull hard to open the heavy car door by its metal handle. Then she had to jump up to sit inside. It was already noon and the closed car was boiling hot. The plastic covering over the upholstered seats was sticky, but Jocelyne didn't care. She sat up straight in the back seat, quietly peeling her bare legs from the plastic, one at a time, as she watched her mother apply her lipstick. The visor mirror bounced as they hit a pothole on the way out of the driveway, and her mother missed her lips and daubed the lipstick tube against the end of her nose. Jocelyne giggled. Her mother sighed and wiped her face with a tissue.

Grandmother drove. She never let anyone else drive, even one of her sons, if she was in the car, much to their chagrin. She didn't have a car of her own, just the rusty old farm truck. She loved to race down the highway in Paul's brand new blue Desoto, even though she had criticized him for buying such an expensive car. When she had finished applying her lipstick, Suzanna gripped the armrest with her gloved right hand and passed a tissue back to her daughter with her left, then motioned her impatiently to sit back in her seat. She put her index finger to her lips to remind her to keep quiet as well.

Jocelyne leaned forward to retrieve the tissue Suzanna had used to blot her lipstick. Her mother knew she liked to open it up and trace the "kiss" with her finger. She would trace the red heart shape over and over, until she tired of it and threw the Kleenex out the open window behind her mother's shoulder, to watch it flutter away in the wind, wondering who might find her mother's kiss.

"A big day for you today, n'est-ce pas, Jocelyne? Nouveaux souliers. New shoe. Dat's what you need to start school in September. You cannot go to school in 'dos old runner. You need a nice pair of good strong shoe, to 'elp your feet grow properly. Oderwise, they grow all splayed out an' you look like a boy. Dis is da bes' time to buy shoe for school right now for shore. We go to my special store an' Jacques will fix us up jus' right. Den my gran-daughter will go to school dress properly on her firs' day to school."

School? What was Grandmère talking about? She didn't know she was going to start school! Holy cow! Her mind whirled as fast as the other cars slipping by on the highway, and she was only vaguely aware of the conversation going on in the front seat.

"This really isn't necessary, Madame Gérard. I could have found her some sensible shoes on sale just before school starts. And Paul must be making good money now, so we don't need to be so careful anymore," said her mother, holding up her hand to look at the ring slipped over her gloved third finger.

She clicked the gold clasp on her purse, took out a metal, pearlescent box, drew out a cigarette, and then reached forward to push in the lighter on the dashboard. The cigarette wiggled between her fingers until the lighter was ready. Jocelyne peered eagerly between the seats, waiting to see the bright orange circle of fire that appeared at the end of the tube from the dashboard. She loved the slight hissing sound as it met the tip of the cigarette, and the smell of the first puff of smoke.

"Pas necéssaire? Pas necéssaire? Lissen I tell you somthink. We didn' come 'ere in Alberta from Québec wid nutink, to build up de bigges' farm in de distric' , practically in de 'hole pro-vince, den to sen' our gran-children to school in dirty running shoe. My chil'ren alway 'ad de bes'. No madder if Papère an' I 'ad to do widout, we make shore of dat. It 'tis a question of family pride for us, ma chère," she exclaimed, smacking the steering wheel with an open hand and shaking her head. Suzanna gripped the door handle as the car picked up speed.

"An' my gran-children will 'ave de bes' too, if my son would just lissen to some sense," the old woman ranted, barely pausing for breath, her eyes glued directly in front of her as the car ate up the road.

"But no. 'E won't stay on de farm. 'E don' like it. An' when I offer to get for 'im an education, no, 'e cannot stick to dat. 'E could 'ave been doctor, lawyer, anytink you like. 'E 'as de brain, jus' not la patience. So 'e goes runs off an' dig a ditch. A ditch digger, you call? What future is dere in dat? Never 'ome wit 'is famille. Always off on de road or sittink in de bar. Now tree kid an' a wife to feed an' not even a decent 'ouse to live in?!" The old woman was out of breath. She cranked the car window open beside her and through the gust of air, found her voice again.

"It t'was only a matter of time before dat shack would burn to de groun', anaway. I always was afraid it twould, but de blessing is, you got out in time. Tanks be to God for dat. But now you 'ave to start all over again. Well, I know what dat is like. We been 'ailed out an' dried out so many time ourself..." Her voice suddenly changed to a lighthearted tone and she glanced back to flash a golden smile at Jocelyne.

"So we go to town an' we buy new shoe an' a new 'at an' we forget about it. We 'ave a nice time in town. We go to my store an' Monsieur Jacques will fix us up, dat's for shore. De Gérard famille 'old it 'ead high in de church on Sunday morning an' in de school 'house too, as al-ways, an' nobody can say any different." She firmly turned the wheel hand over hand to round a corner, then hit the brakes at the first red light on the edge of town. Suzanna and Jocelyne jerked forward, then recoiled back into their seats. Suzanna gritted her teeth in annoyance at her mother-in-law's aggressive driving habits.

"By de way," she said, turning to Suzanna as the car idled, "I tink, me, you should not smoke right now. It 'tis bad for de bébé. I never smoke, myself, but dere was so much smoke in de 'ouse when I 'ad Luc, I am shure dat's why 'e was never strong. 'E cough all da time, an' when de col' weader come, 'e suffer so much. Finally, de pneumonie, it caught 'im an' 'e die. I don' know why all my chil'ren sauf Richard, smokes so much. Dad an' I never did."

"Everyone else does it. Gee, at least I don't drink like the other girls do when they're expecting. I can't believe it when we go to the bar and see them out to here, swilling back the beer. It turns my stomach. But I can't see that I need to give up smoking, though." Suzanna's voice sounded like a whine. She cleared her throat, took a puff, blew the smoke through her nostrils and started again.

"I smoked through all three and only had trouble with Nicolas. The girls were both big and healthy, but he was so sickly when he was born, and he's still pretty tiny. Maybe you're right, though. I should quit. It's a filthy habit, anyway." She stubbed out her cigarette and turned the handle to roll up her window.

Within a few minutes, the old woman handily pulled the huge car into a tight parking stall. Opening the doors only partway, they exited sideways so as not to dirty their clothes on the cars parked on either side. Jocelyne gasped and stared all around her, when she reached the pavement behind the car. They had arrived in "town!" A small city of twenty thousand people, about ten miles from the farm and twelve from the prairie village where Jocelyne had lived. Jocelyne was overwhelmed with the sights of flashing traffic lights, streets filled with cars of every colour and shape, and people dressed in fine clothes bustling down the sidewalks. They stopped in front of a shop with colourful dresses, high-heeled shoes and feathered hats displayed in the window. The door caught a jingling bell as they went inside. Instantly, a man in a dark suit appeared behind a long wooden and glass counter. As he approached them, Jocelyne ducked under her mother's arm, to press her face against the glass, for a better view of the sparkling jewellery inside the cabinet. Her mother wrenched her back to her side, but not before a nose print was left on the immaculate display case. Jocelyne didn't see her mother blush, but felt a pinch on her arm that warned her to be still. Holding tightly to her mother's hand, she breathed in the scent of lemon polish from the wooden counter, and the fresh scents of new leather and cotton from the shoes and clothing on the shelves and racks in the vast space behind.

"Oh, hello, Madame Gérard. So nice to see you," he purred. "And this is your lovely daughter-in-law? Married to Paul, am I right? Ah, and who might this beautiful young lady be?" The tall, thin man stooped down and looked directly at Jocelyne. She was unable to utter a sound.

"Dat tis my gran-daughter, Jocelyne. She start school in September, so we need to get 'er set up for dat. You know what I mean, Jacques? New shoe, new clothe, to look nice on 'er firs' day to school."

"Of course, that's a big day. Well, let's see, young lady, what size do you think your feet are?" The man looked down at her feet. Jocelyne quickly covered one foot with the other, trying to hide her stained, torn running shoes.

Her mother answered shyly. "I really don't know. She's been growing like a weed lately. And running on the farm all summer, as you can see. There's nothing left of these old shoes, I'm afraid."

"Well, let's see here. Take a seat and put your big foot right on this stool. Hmmm. I think we need to measure this foot. Now stand up and put your big toe right up to the edge of this metal plate. See the numbers marked here? That's how I measure to know the right size." Jocelyne giggled as the cool metal tickled the ends of her toes through her thin socks, but quickly regained her composure with one look from her mother. She sat stalk-still, waiting while different shoes were tied or buckled, then walked up and down the aisle from one end of the store to the other, as instructed.

"Such a good girl! Just like a little angel! Well, it must run in the family, I guess!" Mr. Jacques crooned. "Now turn, come forward, stand up straight, now walk again, stand still, Sweetie, while I give a little pinch at the end of the toes. Here, Madame, you squeeze on the sides too. You want to have some room, but these little feet won't stop growing, you know! You'll be in for another pair in no time."

After what seemed like hours, she had not one, but *two* pairs of shoes—a pair of black and white shoes called saddle oxfords that were hard and painful, for school, but also a shiny pair of black ones, patent leather they were called, with a strap and a gold buckle, for church! She didn't really like the saddle shoes, but Grandmère insisted, saying they would keep her feet from spreading out like a boy's.

"You don' want big, ugly feet when you grow up, n'est-ce pas? De feet need to be train' to grow proper-ly, like a lady, by wear good solid shoe. Now, Monsieur, she also need new white glove for la Messe an' yes, let us try dat white cotton dress wid les papillons, 'ow you say, de butterfly. Ah, elle est belle, n'est-ce pas? Look 'ere, Jocelyne, a proper crinoline underneat'. An' she need a 'at al-so. I like 'dis straw one wid de wide ruban. Qu'est-ce que tu en penses, Jocelyne?"

Jocelyne just shook her head up and down, accepting every suggestion her grandmother made. She had never seen so many pretty things. Her eyes darted everywhere, from the jewellery in the display case, to the mannequins in the window.

The old woman opened the metal clasp on her purse with a click and drew out her wallet. Counting out a pile of bills, she noticed Jocelyne staring above Mr. Jacques' head at a golden yellow lace dress, with a pink silk rose at the neck and ribbons on the short sleeves, pinned high up on the wall above the counter.

"You like dat one, don't you, chérie? Imagine-toi, to show up in such a dress on your firs' day to school? Me voici, Jocelyne Gérard! Que je suis belle! Am I not the mos' be-ooo-utiful girl in de worl? Yes? Qu'est-ce que tu dis? We try it t'on?"

"No, Madame Gérard, it's too much, really, and not practical for school at all," Suzanna protested.

"Mais voyons, she 'ave de res' of 'er life to be practical. You're only young once, an' believe you me, you are old a long time. We 'ave a look at dat one, s'il vous plaît, Monsieur Jacques."

Leaving the store with her grandmother carrying two dresses wrapped in tissue paper in a cardboard box, wearing her new saddle oxfords and her wide-brimmed hat, Jocelyne felt like the world belonged to her. Following her grandmother outside, she deliberately pulled the door of the shop back and forth, to hear the jaunty sound of the bell, until her mother reached behind her and pulled the handle firmly to shut the door. Click. Between the cool quiet of the shop into the blinding, noisy sunlight, she could hardly see. It took a moment for her eyes to adjust.

"Oh yes, there's the car, parked up against the sidewalk," she reassured herself, getting her bearings. "I guess it's time to go back home."

What did Grandmère just say? Holy cow, they were going to a café!

"We get to go for doughnuts and coffee, just like the big ladies in the street! Hurray!" she cried.

She stood taller in her new shoes. They felt good, even though the leather was stiff and her feet were pinched at the sides. The old runners had been left behind, tossed in an empty shoebox by "Monsieur Jacques," who had wrinkled his nose and held them out by his fingertips as if he were handling a dead cat. Thinking of which, she could use her new boxes for coffins for the cats. They still weren't buried! Dad had promised, but he forgot. Oh well.

Anyway, she was glad her dirty runners were gone. Runners were fun, but always quiet. Perfect for sneaking around the farm. But hard shoes made noise. Better for the cement sidewalks in town and for school, for sure. They said something. Heel, toe, click, click.

"I am Jocelyne Marie Gérard. I am going to school. I am almost six years old. I am a big girl now. I am going to a restaurant," she chanted over and over silently as she kept pace beside her mother. Click, click. Mama's shoes, click, click. Grandmaman's shoes, click, click, click, click. Jocelyne's shoes. Click, skip, skip, click, click. Shoes clicking down the cement sidewalk, Saturday afternoon, in town. Going to a restaurant. For a doughnut! Yeah! Click, click.

Chapter Eight

Jocelyne dozed in the car on the way home, wrapped in the new sights and sounds she had experienced. The greasy, spicy smell of the store-bought fried chicken in a cardboard bucket on the seat next to her filled her with anticipation of still more delights to come. Mmm, what a day! A glazed doughnut and cream soda pop in a café! Riding in the shopping cart at the "super" market, until it was filled with so much food there was no more room for her. Even though her feet hurt, she hadn't complained that she had to walk beside the cart: she loved standing next to her mother's beautiful dress and hearing the click, click of her heels on the shiny linoleum floor. She had never been on the mysterious Saturday shopping trip, and couldn't believe her eyes: stacks of fruits and vegetables, piled high in rainbows of colour; row upon row of freezers that made your teeth chatter just standing there; aisles of cans with pictures to show what was inside. Even beans!

"Dese can never beat 'omemade, from Grandmère, but we can try dem if you wan', ma belle," her grandmother had laughed, dropping two cans into the cart. Jocelyne held onto the side of the cart as they bumped across the parking lot to the car. Talking continuously, just to hear her voice jiggle, she raved about the wonders of the "super" market. The village store that she knew so well had definitely lost its charm. She had thought it huge, crammed to the rafters with food, tools, clothing and one whole counter of candy. Hah! That was nothing! Wait until Pauline got her chompers on the candy they'd bought her as a treat, which Jocelyne had been allowed to pick out from the racks of treats on display beside the cashier. And another thing: so many people in the store, more than she had ever seen except on parade day in the village. They'd had to wait in line a long time to pay, but she hadn't minded, wishing instead that the day would go on forever.

The motion of the car and the quiet conversation in the front seat lulled her to sleep. The hat came off and was placed carefully on the floor in front of her. Daring to pull off her gloves, she crumpled them in her sweaty hand, lay down on the seat and stealthily stuck her thumb in her mouth.

"Jocelyne, here we are, honey. To market, to market to buy a fat pig, home again, home again, jiggedity-jig! Time to get in for supper." Her mother gently shook her shoulder. The car had stopped. When the cold air hit her face, she was instantly awake, and eager to tell everyone about her day. Avoiding the dog greeting them at the door, she hopped up the doorsill into the kitchen and then carefully unbuckled her new shoes and placed them side by side on the mat. She hurried to climb onto her kitchen chair, perching on her knees as usual to be level with the table. The groceries were put away and the table was set. Jocelyne had been left sleeping in the car and had missed out on all her chores. "Holy cow, am I ever lucky today," she murmured to herself. Her stomach immediately responded to the smell of food. Embarrassed, she quickly leaned into the chrome edge of the tabletop, to stop the growling.

"What tis dat growl I 'ear? I tawt de dog were out-side. Oh non, c'est Jocelyne, telling us she is 'ungry, as usual!" Grandmother teased, ruffling her hair as she came to sit beside her. Everyone laughed, including Chantale.

Jocelyne heaped a spoonful of the canned beans on her plate, reached for a bun and opened her mouth to speak. Grandmère signalled by putting her index finger over her lips, then pointing to everyone at the table, signalled that this was not the time to interrupt. Everyone had to be served and then Grandmère had to give a blessing, before the meal could begin. The family was just passing around the bucket of fried chicken, when Paul appeared at the screen door.

"Well, how was town, girls? Same as always? What'd you think, Jocelyne? Big enough for ya?" he boomed, letting the door slam behind him.

"Oh, Daddy, you just wouldn't believe it. We went to a "super" market. There were rows and rows of fruit, even bananas, and Mom bought me a doughnut and cream soda—it's pink and fizzy! And look at my new shoes over there, and that's not even all I got. Grandmère bought me two pairs, the best ones are the black ones, they're so shiny! And I got two new dresses for school, not just one, and a hat and...did you know I'm going to school?"

"Yes, that's very nice, honey. Pass the chicken. Well, you won't believe what happened to me today. It must have been fate what you said yesterday, Chantale, because I met a guy in the bar and he has a house for rent just outside the village, on an acreage. The chicken plant is across the road, and it's a bit smelly when the wind blows the wrong way, but the house is good enough. So there you go, I took it, and we move in next week. We'll finally be outta your hair, Ma, and you won't even have to wait until our new house is ready. And, Chantale, just before I forget, here's for all your trouble helping with the kids." He reached into the back pocket of his pants, wrenched out his thick leather wallet, and handed a bill to his sister.

"Cent pieces! Mon doux, Paul, c'est ben trop. C'est même pas necéssaire. C'est à ta soeur de t'aider. On est de la famille, après tout! Tu n'es pas obligé de lui donner de l'argent, voyons."

"Non, Ma, she's bitched enough about helpin' out with the kids when we go out, to earn a hundred bucks for the summer. There you go, Sis, sorry for the pain in the ass. Although just what's put a burr under your saddle since we been here, I'll never know. Didn't hurt you to look after my kids once in a while to help your brother, for Chris' sake. I pulled you out of enough jams and looked after you plenty of times when you was little. Oh well, don't say I never paid you back, and just make sure you never ask me for anything again, when you're in a jam. Ever, that clear? 'Cuz this is it, kiddo. We're square."

"Jeez, thanks, Paul. That's great, I mean, really great. I'll be sorry to see you all go, but I do think it's better to have your own place. That's all I meant by it. No offense or anything."

"Well, you could'a fooled me. Anyway, we're out and it's gonna be heaven. You should see this place, Suz. It's kinda a little house—the girls will have to bunk together in one room 'cuz there's only two bedrooms. Nicolas can sleep in the crib in our room for now and when the new baby comes, why we should be in our house by that time. The place is furnished, except we'll have to get bunk beds for the girls. There's an electric wringer washer downstairs and a clothesline right off the porch, so that'll be handy for you. There's even a barn and the yard is huge. There's room for a swing for the kids—I'll have to see what I can pick up at an auction sale. I was thinkin' we should get a dog. I know a fella who has pups to give away. There'd sure be room out there and it'd be good for you to have a guard dog when I'm on the road."

Her father's voice drifted off as Jocelyne tried to make sense of what he had said. They were leaving? Very soon? Before the first day of school even?

"But, Dad, I don't want to go. I like it here at Grandmaman's! There's the dogs here to look after Mom and I get to help with the pigs, and Chantale promised me I could ride the horse pretty soon, and there's lots of stuff to do here and I like it here with Grandmaman!"

"Dat's troo, ma chérie. 'Oo will cook you dose bean you like so much, hein? Ne t'en fais pas, don' you fret, I teach your maman 'ow to cook it t'all before she go. Den you can 'ave it anytime you like, d'accord?"

Jocelyne didn't hear the end of her grandmother's sentence, as she ran from the room crying and threw herself on the dining room sofa. She lay there sobbing while the rest of the family finished their meal. Before long, the dishes were clattering in the kitchen and the cigarette smoke was drifting through the swinging doors, but Jocelyne didn't move, even when they called her for pie and ice cream. No, no, no, she cried silently, kicking her feet against the cushions. The worst day, the worst day ever. Chantale, it was all her fault. Dad had said so. She sobbed until her chest ached.

A while later, her grandmother swung the doors open and entered the dining room. She held a thin, metal tube in her hand. She turned the child over on her back, pulled the little white sock off her foot, and began rubbing her leg and foot with cream she squeezed from the tube.

"Dose new shoe, dey 'urt your feet an' leg, I bet. Not use' to dem yet. Dis is de liniment we use on de 'orse. It work so good on 'dem, I tought, why not try it on de 'uman beean. An' shure enough, it good for us too. I use it on all my kid, 'specially when dey go troo de growin' pain, twelve, tirteen year ol'. Me too, on my poor ol' 'and all crippled up wid de arthrithe. You tink so too? Feel so much better now, n'est-ce pas? Dere, le's do de odder one, hein?"

"That really is nice, Gram. It stings a little but it's a good sting. It smells strong, like medicine. But, Grandmaman, please, please, please, I don't want to go. I love it here at the farm with you. Why is Daddy making us go? Was it what I said at the table about the cats and Chantale got so mad but I was just worried about those cats and I didn't mean it. I'm sorry, I'm sorry. Is that why we have to go?"

"Non, non, chérie. What make you tink about dat? Dat 'ad nutting to do wid it. Your fadder, 'e always want to go 'is own way, dat is all. Never stick to one ting too long at ta time. 'E as to move, always move. 'E always done dat type of ting, an' 'e always will. 'E never sit still, even as a small chil'. Ressless blood, I always tink, Papère always say it twas de blood of les voyageurs, da fur traders who firs' came to dis lan'. Me, I jus' tink it tis a lack of commitment, to stay in one place an' work 'ard, like me and Papère did," she exhaled a deep sigh as she rubbed the liniment even harder into Jocelyne's calves. The child tried to squirm away, but was held firmly by the other bony hand.

"Anaway, what can you do?" She went on, "E does tink he knows bes an' 'im, 'e always 'as to make 'is hown decision an' den live wid it. So, 'e will move you to annudder place, an' you will spend de 'ole win-ter dere because your 'ouse, she won' be rea-dy until next spring, I guarantee. He say de fall. Ha, we'll see. I know workman, me, and I know your papa al-so. But may-be Chantale is right an' it tis for de bes'. Your maman, she very tired, très fatiguée, an' it tis not so easy to rest under anudder woman's rooftop. I can appreciate dat, for shore. But now she will be all alone to look after all of you, wit' a new babe on de way an' no 'elp attall. But dat's your fadder for you. Act in 'aste an' tink about de consequence when it tis too late. Trop tard. So, you will 'ave to do your bes' to 'elp your maman, d'accord? An' you can call me on de phone, any-time. An' I will for shore come to visit you an' bring somet'ink special wid' me, a tourtière, de meat pie you love, remember? Or your favourite bean, hein?"

She kept her soothing voice low so the others in the kitchen couldn't hear. Then with a sigh, she stood up and leaned over to switch on the floor lamp next to the sofa. Its cream-coloured glass lampshade bathed the room in a butterscotch glow. Jocelyne remained on the couch and watched her move to the buffet next to the window, a huge piece of furniture which occupied one whole wall of the room. A length of lace across the top protected the polished wood from dust. Green glass figurines of herons and cranes stalked the surface, among silver-framed photographs. Shelves on either side reached almost to the dining room's high ceiling, each one graced with another figurine made of the same solid emerald glass. The shelves were separated by a row of delicate pillars spiralling upwards amongst carved vines and flowers. The wide expanse in the middle was glazed with a smoky, spotted mirror, distorting the reflection of the ornaments. The lower half of the cabinet consisted of drawers, wide ones in the middle and narrow ones down each side. Jocelyne knew, from watching the proceedings last Christmas, that the buffet held many treasures: cutlery, china, crystal, linen, candlesticks, everything needed to set the dining room table when it was expanded to serve the whole family.

She watched in fascination as her grandmother grasped each of the antique brass handles on the lowest drawer and tugged. The heavy drawer tipped forward once she had succeeded in wrestling it open.

"Look 'ere," she said, motioning for Jocelyne to move closer on the sofa, near the light. "I want to show you dese picture of your ancêtres. I keep everytink in dis drawer 'ere." She withdrew a thick, leather-bound album, joined Jocelyne on the couch and opened the cover. Tiny silver triangles held the corners of black and white photographs, two on each black page. Jocelyne touched the rough paper and breathed in its inky, dusty scent as her fingers moved toward the shiny faces staring out at her. Her grandmother's hand gently guided her tiny index finger to the scalloped edges of each photograph, as she told their stories.

"Dis is Great–grandmaman. Ici, your great-grandpère. Dis is your great aunt Jocelyne. You are name after 'er. I give all you chil'dren your name, from da famille, according to our tradition. Ma famille—on my side, we are among de firs' familles in Canada, straight from France, more dan tree 'undred year ago. We stay in Québec an' all marry in good famille—"pure laine" it tis call, only de bes' of de bes'—notaire, docteur, landowner, even a governor, 'ho knows. Mos' of dese people are dead now, comme ton grandpère. But bot' our family, "pure laine," eider side, meaning pure as lamb's wool, wid' lan' to pass down for generation." Her voice took on a glowing tone. She tapped the picture of her father with her twisted forefinger, and continued.

"Dat de reason why my fadder permit me to marry your grandpère. De fadder 'ad to give 'is blessink in dose time, chérie, or you could not marry. But in de famille of Papère, dere was not enough lan' to go pass down to all de son, an' 'e wasn' de oldes' so 'is fadder could not give 'im too much in any case. Tirteen children in 'is family, what could 'e do, hein? Can you imagine?" Jocelyne shook her head, no, of course not!

"Dey 'ave so many chil'ren to feed, one of your great-aunty was give to de church, to become a nun. 'Ere she is, when she was a young girl wid 'er famille. Soeur Marie-Joseph, almos' fifty year now since she enter de con-vent, poor ting. Ah oui, she is still alive, an' she write to me, souvent, very often, of course what else 'as she got to do wid 'er time? Always ask about la famille, since she 'ad none of 'er hown. Not like me wid' all dose chil'dren!" she chuckled to herself.

"Me, I keep all 'er letter in dat drawer, al-so." She paused, turned to the child staring at her with rounded eyes, and caressed her chin with her thumb and forefinger. Then she withdrew her hand and turned another page.

"Dis is your grandpère, when 'e was much younger, in fac', when 'e arrive en Alberta an' send to me a picture of 'is self taken by a photographe at de train station. 'E come 'ere "un pionnier," like 'is ancêtres did in Québec. Firs' family, mais, en Alberta dis time. Lan' almos' free on de prairie, jus' clear de groun' an' start to plow. Nuttink but dirt an' tree and rock ever-where, when 'e got 'ere. An' jus' look what 'e build! Such good lan', soil like chocolate cake, le gâteau au chocolat, we use to say. Dat's why Papère come 'ere, to 'ave a big farm an' lots of lan' to pass to de next generation. Look right 'ere is de paper to prove it tis our hown lan' now an no-body can take it from us, never! Dat's why you en' up born 'ere. Strange, n'est-ce

77

pas?" She posed the question, but her eyes remained focused on the photograph.

"You mean, I could have been born in Québec, Grandmaman?" Jocelyne interjected.

"No, not really, chérie, because your mudder, she not from Québec, is she? Well, Grandpère, 'e never fear 'ard work an' he wan' to make 'is own way in de worl'. So far from 'ome. So young, only twenny-one year old. 'E could not speak one word of Eng-lish when 'e came—'is Eng-lish, she en' up much bedder dan mine. Dat is because 'e 'ad to work for odder people durink wintertime, jus' to make enough money to buy grain in de spring." She paused, placing her whole hand on the photograph and keeping it there.

"It t'was 'ard, I'm telling you. 'E even 'ad to do dat sometime when de kids dey was small, so we could make enough money to eat, an' me, I 'ad to stay 'ere alone and do everythink by my-self. Toute seule. But we 'ave no choice. Anyway, 'e came back wid some money and some funny story, dat's for shore. One ol' farmer was so dirty, Papère foun' a dead mouse in de teapot one day an' den 'e realize dey'd been drinking tea outta da pot de whole time! So 'e 'as to learn to cook too, or be poison by de ol' man! Dat one always made me laugh so 'ard! 'Is face, all screw up when he tell it, jus' imagine, drinkink tea wit' a dead mouse in de pot! I would not recommend dat recipe, me! But it never kill 'im, which is a pure miracle!" She laughed until she choked, nearly suffocating, Jocelyne happily joining in.

Then she bent over to catch her breath, raised her glasses off her nose with her fingertips and wiped her eyes with her apron, before continuing to speak.

"After five year as a bachelor, cooking for 'is two brudder an' 'imself, 'e en' up a pruddy good cook, for shure! But not as good as me! Tank God Maman taught me to cook, 'specially dose bean wid de maple syrup you like so much, hein? Well, Papère, 'e wouldn' bring me out until 'e 'ad built a 'ouse for us. Not dis 'ouse, but anudder one dat was pruddy good for a firs' 'ouse. My fadder insist 'dat we 'ave a decent 'ouse, or 'e not give 'is blessink for me to go at tall. As it t'was, 'e was not 'appy about it, but 'e finally 'ad to let me go. An' me, when I see dat tree room log cabin for de firs' time, I tell you, I tought it t'was so cute an' jus perfeck! Papère, 'e could build anyting, you know, wid 'is very own 'and. 'Course dere was only two of us at dat time; 'is brudder 'ad move to dere hown lan by dat time. Den after a few year go by, we 'ave Ghislain, den your Papa, den Danielle, you never met 'er, she been gone from 'ome many year now, and den Richard, an' petit Luc 'ho died as you know, an' finally, Chantale. She was our last surprise, wid me already forty-seven year old! We could 'ardly believe it, but it t'was true! Our liddle gif' or 'cadeau,' like a present, n'est-ce pas? Ana-way, dat's what we call 'er when we foun' out de surprise. I never tought to 'ave so many children, me." She sighed heavily, and wiped her eyes again. She wasn't laughing anymore, so why were there still tears, Jocelyne wondered.

"We was preddy crowd' in de ol' farm 'ouse at firs', but we manage until we get de money to build dis 'ouse. My dream, to 'ave a 'ouse de same style like in Québec. But, ton pauvre grandpère, 'e never even live long enough to see dis 'ouse all finish. 'E work 'imself to deat', I tink. Den me, I lef' all alone to finish everytink an' keep it tall going. Tank be to God I 'ad some 'elp from 'de children, but now, dey all leave, one by one. 'Ow could we imagine dat, dat I could end up all alone?"

"No, Grandmaman, you're not alone! We are here now and I want to stay! I don't want to move into the village. I want to stay here with you on the farm, with you and Blackie and I can tame those cats, you'll see, we'll have them as pets for us, and..."

"Papère mus' turn over in 'is grave, even more dan my fadder. 'E would be so disappoint in me, not 'olding a family togedder bedder dan dat. Dese kid, it 'talways like war in dis 'ouse nowaday! C'est pas bon, it's not right at tall. I don' unnerstan! I did my bes', what more could I do? Now, it will soon be all gone—nobody 'as no interest nomore, run off, get marry outside de church, break up la famille. Never lissen. Dey don' want to stay togedder, but dat's what a family 'as to do for de 'eritage, for de strengt', to stick togedder troo good time an' bad. Dat's what I always tought, ana-ways."

Her voice drifted off, in an unending stream, as she gazed down at the album without seeming to focus on the pictures. Jocelyne couldn't understand much except the sad tone of her grandmother's voice.

"What will 'appen to your 'eritage, when I'm gone, hein, chérie?" The old woman clasped Jocelyne's chin in her trembling hand for a moment, pinched her cheek, then flipped another page.

Jocelyne squinted and stared at the somber faces in the pictures. Light passing through the half-sized swinging doors to the kitchen threw shadows across the book. The images in the black and white photographs were slightly blurry, but the eyes were hollow, expressionless and the lips didn't smile.

"Why do they all look so mean, Grandmaman? Why isn't anyone smiling? They look kind of ... creepy. Doesn't it make you feel sad to look at all those dead people?"

"Well, life was 'ard for dem. An' people didn' smile to get dere picture taken in dos time. It twas consider a special event, very expensive too, an' dey want to look sérieux. Dese are de only picture we 'ave of dem, so dey are very précieux. Dat's why I want you to know where dey are kep'. I don' know if anyone else will care about dem, when I'm gone. I wan' you to look after dem for toute la famille. I will write on de back of each one, so you know 'ho dey are, some time when I get aroun' to it 'ere pruddy soon. I got so many paper to look after," she gestured to the dining room table, "but dere is never time." Suddenly, she snapped the thick album shut, rubbed her palm against the cover, then absently traced the designs on the tooled leather with her knobby forefinger.

"Why, where are you going, Grandmaman? Are you going away, too?"

"Non, non, 'ush now. Now look, I want to show you some odder ting, too." She slowly raised herself from the couch. She flopped the book awkwardly back into the bottom of the deep drawer. She had to bend over to force it closed with the weight of her whole body. Then she easily tugged open a narrow drawer in the middle of the bureau.

"Lookie 'ere at dese!" Attracted by the immediate rise in her grandmother's tone, Jocelyne anxiously kneeled over the curved wooden arm of the couch to see. Grandmère held up a small, triangular shaped stone, placed it carefully on the lace cloth, then added another, a bit larger, then another, until the front of the bureau was lined with them, each one unique in colour and size.

"Pointes de fleche—arrow 'ead, you call in Eng-lish. Papère fine dem when he firs' till de soil 'ere, walkin' behin' de plough. You seen de ol' rusty plough, standin' in Blackie's fiel'? Dat's all Papère 'ad when 'e firs' come 'ere en Alberta. Of course, we don' use it any more. But 'e fine dese arrow 'eads, parce que... ben, 'e was de firs' white man 'ere of course. Before dat, nutink, sauf les Indiens. Dey was all gone too by de time Papère got 'ere, but still, I feel sorry for dem. It twas der 'ome firs', an' dey lost everytink dey 'ad. We didn' mean any 'arm, but dey was lef' wid no 'ome and no bison to eat. All gone. Very sad. Now look at dis, too. 'E also foun'... a dinosaur toot. Look at de size—it mean she was a very big dinosaur, walkin' somewhere on dis very spot. Imagine-toi! Just tink on dat a minute! All dis to say de dinosaur, dey was 'ere long be'fore any of us at tall, an' den de Indian an' now us. Incroyable, incredible, n'est-ce pas? Who will be next, in dis place, I wonder?" Jocelyne shook her head eagerly.

"I don't know, Grandmaman. Who do you think?"

"Bein, I don' know. Everytink change, an' some'ow you jus, you 'ave to accept, I guess... Dat's what your Papère say to me, when 'e decide to bring in de pig during la Dépression. La diversité, he say. Dat's 'la reponse,' de answer. Everybody hun'greh, an' de pig, dey not cos' a lot to feed an' bring in a steady income when nobody could sell any grains. So Papère, 'e 'as de pig. I never care for dose pig much, but me, I raise de chicken an' turkey, an' den, les enfants, dey collect de egg an' milk de cow, an' we sell egg an' milk an' meat an' my 'omemade pork pies dat you like too, chérie, "la tourtière," an' we never starve like some I could mention. Non, pas nous-autres! We survive an' not lose our farm, like so many odders. We even make more money, finalement, an' do verry well in de en'. Alors, Grandpère, 'e was right, n'est-ce pas?"

Her voice was bright as she smiled and winked at Jocelyne. The child noticed that her grandmother's green eyes sparkled every time she mentioned "Papère."

"Non, I never like dose pig. 'Ow about you?" She scrunched up her nose and her wrinkled face became even more creased. Jocelyne giggled at her expression, but she nodded up and down that yes, she loved them!

"I can' stan' de mess an' de smell. Colline de bine, ça pu! Even chicken stink is better dan pig, if you ask me. Richard, 'e de only one to keep it up, an' you notice I make 'im keep 'is clothe outside before I will wash dem. Richard, 'e cannot manage de lan' all by him' self, so we 'ave to rent it out, nobody to farm it ana-more, nowaday. I cannot imagine—stranger on our lan', what next? But my boy all say too much work, too much expense, an' risk an' no money in it. May-be, but what about de life? You work togedder, you make a strong famille, an' de lan', she is your hown, it belong to you, no expense dere, ana-way!"

The old woman now stood arguing with her reflection in the buffet mirror, as she patted her fine grey curls. Jocelyne sensed her grandmother's distress, and barely breathed, to avoid interrupting the flow of her words.

"All de res' of de children get marry, move away, run away from life 'ere. Firs' Ghislain, den, Danielle, mon doux! Now your fadder, 'e won' stay needer. We work so 'ard to give dem everythink. At 'ome, four, five generation on de lan', everyone proud of la grande famille, stick togedder an' get strong an' rich. 'Ere, it tis so different. No tradition. Pas de culture. Sometime, I wish I 'ad never lef' 'ome. I break my mudder's 'eart, an' all for what? Jus' sorrow an 'ard work alla da time."

The sadness in her voice had returned. Still facing the mirror, she gathered the arrowheads one by one and replaced them in the drawer.

"I got more paper in 'ere. I jus' 'ave to get dat all sort out one 'o dese days, when I 'ave de time. Le testament de Papère, Grandpère's will, an' all kind o' paper dat need to be look at. Ahhh," she groaned and pushed the drawer closed. After smoothing down the doily on the top of the cabinet, she shifted to the left in front of a bank of even wider drawers. She tugged at the brass handles, twisting the heavy drawer from side to side, but it wouldn't budge.

With a shrug, she grunted in disgust. "I 'ave to remember to get

Paul to fix dat dam' drawer for me. It 'tis alway too 'ard for me to get open. I was going to show you my mudder's silver, dat I brought wid me from Québec. What good is it to 'ave a silver service dat you can never use jus' be-cause you cannot get de dam' drawer to o-pen?" She smacked the drawer with an open hand, exasperated.

Jocelyne started at the sudden movement. She had never heard her grandmother say so much at one time before. The stories she shared were usually short, sprinkled like salt and pepper amongst the daily chores. Jocelyne held her breath, keeping quiet in the hopes that more treasures would appear from the depths of the cabinet. But instead, the old woman turned and returned to Jocelyne's side, perching on the edge of the couch. Jocelyne slipped down from her seated position to lay flat once more. Strong hands started rubbing her legs with the liniment again. She turned her head to face the back of the seat so her grandmother wouldn't notice her thumb wriggling its way into her mouth. For what seemed a very long time, the only sound in the room was the ticking of the grandfather clock. Jocelyne had started to drift off to sleep when suddenly Grandmère stopped her ministrations.

"Dere, does she feel better on your feet an' leg now? You cannot wear your new shoe all day for a while, ma chère, because you will 'ave to break dem in, jus' like a new horse. See, you got a blister on your 'eel all-ready. Come on upstair. We fine a bandage an' den we tuck you in bed for de night. Time for "bonne nuit," hein and to say our prayer? Grandmaman, elle est très fatiguée, so ti-red. An you al-so, n'est-ce pas? Such a big day for a liddle girl. Viens, ma petite. Up we go."

Chapter Nine

Sunday morning. All was quiet. Jocelyne woke, put on her new white cotton dress sprinkled with orange butterflies, white hat and gloves, white socks and black patent shoes. Her foot was sore where the blister on her heel rubbed against the hard leather. She didn't care. Even her beautiful hat and shoes couldn't make her feel better. Her careful footfalls creaked against the silence in the house as she stepped, one by one, down the stairs. None of the usual cooking sounds came from the kitchen this morning: no breakfast was allowed until after Mass. That meant they fasted until noon, sometimes longer. And this was only one of the many discomforts to be endured, as Jocelyne knew only too well. But it was worth it in the end, when Mass was over.

In the kitchen, Grandmaman and Paul greeted each other with a nod and led Jocelyne to the car. They drove silently into town to the Catholic Church. Suzanna stayed home with the younger children, pleading a headache. Anything to beg off from the ordeal of dressing a squirming toddler and a colicky baby and then struggling to keep them quiet for an hour or more, next to her immaculate mother-in-law. Suzanna wasn't even Catholic, but usually did her best to be part of the expected appearance in the family pew. But not today. Chantale had refused to be aroused and, of course, Richard had risen early and was safely busying himself down in the pig barn, where he knew no one would dare come to get him, dressed in their Sunday best.

The mass dragged on endlessly. The pungent aroma of incense and candle wax only heightened the hunger Jocelyne felt gnawing at the inside of her stomach. She sat glumly on the hard wooden bench next to her grandmother, staring at her shiny shoes, swinging her feet back and forth, back and forth, until she received a sharp slap on a bare leg. Grandmère pulled her down beside her, onto her knees, while she murmured prayers, pressing her lips into a string of purple and white beads. Jocelyne imitated her, using the sparkly elasticized bracelet from her wrist and muttering nonsense words. Again, another smack. Now what had she done wrong?

Jocelyne sighed. Grandmaman would tolerate no nonsense in church. Children were to be seen and not heard. "Listen to de fadder—sshht, see—lence, 'ush up." But he was speaking some other language, not French or English. Just sing-song words, which sounded nice but made no sense at all. No matter how hard she listened, she could never understand what was happening at the front of the church, high on the altar so far away. Always a blur of sound and movement that somehow directed the adults to kneel, sit or stand, actions she followed as if she were in a dream.

She turned her gaze to the pictures on the walls around the church, just above the pews. Grandmaman had told her they showed how Jesus had suffered. "Tink how 'E suffer for our sin, an' you can' even wait a few hour for breakfast? Dat is why we fast, to remine us of 'ow Jesus suffer an' die for us. If you cannot sit still, tink on dat an' be gratefool. Beside, when you are 'ungry, it sharpen your mine so you can tink more clear. 'Ush now, tais-toi."

Twelve stations of the Cross. Didn't look like "stations." Did Grandmère mean train stations or gas stations? There were no buildings, so where were the stations? From her place next to her father and grandmother, Jocelyne strained to see the details in the pictures, to no avail. She vowed that she'd look at them before leaving today, instead of being so anxious to get home to eat. She returned her gaze to the front of the church and the statue of Mary in her pretty light blue dress, her hand raised in blessing, wearing her sweet, sad smile.

"Mary looks like my guardian angel in the picture above the bed at Grandmère's... except she doesn't have wings. Why wouldn't Mary have wings, if she was Jesus' mother? How did she get to heaven with no wings? And why is her heart open and bleeding? Eeewuh, yuck." Her questions spun spiderwebs through her sleepy mind.

Suddenly, a bell sounded, and the child jumped. It meant Mass was almost done! Grandmère went to the front to receive Holy

Communion. Seated next to her father, Jocelyne anxiously awaited the collection plate. Men in suits strode up one side, and down the other of the church. With serious, impassive faces, they ladled the cash in the plate by its long handle, reaching to the middle of each pew. By the time it reached their pew, the red velvet bottom of the plate was covered. Still, her father put in Grandmère's family envelope, added a bill from his pocket, and ensured Jocelyne donated the coin he had given her. She loved looking at all the money and envelopes stacked on the round dish. So much money! Piles and piles of cash passed straight under her nose. Did the priest get to keep it all? He must be very rich! She would have to remember to ask.

The passing of the collection plate also signified to her that her trial was almost over. At last, spicy incense drifted through the church as the priest and his attendants proceeded past, and the bells rang outside, announcing the end of the Mass. She was directed one last time to kneel on the padded bench in front of the pew and put her gloved hands together nicely for a moment, before joining the other children in the rush for the door.

At last, fresh air, brilliant sunshine! The light outside blinded everyone after the semi-darkness inside. The youngsters squinted and rubbed their eyes, skipping around their parents, poking anyone within reach. The parishioners took their time, milling about the wide cement porch, stretching their legs and adjusting their eyes and hats, while taking the measure of one another's Sunday best and catching up on the latest news. Grandmaman flashed her white and gold smile from under her feathered hat, but she wouldn't leave until the Father had personally greeted the family. Dad shook hands with the priest and several other men before donning his wide-brimmed black Fedora to shield his eyes.

Jocelyne watched children playing on the grass next to the church. She didn't dare join their game of tag—not in her pretty dress and new shoes! The sun made her thirsty, but she knew better than to complain. A sweet taste rose in her mouth. She had pushed her wide-brimmed straw hat onto her shoulders, but now she snapped it on her head by yanking on the elastic around her neck. The elastic slapped her ears like a bee sting.

"Ouch! Goddamn blastick!" she grumbled under her breath. Her stomach growled in response. "Jeez, I'll bet Mom even fed Pauline and Nicolas by now. Still, I got to come and Pauline didn't, so there. Too bad for her."

Nothing would pass her lips until they got home. When her mother came, she always fed them crackers or cookies that she brought in her purse, as soon as they got in the car. But not Grandmère. She didn't believe in cheating!

When they arrived back at the farm, sure enough, Mom had lunch almost ready and everyone was in a good mood, even Chantale. Grandmaman even allowed Jocelyne to wear her church shoes to play outside, much to her surprise, with no more than a warning to stay on the sidewalk next to the house.

"Oui, I know dat dey are bran' new shoe, Suzanne," Grandmère insisted, when Suzanna protested allowing the child to run around in her new shoes.

"But she mus' wear dem in, an' she like dem so much, it seem a shame not to 'ave dem on for more dan a few 'ours in church," the older woman cajoled. "She take care, won' you, chérie?"

Hurray! She could skip and hop and make noise with her heels on the cement sidewalk until lunchtime. In her church dress and shoes, she could prance up and down like a town lady.

Jocelyne hopped up and down on one foot, two feet, then skipped the length of the walk once, and then sighed and stared down the lane at her favourite pine trees.

"Richard and Dad never did get around to burying those damn cats for me yet," she said to herself in a voice much older than her years. She turned on the base of her heels and headed for the veranda at the front of the house. Lifting her knees high to climb the high steps, she didn't notice the scuff marks appearing on the fronts of her shoes as her toes hit each stair on the way up.

She danced across the wooden deck at the front of the house, delighting in the hollow sound of footsteps echoing against the ground far below. The veranda was level with the parlour windows. By pressing her face against the glass, shielding her eyes with her hands, and squinting, she could just see into the dark room where the piano stood against one wall, below the picture of the horses in the golden frame. Leaving her nose print on the window, she shuffled along to the next window, looking for the doll resting in its place on the velvet chair. Yup, there she was, ugly as ever, just sitting there doing nothing! Well good, no one would want to play with her anyway, with her nearly-bald head and "prokleene" eyes. And there stood the spinning wheel, right next to the door. She shuddered at the sight, thinking of the fairy tale and the princess that bled after touching the wheel. She vowed never to go near it! Through the glass doors she could just make out, in the distant room, the dining table and against the wall, the wondrous, carved wooden cabinet facing the window, where Grandmaman kept all her special treasures. She was just about to turn away and clatter back down the steps, when suddenly the French doors were flung wide.

Chantale entered the room. Jocelyne watched as her aunt headed straight for the doll and picked it up by the dress, hanging it upside down. Holding her breath, she saw her spread the doll's legs and pull something out from under the dress, a round wad of paper. Then, even more horrifying, her aunt grabbed the doll around the neck and smashed the back of its head against the chair's wooden armrest. Then she sat the doll back down, fluffing the skirt around so that it looked like it hadn't been moved. Turning to the piano, she rubbed her hand along the fine, gleaming wood, lifted the protective cover and tapped on a few keys, so softly that no sound travelled outside. Then she carefully held the edge of the wood so that it dropped silently back down.

Lifting the seat on the piano bench, she rifled through many pages before taking out several sheets, folding them and hiding them under her sweater. Finally, she closed the bench and turned to leave the room, looking behind her before shutting the glass doors. Jocelyne feared she had been seen, but her aunt seemed to look through her, even though she was standing right in front of the window. When the doors closed, the child was able to draw breath again.

"What was Chantale doing in that room? And she was the one who warned me about the doll, and then she goes and smashes its head? Holy cow! Grandmaman will kill somebody when she finds out about the doll being broked. She just better not think it was me, because if she does, I'm telling... " Jocelyne thought, folding her arms across her chest with firm determination.

From far away, on the other side of the house, her mother's voice was calling her, to come to lunch. Tripping hastily down the steep stairs she glimpsed the white scuff marks on the fronts of her shiny shoes. Oh no. Oh no, oh no, oh no....

Chapter Ten

Jocelyne had to face the inevitable. They were moving. Within minutes it seemed, she and her family were in the car, about to leave the farm. They were not going far, as her mother kept reassuring her. They would visit Grandmère as often as they could. But they would not live there anymore. No more days in the barn with the pigs and the cats and Richard telling her what to do and then lifting her onto his shoulder for walks down to see the horse. Well, that hadn't happened for a while anyway, but even worse, no more special picnics alone with her dolls under the sweeping branches of the pine trees. Couldn't do that when it was just a visit. That took time to get ready. On visits it was never the same. Always somebody else there, other cousins or aunts or uncles and then she would have to sit inside and be quiet, or share Grandmaman with them, and only get a little time to play on the veranda before the meal was ready. Never the same. And then they would have to leave again. Not sleep in Papa's old bedroom and wake up to hear the... what was it called? The mellow lark, something like that? She would have to ask Grandmaman again.

It was all Chantale's fault. Hatred for her aunt boiled in Jocelyne's stomach. She longed to tell her mother what she had seen her do to Grandmaman's doll, but she didn't dare. Besides, she was already in trouble for ruining her new shoes. Everyone had gone quiet in the house for the last few days, as they were getting ready to move, and somehow she knew she couldn't tell.

"Don't say anything. Just try to pretend like you didn't see. Maybe it didn't even happen. Maybe I saw wrong. Or I dreamed it, like a nightmare. Anyways, Grandmaman might never find out. I hope not. It would make her cry to have her dolly broke. Why, why did Chantale do it? She's just so mean, like that mean black and white dog with the funny eye guarding Richard's bunkhouse. Just like that dog, always growling and barking at someone and ready to bite. Mean ol' farm dog. When I have my dog, it'll be a really friendly dog who will follow me around everywhere. That's right, Dad said we would get a dog! I wonder what the puppies look like that he said we could pick from." Her thoughts swirled like oil on a puddle, dark to light, colour to black, happy to sad, constantly in motion.

Grandmaman kissed Jocelyne through the open car window. Richard waved at the car from the farmyard, busy doing his chores. By himself now.

"More work for me now, Squirt, without my special girl to help me," he had said quietly, while they were standing by the back door waiting for Dad to get the car. He had squeezed her shoulder, then tapped her bottom with an open hand and left to go to the barn, without saying goodbye to anyone else.

Jocelyne straightened her wide-brimmed hat with her gloved hand, and turned twice in a circle to flounce out the crinoline in her dress again, until her mother stopped her with, "Jocelyne, stop that. You'll make yourself sick for the car ride."

As they slowly pulled out of the gravel driveway, with Mom reminding Dad about the treacherous pothole, Jocelyne turned on the seat and knelt facing the back window, so she could keep waving goodbye to her grandmother. Chantale hadn't come downstairs. The tires crunched past the back end of the house, and then her father turned the steering wheel to set the car on the narrow one lane highway that led to the village. Jocelyne didn't like going this way. She liked going down the other driveway, past the giant, friendly pine trees. The road to town.

"Oh well," she sighed to herself, "at least I got to go to town once in my life."

She kept waving out the back window, fixing her eyes on the house. Just before the car turned out of the driveway, she glanced up at the small bathroom window on the second floor. The one room in the house that she wouldn't miss. And in the window, she saw Chantale looking down at the car. Their eyes met. Jocelyne kept her hand in the air, but didn't wave. Her aunt put her hand to her mouth, then held it out flat and blew. Jocelyne, unsure what this gesture meant, moved her hand slightly back and forth before the car turned down the sloping drive. The house was out of sight. The shiny blue Desoto leapt down the path, hogging the road to itself as it hurried toward its new home in the village.

*****

Whew. Gone—at last! Now she could finally move ahead with her plan without worrying about Jocelyne. Not a very nice way to do it, but it had worked and at least Paul's kids were out of here. Had to be done. No more worrying about them. If she hadn't been there that day at the trough... she shuddered. That was close, too close. And Jocelyne, such a sweetie. She had to protect her. Of course, they'd still come for visits. But that was different. Not nearly the same risk.

Now, all she had to do was wait for Carol to arrive. Everything was ready. The extra money from Paul would come in very handy. She'd only managed to stash away fifty bucks before his big payoff. He would never know how much he'd done to speed things up. Good ol' Paul. She congratulated herself for her cleverness, too. No one would have thought to look for her money where she had hidden it inside the doll, away from Richard's searching fingers, for she knew he regularly searched her room while she was at school during the day. She had noticed things moved on her desk and under her bed, and her mother never entered her territory, expecting her to keep her room clean at the very least, as she would say. But Richard had no qualms about invading her privacy. What was one more invasion? She ground her teeth against the sour taste rising in her mouth, as she threw another sweater on the bed to add to the mounting pile of clothes. How would she select just the essentials for her new life? Luckily, she had time.

Night came. A car pulled into the driveway slowly, with the lights off. Chantale quietly slipped down the stairs carrying a heavy suitcase. Counted each step to miss the sixth one that squeaked, as she knew all too well. Mustn't wake Ma, snoring in the room at the foot of the stairs. Luckily, the old woman was going deaf and was a sound sleeper. She could sneak out without waking her. Open and close the heavy interior door, then set down her bag and hold the screen with both hands so it wouldn't squeak or slam. Shut it ever so gently. She could be so gentle when she wanted to.

Good, the damn dogs were down at the bunkhouse. With Richard, where they belonged, bunch of mangy, filthy beasts! Hopefully, he wouldn't hear the car motor until they were out of the driveway. Open the passenger door only, to take less time and make less noise. Flop into the front seat, throw her bag in the back. Point toward the front driveway, past the pine trees. Direct the car, in the dim light of the farmyard lamp, to coast in neutral out to the main road. Whisper, "Hang a left." Head south. Roll down the window. Light a smoke. Suck in a long drag. Laugh. Blow smoke through her nose. Lean over and turn up the radio. Loud. And sing.

"Big girls, they don't cry, yii yii, they don't cry. Big girls, doooon't cry!"

*****

The children's suitcases weren't unpacked until the next morning. The two exhausted parents had spent so much time setting up beds, cleaning the kitchen before getting supper ready, then cleaning some more, that they had just plopped the two girls down on mattresses wearing their undershirts and underpants, covered them with loose blankets and left them to go straight to sleep.

"What's this?" Suzanna held up a stiff piece of cardboard, looked at it and then turned it around to show it to Jocelyne.

"Holy cow... oops, I forgot I'm not s'posed to say that all the time. I mean, hey, what's that doing in our suitcase, Mom? I didn't take it, honest! That's that record thing I was telling you about, 'member? Chantale's special record. See the little girl in the picture sings a song, but like you tol' me you have to have a record player to hear it. What's it doing in our suitcase? Chantale keeps it under her bed. Oops, I wasn't s'pposed to tell. But that's where it came from, in

94

a special box that she hides all her stuff in."

"Maybe she means for you to have it, Honey. She must have given it to you. Why else would it be in here?"

"No, she'd never give it to me. It's really special. But I didn't take it, honest, I didn't."

Chapter Eleven

Carol had convinced her mother to allow her friend Chantale to stay with them until she got her own place in town. From the first meal with the three boys, Carol and her parents crowded around a small table, Chantale was acutely aware of what her presence meant to the family, and inwardly vowed not to outstay her welcome. Each plate came to the table portioned by Carol's mother at the counter. Second helpings were neither offered nor requested. Fried bologna, cooked cabbage, macaroni from a box, creamed corn from a can. No heaping bowls of steaming potatoes and fresh, garden vegetables, beside a heaping platter of prime-cut meat, to which everyone helped themselves. No pitcher of ice cold milk, but a glass each of mixed skim milk powder. Chantale smiled at her mother's voice in her head, "Dat's food for de pig, dat box macaronis. Not fit for de 'uman bean." Along with Carol and her ravenous brothers, she eagerly spooned up the macaroni and cut her bologna with her fork.

"The supper's okay for you, dear? You like it?" Carol's mother asked her shyly.

"Oh yes, Mrs. F. It's the best! How did you know these are all my favourite things? I must be the luckiest girl in the world, to be staying with your family. Thanks so much for having me."

"It's no trouble, dear. We are glad to help out one of Carol's friends. So you and Carol will be in Grade Twelve together this fall? That will be nice, for you to go to school in town instead of on the school bus. It must be a long ride from the farm. I know what that's like. I lived on a farm and rode a school bus for years. I hated it, too. I'm sure you'll like it a lot better in town. Carol usually drives the boys and herself to school now, and I'm sure they'll let you catch a ride with them, even when you get your own place. Are you sure it's what your folks want? You're kinda young to be on your own, to my mind. I'd really like to talk to your mother. You said you were going to have her call me. Make sure you do that tomorrow, okay, dear? I'm sure she'd like to know how you are getting on here."

*****

"Non, M'man. I don't know where the hell she is! What do you think, I'm a mind reader? Especially not that girl's mind! She's such a screw-up! All I know is, she gave my kid a record that belonged to her, and that's it. Didn't she even leave you a note? Have you called the cops? Well, what do you expect me to do about it, then, if they won't interfere? If you want my advice, I'd say let her stew in her juice for a while. She'll come home, with her tail between her legs, when she runs out of money and has no one to bail her out and clean up her messes anymore. She's too damn lazy to look after herself, so what the hell is she going to do? I wonder if she's pregnant. Yes, I know, I know that's not how you raised her, but I saw a hickey on her neck, and Suzanna had a feeling... women's intuition, you might say. What's a hickey? Well, it's... oh, never mind. Anyway, it might explain some of her bitchiness. In any case, leave her on her own for a while to teach her a lesson, I say. Then she might appreciate everything she has out there. She has it a hell of a lot easier than I ever did, as the youngest. Spoiled rotten little brat! She oughta' try being the oldest like Gus and me, and see what it felt like. She's never had to share anything or do any work for anybody. That's her problem. Everybody's always just catered to her. You know it's true, Ma. Always got her own way because she was the baby. I'd just leave it and let her try to make it on her own for a while. You'll see, she'll be back within the week. Une semaine, c'est sur et certaine. Mark my words."

*****

"But why? Why do you have to go? Mom and Dad would let you stay here for as long as you want. They like you a lot and Mom's used to having lots of kids around. She doesn't mind. 'Just throw one more potato in the pot,' as she always says. It's so cool having you here, like a continual pyjama party… or having the sister I always wanted, only better, 'cuz we never fight. Hell, it's only been two weeks, and in one week, school starts again. Grade twelve, we're almost finished! You really gonna leave? Quit school? It's crazy. I know Paul caught up with you at the store and asked you to call your mom. So why don't you, then, just so she'll stop worrying? And then stay here with me? They still don't need to know where you live. You don't have to go. God, Vancouver for Chrissakes! You must be nuts. Why'd you want to travel so far, hundreds of miles away, all by yourself? You'll get raped and stabbed and thrown in a ditch! Don't even think about it anymore, pleease. Remember the old pinky swear? C'mn, pinky swear you'll forget about it."

Silence in the darkened room. Then, from Carol's twin-sized bed, more words erupted.

"Okay, fine. Go. But if you need anything, anything at all, just call me. Thank God Danielle can meet you when you get in. At least you have a sister out there to help you. I can't imagine going to a big city and not knowing anybody. It would be so scary. Chantale, I guess I just don't get why you left home, you and your big sister Danielle both. Your mom always seems so nice and you have a farm with a horse and you guys are so rich. I mean, just look at your house compared to ours. All that gorgeous furniture, and such a beautiful room, with a princess bed and everything! I would just die to have a room like that! You even get to drink as much real milk as you want to! Why'd you leave, anyway?"

No response from the body curled away from her.

"Hey, you still awake? Oh good, I thought you might be dead or something. Well, I still don't get it. But I guess the one thing I never told you is that I don't like your brother Richard too much. He kind of gives me the creeps. I always felt like he was staring at me every time I came to your house. There's something kinda weird about the way he looks at you, too. How come he doesn't go to school, and why does he live out there with all those pigs? He always smells, well, 'piggy' is all you can say, isn't it? Is that why he doesn't live in the house? It's kinda weird to have a brother who doesn't even live in the house with you. Anyway, pigs are pretty, well, homely, is all you can say, isn't it? That part of living on a farm would be kinda stinky, so I guess I can understand why you wanted to run away. But... Chantale?" A pause, a sharp intake of breath.

"Say something, for God's sake. Oh great, I didn't mean to... I sure didn't mean to make you cry. I should never have asked you. It's none of my business anyway. It's your life, and you're almost eighteen so you can do what you want, and you should. I'm sorry, I just feel so close to you, you're my best friend, and I might never see you again, and I just had to try to get you to stay. Shit. Please don't think bad about me, okay? I'll drive you to the bus tomorrow. I'll make sure you get off okay. And then phone me as much as you can, so I'll know you're alright. Reverse the charges, I'll find a way to explain to Mom. I'm gonna miss you so much," Carol sobbed into her friend's stiff shoulder.

Still not a word, not a sound, the shuddering of the mattress the only betrayal of emotion. Hot tears dampened both pillows, and left their stains in the morning.

*****

"Non, Ma. She up and quit her job at Woolworth's Five and Dime yesterday. Told them she was leaving town. Just pure luck that I even ran into her there. I never shop at that cheap store, but I wanted some trinkets to bring to the kids so I stopped on my way through town. Was she surprised to see me! Tried to hide behind the counter, but I caught her! Non, elle n'a pas laissé d'addresse. Non. She obviously doesn't want to be found. Well, yes, we could report her missing to the police again. I doubt they'll do anything, but sure, why not? It's worth a try, j'imagine. She's still under age and in school, so they might take it seriously. But it's not like she was kidnapped or disappeared or anything. She left, of her own free will. What can the cops do? Force her to come home? I don't think so!"

He took a drag on his cigarette to calm his nerves and listened before shouting into the receiver again. His mother's demands seemed interminable and always left him craving a drink.

"Calisse, I got my own kids and wife to worry about, Ma! I can't go chasing after her. I wouldn't even know where to start! If she made up her mind to leave, let her leave. She'll come home, wagging her sorry ass behind her, you'll see. Oui, Maman, je sais, mais maudit, qu'est que tu veux de moi? Je travaille à temps pleins, j'essaie de surveiller la construction de la maison. J'peux pas tout faire, tabarnak! I got a house to build for Chrissakes! I hate to say it, but it's your own fault for spoiling her so much. It's not fair, why do I always have to play the big brother? Why don't you get Richard to do something for once, besides shovel shit? He deserves some of the blame too, always antagonizing her. Those two were like fire and oil. I couldn't stand the way they fought all the time and I sure as hell don't understand why you put up with it. I always tried to treat her fair and square and help her out, and what did she do but spit in our faces, make Suzanna feel like dirt. So to hell with her!"

Silence while he listened, then assumed a gentler tone. "Oui, oui, je sais. Sorry, Ma, I know I wouldn't like it if it was one of my kids. She just makes me so damn mad, causing all this trouble. Yes, yes, I said I would and I'll do it, take the picture downtown and report her missing right away tomorrow morning. But, in any case, she has no right to do this to you, Ma, or me neither, come to that. It really stinks. Just wait 'til I catch up with her, I'll tan her ass! Took a page right out of Danielle's book, didn't she? It wouldn't surprise me to find out that she's hooked up with that bitch somehow. I just wish I knew where she was, and Danielle too, come to that! I'd tear a strip off both their hides, by God!"

Chapter Twelve

So quiet. Not a sound. She smiled, a slight, crooked movement of the lips, remembering a time when she had longed for peace and quiet. With six children, the spacious wooden house had rocked on its cement foundation, crammed to the rafters despite its size. Feet banging upstairs, downstairs, doors slamming, dishes clattering, music blaring from the radio, voices arguing, a dog's tail thumping on the kitchen floor as another family member swung open the creaky screen door and strolled in... Never still, day or night. Now, suddenly... dead silence.

She wandered through the gloomy parlour into the sitting room. As she passed through the wood and glass doors, her hand distractedly turned the spinning wheel standing idle in a corner. The balls of wool in the basket beside it were discoloured with age and dust. The smell of musty upholstery and mothballs permeated the chilly air and caught in her throat, making her cough slightly while her feet carried her silently across the carpet into the dark space ahead.

This room extended the entire length of the house. A wall of paned windows offered a view of the lawn, separated only by the oak door to the veranda. Starting with these first cool days of autumn, the room huddled behind its heavy velvet draperies from morning until night, to keep in the small amount of steamed heat that puffed out of the registers. Emile had said that so many windows would be impractical and let in all the cold of the Alberta winter. But Marie-Eve had insisted, for beauty's sake, and he had not lived long enough to hear her admit that he'd been right, all along. The imported rosewood table that could comfortably seat twelve complete with all her silver trays and crystal goblets, stood abandoned in its lace clothes. The dining room table in the other room, close to the fire, had hosted most of their special occasions. Still, she loved this space.

It housed her finest treasures and was always kept immaculately clean, in case someone such as the priest should visit. In the past, on warm summer days, she had served coffee here to her lady friends from her best silver and china. Then they had raved about the refreshing coolness of the room and her pride found its place.

"But who comes to visit nowadays?" she thought, her thin lips forming a pout.

She sighed and reached for the chain on the stained glass lamp on the piano. Lifting its curved, polished keyboard cover, she plunked at a few keys. As a child, she had played quite well, but her twisted, arthritic fingers were long out of practice. No matter. A piano was still an essential in the best homes. When she had inherited it from her mother, it had been brought by train from Québec to Calgary, and the rest of the way by wagon, to arrive in Central Alberta on the homestead. The freight cost more than two new pianos, Emile had dared to observe. Why spend the money, when there was certainly no cash to spare for such an extravagance? She herself never found time to play. It had been left quietly holding up the wall in the sitting room for years, until Chantale, the youngest, had been offered lessons by the dear sisters at the convent. But the girl had soon tired of practising and she constantly complained that the nuns were too strict; they smacked her fingers with a wooden ruler whenever she made a mistake. How else were you supposed to learn? her mother had wondered at the time, and still did. But Chantale had crossed her arms, stamped her feet and refused to continue. That was that. Fini.

The old woman shook her head and exhaled sharply through her nostrils, pinched tight by the glasses that had slipped down her nose.

"What was the use, giving them anything, everything? They all left, in the end. Only one at home, and even he just takes, takes, takes. Eats, falls asleep on the couch in front of the television, and goes back to the bunkhouse. Why choose to live in the former hired man's shack, rather than in his cozy room upstairs? All he does is work, to earn money for himself from those stinking pigs!" Automatically, her face grimaced in a sour expression.

"No thanks, no appreciation from Richard or any of them for our years of sacrifice and hard work. No love lost, as they said in

English. What did it mean exactly, 'no love lost?'" she wondered, separating her fingers to play the few chords she remembered from childhood.

In the lamp light, the veins and bones of her hand strained against the wrinkled, bluish flesh. Whose hands were these? Surely not the delicate hands of Marie-Eve de LaSalle, that had once slid so effortlessly into the tiny kidskin gloves she had worn on her trip West? Those gloves which had remained draped on the hat rack in her room, though they hadn't fit her for years. Whose fingers moved along this yellowed ivory keyboard? The light captured the golden gleam of her wedding band that would not come off over the knobby joints. "If you want it when I'm dead, you'll have to cut it off," she used to say teasingly to her sons, which Paul in particular found a tasteless remark. She knew that her wedding ring would be buried with her. But looking at it reminded her of another piece of jewellery in her jewellery box, an old silver brooch Emile had been given as part of his mother's legacy, when she had passed away many years ago. Even after she had polished it to remove the tarnish, and had removed the dirt of ages from some sort of precious stone at its centre, she had exclaimed to Emile, "I wouldn't be caught dead wearing that hideous thing!" But she knew it had been passed down through the family for generations, so she had held onto it.

"Jocelyne," she thought suddenly. "I know! I will give it to Suzanne to pass to Jocelyne, when she grows up. At least she will appreciate something from her heritage, that one! I will make sure the child gets all my jewellery. My own daughters don't deserve it anyway!"

She smiled to herself over the decision, bringing her hand to her throat to grasp her other precious memento of Emile, the emerald ring hanging from a gold chain around her neck. She raked it up and down along her neckline, as was her habit. With her hands constantly in water, dirt or slop, she had feared losing the stone, but she couldn't bear to put it in a box so she wore it as a pendant. It had become her amulet. Such a comfort, in times of stress.

The fingers of her right hand hit the black keys. The black keys seemed to make a sound to match her mood. Then, trailing her left hand down the length of the keyboard from one end to the other, her eye caught the doll sitting askew in the velvet armchair. She rose from the piano bench and gently brought the doll to her chest. Easing into the deep, velvet cushions, she plopped the doll onto her lap.

"Ah, petite Jeannette. How many years have we sat together and told each other our secrets, hein?" she asked her childhood friend, turning its body to face her.

The head lolled forward and she saw... the wound. The back of the doll's head was crushed, the porcelain falling inward, the holes in the back exposing the workings for the eyes. She rocked its white, balding head back and forth, watching the eyes open and shut, open and shut, while tears streamed down its porcelain face. She ran her fingers along the cool cheeks, frowning in puzzlement at the dampness there. Where were the tears coming from?

She hadn't wept for many years. Not even at Emile's funeral. Young as she was but ever curious, three-year-old Chantale had asked her, "Maman, you don't cry for Papa?" And she had replied, "Non, ma petite, it's not seemly to break down in front of the neighbours. I have cried all my tears already." Her lips unknowingly formed a sad smile, recalling Chantale's puzzled expression. How could a child understand?

She had been taught to keep her feelings to herself. It wasn't right to make a spectacle, or to question God's Will. No matter what, she had to believe Emile was at peace, with the Heavenly Father. Now, it was her duty to carry on, thank the neighbours for coming, ensure the children were polite to their guests, and maintain her decorum.

It had been so much harder not to collapse when they had lost Luc, maybe because Emile was there to be the strong one, her rock, as she always called him. Born the terrible winter of 1930, Luc had never been healthy. She had always blamed his weakness on the fact that her bedroom, where she had given birth to him, was freezing cold. His lungs were never strong. Five winters later, he caught pneumonia and died.

Those dark years, a blight on her memory. Back then, she was sure her heart would break. But it would not, no matter the number of injuries inflicted upon it. It kept beating, beating, keeping time to the death of her son and then her beloved husband. A monstrous accident, so unfair! Emile cleaning his gun, to have it blow up in his face like that, how was it possible, how could he have been so careless? Leaving her alone to manage the farm and the household both, with only the children to help. At first, they were willing partners, working hard alongside her and she was sure she could keep it all together. But as they became teenagers, they defied her at every turn and the more she tried to involve them, the further they pulled away, screaming that they wanted out, away from the hardship of failed crops, unstable prices and endless labour. They had abandoned the homestead one by one. First Ghislain, then, Danielle, next, Paul, and now, Chantale. Unbelievable. Incroyable.

"What good are tears, anyway?" she thought viciously, rubbing her face with clenched fists. "What do they change? Rien. Chantale, Danielle, Richard, all gone away, or as good as lost. Ghislain, married, living a hundred miles away, earning 'big bucks' as he boasted, in the city. Paul, always on the road. Richard, unable or unwilling to commit to the effort of keeping up the whole operation. With three sons, you would have thought at least one would take it on. Why not? Don't they understand what it means?" Unconsciously, she let out a soft moan.

She had always tried to make them value their heritage, in spite of living out here in Alberta, where there was no culture at all. But how could they understand what they'd missed, when they'd never even been "home." Growing up in this backwards territory surrounded by immigrants and English people who knew nothing about the finer things in life, what could you expect? How could they learn to appreciate a legacy going back generations? Their family in Québec had fought so hard to maintain their language, religion and culture against the English invaders. She had done her best to impress her children with the importance of keeping French alive in the house, despite the rules against it at the children's school in the village. It was vital to hang onto who and what they were, even though it didn't matter a tinker's damn to anyone else. She had been determined, despite the hardships, that the family would be strong and become as wealthy and powerful as they had once been in Québec. Her grandsons would be doctors, priests, professors. Anything was possible in this new territory, if they stuck together and built up their holdings! Land, land, land. That's what it took to survive. Why couldn't they see that?

Deep down, she still believed it could happen. After so much sacrifice, there must be a legacy to leave behind. Maybe Paul would finally be the one to take it up, if he would only grow up, develop a backbone and stop rambling around, put his feet on the good, black soil of their farm. Well, at least he kept his family close by. Paul had finally made one good decision, and settled his family in the village, where she could keep an eye on them and lend a hand. What was family for, otherwise? She had been forced to move so far away from her mother and had missed her support all her life. How many nights had she secretly cried herself to sleep, longing for her mother, while the wind whistled through their log cabin? Who would deliberately choose such a fate?

Her poor mother never even met her grandchildren. She counted herself lucky to have Paul's dear little ones nearby. Jocelyne, who seemed to take to the French Canadian food and culture more than any of her own children had ever done, so adorable with her quick mind, vivid curiosity and eagerness to help. Marie-Eve's secret favourite, among all her grandchildren, including Ghislain's noisy brood of three girls whom she rarely saw, growing up a hundred miles away in Calgary. Pauline, well, too young to tell how she would uphold the family traditions. Fortunately, there was Nicolas, a boy to carry on the Gérard name, and perhaps another son on the way. Maybe one of them…

"Pray for a boy," she silently reminded herself, automatically making the sign of the cross across her forehead and chest.

Easing the doll down beside her, she grasped the carved right arm of the chair and slowly eased her body upright, while pressing her left hand against the small of her back. She turned around to carefully arrange the doll's faded lace dress and cross its tiny booted feet, to make it appear as though nothing had happened. She tipped the doll's head forward so that its eyes closed, then gathered up crumbs of broken porcelain from the red velvet cushion. A tug of the chain on the lamp above the piano plunged the room back into darkness. She waited for a moment until her eyes adjusted, then slowly made her way back into the dining room, and switched on the television. With a clenched fist, she angrily swiped the dust from its wooden cabinet, before taking her customary place on the sofa.

She watched the dot in the middle of the black glass screen begin to slowly expand. The humming of the tubes inside the cabinet grew louder as the television set warmed up. Her thoughts raced ahead until images in black and white could appear to distract her.

"That pair of ungrateful daughters of mine, they know nothing about life, nothing at all. Why do they have to learn everything the hard way, when Papa and I tried to make it so much easier for them, by our sacrifice? Don't they understand what they have done? To leave me without a word, not knowing where they are or what has become of them? Danielle, no word in fifteen years, and now Chantale? What did I do to deserve that? I work and I slave and for what? Selfish, just selfish…" She bent her head and pulled at her own thin hair, angrily brushing the tears from her face and the front of her dress. She couldn't hold back a deep, deep sob. She brought her left hand up to rest it on her breast. Sure enough. Still beating.

"Where, where is that damn girl? Why, why did she go? Chantale, ma petite, please, please come back. Reviens à ta maman!" her mind cried until suddenly the television blared to life. She jumped in her seat. At that, she felt that her heart might really have stopped and she burst out laughing.

Chapter Thirteen

"It's in the blood. That's what Maman would say."

Marie-Eve switched off the television and turned to glance out the window to the yard, illuminated only by the eerie yellow glow of the yard light. It was well past seven o'clock. The autumn light had already faded from the sky. Time to make supper for Richard. Unaware of the chill in the house, feeling no pangs of hunger, she kept teasing at the knots in her mind. Each time she tugged on a thread of memory, she became more entangled in the past.

Her head ached. She pinched and massaged the bridge of her nose under her glasses and suddenly noticed her nose was running. A clean, monogrammed handkerchief was always ready in the sleeve of her dress, a habit she had acquired early, from wiping children's snotty noses. Dabbing the tip of her nose and tidying her hair in front of the mirror above the china cabinet, she spoke to her reflection in the mirror.

"My side of the family was not to blame! Jamais de la vie! And Emile? Non, pas lui, a prince among men! It must go further back than us, I'm thinking. But who?" For his family, like her own, were "pure laine," dyed in the wool French, from France, descended from the first families to arrive in Canada over three hundred years ago. Untainted, like so many others, by English, Scottish or Native blood, their union was blessed. The bishop himself had confirmed it, by tracing the baptismal records, which was why her parents had favoured the match to Emile, even though it meant they would surely lose their daughter to the faraway West.

Emile's handsome face smiled back at her from its silver frame on the cabinet. Such a hard worker, on their farm or someone else's place, doing anything he could to make ends meet. Never complaining about so many mouths to feed, but instead proud of his growing family. And why not? They were beautiful children and with four sons they had begun a dynasty!

"Everything must go into the land, chérie. We have to homestead enough land to pass down a goodly share to each of our boys. I won't see them disinherited, as I was. We have to file as many claims as possible, nearby, before they are all gone. Then we will keep our family together as one unit and we will be strong." His voice sounded so clearly in her head that she turned around to look, as if he would come through the parlour doors behind her at any moment. No. Jamais encore. Never again.

She put her index finger to her lips and then pressed it to the photograph behind the glass. Through everything, all the hardships of drought, debt, the Depression, she had never lost her faith in him. That is why it was such a shock that he might have, well, it seemed that he had...

No... stop that thought right now! she admonished herself. An accident, that's all. It had to be. He had loved her and the children. He would never deliberately abandon her, all of them, and worse, curse himself to Hell everlasting for... No, never—jamais de la vie!

She had been certain their dreams would really come true if they just worked hard enough and trusted in God. It had seemed so real, within their grasp, as it never would have been at home. They were truly among "the first families" in Alberta, with a domain of their own. How proud Maman would have been. Marie-Eve had longed to bring her mother out West, to see all they had achieved and show off the children. She shook her head, chastising herself, remembering how she used to beg Emile, even though she knew the expense was far beyond their means. It wasn't fair to him. But she had missed her parents so.

"Will I never see Maman and Papa again?" she used to lament, disregarding the pained expression on her husband's face, in her need to vent her sorrow.

Non. Jamais. Twenty years passed with no more than correspondence to maintain their loving ties, until one day, both Maman and Papa were gone. But her inheritance had built this house, a showpiece of culture, grace, and style. The villagers and farmers would never understand and she had bristled at her neighbours' obvious jealousy and harsh judgement. After their universal suffering through the Depression, the house had set her apart once more. All she wanted was to create a reproduction of home, a two-storey, six-bedroom house constructed in the traditional Québec style, with gabled windows and a high, steeply slanted roof to keep the snow off, which was only sensible. And of course a wide, elegant "galerie" on the front, with room for a swing and a rocking chair, to sit out in the evening and enjoy the cool breeze. Never mind that she had to add an oak staircase, hardwood floors, hand-etched glass French doors shipped by rail from the east, two stone fireplaces, a crystal chandelier, wool carpets, velvet upholstered chairs and antique tables. At the same time, she had insisted on equipping her new home with all the modern conveniences. Indoor plumbing, electric refrigerator, gas stove, the works! Everything designed to lighten her workload and offer the family the comforts they could now afford.

"Bah! Too bad, she would say," when the children came home with stories of criticism from the village.

"We Gérards don't care what they think! Who are they but peasants, anyway? They can't help it if they don't know any better."

On all the farms, in most of the small homes in town, and even at the church, outhouses were still the norm at that time. Bah! What did they know of culture, of civilized living, of style? The Gérards even had a free-standing tub, with hot and cold running water! They could take a bath whenever they wanted, while most people still had to bathe in a washtub in their kitchen, heating the water on the stove!!

Marie-Eve smirked to herself now at the sense of pride she had felt while touring the neighbour ladies upstairs to see the luxurious bathroom after her "house warming" coffee party. She blushed now at her foolishness. If only she had known then... her poor Emile had never even lived to see the house completely finished, in all its splendour. How could she have known that their dream house was to be his mausoleum? With so many children, she and Emile should have lived in a house full of joy for many, many years to come.

Had he just given up? Were there more pressures than he had

shared? Was it pride that caused him to... fall? If only she had seen it coming! If only he had told her what was wrong! Yes, there were debts, but they were paid, eventually, with help from the children and everyone working together after... the accident. All could have been well if only he had... waited. How bitter she had been! Her deep faith had been sorely shaken. Why did God have to take him from her, leaving her with young ones still to raise, a huge farm to run, all on her own? In her room, she would curse God, beat her pillow and scream into the depths of her mattress. The majestic house was bereft, empty. Drafty too, just as Emile had predicted. Damn him. Yes, God Damn him! Oh, what have I said! No, forgive me! No, no, it was not his fault. Nor God's either, of course not! The Devil had made such a thought appear in her mind. It was an accident. The gun had gone off when he was cleaning it and he had just forgotten to unload the weapon first. That could happen, with all the distractions in life. Even to an experienced hunter like Emile, as the priest had reassured her. Un accident, c'est tout. That's all. That's ALL! She crossed herself again vigorously and lifted her eyes to heaven.

This carousel of negative thoughts had spun in her head for years, yet she never allowed herself to display emotion in front of her children. She believed she had to be strong, to keep the family together, and she never criticized Emile, to anyone. Thank God, really, that he hadn't lived to see these days. Maybe he would blame her.

"Non," she cried, pounding her fist on the bureau in front of the photograph. She had always done her best, with no help from anyone. She had sacrificed her life's blood, God only knew. It was not her fault that her family had fallen apart, that the legacy meant nothing to young people nowadays, that they couldn't see. Everyone had abandoned her, in the end. Anger tightened her throat. Her bony hand shook as she ran a finger across Emile's black and white face.

What poison had ruined such a proud, distinguished family? She picked up the old family photograph propped next to Emile's, also in an ornate, antique silver frame. She blew at a thin film of dust that made her sneeze, then breathed on the glass and rubbed it against her dress. When was the last time the cabinet had been dusted? Ah, since before Chantale had left. It had been just one of the jobs that she found tiresome. But then, what didn't she complain about, that lazy girl? Now, a fine layer of dust shrouded all the glass ornaments on the cabinet. Oh well, what did it matter?

She stared at the photograph. There they were, the proud Gérards. Emile in the middle of his brood, his sideways grin lighting up his broad, handsome face. Even in the black and white photograph, his hair was starkly white. He might have been mistaken for the grandfather, rather than the father of the six youngsters gathered around him. He had not married young, waiting until he had been established on the land before sending home for his bride and, in any case, the black hair in his family started to turn gray at eighteen. She smiled, remembering how he had always joked about it, calling himself "the silver fox." How old was he in this picture? Chantale must have been, maybe, eighteen months. Meaning he was, already, how old? Fifty-five? No, fifty-six. Yes, that made sense, since he was twenty-eight when they got married. She painfully calculated the years in her head.

Hard to believe that times so important could just fade away, like a dream, she mused. Who was that woman standing next to Emile, wearing that elegant feathered hat? She brought her index finger to each of her children's faces, one at a time, as if to reassure herself that they had all really been there. The eldest sons, Ghislain and Paul, standing on either side of their parents, Danielle and Richard, placed next to their brothers, and there, Luc, right in front, his mother's hand placed protectively on his shoulders. And petite Chantale, cradled in her father's arms. The jewel in the old lion's crown, he would say when he introduced his family. Such a crude reference had made Marie-Eve blush, but he persisted in his fond nicknames for Chantale.

"Isn't she my chubby little cherub, with her golden curls? You can almost see her wings! See, there they are, right there!" and he would tickle her back and ribs until the baby was breathless from giggling. Well, his angel had flown away. She drew in a ragged sigh. What would he say about it, if he had a voice to speak?

"May your guardian angel protect you now, little one," she

whispered to the picture. She had to admit to herself that the bubbly child in the photograph had been gone a long time. At least five years ago, from about the time she had turned twelve, she had changed. Morose, confrontational, sad all the time, and so overweight, even though she never seemed to eat at the table.

Paul had said it was a teenage phase. The priest had agreed. "Don't give in to her. She just wants attention. She is the youngest and is bound to be spoiled. She'll grow out of it, don't worry." Such good advice. Why had she listened to them?

Something was wrong! Girls just don't up and leave home, without a very good reason! First Danielle, so many years ago. Yes, she had been much older, but what was wrong with keeping in touch, letting your mother know if you were alive or dead? She would be, what, almost thirty by now! Did she have a family of her own? What had become of her? Then to lose Chantale! Mon Dieu!

When she herself had left home, at twenty, to marry Emile, she had been heartbroken to leave her family behind. Yet her daughters didn't even tell her where they were going, and they didn't leave for a good reason, as she had. Unthinkable! Had she been wrong to discipline them? She had been determined to be firm but fair, teach them the meaning of hard work and sacrifice, give them a secure home, food, clothing, anything they wanted. All her energy had gone to one purpose, to keep the farm and the family together. And yet... no! It was not her fault! Who, who was responsible?

Tugging hard on the heavy oak cabinet drawer, she heaved out the faded black and white photograph album. Of course, this didn't represent them all, only the few family members on both sides who could afford to have a photograph taken, way back when. The pictures had been left to her by her mother and Emile's family. No one else had wanted them.

She thumbed through the thick black pages. Hard, stern faces with cold, dead eyes stared back at her. Jocelyne's voice echoed in the room. "They look mean, Grandmaman. Why do they look so mad?" She smirked again as the child's naïve question played in her mind. Maybe she was right, after all. Maybe they were mad. She bent down to examine their faces more closely.

She suddenly recalled the advice her father had given her more than forty years ago. In the weeks before she left, the reserved old man spoke to her more than he ever had in her life. He believed it was his duty to arm his only daughter against the hardships he imagined she would face in the West. From morning until night, his voice droned on, until she wanted to put her fingers in her ears and scream. She didn't dare. She had to nod and smile and respond with "Oui, Papa" for every "Tu compends-tu, ma fille? You understand me, my girl?" He especially feared that as a woman travelling alone on the railway journey across Canada, and then even more in the vast wilderness of Alberta, she would be forced to rely on strangers for help. How would his little daughter from Québec, who had never been more than ten miles from home, only able to speak French, know whom she could trust? He desperately tried to pass on his knowledge of men, gained over a lifetime.

"It's in the eyes, Marie-Eve. Look carefully at a man's eyes. That's how you will know his character. Too small, too close together, with no light in them... that spells trouble. Don't ever trust such a man." Hearing his words, her lips had curled in a sideways smile, as if Papa had ever wanted her to trust anyone.

"Don't trust foreigners, politicians, salesmen, and especially not "les maudits Anglais!" Watch those English carefully and always question their motives." Outside the family, everyone was suspect and even then...

"Don't let your guard down around a French Canadian, either. The bastards will steal the wool off their own brother's back! And jealousy, beware the jealousy of your neighbours. Play your cards close to your vest, as we say in poker. It's good advice. Keep a poker face like I've tried to teach you—don't let anyone see what you are thinking, ever! Don't fraternize with anyone who works for you—you can never trust them! Don't talk about your money with anyone outside your family. When you pay for something, take out one bill at a time, hide your cash, and sleep with your handbag under your head. Oh yes, and n'oublie pas... "

Her father's wealth and prestige in the county gave him the influence to easily convince the Bishop to come from Québec City to

La Beauce, to hear Marie-Eve's confession and bless her journey. The Holy Father, too, had many exhortations for her, especially about the French language. He made her promise to speak to her children only in French. "Qui perd sa langue, perd sa foi," he insisted, basically telling her that if her children lost their language, they would burn in the fires of Hell. He assured her that on behalf of her father, he had already contacted the Mother Superior of a French convent in the vicinity of her new home, to make the wedding arrangements and see to her ongoing spiritual guidance. At the time, focused on her dreams of a new life, she couldn't fathom what it would be like to have children, and she blushed at the very mention of it. In front of her parents, how could he?

Obediently bowing her head, then kissing the proffered ring, she secretly scoffed at their old-fashioned attitudes. Their warnings increased her inward fears, but she tried to close her mind and maintain a brave face.

"Papa is such an old fuss-pot," she complained to her mother. "I love Emile and I must go where he is. It could be worse. What future would we have remaining here? He would have to go to Montréal, get a job in a filthy factory! We would live like paupers! Georges and Maurice will inherit the land from Papa, so what is there to keep me here? This way, Emile will acquire his own land and we will be in charge of our lives. Two of his brothers are already there and young François has written to assure me that it's not as rough as we imagine. There are no wild Indians roaming about. They're all on their own reservations now and the land is practically free for the taking. The place has been a province for fifteen years already, and there are roads and schools... it's 1920, after all! The war is over, and if we don't move quickly, the homesteads will all be gone," she wailed.

"Think of it, Maman, the chance to own 160 acres for just ten dollars! One quarter section of prime farmland! Yes, of course there are conditions, but we will certainly be there for the mandatory three years, and clear the brush for planting. That's the whole point, for heaven's sake. Just think what we can accomplish! Emile has prepared a home for us, and we must start our life together, don't you see? Please, Maman, don't cry anymore or you'll start me bawling again, and I have to look nice for the train. Be happy for me. I will write you every week, I promise, and maybe sometime you can even come for a visit."

On the platform, her father had crushed her so hard she thought the stays on her corset might pop apart. She had backed up, teasing him about this unusual bear hug. He said nothing, but wiped his eyes with a handkerchief, then reached into his suit pocket. He grasped her gloved hand and closed her fingers around a white velvet box. When she moved to open it, he shook his head and pointed to the train, noisily blowing its whistle to indicate it was about to leave. Hastily, she leaned in to give her father the traditional kiss on both cheeks, and turned to press a loving caress with the back of her gloved hand on her mother's tear-stained cheek. Then she nodded at the conductor and accepted the support of his arm to embark. Placing her tiny booted foot on the portable step, she turned once more to say, "Don't worry so much, Papa. Ne t'en fais pas! You know Emile is a good man, from a fine family. I'll be fine, we'll be fine, you'll see... " Her voice was drowned by the burst of steam and the screech of the iron wheels as the train started to pull away from the station. She hopped into the compartment, rushed to a window and craned her neck out for a final glimpse. Her father waved his handkerchief. Then she saw him turn and hold the white linen over his face. Her mother leaned into him and stretched her arm across his broad back. Never had she seen her parents display such emotion or hold each other so close. As soon as her bag and hat had been safely stowed away, she settled in her seat and expelled a sigh of exhaustion.

Then she remembered the gift she had so quickly tucked into her small velvet handbag. Looking around to see if any of the other three passengers in the berth were watching, she tugged at the soft rope fasteners, slipped the box out and laid it on her lap. Her eyes widened and a gasp escaped her lips. On a bed of blue velvet lay a rosary of amethysts and pearls adorned by a crucifix of eighteen carat gold. Its beauty and significance took her breath away, for she knew it meant that her father never expected to see her again.

As the breathtaking scenery sped by the window, she kept the rosary clutched in her kidskin gloves, working the strand up and down her fingers. Five days from Québec City to Calgary, passing from miles and miles of forest and lakes through to an endless sea of prairie—who would have believed Canada was so big? She thought herself fortunate that her father had paid for a first class ticket, which included meals in the dining room, as she observed many a young woman, some with babies, sitting up on hard wooden seats for the entire journey, with nowhere to rest. Each night, tucked in the cozy berth above her upholstered seat, she recited a prayer over each precious bead on her rosary until she was lulled to sleep by the gentle rocking of the train.

Now, over forty years later, Marie-Eve stood alone in her Alberta farmstead home and wished she could speak to her father once more. She flattened her wrinkled hand gently on her father's faded image in the photograph, muttering aloud, "Merci, Papa. Je t'aime toujours. You must have known… you were so right, in more ways than one, though I would have hated to tell you so. Now that my daughters are gone, I finally understand how you and Maman must have felt. Like me, you always did your best for your children. How lonely you would have been, with me so far away! Mon Dieu! You must have been so afraid for me and there I was, resisting every word, just anxious to start my new life. I was so excited, remember? I wouldn't listen to anybody. Stubborn and headstrong, like you always said."

When Emile met her in Calgary, she was refreshed and happy, and when she saw his shining eyes she knew she had made the right decision. He lifted her from the train step and swung her in a wide circle. Without a word, he carefully removed the glove on her right hand, kissed the inside of her wrist, then encircled her ring finger with a delicate band of gold. A bevelled emerald set between two diamonds sealed their engagement.

"Regardez, the stone is the exact colour of your eyes. Merci, merci for coming. I can't believe you are really here. It's probably not fair of me, and it will be hard for you, but I need… " he stammered. She placed a finger over his lips. She noticed a nun standing nearby, watching them with a benign smile. Thoughtfully, the Mother Superior had sent Sister Anne to welcome her to Alberta and, more importantly, to accompany the unmarried couple back on the eighty-mile buggy ride, with two forced stops in hostels along the way. The roads were of graded-up soil, cars were not dependable, and in any case, Emile could not afford such a luxury. But with the nun along, despite three people being crowded onto the seat, Emile felt they would satisfy convention and reassure her parents that the demands of propriety had been met. Upon their arrival, she would stay at the convent until the wedding ceremony could be performed. Two weeks later, she arrived at her new home as Madame Emile Gérard.

She soon learned to appreciate the simple log cabin Emile had erected, when she saw the sod shacks Emile's brothers and so many other pioneers still occupied, even after years on their homesteads. Compared to them, she was beginning her new life in luxury. Still, the winter of 1920 turned out to be one of the coldest on record and tested every bit of strength she possessed. In the evenings, she wrapped herself in blankets and by the light of the coal oil lamp, wrote long, cheery letters to her mother. She told of her vain attempts to make bread, the calico she had bought to sew curtains, the new stove that had been purchased through the Eaton's catalogue. After her optimistic promises to her parents, there was no room for complaint.

She joked with Emile about the stubborn streak her father had complained about. "Le Bon Dieu savait que j'aurais besoin de ma tête dure. God provided me with a stubborn streak for a reason. Don't worry, I won't break. I'm tougher than I look!"

As Emile toured her around in "the democrat," their "sweet little buggy" as Marie-Eve called it, to meet their neighbours, she was surprised and relieved to meet other French-Canadian families who had also settled in the district. She knew there were many French colonists further north, but as tracts of land were opened in the central parkland, pioneers came from Québec, Ontario, even l'Acadie. Not "pure laine" like the Gérards and the De Lasalles, of course. Poorly educated or with no schooling at all, they spoke "joual," French peppered with English and bizarre idiomatic expressions.

"No matter. We understand each other, and our children will grow up with French. Necessity makes strange bedfellows," she assured her parents in her breezy letters. "It's a matter of survival, for us to stick together as French Canadians. Though you wouldn't want to stick too close, some of these old bachelors never bathe! But they help us immensely, and a few can fiddle a lively "jigue," so we don't get homesick. Le mal du pays, I think that must be the hardest for those who are more isolated. I have heard of some who lost their minds or even shot themselves, from sheer loneliness in the early days. We are so lucky!"

The tiny community of Francophones formed their own island, with Marie-Eve the unofficial social convener. "Après tout, we are de only true Canadiens, nous autres, aside from the Natives. Us, we arrive here long before les maudits Anglais even heard of Canada, an' for sure we 'ave our rights," they assured themselves, when they met for strong coffee and conversation chez Marie-Eve.

Fortunately, a Catholic Church had been built, attended faithfully by pioneers from Québec since the days of holy Père Lacombe, the great priest from Saint Suplice, Québec who had done so much in the late 1800s to establish the Catholic Faith and keep peace between the natives and the white settlers, in the new western territory. French Canadians continued to mourn the missionary's passing a scant four years earlier, referring to him as "notre vieux connaissant," our wise elder. Since Father Lacombe had successfully founded the Church, and every Catholic family in Québec and even in France still offered up at least one of their many children to God, inevitably, some found themselves shipped out West. The nuns and the parish priest comforted and sustained the young married women and, in turn, they tenaciously maintained their traditions. Thus, the parish grew and remained strongly French in language and culture. Marie-Eve's fondest hope was to eventually have a French Catholic school for their own children. Until then, they were forced to conform to the dominant Protestant rule.

At the village school, however, all children were forbidden to speak any language other than English, even to each other at recess time, in order to learn English properly. To be caught meant the strap or a slap across the face. Any French or other "foreign" names were immediately Anglicised: "Ghislain" became "Gus"; "Richard" became "Ricky." The teachers dismissed Marie-Eve's protests out of hand, even when she tried, in her best English, to explain her reasons for wanting to keep their names. "How will they ever fit in?" was the standard question. The children soon lost their French-Canadian accent when speaking English and readily accepted the nicknames. They wanted to be part of the group. Emile didn't seem worried— he was too busy keeping the farm afloat to trouble himself with such details.

Despite the resistance from all sides, Marie-Eve insisted on maintaining her family's French Canadian culture. She managed to scrape together the money to send a son to the French Oblates' seminary in Edmonton. She and the priest were not just encouraging Paul's further studies in French and Latin. They hoped he would find "la vocation" to become a priest. He lasted a year. He quit school and left the farm, to make easy money in road construction.

"What do you want from me, Ma? To remain celibate all my life? Bah! That's not the life for me. And besides, some of those priests well, let's just say, je me suis serré les fesses près d'eux... they made me nervous, and I heard stories... En tout cas, anyways, I've had enough schooling, more than you or Papa or anyone I know. It's time for me to hit the road and make my own money. I want to buy a car. After all, I'm seventeen and a man now."

The priest had tried to console her: "What is to be done with this new generation, ma petite? They don't understand commitment, sacrifice, loyalty. Pas comme nos ancêtres."

"I wonder, mon Père, I wonder," Marie-Eve shuddered as she once again sensed the weight of the album in her hands. She opened and closed her stiff fingers, then slowly turned more pages, bending down closely to study their faces in the dim light. The eyes were cold and impassive, looking off to some great distance, reflecting only a tiny pinpoint of light from the flash. Who were they really? What were their lives like, at this moment when their image was caught in time? Not one seemed young or carefree. Yes, Jocelyne had sensed it: they looked fierce. Maybe they had to be, for in those times, as she knew from her parents, life had been even harder. She glanced up at her own reflection in the smoky mirror in the centre of the buffet. Leaning forward, she touched the frown lines between her eyes, the crow's feet, the thin, pale lips.

"Hmmppf," she exhaled, raising an eyebrow which she then smoothed with her wrinkled index finger.

Returning her gaze to the family photograph on the bureau, she wondered about the others, all the past Gérards and de Lasalles, who were known only as a name in the family Bibles. They were all somewhere in the picture, though they couldn't be seen. Ghosts, like Emile and petit Luc. As she would soon be. Maybe she was actually in that photograph, at this very moment. She closed her eyes and there, yes... the sun warmed her shoulders in front of the church, she smelled the freshly mown spring grass, she put a hand up to balance her brand new Easter hat in the breeze, her polished black boots, laced up to her ankles, pinched her toes, the starched collar of her dress scratched her long, smooth neck. Emile's arm held her firmly around her waist...

Lost in thought, she didn't hear the kitchen door slam. She felt a sudden draft, and a shiver snaked down her spine.

"Maman, qu'est-ce que tu fais, donc, icitte dans le noir? It's dark as a tomb in this goddamn house! Christ, it's freezin' in here! C'mon, let's put some heat on and get supper goin'. J'ai faim, moi. Some of us have been workin' all day. No use mopin' around the house in the dark. Life goes on, tu sais ben. 'Y un bout à tout, comme on dit. Enough is enough, calisse!"

Richard threw the switch for the chandelier over the dining table, flooding the room with harsh white light, before flinging his way back though the swinging doors into the kitchen. Whistling out of tune, he filled the aluminum kettle with water from the tap, then slammed it onto the metal burner of the stove.

His mother closed the leather-bound photograph album. She lowered it with both hands back to its place in the drawer and covered it carefully with a linen cloth. The drawer didn't quite close when she shoved it with her knee. With a shrug, she headed for the kitchen, flipping the light switch to plunge the room into darkness behind her.

Nouvelle France, 1642
The Stone Thrower

He stood at the edge
of a pool so still
a sigh would shiver its skin,
unmarked by tip of wing, or breath of wind or hand of
man.
His moccasins sucked mud
from the roots of the cattails on the shore.
Sweat streamed from his
brow into his eyes, stinging
like tears.
His legs trembled
from walking doubled over with the weight
he bore
on his back the bundle of furs singing
with flies.
Bones cracking,
he twisted to one side
dropped a shoulder and flung his treasure
to the rocks at his feet.
Sound
assaulted silence
broke open the clouds of insects hovering in the reeds, wafting
them to
his orifices,

seeking salt.

He whipped his face with greasy hair.

Spat.

GOD DAMN THIS PLAAAACE!!!

His aching back screamed silently, cursing the dreaded

portage... when the river turned to rock and rapids boiled the

water to seething froth there was nothing for it but to haul ass

out of the stream and

walk

with everything strapped on or carried above the shoulders

while a tightly wound sash kept the guts in place, for if they fell,

you were done for.

Day upon year stumbling through the

wilderness of trees

crippled by weariness that sapped the will

to go on.

And yet,

when the bundles of furs were finally stowed

in the prow of the sturdy canoe... Oyay, oyay!

Le voyage!

One of eight men chanting as one body striving forward with

one song,

Propelling upstream such rich bounty wrested from the wild

by the teeth

by the sinew

by the skin....

Everything to be gained in a land fresher than any

woman who could be bartered and won,

then savoured, tasted,

caressed, denuded, devoured, despoiled, revered,

exalted in … . possessed.

His mind buzzed like the insects in his ears,

thoughts clenched tight against pain like the rotten teeth in his

jaw.

He stripped,

stumbled toward the water,

thrashed, submerged, splashed, gulped, spouted, laughed aloud,

lay against the reeds, relaxed, breathed, closed his eyes,

rested…until at last he

raised his head, squinted back at the shore and saw himself there,

and that

first vision

of the shining disk

shouting sunlight to the trees.

Still.

Carefully he stepped out.

The pool relaxed its shoulders.

Humming softly, he slipped on his boots and began searching,

 looking for just the right size and shape, laid his calloused hand

to many, tested, balanced, dropped a chosen few, until one felt

perfect in his palm.

Turned, fixed his gaze and with a roar let go and

Shattered the mirror

to glass.

Ripples bounded wildly from the centre

Ripples trembled, capturing light, air, sound...

Robbing the pool

of colour the ripples

Sliced, split and tore the water's lip to shards,

Stillness bounded to madness

Spiralling outward in a broken, yet perfect

pattern

ever since...

Part II

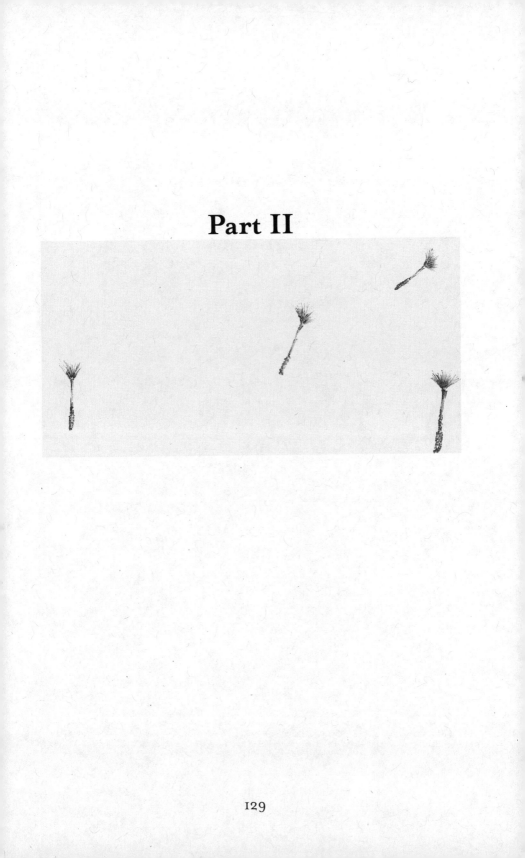

Chapter Fourteen

Well, there was nothing for it. The door must be opened, like it or not. Couldn't leave him standing out there freezing to death. He would already surmise that someone was home, what with the smoke rising from the chimney and the dog barking like mad, so what choice did he have but to let him in?

Tabarnak, he cursed to himself. Life had been so good before the damn Black Robes came. Ah well, no escaping the Church. Pas en France, ni au Nouveau Monde. God is everywhere, as they said.

"Maudit crisse de la tabarnak... Ah bonjour, mon Père. Comment-allez vous? Entrez, entrez. As you know my cabin, she is rustic, but you are always welcome for une petite visite. Here, let me help you brush that snow off your cassock. Take your boots off—your toes must be froze solid. Have a seat, oh let me just take that dirty old coat off there for you. Get down you goddamn filt'y, stupid dog, don't jump up on the Father like that." The mangey cur received a sound smack with an open hand.

"Excusez, mon Père. Well, well, have a seat, as I said. What can I offer you, a cup of herbal cider, a drop of brandy, perhaps? Non, well don't mind if I do, hein? I've been out checking my traps and all that tramping in the snow would freeze the balls off a man without a little liquor to keep the blood flowing, n'est-ce pas? Why, I could hardly put one snowshoe in front of the other by the time I got back. By God, she's a cold winter! Seems they get colder every year."

He laughed nervously and turned to another person in the cabin, lurking in the shadows next to a hanging blanket that served as a curtain.

"Woman, get over here," he shouted in Algonquin, the native tongue which the priest was beginning to learn. Then, switching back to French, he commanded, "Pour me a drink and get something to eat and drink for the poor Father. He must be starving and half froze after walking all this way to pay us a visit."

He tapped his clay pipe against the table to clean the bowl, and then began refilling it from a pouch of tobacco at his waist.

"Well, well, to what do we owe the honour, hein, Father? I know I haven't been down to Mass in quite a while. It's pretty tough to get there in the wintertime and, well, in the summer, we are so busy getting ready for the winter and all....It's been a terrible year, vous savez ben, with the fur getting scarcer. It seems old Jo and me have to walk further into the bush every winter to scratch a living. Thank God I can make up for it in the summertime, by cutting trees and chopping cordwood, but I don't know how long that will last. The old back and legs are giving out on me, *he, he*," he attempted a laugh, which became a wheezy cough. When he finally caught his breath, he tossed more brandy down his throat, then heaved a deep sigh.

"Not much to show for all my travail, after so long, but it's been a good life. You know I was with the *Companie des Cent Associés* for more than ten years, hein? Started when I was just a boy, fresh off the boat from La Normandie. Still wet behind the ears, *he, he*. Them were the days for certain. Time I was twenty, why, I could haul, me, two-hundred pound on my back and paddle upstream through rapids for fifteen hour a day and then make love to three squaws a night... Ha, ha, ha, uhhmm. Well, you don't know what it was like, do you, Father? But now, well, hhhhmm. The land, she is so much more civilized now, n'est-ce pas? It seems all good things must come to an end. I heard we even have a Seigneurie now, down in the settlement. Almost five hundred people, or thereabouts? The Iroquois haven't managed to kill us off or send us running back to France, have they, much as they have tried? Ahh, bien!" He puffed the words out with the smoke from his pipe.

The priest smiled into his mug of cider, which he held firmly to warm his hands. He shook his head as if to agree, but said nothing, waiting patiently for Gérard's chatter to wear itself out. Sensitive to the old coureur de bois' discomfort at his presence, he did not interject with words of pious wisdom, nor react physically to the rough language and manners. He ignored the filth accumulating on the hem of his robe every time he shifted in his chair. He averted his eyes, too, from the young girl waiting on them both. As expected of her, she strove to remain invisible.

He revelled in the steam bathing his chilled face, and let his brown eyes wander above the rim of his mug. Despite the sunlight sparkling on the snow outside, the cabin was gloomy, lit only by the light of the smoky fire and one candle. The sole, tiny window near the door was shuttered against the cold. It was glazed with hide, not glass, and would provide only a sliver of light even in summer. Clothes, animal skins of all shapes and sizes, and thin slices of meat suspended on ropes stretched from one end of the cabin to the other, drying in the heat overhead. Low shelves near the hearth were loaded with baskets, pewter and clay dishes and iron pots. Barrels near the fireplace obviously contained an assortment of winter provisions: peas, corn, salt, flour, and perhaps more than one held "eau-de-vie," the brandy that was the fur traders' stock in trade. An infusion of herbs boiling on the fire would eventually be fermented for homemade cider. The girl constantly drew logs to stoke the fire from a wooden box which overflowed with dry, split wood. As he studied the fireplace more closely, he was startled by its size and beauty: huge boulders and small rocks created a patterned façade from the floor up through the roof. The hearth was large enough for the dog to stretch out and doze, without getting burned. Three pots hung over the flames on a spit, and a side panel lined with iron served as an oven. The girl ladled something from one of the pots into a bowl, plopped a biscuit on top and gently placed the meal in front of him.

Greedily, the young man took up his wooden spoon and, to his delight, tasted venison and dried berries in rich gravy. He slurped up as much as he could, eating like a starving dog, and then wiped the bowl with the last of the warm bread before popping it in his mouth. In the struggling colony, there was never enough to eat, and the Jesuits in their monastery subsisted on meager rations in any case. He peeked out from the rim of the bowl under his eyebrows, chagrined by his lack of manners. His host merely laughed heartily and signalled to the girl for the bowl to be replenished.

"Never let it be said that a man went away hungry from my table! And least of all our priest," he exclaimed.

As he asked if he might have more bread, the priest silently allowed himself one more reason to be thankful he had made the trip up the wooded embankment from the colony by the river. The sturdiness of his cabin, his well-stocked larder, and the solid craftsmanship of his fireplace and furniture bore witness to Gérard's resourcefulness. His possessions exceeded the standards of self-sufficiency and utility, reflecting his pride in creating a home, un foyer, a hearth. Very good. These observations reassured the priest that his goal was worthy and deserved. And as for his "girl" and her cooking! Of course, such relations with the natives were frowned upon by the Church but...

Again he smiled inwardly, savouring his second helping of stew. It was not his place to judge. But still, he had his duty. Perhaps this very mission was the reason he had not yet attained his dream of helping the colonists of the new settlement of Ville Marie, as he had intended when leaving France two years earlier. The Lord did move in mysterious ways. He gathered his courage with a deep breath, as the other man chuckled, thinking the priest was still sighing over the food.

"Oui, Paul, the times are different now, for certain. More of our people are arriving from France every year to establish the settlements at Québec and Trois Rivières and even Ville Marie on the island, which is where I long to go someday. You should come down to Beauport more often and then you'd see the dire straits the Huron are in, wandering around like lost sheep. We can't do enough on our own, the Church, despite our best efforts to help them."

He kept his voice low and even, while the other man pushed back from the table and folded his arms, clasping his pipe between his teeth.

"A decree has been issued for all Jesuits to warn 'les coureurs de bois' to stop trading brandy for furs," the priest continued hastily. "Something must be done to stop this heinous sin. Excommunication even. Don't scoff, it may come to that. You realize what that would mean: eternal damnation in the next life, and grave difficulty in this one, for the merchants would not be allowed to deal with anyone so condemned. We believe it is our bounden duty to convert and protect the natives, not mistreat and corrupt them. They are as children in the eyes of God. And as Jesus said, 'He who would abuse a child should have a millstone tied about his neck and be cast in the river to drown.'" He crossed himself and cleared his throat.

"I trust you don't hold with such ways, Paul. It's the younger men mostly, demanding more and more furs, for the same amount of trade goods, and the natives have no choice but to comply. The traders keep insisting they must use drink to keep the natives on our side and away from the English, who have no compunction at all it seems about plying them with rum. Some even state that it is the only way to convert them! True, they resist accepting our Saviour, but it is certainly to the white man's advantage when the natives give everything away once they are drunk. Then they wake up the next day to find their furs all gone, with nothing to show for a whole winter's worth of work and their children are left to starve. We must then shelter the poor wretches at the monastery and the convent, and we have little enough ourselves. It's devastating for their people and ours. The older men must set an example and stop this practice, n'est-ce pas?"

Paul didn't reply. He just shook his head, puffing out smoke and continually tipping his mug of brandy between his bearded lips. The priest went on, eager to finish while he still had a listening ear.

"Now the traders are advancing into the interior, to 'le pays d'en haut,' since the Companie des Cent Associés has failed and the furs are becoming more scarce. What are you thinking to do now, for yourself? Not join them, surely, at your... hmm..."

His warm brown eyes searched the dark face of the man tipping back his chair. The old voyageur grunted and raised his mug in a silent toast. His ruddy skin glowed in the lamplight like a leather mask. His crooked back forced him to lean on the table to support his drinking arm, which shook slightly as he lifted the cup. He swallowed loudly, wiped the back of his sleeve across his mouth and raked a knobbly hand through his lank grey hair. The priest guessed his age at about thirty-eight years. He narrowed his eyes at the priest.

"*Et crisse, here it comes. I knew he was up to something, this crafty devil in black. What in God's name is he getting at?*" he wondered to himself. Aloud, he hawked up a gob of mucus, spat it into the hearth and murmured, "Well, Father, I agree that The People don't deserve such treatment. The Church is right to intervene, je pense ben!"

Drawing deeply on his pipe for pause, he then roared, banging his mug at the end of each sentence, for emphasis.

"By God, if it hadn't been for them, we would never have survived our first winter. What the hell did we know of snow so deep it could bury you overnight? We knew nothing, coming straight from France. They taught me to live as a woodsman, how to trap, how to break a trail, how to find my way in the bush. I shared a drink with them always, sure enough, in the same way they would share tobacco with me. It was tradition. But I traded for goods, fair and square. I couldn't afford to lose their trust, now could I? That's how I got my little woman here, in the first place," he laughed, and pulled the girl toward him, throwing his heavy arm about her waist. Years of paddling and portaging had made his arms disproportionately large compared to his short, sturdy, body.

"Cost me a musket, but worth it. A man doesn't live by bread alone, in my book, Father. If some say it's wrong, well, let them try to live out here with only men for company, and see how long they last. Fine for you priests, but as for me, well... " he paused, had the decency to blush, stroked his beard, and then added, "And, Father, we are awaiting our first babe, come spring. That is my good news!" His voice cracked with pride as he drew the girl closer to his shoulder.

"You will baptize him, won't you?" he pleaded. "I'm likely damned already, but my son should have a clean slate and a chance at Heaven."

"I don't believe your... woman... is baptized, Paul. That must be done at the same time."

"I suppose that means we have to get married, too. Oh well, no matter. I'll explain it to her somehow and she'll come around. She has a terrible fear of the Church, Father, and can't abide the sight of the crucifix. I don't know why. But we will make sure to come to Beauport for that, I promise," he assured the young man, wiping his brow with his sleeve. The priest nodded his assent. Sighing deeply,

Paul gently tapped the burnt tobacco out of his pipe against the table's edge, onto the floor. The girl stooped to sweep the mess into her hands and dumped it into the fire.

"As you say, the furs are running out around here and no mistake," he grumbled. "You can't really blame the traders. They're desperate, too. What can they do? The damn smallpox killed off a lot of our traders and now the goddamn Iroquois are horning in on our territory. They hate our guts anyway, all of us. My little one here, why, she lost her whole clan to those bastards. You watch yourself too, Father. If they catch you, they'll eat you for supper. I hear tell they relish the taste of a Black Robe."

He laughed dryly until he choked on another cough. He leaned toward the fire and spat again. The dog sidled over to investigate, sniffed, then flopped back down full length in front of the fire. The woman stepped over it to stir a pot and then stoked the fire once more. Sparks shot up the chimney. The priest opened his mouth to warn her against building the fire too high, as cabins in the village were known to burn down for this reason, but he never got the words out.

"Now that the Church has come, well, you're converting the Huron to civilized ways, aren't you, Father? They'll soon shape up. They'll get used to 'the water of life,' like we are. Hell, just as fine as mother's milk to us! Don't give us many ill effects. 'Firewater,' some call it. Voyons—go on with you, now! Keeps a man going, especially in the wintertime, I say! Caaalisse de crisse, I've used it for everything from polishing my flintlock to cleaning dirt out of a wound," he exclaimed, making his point by taking another swig from his pewter mug.

"Hmm hmmm, excusez-moi, Father, but you know what I mean. In any case, we are forced further into the bush, north and north-west, in search of furs. Me, I'd love a chance to see what it's like further west. "C'est l'aviron, qui nous mène, qui nous mène, c'est l'aviron qui nous mène en haut!" He burst into a traditional rowing song, paddling an imaginary canoe, iron muscles bursting against his buckskin sleeves.

"Singing and rowing fifteen, eighteen hours a day! That's what

I've done since I left France, Father, accumulating the wealth which you can plainly see around you. " His arm formed a wide arc with mug in hand. At the end of the circle, he tipped it back into his mouth, frowned and slammed it on the table once more.

"Woman, get me some more 'eau de vie.' Keeps the blood moving! Otherwise, it'll freeze in your bones, for sure. Ahh ... well, if this doesn't warm you up, you are dead already! But, even with a good fire, she's colder than hell in here, I find. I'll join the Father in a plate of that stew. Throw some more biscuits on the table too, voyons. Father needs more food to fatten up!" he hollered. The girl jumped to do his bidding.

"Take note, Father! You see, she is learning French. I am determined that my sons will have both our languages, so they can travel wherever they wish in this land, just like their papa! Even if I have to go further upriver, I will come back, rest assured. My sons will not grow up as some cast-off bastards, unlike some I could name," he mumbled with a pained frown, showing off his strong white teeth. Then he leaned over his plate, encircling the rim with his arm and began spooning up the stew, ignoring the gravy dripping down his beard.

"Well, as it happens, I have a proposition for you, from the Seigneur himself, which could keep you closer to home. You see, as an educated man, who can read and write, you have prospects you have not considered. Seigneur Giffard, Sieur de Moncel, is authorized by the King himself, Paul, to name you a notary and offer you land right on the river. Wait, wait, hear me out," he said, as he saw the older man lean forward with his mouth open, to interrupt.

Raising his hand against all protest, he continued in a firm tone, "I have brought you a letter and a grant of land, in writing. All it needs is to be officially notarized in Beauport ... un arpent de front sur dix en profondeur, imaginez-vous! Just think of the size of it, right on the riverfront, with free access to the water! We Jesuits are organizing the land grants and with your ..."

"You can't be serious! What in God's name do I know about farming? I wasn't born to be a peasant! That's one thing my mother did teach me, at least!" Paul shouted, half-rising to his feet. His abrupt movement startled the young woman, who dropped the spoon in the metal plate with a clatter.

"Me, strapped to a plough behind a goddamn ox? Worse than death! What in the hell would I want to live in town with all the newcomers and their fancy ways? Maudit, they look down on me bad enough when I haul my furs in with my woman here, to get supplies. The old folks, they don't bat an eyelash. But this fresh lot, with their French wives, taking on airs ..." He paused for breath.

"I'd show 'em a thing or three. They wouldn't 'a survived one winter here in my day. You never knew what might happen, and a man could do anything, anything I tell you, and not a soul to say a word about it. Not a soul would either! That's what I loved about it. Among the Huron, it's live for today and let tomorrow worry about itself. Damn it all to hell, we were kings in them days. We lived better'n kings! Free men in a new land. Back home, I couldn't breathe. Here, the pure air filled us up and made us strong! Not like those simpering pussies surrounding His Royal Highness at Court! I seen enough of them as a lad, and as it all turned out, I'm thankful now that I was sent away. My mother wanted to rid herself of her bastard son, and I can't forgive her still, but I have to admit, it was the making of me, I swear!" Paul exclaimed, beating his chest with both fists. The priest drew back from the table in retreat.

"I'm sorry, Father," Paul softened his tone. "I know I have a filthy tongue, but I been here a long time and I seen things you can't imagine. I busted my back to keep my freedom. Civilization, bah! What did it do for me? Mon Dieu, I can't see me and her living anywhere near town, Father."

The brandy had taken hold now and a few tears were slipping along the creases of the high cheekbones, sliding down into the grizzled beard. There was no move to wipe them away. The priest had learned that the voyageurs showed their emotions openly: joy, anger or sorrow, without shame, for in the bush, the social graces meant nothing. He had observed that their raw courage and force of will assured survival and, at the same time, cracked open the spirit to feel more deeply. It was powerful and terrifying for the young émigré from a refined life in Paris. He had quickly learned to tread carefully through this wild domain, offering a gentle word here, a suggestion there, a smile, a helping hand ... all to serve God's purpose and preserve his shaky authority.

A trace of movement in the corner of the room caught his eye. Père Thomas turned and saw the round, tawny face peeking from behind the tattered curtain. Through wisps of black hair, her liquid brown eyes sent a message. The girl's distended stomach created a shadow at the waist of her soft buckskin dress. An unborn soul silently begging to be saved. The young man dug his fingernails into the wooden armrests of the chair.

He opened his mouth, but Paul interrupted by rising to pace the room. He shook his large head and his words came out slurred.

"Besides, how would my woman fit in down there with that lot? Elle n'est pas apprivoisée, vous savez. She's still wild, this one—a savage as they would say. How would that life suit her? She's nothing like our women, which pleases me just fine! I know what it's like to be an outsider, believe me!" He threw his hands in the air with a wild gesture, stretching to catch the girl's arm and pull her out from where she hid behind the cabin's supporting pole.

"Look at this little hand, Father," he murmured softly, placing her palm against his huge, callused paw.

"I'm guessing she's what, maybe fourteen? Not too young, by God. Even old Champlain's bride was only twelve, don't you know, and she lasted no more than four years when she finally got out here. Scurried her fancy ass back to France and swore never to return, as I heard tell. Poor bastard, after all he'd been through to settle this country. It's thanks to him you Jesuits are even here, since he was the one who first brought you out. I attended his funeral, what, fifteen years ago now. Can't say I agreed with everything he did, but at least he understood the nature of the place. The King and the Church decree nowadays that we mustn't 'have relations' with the native women. Why not? What better way to colonize a country and make a strong people for the New World? That's what Champlain thought and he was right, too. No, they're not 'pure,' they insist. Bah! This one can catch, skin, clean and cook a man's dinner in the wink of an eye. Helps me with my traps, mends my snowshoes, tans hides, and sews our clothes. A true little partner to me ..." He gently brought her hand to his cheek, kissed it, and then released his grip. His eyes softened with moisture as he watched her kneel before the fire.

"She would be very unhappy, in a house in town. This is hard enough, away from everything she knows, her people all dead from the Iroquois or the smallpox. It's lonely for her. Maybe she would up and run back into the bush and where would that leave me? But for my son, yes, if when I have a son ..." he hesitated, tipped back in his chair and sucked his empty pipe between his teeth.

"Notaire, now you say, Father. What would be the duties, exactly?"

The priest waited for a moment, his air of calm betraying the rush of his thoughts. The drink lent an element of uncertainty to the situation. Besides, he had to leave before nightfall. The settlement wasn't far, but still, darkness fell early, and wolves and Iroquois might track him in the woods. He shuddered.

"Notaire, yes. Quite the title, Paul. The duties would present no problem for you at all. You would bear witness to business transactions as a trusted servant in the name of His Majesty. I didn't say you'd have to farm the land yourself. I'll bet you have enough of a stake to set yourself up in a fine house and hire some young men to work for you, get yourself a horse even, some cows too and set out every morning and just supervise the work on the farm. Help the Seigneur, witness marriages and baptisms, pay your fealty duties and live a long, happy life. And your mother ..."

"My mother! Why bring that whore into this? What do you know of ..." Paul cut him off with a shout, his face suddenly inflamed in the firelight.

"Well, a courtesan, yes. But, in the court of the King of France, where the position she gained can now help you and yours. In any case, I understand that she mended her ways, in the end, renewed her faith and died with the Holy Sacrament on her lips. I have your mother's last letter here for you also, Paul. The Seigneur was given the authority to grant you a section of land, by the King personally, as your part of your mother's legacy. Consider carefully, my son."

"I don't want any favours. I made my whole life on my own so far, with no help from anybody. Swear fealty to a Seigneur, I ask you, no better than me, not fit to kiss my..." his mumbled monologue continued a few syllables behind the priest. It was as if the bear hide nailed to the wall had sprung to life.

"...Drafting documents, writing letters for people, witnessing signatures, simple matters, to ensure the security of your family, Paul. By baptizing your wife and child, the Church will support them to grow in God, amongst the townspeople. You do understand that, don't you? You would adapt, just as you have done up to now." He let his voice trail off.

"Well, think about it anyway. Not much will be happening now until spring, in any event. Hold onto these papers, and bring the document for me to witness, before the Seigneur, if you change your mind. In any case, be sure to stop by, the next time you come in for supplies. May I give you both our Blessing?"

The older man straightened and blinked. He squinted into the smoky light and then asked, "Pardon me, Father, what was that you said?"

"You will receive our Blessing, before I go?"

"Oh, yes, of course, oui, eh ben, of course. Yes, you must hear my confession, too. It will take a while, because it's been a long, long time. I can't remember how long, exactly. But I have all winter to catch up with my penance, so I will accept whatever the Lord decides. I'll need all your prayers this winter, Father. The traps are too often empty now. The game, she is getting scarce, vous savez. And, of course, there's the little one coming to think about. The first Gérard in Nouvelle France, eh, Father? Maybe, if it's a girl, I will name her for my mother. Wouldn't that surprise the old harlot! And if it's a boy, why, how about Louis, for his Majesty the King? Joking, just joking!" he chortled, grinning at the priest's startled expression.

"Ah well, I'll give your proposal some thought, Father. Don't know as I like the notion of moving into Beauport, at all. We'll see, when it comes time to baptise." He reached out his hand and yanked the woman down to her knees beside him.

"Well, my girl, might as well get some practice with this, especially if we end up in town. Then, we will have to be in Church every Sunday. See, we kneel before the Father. Beside me, right here, that's good. Bon, bon. Now put your hands together like so. We pray, and then you hear my confession, d'accord, Mon Père? *Bless me father, for I have sinned. These are my sins...*"

Before he shut the heavy wooden door on his way out, the Jesuit hastily withdrew a sealed parchment from the pouch at his waist, and pressed it into Paul's hand.

"Jesus asks us to forgive, Paul. Find it in your heart, also, my son. Do not cut off your nose, to spite your face," he said softly, as he wrapped his heavy woollen scarf around his neck, covered his tonsure with a fur cap and struggled to extract the hood of his cassock from beneath his coat, as an additional shield against the cold.

The sun was already bending low toward the horizon when the priest strapped on his snowshoes in front of the cabin and headed down the hill. Still, he faced his trek eagerly, his heart surging with pride in his newfound skills of traversing the deep snows as easily as he had walked down the cobblestone streets of Paris. He whistled one of the voyageur's common ditties to keep a steady rhythm as he trudged along, just as they did while rowing. The fresh air seared his lungs while the blood rose to his cheeks and his breath formed sparkling clouds before his eyes. Under his fur cap, his ears burned with shame as he remembered the weakling he had been during the Atlantic crossing from France to the New World, just a few years before. How unprepared he had been for the hardships of the journey, let alone for life in the young colony...

Once again he felt himself clinging to the edge of the hammock, spitting yellow bile onto the heaving floor. There was no solid food left to release from his stomach, from one end or the other. Still, the nausea overtook him, as he was tossed to the other side of the hammock by the force of the ship's rocking motion, causing his guts to spasm again. The pounding in his head matched the rhythm of the waves against the wooden hull. His view consisted of no more than the planks only inches above his face, and they were a constant blur. He gasped for air in the close, stinking hold, and longed to see the sky and sunlight. The shores of France and the beautiful town of Dieppe existed only in his fevered dreams. Had he left them behind less than a week ago, on a bright, spring morning? Would he ever see the sun, the sky, the land again?

"Lord, how much longer can I endure this? Give me strength, I beg you," he moaned aloud. Tito, the cabin boy, took pity on him, and brought him some water to sip. Though his parched mouth begged for more, he barely wet his lips. Otherwise, the vomiting would start again. His stomach muscles tightened around his core like shipping line, cutting off his breath at the very thought.

Why, why, why had he been motivated to do this? Silently he posed the question, rolling his head back and forth against the netting that was his berth. Because, he answered himself, you had no idea what the voyage would be like. No one had ever told you that a fellow could be sick the entire journey! The sailors had assured him that after a few days, he would get his "sea legs." "Sea legs!" He couldn't imagine ever being able to place both feet on firm ground again! How would he stand upright, after weeks swinging wildly in little more than a sack tied to a heaving monster that wouldn't let him eat, sleep or even relieve himself with decency? And worse, the humiliation of being the only passenger unable to rise from the depths and actually enjoy some of the trip, in the bracing winds on the deck!

His mother had warned him of the dangers, known and unknown, and begged him not to go. His dear sister had screamed and cried and rent her hair, until she at last collapsed at his feet in exhaustion.

"No, do not say it once more. You must not, you will not abandon us! What will we do without you here, to protect and guide us? You are all we have left! The Church will care for you and ensure that we are supported as well, in your very own parish here in the city. Someday you could rise to become a Bishop. Fifteen years, fifteen years you have struggled to be fully ordained and now, just when we thought that you had accomplished your dream..." Claudette struggled up from the floor, to stand, pace and gesture wildly as she continued to admonish him.

"You say God has called you to this mission? No, Brother, it is your own selfish arrogance that is leading you to undertake this foolish cause, to convert the savages. Did you hear me? Savages. Why do you think they call them that? What do La Dauversière and De Verneuil know—have they even been there? Certainly they have been persuasive, managing to gain access to a whole island. An island, far inland, where there is no one *but* savages. Cartier landed there over a hundred years ago and no one has lived there permanently since! Fifty of you, against how many natives, who know the land, and will conspire to throw you out, or worse? Bah, let De Maisonneuve lead them on their fool's mission, everyone is calling it so! Everyone with any sense!" She took a ragged breath and persisted in her pleas.

"Would God really ask you to desert your family and your moral and spiritual obligations to us? Leave other men to go if they wish! No, I will not have you calling it blasphemy to speak against this mission on behalf of the Virgin. Even she was a mother, and a sister, and she would have agreed with me, I am sure! Perhaps others leave no one behind. Or perhaps they are doing some penance. But you are a gentle soul, Thomas. We need you here, and surely if you go, we will never see you again. As Mother says, you have never been physically strong. How do you expect to survive, with no one to care for you as Mother and I do, when you are ill with your winter cough, or simply exhausted from work? And it is well known that the winters there kill our men without mercy, for we are not used to the bitter cold, the snow as deep as a house is tall, not to mention the lack of food. The deprivation will kill you in no time, Brother, and where will that leave Mother and me? You are heartless and cruel beyond belief, if you persist in this venture. Please, reconsider your decision; I am begging you, in our dear father's name! He would not have wished you to go off into the wilds of New France, leaving us behind to grieve your loss. Surely there has been enough grief in this family, with the loss of Father, has there not?

"Please, Thomas, I beg you, do not leave us! Let De Maisonneuve go to New France, to set up his settlement in the name of the Virgin! A fool's mission! Didn't I say so before we left home and here in Dieppe everyone agrees with me! And you, a bigger fool for not listening! The natives don't know of Her and don't care—why should you risk your life to save the souls of strangers, when your own family needs you so?" Her voice cracked in a sob.

"The cold, the snow, the deprivation, Brother, you will die of one, the other or all three at once! Why are you determined to kill yourself? Martyrdom? That is your desire? Bah! You will not live long enough to be a martyr! This is suicide, plain and simple! Suicide is a sin, is it not? If you step on that ship, you are committing suicide, and breaking your mother's heart as well."

Nevertheless, he had left the port of Dieppe on the third ship, together with fifty other colonists, for the mission to build Ville Marie in New France. His fervor to serve God by converting the Natives to the one true faith was unshakable, even against the storm of his sister's wrath and his mother's tears. But now he doubted his own strength to live until his feet touched the earth once more. Perhaps he would rest in a watery grave at the bottom of the ocean for all eternity. He shuddered as a chill ran down his bony spine. His teeth chattered though he was drenched in sweat. Tito wiped his face with a damp, sour-smelling cloth, and muttered soothing nonsense words. The boy's soft, sweet voice calmed him. For the first time in all the days the boy had been attending to him, he really looked at his face. He was shocked to see that the tip of his nose was missing, but also startled by the delicate features, smooth, hairless chin and the eyes as clear blue as a calm ocean. The lovely child had probably lost his nose in a fight with one of the other cabin boys, or with one of the men, for he was well aware that the rape of pretty boys was common onboard ships. The sinfulness, crudeness and stench of the sailors turned his stomach perhaps more than the roiling sea. Poor Tito, what was his story? Suffer the little children...

"Tito, you are so kind to me. I don't know what I would do without you. You have been better than a sister to me. Someday, I will repay you, God willing."

"Not at all, mon Père. It is my honour and duty to serve you. How fortunate I am to be an instrument in God's divine plan, I who am nothing. Do not trouble yourself about me! The Lord has brought us together and I will see you through. In perhaps forty days, you will attain your purpose to begin your mission in the New World, to bring the blessings of our Holy Mother to the Savages there! Look, we will count them together, for I am marking each sunrise with a scratch right here on the floor beside your hammock. See how many there are already? Fear not, your Tito is here."

What satisfaction his sister would have felt to see him suffering aboard ship! It almost made him smile to think that, for once, he would not hear her say, "I told you so. Didn't I tell you so?" He made up his mind that if ever he had the chance to write to his family about his journey, this part would be omitted. He wouldn't exactly lie, but he would never admit that the women had been right, and his body had let him down, once again.

Even in his delirium, he overheard the crew's careless comments as they flipped themselves lightly into their hammocks nearby. "Observe the poor lamb, my friends! How will this one ever manage in the wilds of New France, hein? So soft, he will soon find himself cooked in his own gravy by the fierce natives. Wouldn't they delight in his buttery, white flesh? Though he will be naught but skin and bones if he keeps spilling his guts on the floor. Ah well, he might make a good broth for some hungry Savages on the island, if he even gets that far."

They continually bantered back and forth at his expense, knowing he was too weak to respond and delighting in adding to his misery to break the monotony of the voyage. They had no concerns about reprisals, for they knew the priest was at the mercy of their skills in bringing him safely to the other shore, and they were bound to enjoy the fact that the tables were turned, for once. While he understood this, and struggled to forgive them in his heart, as Jesus would wish, the words seemed to bring his inner doubts to light, for all to witness.

The taunts rang in his ears as another cramp coursed through his gut like icy water. Without warning, his bowels let go, and warm liquid soaked his naked legs and his wretched blanket, spilling onto the filthy floor below.

"Poor Tito. Excuse-moi. I am sorry to be such trouble to you. Thank you for your kindness in caring for me. I don't know how, but someday, I will repay you," Père Bilodeau croaked, as the boy swabbed up the mess once again, and helped him to rise to his elbows and force down some dry biscuits.

"Not at all, mon Père. It is my honour to serve you in your hour of need. Do not trouble yourself. We have been twenty days at sea and in less than forty, we will arrive in the new world, where you will begin your mission. In the meantime, it is my sacred duty to ensure that you arrive there alive and well. The capitaine has given me this task and I intend to carry it out. You must focus on the end and not let this momentary discomfort dissuade you from your divine purpose. Do not lose heart and do not listen to the others. Tito is here."

The lad kept murmuring words of reassurance as he disentangled the emaciated priest from his hammock and stood him up on the sodden boards. Leaning him against a plank on the outward curving wall of the hull, he sluiced his backside down with a bucket of sea water, and then balanced him against his chest while he deftly removed the soiled nightshirt and wrapped the thin white body in a woollen blanket he had stuffed under one arm.

Père Bilodeau endured the indignity in silence, as the boy stuffed him like a rag doll into a clean nightshirt and helped him stumble back to the swaying hammock. Pride had been evacuated from his system along with his bodily fluids, over the past three weeks. Remembering Tito's thorough ministrations now, however, he blushed to his toes, so that the very snow beneath his feet threatened to melt. How he had been fooled! The only consolation he had is that he was not the only one. And had it not been for the nursing he had received he would certainly have joined the ranks of the dead. That fear remained throughout the journey, lurching continuously from side to side like a stone in an empty cauldron. It rose to his gorge each time another corpse tied in a sack was dragged past his berth, up the stairway and into the light above, to meet its fate in the icy sea. Death posed no threat to him, for he knew the Lord would meet him in Heaven, but he shuddered to think that the wasting disease taking the lives of passengers and crew could just as easily choose him next. Maybe he had it already, he thought, his teeth chattering anew as he pulled the blanket up to cover his nose. If so, his dream of joining De Maisonneuve at Ville Marie to build the new colony dedicated to the Blessed Virgin would drown in the deep unknown. Surely the Holy Mother would not wish that. Perhaps it was too late, and the colonists had already left Hochelaga. If so, he would have to summon his courage to make the journey on his own, with only natives to guide him down the mighty Saint Lawrence River to the island of Mont Royal. Would God make that possible?

He summoned his limp right arm upwards, to cross himself, and began to pray to the Virgin Mary, remembering the sailor's creed.

"Si tu vas en guerre, prie une fois, si tu vas en mer, prie deux fois."

Since he was going to war against pagan gods, crossing an ocean on behalf of Christ and in the name of his Holy Mother, he would pray more than twice. He would pray a thousand times, if necessary...

And how he had prayed. And as usual, God had answered. Now, as his strong body carried him vigorously back toward the settlement of Beauport that he was helping to establish, he had to battle against the sin of pride in his accomplishments. He had kept his promise of help to Tito, despite the awkwardness of the situation. He was making progress amongst the faithful in the village. Even this excursion today had not been in vain, for he was sure he had planted the seed of forgiveness in the old voyageur's heart, and he had successfully delivered the letter, as promised. Perhaps it would find its mark. At the very least the native woman and new babe would be converted to the faith. Every soul counted in God's eyes, and the saving of souls was his prime responsibility, here or at Ville Marie sometime in the future. He would put it all in his report to the Bishop. The glow of satisfaction enlivened each stride and before he knew it, he had reached the first stone cottage of the settlement, the light from its tiny windows beckoning through the tall pine trees.

*****

An anguished cry resonated through the smoky cabin, as the piece of parchment hurtled through the air. The Huron girl jumped like a startled rabbit and backed into the corner in terror when a chair was sent flying, barely missing her head before smashing against the stone fireplace. Scurrying behind the curtain, she threw herself on the wooden pallet to hide under the fur coverings. But he didn't come near her. Lately, he had been gentler and was always sorry for hurting her afterwards. He would cry, make excuses, and do all her chores for the day. It only happened when he had been drinking the firewater. And that was only when the nights were long, during the cold, dark winter. In the spring, summer, and fall, he was much too busy with his work.

Long after the sun set, she heard him wailing, bawling, cursing and spitting. The cabin door opened and closed as he left briefly to relieve himself. When he came back inside, he helped himself to more firewater, lit his pipe and kept talking, as though she were listening. She didn't understand a word of his slurred ravings. In her womb, the baby kicked. Rubbing her stomach with the palm of her left hand, she stuck her right thumb in her mouth, curled into a ball and rocked her body back and forth, back and forth. The rhythm of her movement and the song she hummed were meant to ward off disturbing dreams, and lull both of them safely to sleep. But often, in this isolated cabin with no one to talk to, no one to tell, she had nightmares. And most of them were real.

Chapter Fifteen

Early Summer, Huronia, 1636

"Wha…! It can't…I can't…" A mouthful of water swallowed further exclamations. She struggled against the current, flailing her arms while reaching with the tip of her toes for the rock-strewn riverbed which had been beneath her feet just moments before. She had lost her foothold and suddenly the water seemed to be rising past her eyes. Then she was in over her head, too deep to recover her balance. With eyes open underwater, she was nonetheless blinded, for her feet had disturbed the clay of the riverbed. Her loose hair swirled and streamed into her open mouth. Instantly, she regretted having taken out her braid before her swim.

"Foolish!" she thought, just as the water seemed to lift her up and place her back on solid ground, at the spot where the sinkhole had appeared. Coughing and sputtering, she became aware of a small hand in hers, which yanked her across the rocky bank and then let her fall. The hair was pulled back from her face, her eyelids were forced open, she was pushed upright and then her back was pounded until it stung worse than the pain in her burning chest.

"Yellow Bird! Yellow Bird! Can you hear me? Can you breathe now? Aiii, you were almost gone. I saw you go under and I just grabbed you or the river would have taken you away forever. How did it happen? We always cross here. It's never been deep there before. Oh, we are in for such trouble!"

Still struggling for breath, Yellow Bird raised her head and stared uncomprehendingly at her younger cousin. The girl was talking, but only dull sounds were coming out of her mouth. She realized that her ears were plugged with water. She inclined her head side to side, banging her temple with the heel of her hand. Meanwhile the child started slapping her on the back again, until she roughly pushed her back with her elbow. Suddenly, hot water flowed from one ear, and her cousin's voice came through as a scream. Bending her neck, she tried to clear her other ear and her mind. She raised her knees to hold the weight of her water-logged head.

"Mustn't tell," she managed in a raspy voice, gazing down at the blur of rocks between her thighs.

"Not a word to anyone, especially not to Mother. I'll be all right, just let me lie here for a while. Go pick some berries and then you can braid my hair before we go back. Stay close."

As soon as she heard her cousin rustling in the bushes for her clothes, she flopped back onto the stony bank, heedless of her naked flesh. What did a few bruises matter, when she had almost drowned? Her stomach ached with the wrenching feeling of that first drop, when her foot had sought the familiar river floor and found... nothing. She retched and threw up foul-tasting water, then shivered as she re-lived the terror of sinking, stretching to find bottom while the water filled her nose, her eyes, her ears, her lungs. Unbelievable! How could she be suddenly struggling for air, kicking against the current, fighting to live in the place where she always played, splashing and laughing in the sun? The river had become her enemy. She knew that but for her cousin's quick action, she would have drowned. How had the smaller girl managed to pull her back from the whirling waters of the sink hole? Teeth chattering despite the heat of the summer afternoon, she forced herself to her feet, stumbling across the rugged bank in search of the deerskin dress that she had carelessly tossed in the grass. As she sat to pull on her moccasins, her father's voice came back to her.

"You girls must be careful at the river. You may bathe, but only near the bank. The river constantly changes and you must be cautious of the currents. Don't attempt to cross it on your own. Listen well and do as you are told, Daughter. You don't know the dangers. And keep your eyes on your cousin. When you are out, she is your responsibility."

What would he say if he knew that it had been Sunrise who had saved her? Shaking her head, she again said to herself that her parents must never know. She would find a way to make it up to Sunrise—yes, those earrings she had admired would indeed be hers. To convince her to keep her mouth shut, that would be the tricky part. Everyone said that "Squirrel" would have been a better name for the little chatterbox.

"Feeling better now? I hope you don't cough anymore. That must have felt terrible. Well, here are all the berries I could find. It's hot in the bushes. Look, my legs are all scratched."

Yellow Bird did not look at her cousin's legs. She saw instead the pitiful quantity of berries in her little basket. She stumbled over to retrieve her own empty basket from the grass, grabbed Sunrise's basket and dumped half the berries into it. Oh well, too late now, she shrugged.

"Quick, braid my hair. You know how it turns out when I do it myself. Here are my ties. Then we must get back—Mother will be waiting for us. Remember, no stories. I'll give you the shell earrings Papa brought me from the last trading. But don't say anything, or they'll never let us come here by ourselves again. Understand?" her voice rose, pleading. She grabbed the smaller girl and held her to her chest, patting her back reassuringly. That trick sometimes kept her quiet.

When they arrived back at the camp, her mother said nothing as she looked at the paltry amount of berries the girls had collected between them. Her face said all there was to say. Yellow Bird looked at the ground as her mother dumped the berries into the cooking pot, to mash with the meat.

"Go, there is a hide strung, for scraping. You can work on that. Show me that you can be diligent. You have obviously wasted your whole afternoon. Yellow Bird, the time has come when play is over. There is much work to be done and a woman must show her value. I see your hair is still wet from the river. All very well to bathe on a hot afternoon, but I expect more from you. How will we eat if there is not food put away for the long winter ahead? Think about it, while you prepare the moose hide for a winter coat for your father." Her voice was soft, controlled, but the reprimand stung Yellow Bird like the slap of a stray branch in the forest. Physical punishment might have hurt less, but would never have been considered by The People.

No more was said, even at dinner, around the fire. Her mother had obviously told her father, who disciplined her just as sternly through silence and reproachful glances. Yellow Bird's face flared from the heat of the fire and her parents' ill regard. She could barely swallow her food. She longed to shout in defense of herself.

"Do you have any idea what happened to me today? That you almost lost your Yellow Bird? I could have drowned you know! It was awful! I felt the water over my head and the current swirling at my feet and I wasn't strong enough to fight it. If it hadn't been for Sunrise, you would be mourning me now! But instead, you are reprimanding me for not picking enough berries. The Strawberry Festival, that's all everyone cares about. What is fruit, compared to my life? How did I know the river would change, right under my feet? I just wanted to ... oh, you don't understand. You will never understand!"

She swallowed the words with each spoonful of her corn mash, watching the fire without blinking until her eyes filled with tears. The thick sagamité stuck in her throat. She turned away to spit it surreptitiously into her hand, for if she were caught wasting precious food, the punishment would be worse. She then collected the clay bowls and went about her chores, while the night sounds filled the long house, and other families laughed merrily with their children around their own hearths.

As soon as she could, she escaped into her section of the summer pallets attached along the full length of the longhouse. The river water rose again in her gorge. She leaned over and threw up on the earthen floor directly below her bed. She leaned over to cover the mess with dirt, then curled into a tight ball under a pile of tanned hides against the outer longhouse wall. Close by, her mother was humming the Strawberry Festival song. So pretty...

*****

The animal's legs were so high that she had to stand on a tree stump to mount upon its back. She threw herself aloft, then shimmied forward to grasp a trailing lock of stiff hair. Astride the animal, the animal's fur scratched her bare flesh, creating a heat between her legs that she had never known. She wanted to itch there, but suddenly the creature threw back its head and took off at a run. She clung on desperately, squeezing her knees together as the wind whipped through her loose hair. Had she neglected to braid her hair again? What would Mother say?

She and the beast exploded out of the forest, to an open field where they joined a herd of similar animals of every colour—black, beige, spotted, brown, grey. The white one she was riding led them in a wild race. Hooves barely touching the ground, at the speed of the clouds racing across the blue sky, they came upon a cliff. Far below, she could see crashing waves. They veered away just in time and their companions followed. Turning them all away from the edge, the leader sped across a wide, green plain dappled with flowers. Icy wind stung her face. For protection, she nuzzled down into the animal's back, gripping its warm muscles with straining fingers. She glanced to either side at the other animals, determined to keep pace. She tried to stretch out her arms and touch their shiny coats. As fast as they might run, ears pinned back, nostrils flaring, eyes bulging, they couldn't match her mount.

Then, without warning, she lurched forward. She was thrown to the ground, landing on her back. Gasping for breath, she rolled over onto all fours. Pain stabbed her abdomen as she crawled forward to see what had happened. The strange animal was caught in unyielding strands of bright cord, woven with sharp, pointed claws, attached at intervals to posts driven into the ground. The claws had torn his broad chest to shreds. No longer white, his red coat heaved and trembled as blood pumped from deep wounds. She placed her hands against the cuts, trying to staunch the flow, sobbing. She felt the warm, sticky blood on her hands. The animal raised his head and screamed into the wind, a cry that stabbed her to the heart. She tried to call out, but pain strangled her: no sound came. She raised her hands to her face, inhaled the smell of fresh blood, and woke up.

Her hands, her legs, her furs were soaking wet. In the darkness, she could not see the blood, but she knew what had happened. Mother had prepared her for this. But why, why did it have to happen in the middle of the night? She didn't want to wake her mother, for that would wake Father too, and the humiliation would be too great. He would find out soon enough, but not this way. What to do? What to do? She couldn't lie like this until morning—that would be worse. Everyone would make a fuss... no, she couldn't bear it. She raised herself to her knees, clasped the wet furs around her, and rolled onto the ground. Trying to stand, her abdomen locked as a cramp took her breath away. Waiting for a moment until it passed, she allowed her eyes to adjust to the dim glow of the smoking, banked fires. The doorway nearest her family's quarters was close to her grandparents, but luckily they slept soundly and her grandfather's snores would cover any sound she might make going outside. Her bare feet slipped soundlessly across the earthen floor. She hurried silently through the door of woven bark and stepped into the early morning light. The women's wigwam awaited her about a hundred footsteps away, close by the stream. Hunched against the pain tearing across her belly, she hurried down the path, oblivious to the pebbles and sticks beneath her hardened feet.

Next to the hut, a bucket stood waiting. Before going in, she grabbed the hide pail and rushed to the stream. Stooping to fill it, her furs slipped off her back. She leaned over, naked, threw the fur in the water and in the half-light saw the dark liquid swirl away. She rinsed her hands and tossed the icy water between her legs. The sticky blood washed away, but more dripped hotly onto the ground. Another bucketful of water dissolved the blood into the earth. She hoped it couldn't be seen, but she knew the dogs and maybe other animals would come to smell it. Her heart began to race. She must hurry inside, to staunch the flow with the moss prepared for that purpose, before the blood contaminated the ground. Flinging aside the tanned leather hide covering the doorway, she stepped foot for the first time into the women's hut.

All her mother's and grandmother's teachings hadn't prepared her for the rush of emotion that overwhelmed her as she collapsed onto the matted floor. The earthy scent of moss and herbs in the small space went to her head like smoke, as she numbly searched out the supplies she needed from the birchbark trunk. A comfortable pad of moss secured by a leather thong reassured her that there would be no more mess to clean up, but she started to shiver in the damp, dew-drenched hut. Teeth chattering, she crawled under a pallet piled high with furs and wrapped herself in her own arms for warmth.

"Too cold to make a fire. Besides, Mother or Grandmother will bring me something, as soon as they realize..." Her nose buried in the furs, she thought she could smell the wind-blown scent of her wild ride in her dream once more.

She awoke with a start to a persistent scratching on the leather door. Sunlight streamed into the space, blinding her as she rose on both arms to greet whatever female family member had come to find her. Squinting, she called out, "Yes, yes, I'm here," in response to her grandmother's voice, whispering her name.

"Ah, then it's true. Our little one became a woman overnight. I thought I heard you moving about. You know I would have helped you, my dear. You are the headstrong one, always determined to do everything for yourself, aren't you? Well, you seem to manage your way out of any situation, so I suppose this is no different. Here, let me start the fire for you at least. I've brought you a hot infusion, for the pain. Is it very strong, child? Why, I remember, so long ago but it seems like yesterday, my first moon times. And your mother's too. Sore back, yes? And cramps? Here, roll over and I'll rub your back with this balm. It will help right away. Then we'll get you dressed in a warm robe and keep you tucked up here nice and cozy."

The old woman's tone soothed Yellow Bird, as always, and the warm massage and herbal drink lulled her into a state of deep peace. She snuggled deep into the furs as she watched her grandmother light the fire in the center of the hut. The smoke rose lazily toward the vent in the roof and soon the air was filled with the sweet aroma of maple wood. Yellow Bird's stomach growled in response. She giggled.

"Ha, well you are hungry at least. That's a good sign. Some women become famished, while others can barely eat. Me, I always think it's better to eat. Settles the cramps down and keeps up your strength. Here, this is now your own little cooking pot, just for you, to use at your moon times. Cook yourself some sagamité. I brought some corn cakes, too. Eat whenever you want. I'll bring you some broth later and your mother will be down soon with a maple sugar treat, if I know her. She always did spoil you!"

"I think she is still angry with me. She was so upset yesterday..."

"Not angry, just disappointed. She wants you to learn your duties, so you will make a good wife and can look after your mate and your children. Now, you see, that becomes more important than before. Your days of dreaming with your eyes open are done, little one."

"Ah, speaking of dreams, Grandmother. You must hear the dream I had last night. I was riding on the back of some tall, wild animal! It was like flying on the back of a bird—so fast! Isn't that wonderful?" Yellow Bird described every detail she could remember of the dream, as she always did for her grandmother and mother. Dreams were meant to be told, upon awakening, to discover important messages. Family members spent time each morning recalling and even acting out their dreams, then interpreting the "soul stories" together. If a dream seemed especially powerful, it was brought to the shaman for consultation. Grandmother shook her head as Yellow Bird finished with the question, "What hurt that animal, do you suppose? And what kind of animal was it? Here, let me draw it in the sand for you. You see? I have never seen anything like it, have you?"

The old woman squinted in concentration, as was her habit. She constantly rubbed her eyes and blinked, to fight the blindness that plagued all the elders in the longhouse, caused by the constant smoke trapped indoors. She clucked her tongue as she tried to think of an answer for her granddaughter.

"Strange indeed. More potent because it came to you on the night of your first moon time. This must be your totem animal. A very strong dream, to be sure. I can't say what it might mean. I will bring it to the shaman and see what he has to say. To me, it means that you will travel far away from us, perhaps to the white man's territory. That's my feeling and it makes me very sad. It bothers me too, that you fell and the animal was hurt. While you are here, try to bring him back in your dreams, heal his wounds, and walk him slowly back to the forest. That would be best, I think." She smiled and patted the young girl's cheek.

"You have plenty of time to focus on it—at least ten days, it just depends how long your flow lasts the first time. I brought a lot to keep you busy, hides to scrape, weaving to do, some baskets to repair. A woman never lets her hands be idle. Your aunties will show you everything you need to know, so that when you come back to the longhouse, you will be ready to join us. A special occasion. Why, I mind the time I tended to your mother. Such a moaner she was, claiming to suffer too much to do anything!" The memory made her chuckle to herself, while Yellow Bird listened intently.

"Whining and complaining that she would die of the pain! Hah! She learned different! Never killed any woman that I know of, but you should have heard the carrying on. Crawling around on all fours and howling like a wolf cub! My word! I told her then and I'm telling you now, as my mother told me: the pain is a gift, preparing us to endure childbirth, and more."

The old woman leaned over to stoke the fire, flipping her long grey braid over her shoulder. With a crinkled smile, she gestured at Yellow Bird with a stick, drawing it against her bare wrist in a cutting motion.

"You have seen the young men, cutting and burning themselves, so that they will be strong to endure the wounds of battle? Yes, I see you have noticed that. Well, we have no need to do so, for our moon time gives us power. Especially precious is the time you will spend here by yourself, when you will pray, dream and seek your own answers. The longhouse is a beehive, always buzzing with noise and activity, and you are never alone. Here, for a few days, you can move to the rhythm of your own beating heart, listening only to the wind in the trees and the songs of the night creatures. Ah, so peaceful, I recall..." her voice drifted off.

Distractedly, she began to sing as she poked the stick into the fire. Then she interrupted herself, as if remembering something.

"Make sure you wait until the clan is asleep, then stand naked and bathe in the light of the full moon as often as possible. The moon is a woman, too, and knows the secrets of your heart. When she is fat and happy, she is joyous and ready to share her gifts with us, but when she is thin, her husband is angry with her and she is very sad.

At that time of the moon, your energy will wane also, and you must rest and not undertake any new projects, but rather, finish something you have already started," she said as she handed the girl a half-sewn moccasin.

"When your flow has stopped and you return to the longhouse, you will feel refreshed, happy and calm. That is the magic of the moon's cycle. Tut, tut, don't look so worried, my dear: women's ways will soon be your ways, too. When the leaves change colour, very soon, you will accompany your father to the meeting of the clans, and there he will seek a husband for you, from the people of the Rock or the Cord clans. They are not as strong as us, the Bear, of course, but they are The People, just the same. Won't that be exciting? What is that look? You won't have to keep him if you don't like him! But it will be fun to try him out. Just you wait and see." She laughed brightly, like a young girl.

"Ah, my little one, youth passes so quickly. I wish I had mine to live all over again. Your life is just beginning! All the "firsts" you have to look forward to: today, your first cycle, soon your first love, first mating, and your first child, each a moment to be celebrated. Why, I mind the time..."

Chapter Sixteen

Her ten days of quiet contemplation flew by and soon she rejoined the family and returned to regular duties. Yellow Bird rejoiced when it rained, for it meant she did not have to haul water from the river for the plants, nor weed the garden in the hot sun. One stormy summer afternoon, the five families of the Bear Clan longhouse had gathered around the central hearth. All eyes were glued to Taretande, as he was about to recount one of the sacred stories of their people, to introduce it to the very young, reinforce it in the minds of the children and keep it alive among the elders. The thunder in the heavens and the rain pelting on the thick cedar roof high above would only add to the drama of the tale. The dark roiling clouds hovered menacingly over the slim roof vents. At a length of four hundred paces, the interior of the one-room structure was gloomy, illuminated only by firelight. The damp outside held the smoke within, creating ghosts amongst the furs and dried corn hanging from the rafters. Babies rested quietly in their cradleboards, while youngsters cuddled down into their mothers' laps. The close scents of meat, herbs, furs and body odour generated feelings of calm and harmony within the community. Everyone huddled together around the roaring fire, breathing as one, in anxious anticipation.

Too old to sit in her mother's lap, Yellow Bird rested on her shoulder and gently rubbed her baby brother's arm, to keep him quiet. She smiled and nodded her wordless assurance to her grandmother, seated at her mother's other side. No one must interrupt the speaker and no one would. This time, she was determined to listen even harder and memorize every word. Yellow Bird shivered in anticipation of her father's resonant tones filling the cavernous space. Taretande raised his arms skyward and began to speak.

"Brothers and sisters, listen. We are the Ouendat, the People of the Island. We are blessed by the Big Turtle, whose shell became the surface of the Great Island, which is the Lower World. We descend from Sky Woman, who fell from the Upper World when she ate the flowers of the Tree of Light. Long ago, we lived in a world above the sky, where there was neither sun, nor moon nor stars to shed their light. We basked in the light of the yellow flowers on the Sacred Tree which grew next to the longhouse of Hoo-wa'neh, chief of the Upper World. One day, when her husband the chief was out hunting, his wife, Aataentsic, took some flowers and put them in her mouth, to taste them." Taretande paused and looked at the rapt faces highlighted by the fire's glow.

"Ah, brothers and sisters, the light immediately faded from the world, and twilight fell. Much afraid, the woman ran away, back to her own people, sick from having eaten the flowers." He dropped his voice to almost a whisper, in a tone of sadness. Then he shouted, to drown out the pounding rain above the heads of his audience. Yellow Bird imagined the beautiful golden flowers and she knew that she, too, would have been tempted to grasp them, drink their scent, and taste their sun-kissed petals. How could anyone resist?

"Hoo-wa'neh cried out in anguish and dropped upon his face on the ground at the foot of the Tree, refusing to eat for many days, hoping that by his prayers, the Tree would again come to light up the world. But it did not. Then he turned to the priests and begged them to help his wife, who was heavy with child. The priests thought they would find a cure among the roots of the Tree of Light, so they laid the sick Woman beneath the branches of the Tree and began to dig. Suddenly, the Tree of Light and the ground around it sank and broke through the Upper World, creating a great rent in the fabric of the Upper World. The only thing the Woman could do was to grasp its branches and hang on for dear life, as it fell further and further. She looked up and saw that the tear above her head had closed and she was shut out of the beautiful world above the sky, forever."

Taretande paused and once again turned his gaze from left to right, right to left, including everyone in the story. He poked at the fire with a stick, sending a shower of sparks into the air, before continuing.

"Now, my brothers and sisters, in those days the Great Water covered the Lower World. As the Woman fell, Heno, the thunder god, rolled a great crash of thunder." As he spoke these words, a clap of thunder shook the very timbers of the longhouse. Everyone looked skyward in awe.

"Two swans looked up and saw the Woman as though she were standing in a broken sky, her arms spread wide, about to fall in the water and drown. The swans swam side by side and caught the woman on their backs. But they did not know what to do, for there was no land to put her down upon, and they knew they could not carry her much longer. So they called a Council of the water tribes, the first Great Council.

"But none of the swimming animals knew what to do, not even Big Turtle, who was their chief. The Tree of Light had landed on the bottom of the sea, shining like the sun, with the broken earth floating around its branches.

"At last, Big Turtle decided what to do, and told the others, 'Get a little of the earth that lies at the root of the Tree of Light and place it upon my back. There it may grow into a world where the Woman may live.'"

Taretande motioned with his hands, to show how the animals might spread the earth on the round shell of the turtle. He waited until the children nodded with understanding and not until they had begun to squirm with impatience did he speak again.

"Well, the animals drove deep into the Great Water to bring up the earth, but they could not. The beaver, the otter, the duck: one by one they tried, but each swimmer failed and some drowned in the attempt. Finally, Toad said she would try. The other animals did not believe she could do it and were afraid when she was gone such a long time. When she floated to the surface of the water, she was indeed dead. But in her mouth, she carried the shining earth," he said, grasping a handful of clay he had hidden on the ground beside him and holding it high. He dipped the fingers of his left hand into the mound of earth and demonstrated the next part of the story.

"Little Turtle took great care as he spread this earth around the edges of the shell of Big Turtle, where at once it grew into the Great Island. The two Swans gently placed the Woman upon this Island to live and there she gave birth to two sons, Tawiscaron and Youskeha. Children, listen. Still today, the Big Turtle stands on the bottom of the Great Water with the Great Island upon his back, which is the land of the Ouendat. And because Toad was the one animal which succeeded in bringing some earth from the depths of the Great Water, we love her, as our cherished Grandmother. We are The People of the Great Island. Upon the back of Big Turtle, we make our home, now and forevermore." He patted the ground emphatically to make his final point.

A collective sigh emerged from the listeners in the circle. Yellow Bird lowered her head and hid behind her hair, so her family would not be shamed by the pride radiating from her face at her father's great powers of oration. She never tired of the story, nor of her father's voice as it marked the measured rhythms, line by line.

Everyone knew the tale, but he made it more beautiful, more vivid in the telling. His gifts of speech and persuasion made him a worthy chief in the eyes of the matriarchs, the clan mothers, who had named him to his position. Generosity, wisdom and impeccable character kept him there. Along with high prestige, came the responsibility to maintain the Great Law. He was expected to settle minor disputes in the customary soft, yet decisive manner and to lead discussions at council meetings for important decisions, where accord would be reached for the welfare of all. Everyone knew that if he failed in his duty at any time, he could be unseated.

Yellow Bird peeked out from her lowered eyelids to watch each male clasp her father's arm in fellowship before returning to their own fireside.

"My father is like Big Turtle," she suddenly realized. "Upon his back lies the safety of the whole longhouse."

When her turn finally came to wish him goodnight, she threw her arms about his neck and hugged him hard. He laughed in surprise. He caught at her long braid hanging in front of her shift, tickled her chin with the end of it, then released her and motioned for her to head to their hearth. She skipped lightly over his crossed leg, grabbed her little brother's hand, and swung him to her hip as though he were weightless. He giggled at the swinging motion and said, "'Gain? 'Gain?" which meant he wanted her to do the same again. She swung him around in a circle by holding him under the shoulders, taking care not to smack his feet into one of the passersby. Tonight she knew that it would not feel like a chore to tuck him under his furs, lie beside him and hum a tune in his ear until he fell asleep. She glowed from within, as if she too had eaten of the Tree of Light.

Just as she was drifting off to sleep, the sound of the rain drumming out the whispers of the other members of the longhouse, Yellow Bird's heart was seized with a tremor of fear. She gasped as she felt herself drowning once again. Maybe the dead Tree of Light was caught at the bottom of the river and had been trying to pull her under by grasping her ankle with one of its branches. She sat bolt upright, trembling with terror. Her grandmother, banking the fire for the night, noticed the sudden movement. Yellow Bird reached out her hand to pose an urgent question.

"Grandmother, is it possible that the Tree of Light is still there, below the water, angry with the People for stealing its power?"

"Yes, I suppose so. I have never thought of it that way. I have always focused on how our land came to be, how the animals helped Sky Woman and the debt we owe them to this day. It is true that Sky Woman ought not to have eaten the flowers, but if she had not, where would we be? Who knows, the Tree of Light may have fallen all the way into another world, and be shining somewhere else. It is not for us to question. Hush now and rest your head," she crooned, rubbing Yellow Bird's back. She held her close, tucked her into her furs and kissed her goodnight, then groped through the dim, smoky light to her own sleeping pallet. Yellow Bird drifted to sleep with the rhythm of the raindrops tapping against the elm bark roof overhead.

*****

"Huh, uuuhh!" she groaned. The urge to urinate pressed against her pubic bone and she feared she would not make it to the pot. It was still pitch dark and she never drank much before sleeping, so that she could last until dawn. Why was the pressure so strong and why was her stomach so hard? As she rolled across the wooden bedframe, her awkwardness reminded her. No, she was not in the longhouse. She was no longer a child, but was about to become a mother, with neither a mother nor an aunty nor a grandmother to help her. All dead, and she alone here in a small cabin in the woods, surviving among white-skinned strangers from across the big water. Wendake, her homeland, had been destroyed; the People, killed, enslaved or scattered to the four winds.

She squatted on the bowl kept beneath the bed for night use, and sobbed quietly into her hands as the hot liquid ran between her legs. Behind the curtain, the man was still raving. Amazingly, she had slept through it and re-lived so much of her past in dreams, dreams that she had no one to tell. What did he have to cry about? How could his sorrow possibly compare to hers? A piece of crockery smashed on the wooden floor. He swore even louder. Frightened that he might hear and come in search of her, she stood up and wiped herself with the back of her left hand. She crouched over the bed, scrambled back under the furs and poked her fingers in her ears. No matter. She could still hear his moaning. She felt no sympathy. All it did was remind her... She unblocked one ear and wriggled her index finger under the bottom blanket near where she rested her head, until she felt her amulet and clasped it tightly in her palm, even though the pointed end pierced the skin. She wanted to feel pain, to bleed. She didn't want to remember...

*****

The men had cleared away the trees outside the palisade, the women had prepared the soil and planted the seed, and now the daily task of minding the gardens fell to the girls. Weeding, watering, and scaring away the crows occupied most of their hours from spring to late summer, until harvest time. The precious crop of corn, beans and squash, known as the "three sisters" was planted in hills to shield the fragile seeds from the sun, wind and marauding birds or mice.

The plants would flourish in the rich soil, supporting one another as they grew: the squash at the base, protecting the young beans and holding in place the corn, which would in turn provide a sturdy stalk for the beans to climb upon. Separate mounds held sunflowers, just now starting to poke two round leaves toward the sky. In the humid summer heat, the plants would soon blossom and bring forth sustenance to last throughout the dark winter months, when meat was hard to come by.

Yellow Bird knew this well: her family had never starved, but she remembered the hungry days in the depths of winter when the stored food was portioned out in small quantities because supplies were running low and the deer were nowhere to be found. Often too, her people prospered, for they grew enough food to trade with others: the Neutral, who grew the finest tobacco, and the Petun, who crafted breathtakingly beautiful shell jewelry. Her clan was known far and wide for the quality of its crops. Still, she hated gardening. Her hands and feet would swell and itch if she even touched a thistle with her bare skin, so she relied on her gardening stick and used her moccasin-clad feet to form the dirt into hills, unless her mother caught her. Then, a look would send her instantly down to all fours. Itchy skin, which could quickly be eased by Grandmother's healing balm, was nothing compared to suffering frosty disapproval for lack of due care and attention to her duties.

When no one was watching though, she allowed herself to be lazy, and daydream about joining her brother and his friends in the front yard. She poked lethargically at the dirt with her stick in one hand, waving a fly away from her ear with the other. The raccoon oil covering her skin never sufficed to keep the insects away from her, it seemed. Her grandmother always teased her that it was because her smell was so sweet! With one of the two pointed ends of the hoe, she speared a weed and deftly flicked it into the air to land in the pile behind her. Rather than bending down as she should, to cup the earth protectively around the plants, she patted the tiny hill with the instep of her foot, and quickly moved on to the next mound.

"Why can't I learn to hunt? It is a useful skill, and I would be better at it than I am at this," she grumbled under her breath. In secret, she had practiced with her brother's bow, and she was sure that the strength in her arms from swimming in the river lent her arrows much more speed and accuracy than any of the boys'. Her brother would never make a warrior, for one thing. All he wanted to do was play with the dogs and their puppies!

Yellow Bird resented the fact that the boys never had to do anything except fool around together, while she and the other girls had to learn to do everything their mothers did: to sew, cook, smoke meat, clean hides, garden... the chores never ended. The prospect of womanhood held no magic for her. Just more of the same, only even less freedom, as she would be expected to work side-by-side with the women and join in with their gossiping. Grandmother had spoken of a husband, but she didn't want a husband. She wanted to move freely through the forest, to travel across the water in a canoe, to bring back precious meat for the clan and furs to trade, even to fight the Iroquois. Why had she been so unfortunate as to be born a girl?

She kicked her toe into one of the hills and as the soil cascaded downward, a shiny object fell at her feet. She reached down and brushed off the dirt to examine it. It felt cool to the touch. It sparkled in the sunlight, hard and flat, like a rock, but covered in strange markings on the surface, like waves. Its oval shape fit exactly into the palm of her hand. When she turned it over, the back was smooth, but there was a sharp stinger attached that drew blood when she pressed the tip against her finger. Its bite made her lose her grip. The thing hit the ground with a muffled thud. She crouched down and gathered it up with two fingers this time, pointing the stinger upwards as she dropped it into the pouch at her waist. It thudded against her thigh as she ran back to the longhouse to show her grandmother.

Halfway there, she suddenly stopped and sat down cross-legged on the path. She did not dare to take the object from the pouch tied to her waist, under her sleeveless summer tunic. Someone might see her. She tossed the leather bag from hand to hand between her thighs, as she thought about what she should do. Her impulse had been to show it to Grandmother immediately. But if she did, Grandmother would no doubt take it to the shaman, and she might never get it back. It would then belong to the clan. Perhaps that was right.

On the other hand, it had been given to her. How many women had worked that soil before her and never found it? Why had it come to her? What was it? Surely no one from the clan had lost it, because such a strange thing would have caused a stir long before now. It was not a stone, or a shell or a bone or a piece of bark. Even though it could sting, she could tell it was not alive, for it did not move on its own. But maybe some creature had made it. She slipped her fingers into the soft leather bag, to carefully touch the rough surface of the object, taking care to avoid the sharp tip. It was covered in curls and ridges, like a shell, but it was too hard and shiny to be a shell. Suddenly, she heard a shout, and instantly made a decision.

She scrambled to her feet and raced into the trees, pulling strands of hair moss from the lower branches as she crashed into the bush. Her heart pounding, she searched about for a safe place, but one she would remember and could easily find again. Looking desperately about, she noticed that one spruce tree up ahead had a long, crooked limb standing straight out, perpendicular to the ground, sprouting another, smaller tree.

"Perfect," she said out loud, rushing forward to throw herself at its base. She quickly made a little nest out of the moss, and then clawed a hole out of the soft dirt underneath one of the tree's thickest roots. When the space had been cleared, she reached into her pouch. She carefully wrapped the object in the moss and stuffed it into the hole. She was patting the earth gently back over the root when the cries in the distance became louder and more urgent. She thought she heard Sunrise scream.

"Yellow Bird, where are you? You must come quickly and get inside the palisade. The Iroquois are coming. They will kill us all. Yellow Bird, be quick. I must go and warn everyone in the fields. Please, hear me and fly like the wind!"

*****

The wailing and moaning of the survivors drowned out the raucous cawing of the greedy crows, gathering overhead for a feast.

Stunned mothers who had escaped the fire wandered in circles, searching for their lost children. Men stumbled over the smoldering wrecks of the longhouses, picking out charred human remains from the ashes and hugging them tightly. Every family had to attempt to collect enough remains of each slain member, to create individual bundles. But how could they be sure they weren't mixed up? The spirits of the dead might be confused and not find their way to the sacred lands in the West, and peace. That would only deepen the tragedy.

The Iroquois war party had prevailed, attacking unexpectedly and with their customary force. The ancient enmity between the two tribes had escalated with the arrival of the white strangers from the east, whose insatiability for furs drove the competition for territory to new heights. The Iroquois had long despised the people of Huronia, but truly abhorred their collusion with the white men who had tricked, humiliated and exploited their people since their first encounter. As one, they vowed that the Ouendat would regret trading with these white faces, with their crosses and bizarre rituals. With fierce determination, their Confederacy planned to wipe their enemies from the face of the earth.

The crops surrounding the village had been destroyed, the longhouses had been immolated with the women and children inside, and most of the old men and young warriors had been either killed or captured. Yellow Bird had arrived too late to run inside the enclosure, and so had hidden in the trees while the raiders carried off many children, among them her older brother. His screams wrenched her heart, as his dog and her puppies were thrown into the fire, before his eyes. The tears streaming down his face brought nothing but derisive laughter from his captors. Yellow Bird's eyes stung with tears from the smoke and her guilt at the jealousy she had harboured against the boys, as she watched them being dragged away.

Against her will, a strange laugh had erupted from her throat when she saw her second youngest brother vomit all over the man holding him around the waist. Had she moved to save him from the axe that had rent his skull in two? No. For all her imagined strength, she had been paralyzed with terror. Now she would never see her siblings and cousins again. She knew they would certainly be beaten or forced to run naked through the gauntlet of the Iroquois village. Could they stand the abuse? If so, they might be adopted into the Iroquois tribe as slaves. If not, their captors might torture them, until, tired of their sport, they would be put to death. They might even eat their flesh, she thought, shuddering.

Horror stories told around the fire of their rivals' treatment of captives echoed in her mind as she helped her father sift through the ashes of their home and her family. Fortunately, most of the strongest men had been away, hunting in the forest. The enemy had taken advantage of the village's weak defenses and struck hard, with fire, dagger, hatchet and club. Yellow Bird's baby brother would have been immolated in the scorching fire that had swallowed the longhouse, along with all the other young children and the women. The spiritual leadership of the community had perished with the clan mothers and the shaman. All the survivors deeply mourned Yellow Bird's grandmother, Haronhaiya, head matriarch of the Bear clan. Without her wise counsel, they whirled about aimlessly like dust in the wind.

Yellow Bird sat cross-legged on the ground with her father, Taretande. He cradled what he thought were his wife's scorched bones in his arms, moaning. Yellow Bird clung to the charred skeleton that she believed had been her laughing grandmother. It was impossible to be sure whose remains they mourned over. The girl sent out a keening cry. Her father caressed the grey sticks, which he had retrieved from the hearth nearest the front door. His tears traced rivers through the ashes he had rubbed across his face. He called his wife's name and told her the details of the attack, that their eldest son had been captured, the other killed and that there had not been enough stored water to extinguish the fires in time to save the mothers and their babies. He swore vengeance to the spirit of his dear Blue Flower, for he knew one of her souls lingered there beside him, to hear his words. The other was already on its way toward the setting sun and the village of the dead. Yellow Bird's heart cracked as she watched the strongest, most gifted warrior and orator of their clan rocking in the dirt like one who had lost his mind. She trembled in fear, for if her father could not lead and protect the surviving people, who would?

"Remember how excited you were, Grandmother, about my 'firsts?'" she asked the shattered bones in her lap.

"You forgot to mention 'first murders' and 'first kidnappings,' did you not? You always warned us of the danger from our enemies, but what herbs must I gather to heal my father of a broken heart?"

She searched her father's unseeing eyes and was startled to feel anger against his lack of strength. Shouldn't he be comforting his one remaining child in his arms, telling her that everything would be all right? She shook off the selfish impulse and turned her gaze back to the devastated village. Her heart continued the dialogue with her grandmother.

"Tell me, Grandmother, how do I go on? I wish I had been with you, for you would have held me tightly and our spirits would have traveled westward together, maybe upon the back of the animal in my dream. Do you remember that? You told me to find him again and I didn't even try. This was my fault! I should have been paying attention! I should have been a better daughter! Instead, I wished to be delivered from working in the garden, and now it is gone, burnt up! What will we eat? All the stores in the longhouses are ruined: our clay pots shattered from the heat of the fire. Those of us who weren't killed will surely starve!"

Her despair was interrupted by her father's croaky voice.

"There are no furs to wrap them in, to bundle them up warmly while they await the Festival of the Dead. With so many gone, who will organize a festival to release their souls? Only the Elders of all the clans together understand the cycle and know the proper interval and rituals. I have attended one Festival, but was too young to learn the Death Song. I simply revelled in the joy of dancing and feasting, foolish youngster that I was!" he reproached himself, slapping his naked thigh. Then he stood, still clutching the loose collection of bones in his arms, and pronounced, "Daughter, we must leave. We will each bind the remains of our families with whatever cord we can find and carry them in our canoes and on our backs, to the next village to the south. We can only hope they have not also been attacked, otherwise we must find the Petun, further west, or the Oddawa, further away still. We will seek refuge amongst another clan and plan our revenge," he growled. Yellow Bird leapt to her feet at his decisive tone, prepared to follow any orders.

"Gather everyone you can find. Sift through the fire pits and the broken vessels for whatever food you can, even if it is spoiled. How to carry it? Wrap it in your tunic if you have to. Be resourceful and think! Hurry, scouts may be watching and may send back another party to finish us off. We will travel as soon as the moon rises. In the meantime, the warriors and I must retrieve as many arrows and war clubs as possible. I vow that someday we will return to slay our enemies with their own accursed weapons."

With her father's voice still ringing in her ears, a kick from the baby brought her back to the cold, darkened corner of the room. Paul still howled and cursed to himself, next to the fireplace.

"Taretande. Taretande, where are you now?" Yellow Bird cried softly under her breath, as she placed both hands on her belly and rocked herself and her unborn child to sleep.

Chapter Seventeen

"Come, Daughter, wake up. Are you feeling better now? I hope so, as I plan to take you with me to the trading post. How does that sound? It may shake this lethargy out of your bones! And I can use the help on the way, to prepare meals for the men. It's time you took up your womanly duties, as your mother would have wished. Quickly now, look lively, unless you are too ill to go..." Her father's voice trailed off, with a tinge of worry. His love for his unruly daughter ran deep, though he tried to keep her on the right path by being as exacting as he could in his instruction and supervision.

With her mother, grandmother and kinswomen all dead or captured by the Iroquois, Taretande alone carried the burden of his daughter's upbringing, along with responsibility for the scant remaining members of his clan, residing here among the Odawa, their distant relatives. All winter he had directed the men to kill beavers, wolves and muskrats, not for meat, but for their furs. He knew that the white traders, with whom the Odawa traded, were hungry with desire for the gift of life from more animals than could be eaten or worn by an entire village. The waste of meat, left dripping on the ground for the dogs and scavenger birds, splintered his heart like the broken shaft of an arrow. They had no choice but to squander this abundance of food, since the wolf they could not eat according to their law, and they killed more than they could possibly consume or preserve. He soon stopped asking the traditional forgiveness from his fellow creatures; shame stopped the words in his mouth. Compelled by the need to prepare as many furs as possible, in time for the spring trading expedition, he and his men hunted deep into the snow-bound woods, determined to prove that they were not beggars, and would repay their brothers for their kindness in giving them refuge. On the journey, he planned to seek out any surviving members of his tribe, to help him rebuild the devastated village that had been part of Huronia. He did not know that there were none to be found. Any of The People not killed or captured by the Iroquois in their last great attack had scattered in all directions, like himself and his clan. Huronia was no more.

Taretande had never been to the white man's trading post. He both feared and looked forward to the long journey to the meeting of Three Rivers. Unlike many others of his tribe, his clan had always remained within their ancestral territory, and thus avoided contact with the white traders and the dread diseases that always followed in their wake. But the Odawa lived near the Great Water and had continuously maintained a partnership, which now, on Taretande's closer consideration, seemed to be advantageous. They had many possessions that Taretande intended to acquire for his people: iron cooking pots, sharp knives, woven cloth, but most important among them, the killing stick that shot fire great distances to cast down an animal, or the enemy. He had plans for this new weapon; images of vengeance appeared in his dreams during the restless and lonely nights in a stranger's wigwam.

Now that it was spring, and the river had once again become an open highway for birchbark canoes, he was restless to stow the many bales of thick, luxuriant fur that had been so painstakingly gathered and preserved, and set off with a flotilla of his own. But to his surprise, he found himself unable to leave behind the only member of his immediate family remaining alive. If he were to die on the trip, she would be left without his support, and while their hosts had been generous so far, who was to say that without his strong presence, they might not enslave or trade off his only daughter, his precious Yellow Bird? And besides, she would see a broader landscape and perhaps rise out of the deep mire of her grief. She had become so thin that the bones under her neck resembled a hunting bow! And the dark circles under her eyes troubled him. He missed the ring of her laughter, so like her mother's... He shook his head to dispel the sound that echoed in his ears and made his decision. Yes, Yellow Bird must come, so he could keep an eye on her and she could learn to make herself a little more useful. Surely her mother would agree that it was time for the girl to assume her duties. If only she were here.

His jaw set with determination, Taretande ordered the last of the bales to be loaded for proper stability in each of the seven canoes. He double-checked that their supplies and necessities were in order and then led Yellow Bird by the hand to his canoe. Ten strong, bare-chested hunters, five on either side, deftly paddled backwards against the current to direct each vessel toward the centre of the fast flowing waterway. Taretande too felt his spirit soar for the first time in months, as he saw himself actively pursuing his plans for revenge against his enemies.

Knowing it was useless to argue, Yellow Bird had assumed her place in the canoe with her head bowed in resignation. After all he had endured, she would not shame her father by resisting his orders, even if the pain of her monthly courses had not been subsiding. And, though terrified that they might encounter Iroquois on their way to the trading post, she was deeply honored that she had been chosen to accompany him. She felt relieved, too, at the fact that she would be absent from the chattering women for a time.

How stupid they were. Not one could match the wisdom of her grandmother, yet they squawked incessantly like rooks in the trees. They did not maintain individual plots of land for growing the three sisters—corn, squash and beans—to harvest and store away for the winter. Their people subsisted on what roots and berries the women gathered, to supplement the meat and fish the men were able to provide. In times of plenty, they feasted. Otherwise, they nearly starved. Yellow Bird thought they had become even lazier than they were naturally, from using the strange cooking pots and utensils that "saved" them from the crafts of making their own baskets and spoons. Girls her own age would smile at her with ill-disguised smugness as they leisurely walked past her wigwam, where she sat weaving basket after basket. Her nimble fingers craved the occupation and her lonely mind needed the distraction. She cared nothing for the shiny foreign beads the girls sewed onto their dresses or wove into necklaces and bracelets, which they then flaunted in her face.

Possessions meant nothing to her. All things, even people, could be turned to ashes in a moment, as she well knew and longed to shout at them. But she lacked the will to voice her angry thoughts and they too turned to dust in her mind, and blew away. The obligatory fasting before weaving required no effort on her part: she ate little. The older women of the tribe brought her food as she worked. At first, the dogs and magpies would slink up to steal the untouched morsels from her bowl. Now they waited just out of range of the woman delivering the meals and as soon as her back was turned, boldly hopped or trotted away with chunks of cooked meat. Eyes glazed over as if in a trance, Yellow Bird failed to notice. She wove white sedge grass, black bull rush roots, reddish-brown redbud roots and long strands of sweet grass into beautiful patterns more by feel than by sight. As she entwined the strands through her fingers she repeated the only part of her grandmother's weaving prayer which she could remember.

"...Thus weave for us a pattern of brightness, that we may walk fittingly where birds sing, that we may walk fittingly where grass is green, Oh our Mother Earth, Oh our Father Sky."

Often, tears were woven into the very fibers of her baskets while she worked. The song brought back memories, which were her sole possessions now. Each time she wound the final row and tucked the ends in neatly to complete a basket, she momentarily startled herself with the outcome. She would hold the object on her lap and stare at it as if it had indeed been dropped there by Father Sky, and she would marvel at its beauty and utility. As soon as she set it aside though, the joy would evaporate like a raindrop in the sun and she would quickly reach for another handful of fresh supplies that the grandmothers kept heaping by her side. They praised her work and their kind words and smiles soothed her heart. Wrinkled hands smoothed and braided her knotted hair and caressed her chapped fingers with oil, before collecting the latest container for their own use.

But her young body needed more activity. After sitting so long in one position, her backbone had become as brittle as cured birch, and she had to carefully unfold each leg and then stamp her feet hard on the ground before she could walk away from her wigwam to relieve herself or join the others for a seat at the fire when the light had faded. This she was reluctant to do, unless her father, the great orator Taretande, was telling a story. More often than not, she merely stood for a while to warm her tired body, then returned to her tiny shelter for sleep. She soothed herself by rubbing the soft fur between her legs until it throbbed like a rabbit in her hand, then drifted off to a thankfully dreamless sleep. For if she dreamt, it was always of home.

She would return to the garden that fateful day of the Iroquois attack and relive the memories of terror, smoke and slaughter. She would awake drenched in cold sweat, unable to chase the images and sounds from her mind: her baby brother crying, her younger brother yelling at her to run, Yellow Bird, run, the war whoops of the enemy, the crackling of the fire as the longhouse flared in the fires of destructive torches, the moans of the survivors searching through the smoke for family members, the heart-wrenching sobs of her father, holding his wife's charred bones in his arms. The smouldering ruin of the precious garden.

The garden. She remembered how she had hated working in the garden in the humid summer heat. Now that was all she wished for, to be back tending to the three sisters, the corn, squash and beans that sustained The People, and to be teasingly chided once more by Grandmother for her laziness. She longed to toil in the sun with the sweat of her brow stinging her eyes, nurturing the tender shoots to bring forth life from the rich earth. She held fast to this secret desire now, as the canoe backed away from the shore. Father had unknowingly given her a chance that she could only have wished for, never requested. Somehow, en route to the trading post, she would convince him to return to their former village, to scavenge seeds from the dirt, and also verify the security of the bones of their family members.

After the raid, the survivors had left so quickly that it was impossible to ensure that all had been properly done to care for the remains of their clan. And the bones had to be preserved until the Festival of the Dead could take place, sometime many years hence when the survivors settled in a new village of their own. Yellow Bird imagined herself sitting among the ruins of her home and conversing with her mother and grandmother in spirit. They would advise her on how to survive amongst the Odawa, with their hideous tatoos, pierced noses, and lack of common sense. For regardless of her feelings of scorn for their ways, combined with humiliation at accepting their hospitality, she knew that their village was her only refuge. She was sure that Taretande, her wise father, would see the wisdom in teaching them to farm.

Yellow Bird lifted her hand in a shaky farewell to her cousin, as the sturdy birchbark canoe bounced up and down before joining with the current. Her heart rose to her throat when the wind caught her full in the face as the prow of the vessel dipped into the waves. The memory of her last canoe trip shimmered before her eyes. She tasted the bitterness of that time, but she deliberately clenched her teeth against spitting out the vomit in her mouth. She would not shame herself, or her father. She smiled at his glowing copper shoulders spread like a hawk's open wingspan just in front of her, the muscles rippling with exertion as he rowed. Strongest of all the warriors, he would keep her safe. Swallowing hard, she reminded herself that this time she was on a journey toward something, rather than escaping from death and destruction. Soon her thoughts succumbed to the rhythm of the forward motion and she dropped into a contented slumber.

*****

The trading post. The course sounds of raucous laughter and strange voices assaulted her ears, while eyes the unlikely colour of the sky and the trees watched her every move. She ducked her head and retreated behind her kinsmen in fear. Some protectively put their arms about her shoulders and stood in front of her like older brothers, ready to take on all comers. They had grown increasingly fond of her during the journey, when she had made herself so useful, fetching and heating water, snaring rabbits and gathering berries for the evening meal when they were too exhausted to move from the shore after a day of strenuous rowing. She had kept them well fed and cheered with songs as they rowed toward their destination. At the shore they had warned her once again to stay close beside them and keep her head down, reminding her of the deadly fever that had already wiped out half of their tribe. Sternly, they advised her not to eat or drink anything that may be offered to her, nor to go near any man wearing a long black robe, for their touch brought the sickness. These were the sorcerers of the white men, bringing death to The People.

Yellow Bird had not known such waking fear since the Iroquois had burned, slashed and launched their arrows in a frenzy of destruction. Only a few days before arriving at the trading post, she had sifted through the ashes of her ancestral home, looking for undamaged seeds and collecting any bones to be properly cared for. She had also searched for, and found, the shiny, stinging stone she had hidden under the forked tree, that terrible day. Furtively, she had tucked it in her deerskin totem bag around her neck, under her tunic. She clutched it now as if seeking its protection. Since her arrival at this camp, she had come to understand that her treasure was not a natural object, but made of the same material as the white man's knives and fire sticks. When she took it out to hold it in her hands, it was as cold as river water. It had a sharp point which pricked her thumb like a bee sting but also drew blood. She didn't mind. She soothed the tiny wound with her tongue while the pain brought back the faces of her brothers, her mother and her grandmother, and reminded her of the blood her clan had lost to the enemy. But were these white men no less to be feared? Were they worthy of trust?

Her father seemed to think so, as he eagerly disposed of the entire winter's worth of furs they had so painstakingly prepared, to acquire cooking pots, hatchets, needles, blankets and other treasures. He smiled as he tied a beautiful beaded bracelet around her wrist, but Yellow Bird felt nothing but shame at his demeanour. Somehow he stood a little less tall as he negotiated with the white men, for he keenly desired the objects on offer, and was not confident of the worth of his goods. Yellow Bird knew that his lack of experience in the process was costing him his pride, for he was used to being the leader of his clan. When, in the early evening, a member of the Odawa scoffed at his inability to bargain more strenuously, he had taken out his knife and brandished it in the Odawa's face. Yellow Bird was shocked at her father's lack of customary restraint. The feeling that she barely recognized him anymore left her with a wrenching dread in her stomach as she hastily prepared the evening meal of venison stew.

That night, while she cowered in a makeshift teepee behind the circle of men around the fire, she listened to the click of gambling stones thrown on a mat and subsequent hooting and shouting that became louder as someone mentioned "firewater." In vain, she strained her ears to sift out the deep tone of her father's voice, to see if he too was foolishly gambling away the hard-won earnings of a whole season's work. The concentration combined with exhaustion from the day's work and excitement finally allowed her to doze off. Within moments it seemed, she was startled fully awake by a clash as loud as thunder and a flash of light. Heart in her throat, she crawled to the opening of the teepee and peeked out.

Dawn was breaking in the east. Men lay sprawled in disarray, mouths open, snoring and drooling in their sleep. One sat gazing vacantly into the fire, nursing a bleeding hand and moaning in pain. The banging sound had come from the edge of the clearing, where her father stood with a white man who was showing him how to use the fire stick. His head was turned at an awkward angle toward the stranger. Her father Taretande seemed to weave unsteadily on his feet as he attempted to shoulder the weapon. The man held him by an elbow to support him. Never had Yellow Bird seen another man dare touch her father unbidden. Her shock at the gesture was interrupted by the continual groaning of the man at the fire. She sat back on her haunches, reached for her medicine bag and crawled on all fours out of the teepee. She approached the fire by wending her way around the unconscious men on the ground.

"Grey Cloud, what happened? What is wrong with your hand? Let me try to help you."

"Cut....cut off..." he mumbled and pointed with his elbow toward his foot. Resting on the blade of a tomahawk was a bloody finger, the smallest finger of the warrior's right hand.

"Bbbut how?" sputtered Yellow Bird as she fumbled for dried moss in her pack to staunch the wound.

"Gambled...and lost," he replied dejectedly, as if his answer made sense.

"You gambled your... your finger? Why? What happened to all

your trade goods, as if you should gamble those, but don't tell me..."

"Gone, all gone. Only a finger left to gamble and now that is gone, too. So I won't be returning with you, Yellow Bird. I must stay and pay off my debt to the white men. Tell my little ones goodbye for me. Don't say anything to my wife, I beg you. Ah, that feels better. Your salve may heal me so I do not lose my hand. If that should happen, I am truly finished."

Yellow Bird shook her head in disbelief as she packed a dressing on the gory wound. Behind her, Taretande approached, still speaking to the white man. With a distant look in his eyes that chilled her spine, he greeted his daughter when she stood and rushed toward him. He stretched out both arms to catch her by the shoulders.

"Good morning, Yellow Bird. I am glad to see the night has kept you well. Thank you for tending Grey Cloud. I knew you would be able to help him. Such foolishness. But young men will be young men and they have held back their blood lust for far too long. This is the result. They had been warned against eating and drinking of the white man's food and water, but they chose not to listen. I have no control over them anymore, it seems," he sighed.

Yellow Bird felt relieved that her father was not suffering the ill effects of the white man's firewater. He was awake, sensible and speaking in measured tones, as always. But something was wrong. Maybe he was just tired. Obviously he was as disgusted by the clan's behaviour as she.

"Daughter, I have good news. This white man wants you in exchange for the fire weapon and the many axes and things we need for our people to survive another winter and rebuild our village. Your hand-clasping honours our clan with status and riches. We will now have the power to mount a strong defence against the enemy, with this fire stick. Our own weapons are useless against them, for they kill at a much greater distance and force than even our greatest warrior can shoot an arrow."

What? The enthusiasm in his tone rang as hollow as the hoot of an owl in the distance. What was he saying? Had she heard correctly? Her mouth was suddenly dry and she could not swallow. Was she truly betrayed? Sold for a stick?

"Now, Yellow Bird, do not shed tears. You knew this day would come and better sooner than later. Your mother and grandmother would be proud of the match, for it is a rare and special honour to be chosen by such a wealthy stranger with fine gifts for our people. He calls himself a single word, Pole. I don't know what it means but he is obviously a strong man and a leader, for he has the most valuable goods to trade. Maybe it means "tall" for he surely is that, and strong, by the look of him. His clothes are made of the finest buckskin, his teeth are white and his eyes are wide apart, deep set and free of ill intent. He seems to respect us and deals in an upright manner, without resorting to trickery. He knows the rudiments of our language, so you will be able to understand each other from the start. In our trading talks earlier, I spoke of you when he asked, as my one remaining child, telling him how clever you are, not only able to cook, sew and weave baskets but also skilled in the healing arts you learned from your grandmother. I did not intend this outcome: it was only a father's pride in his beautiful daughter speaking. But now I see that it is a fair bargain for all. I am no soothsayer, but I foresee a bright future for you, travelling to new territories with this man, becoming rich in the knowledge of the white people who have so much to teach us. Better than tending a garden for me until I am an old man, don't you see?" he cajoled in response to the expression on her face.

"Your dislike of gardening is well known," he added lamely.

Yellow Bird's hands turned to ice. She dropped her precious medicine bag to the ground.

"Aiee, Father, how could you? Better you had cut off your finger like Grey Cloud, than to trade away the only child you have left. No, please, unmake the bargain. Anything, do anything, but do not leave me here." She fell to her knees and clutched her father's legs, bathing his moccasins in tears.

Abruptly, her father backed up, grasped her forcefully by the arms and hoisted her to her feet. His voice turned from gentle to stern in an instant, backed by the power of his orator's gift.

"Yellow Bird! You shame me! You shame yourself and the People. You will do your duty as I have told it to you. I have considered well and my decision is final. You will accompany this man Pole on his life's journey wherever it may take him and be a good and obedient wife. You have no womenfolk left to teach you or support you anymore. You and I are alone and we must make our way the best we can. I have determined that this is the safest and most favourable path for you. You will obey me as your father and leader of the People, few though we may be. There could be worse than this, for when the Long Dark comes again, I fear the red sickness that has already killed half the Odawa. Our medicine cannot cure it and I cannot bear to lose another member of my family. I would be certain you are far removed from the danger, than risk your death. This man and his fire stick will protect you from our enemies, also. Remember always that you are Yellow Bird, beloved daughter of Taretande and Summer Moon. Uphold the dignity of the Bear clan. Go in peace and with my blessing."

He placed his right hand gently on Yellow Bird's head, while the white man stood waiting with what Yellow Bird interpreted as a stupid expression on his face, his white teeth gleaming between his hair-covered lips. She shuddered with revulsion. The marriage ceremony was over when her father placed her hand in the white man's and bound them together. Without another word, Taretande turned and headed to the canoe where the Odawa men and her own kinsmen were waiting, averting their eyes. Not one raised an arm in a gesture of farewell. Still sobbing, but gritting her teeth to keep from screaming, Yellow Bird stumbled behind the tall Pole man, as he led her away from the river's edge, to his own tent. Behind her, she heard Grey Cloud moan, vomit and topple to the ground next to the cold firepit.

*****

She awoke shivering despite the heavy fur cloak that had been draped over her shoulders. Her breath formed a cloud of vapour as she awkwardly rolled out of the wooden bed. The fire was nearly out. The dim light in the cabin told her that the sun was rising and she knew he would be out checking his traps. No matter what happened during the night, Paul rose early and attended to his duties.

"Better than me," Yellow Bird silently reproached herself, as she poked the fire with the metal stick that revived the embers and added more wood. She hated mornings at the best of times and, now, felt even worse at the start of the day. Paul knew this and let her sleep as long as possible. He had already stacked wood by the fireplace, filled the pots with snow, emptied the chamber pot, and set out her dry biscuits to soothe her morning nausea.

"A good man. A thoughtful man. Maybe Father made a wise choice, despite himself." She knew that no warrior of her clan would have been so solicitous. But then, they didn't have to be, for the mothers, aunties, and grandmothers would care for an expectant mother. And she was all alone. Except for Paul.

As she sat munching her biscuits, she smoothed her free hand across the skins with markings that had so upset him last night. That the Black Robe had delivered. Those gaunt, hideous creatures lived up to their reputation, bringing ill fortune wherever they went. She felt its presence as an evil spirit. Maybe she should burn it in the fire, to cleanse the air and release Paul from its power. The spell it had cast was bad for the baby, too.

She was just about to place the sheets of vellum on the flames, when the door opened behind her, blowing in the snow and Paul, bundled in furs so that only his eyes were visible. His muffled roar startled her and she dropped the document into the fire.

"What are you doing? No, you mustn't," he managed to sputter into his scarf, as he crossed the room in three paces and knelt to retrieve the letter. He cooled it between his thick fur mittens, placed it back on the table, and turned to Yellow Bird.

"There, there, don't cry, Sweetheart. It is fine, no harm done. I was just surprised is all," he said in Algonquin, placing an arm across her shoulder.

"I thought..."

"I know it frightened you. My reaction to it, I guess. But it is from my mother, all I have left of her, you see? Even if it upsets me, I have to keep it. These markings tell a story. Here, let me get undressed, we'll share a hot mug of spruce tisane, you know how that settles you, with a wee drop of brandy for good measure, and I'll try to explain. For it means some changes, come spring."

Chapter Eighteen

How to make her understand? She knew nothing of noblemen and whores, birthright and bastards. He would have to re-read it and then interpret for her in terms she might comprehend, but he had folded and unfolded the parchment so many times through the night that he feared it would no longer be legible, especially since the ink might have run from the sweat of his hands or the salty moisture of his tears. Twice, he had fashioned it into a small packet and made to throw it into the fire himself, before he had even read it, but his curiosity had supplanted his former resolve never to communicate with his mother again.

He bent down to light a precious candle from the fire, for the winter daylight was too dim for reading. He held the parchment at arm's length, and brought the candle closer.

Le 20 Avril, 1648

Mon cher fils Jean-Paul,

Please do not disregard this letter, I beg you. I know and appreciate that it may be unwelcome to you. Therefore, I send it with the Jesuit, whom I know to be coming to the New World, trusting that he will prevail upon your good conscience to read it at the very least. The Jesuit might admonish you with, "Honour thy mother and thy father." I will not, I assure you, for thy father is as unknown to you as to me, and as for thy mother, what honour do you owe her? Not much, you would no doubt reply. Still, I gave you life, and I wish hereby, to make up for some of my neglect. I am old and the fear of Hell weighs heavily on my heart these days.

You had some happy times as a boy, did you not? And you were always fed, clothed and kept warm by the kitchen fire. A better life than many unfortunate boys I see in the streets outside these convent walls. What is more, you had the chance for learning, which is more than most and that should hold you in good stead in the New World. Although no thanks are due to me, I was always somehow proud of your quick mind, when your tutors mentioned you to me and his lordship. I thought of you then, though not often enough, I realize now.

Ah, my poor son, you might as well have been born of a cat! I was never meant to be a mother. I could not trouble myself with the needs of others. I thought only of myself and my own interests and pleasures. Such pleasures, the likes of which I could never have known, but for... sin itself. Pleasure is sin, sin is pleasure. Did God make it so? I have yet so many unanswered questions that I dare not ask.

How painful this long time of reflection has been for me. Although I have not looked in a mirror for many years, I have faced my past every day in my heart and stared at darkness in my soul. You may smile at my suffering, believing it no more than I deserve. I only pray that the pain I feel now will not be eternal, in the fires of Hell. God is merciful, the sisters tell me. If I repent, I will receive forgiveness. I ask forgiveness of you alone, my son. Your exile to New France, never to return, frightened me more than words can say. But at the time, self-possessed as I was, I convinced myself that it was for the best, that his lordship was right to thus dispose of you, consigning you to the Jesuits. I could not come to the ship to say farewell—how could I? I wished you well in my heart, though. You must believe that.

Now, my dear boy, you are daily in my prayers and I long for word of you. I wonder where you are and if you are thinking of me. I dream of you as a baby, I smell your sweet head, and I awaken in tears, the weight of your body as a newborn still heavy in my empty arms. I did care for you, as a baby, you need to know. I felt such joy at your birth, like you were the most perfect child ever born. But soon my duties took over once more, for duties I had, to support us both. Your wet nurse could care for you better than I, I convinced myself, and soon I was caught up in my own life again. I am aware that my words may hurt you, but at least they are the truth. Before my son and God, I speak the truth.

Now I am alone, a broken shell, living, like you, in exile. Who would have believed that I, la belle Jeannette, should ever be abandoned and alone? Impossible! I hardly understand it myself. Yet here I remain, wearing grey robes, my shorn hair is the very colour of my habit, repenting and serving God. My days of serving men are done, thanks be to God.

The sisters here have been kinder than the priests at Court ever were.

"Remember the Magdalene," they remind me. "Our Lord and Saviour did not condemn her. All is forgiven in the eyes of our Lord, for those who ask his Mercy." And so I ask, I beg on my knees, but shall His Will be done?

I have sinned, mais oui! You know it and I know it. Yet the priests held me in such contempt that I avoided the confessional, or lied to the figure behind the screen in that suffocating box. I never believed that God himself was present, listening to me. Blasphemy, I know. I always sensed the priests' judgement against me. But how could priests possibly understand the motives of a peasant child, sweeping a filthy cottage one minute, dancing in a grand ballroom the next? Being men, what did they know of the heady joy of sudden power, resulting from my beauty and my "cunning wiles," as they called them? And what of the several priests, who delighted in me, then tossed me aside? Was not their fornication a sin? Nay, said the priests, for I tempted them against their will. True, I was very beautiful.

What choice did I have and how was it so wrong, to use my gifts for my betterment and in turn, provide for my son? I still cannot reconcile that. My looks came from God, did they not? No, say the priests, I was put on this earth to tempt men's souls, like a serpent. Then how could I have prevented that? The Lord of the manor noticed me, still a child, and took me from squalor to luxury, for favours rendered. It's true, I swear it! It was easy to comply. Would I not trade the simple use of my body for the provision of warm food, beautiful clothes, comfort and constant praise? My vanity knew no bounds. The mirror soon reflected a plump, painted goddess, whom I admired as much as the men I taunted and teased. Her crystal laugh now shatters like glass around my ears. But once, it was so beguiling it brought men to my skirts like butterflies to a flower.

My beauty ensured that you were not raised in a sty, as I was, but in the finest palaces in France. Your benefactor, and my lord, smiled on you for your own sweet, good looks and encouraged your education in company with his own sons. Was that not also a gift from God, thanks to my position? Not your fault that you quickly surpassed them and sparked their jealousy.

Now you are no doubt saying, "There she goes again. Justifying herself. Jeanette, Jeannette, that's all that she thinks about." Peut-être. Perhaps. It is easy for you, and all men, to judge me as a depraved, fallen woman. Fallen from where? From the squalid existence my mother endured, a drudge no better than a milk cow. Burdened with ten children, relegated to an early grave, and not so much as a stone to mark her passing? That is why I wanted no children, to end up like her. The accident of your birth happened but once. Ever after, I prevented life from escaping my womb. I shall burn in Hell for that alone, never mind the rest.

But children would have kept me from a life where I bathed in the glow of a thousand candles, clad in silk, glistening in jewels, awakening warm and safe in a nobleman's crisp linen sheets... I could not afford to sacrifice my beauty, my sole currency. Did I understand how little I really possessed that was mine alone? No.

My memories of that time torment me. The priests used to tell me I was awash in sin.

Yet, I would happily have drowned in pleasure. I sparkled like a jewel in the light of the chandeliers. If only I had died young, before my teeth began to rot, my skin to sag, my eyes to dim! I came close to dying more than once, when the wise woman prevented the birth of a sister or brother for you, with purgatives or needles inserted in my womb. This cost me dearly in health, I assure you, and you may be happy to know that I am paying still.

I recognize that this missive is the most I have spoken to you in your life, for I never knew what to do with you, what to say. I entrusted your care to the servants. They loved you like a pet, you remember, Jean? They treated you well, did they not, and in the kitchen, you learned many things, even to cook, if I am not mistaken? I still see you, a little boy covered in flour from head to foot. How you made me laugh, such a little imp, when I visited you and the cooks in the kitchens. I had faith that they would do a better job of mothering than I. You are the living proof that it is so.

I know you still blame me for rarely visiting you, but you must remember, my life was nocturnal. I slept all day and woke at twilight to dress. I still adore the night! I cannot sleep when the stars are out. When I do sleep, I awake drenched in sweat and the heat of unspent passion. I constantly relive my former life, dancing alone in my cell. Once more, I am twirling at the masquerades, at the height of my glory, where one courtier after another would sweep me from the floor to seclude me in a cubicle for a thrilling encounter!

You might wish me in Hell, as the mother who abandoned you. Be assured, I am already there, for layers of powder and wax could not hold back Time. Men, in their power, may choose the best. They stopped choosing me. Too soon, I was one of the "matrons" left covering the hair on her chin with her fan. Good for nothing but gossiping on the sidelines, while the beauties swirled past me, as once I had done. ME, becoming one of the "grand dames" whom I used to ridicule and revile! I refused. I could not bear the humiliation. Better to be locked in a nunnery than to wither away in front of them all. God's punishment is to keep me alive still, like a wilting flower.

All this to tell you, my son, that while I cannot change the past, I can make the future better for you and any children you may have. I leave you a legacy of money and a letter of recommendation that I wrested from His Majesty's office, for the new Seigneur. Do not be a fool and deny your inheritance. It was hard-won, and not in shame, but in joy, though that be deemed a sin in the eyes of God, or the Church, I am still not sure.

Take what is offered to you in faith, as I did. Remember that had I stayed "in my place" and kept to my "destiny," you might very well now be scrabbling in the dirt in the fields of Deauville, as did my father and his father before him. That desperate past too is part of your heritage, mon cher fils. I know there is no redemption in poverty, though the priests insist the poor earn a better place in the next life. Bah! I will believe it when *someone comes back to tell me it is so. Until then... ah, but I blaspheme again. I cannot help myself, it seems.*

You, my son, have a chance to start a new legacy, in the New World, free of the bondage you might have known here, as the son of a courtesan fallen from favour. Be assured that I admire your courage and am secure in the knowledge that you have the will to endure, in the face of any trial. My strength flows in your veins.

Temper your stubbornness with good sense, my son, and do not allow pride to cloud good judgment. I gloated over my looks, my fine clothes, my jewels, my skills at seduction and manipulation. At my age, one comes to understand that pride is perhaps the greatest sin.

All the worldly goods I struggled so hard to attain are now yours. I no longer need them. May they give you the power to establish yourself in New France and thrive in your new life! It is all I have to leave you, as your mother, if only in name. Remember that as a woman, not all choices were my own. You were not one of them, yet you live, and I am glad of that. You will be the best outcome of all that I have done. I pray for you day and night. Would that I could kiss your sweet face once more!

Blessings and peace be upon you, now and always, Jean-Paul.

Sincèrement, votre mère,

Jeannette

Struggling for words, Paul tried in vain to convey the significance of the markings on the parchment to Yellow Bird. His description of the carelessness of his mother and his lonely life as a boy, with only a dog for company, brought them both to tears. Yellow Bird, who had been surrounded by the love and attention of a whole community, could not fathom such treatment of a child. Paul sobbed as though his spirit would shatter like a clay pot dropped on the hearth. Ashamed, he buried his face in his crossed arms on the table. Finally, after she had soothed him by petting his hair and encouraging him to swallow a warm glass of brandy, his emotion subsided enough for her to lead him to bed, though his tears still spilled on the wooden floor and his nose needed wiping. This she did, then tucked him fully-clothed under the furs and hummed the Strawberry Festival song. Paul took Yellow Bird's hand and thanked God for giving her to him. He started to re-tell his memories of the day they met, smiled and fell asleep.

*****

Paul grinned broadly as he raised his arms high across his chest and dipped his oar into the crystal water. What a successful trip this had been! Stowed safely in the prow of his canoe were bales and bales of high quality "made" fur: beaver, fox, wolf, muskrat and otter, all cured and ready for shipping to France. He carried a cargo worth a small fortune and seated on the supporting crossbar just in front of him was his new wife. His wife! At last, a helpmate for all the work that awaited him back at his cabin. Someone to cook, clean, repair his clothes and sew coats and moccasins for winter. Not to mention the other benefits: a warm body next to him for sleep, after the sweet delights under the furs! The previous night, he had tried his best to be patient, as the girl told him clearly with her wide doe eyes that she was a virgin, and terrified. He had caressed her gently and spoken softly, but in the end his excitement held sway and he had exploded in a volcano of delicious passion. Now, his body responded immediately to the memory, and joy arose in his throat, forcing open his mouth in a rowing song.

"V'la le bon vent, v'la le joli vent, v'la le bon vent, ma mie m'appelle,

V'la le bon vent, v'la le joli vent, v'la le bon vent, ma mie m'attend!

Ah the lovely wind, the beautiful wind, my love is calling, my love awaits…"

Startled, the girl turned to face him, her brows furrowed in perplexity. Taking her expression as an invitation to continue, he virtually shouted the remaining twenty-odd verses of the song, which he knew by heart as one of the many rowing ditties he and his fellow voyageurs would sing to keep up a steady rhythm during their fifteen to eighteen hours of paddling on the river. Alone, he had to do the echo parts as well. He thought she might be impressed by his strong, deep voice, which did not lose volume no matter how hard he had to row.

"Derrière chez nous 'y a t'un étang, *derrière chez nous 'y a t'un étang*,

Trois beaux canards s'en vont baignant, aaaannt, aaaaannnt!"

Yellow Bird had her own impression of that day, at great odds from that of her husband, but which she would never share. After her initial surprised response at his howling behind her, she had turned to face forward once more, shaking her head in disbelief that any warrior would be foolish enough to announce his presence to enemies that might be lurking in the forest. Apparently, he had no caution or sense at all, she thought, relying solely on the fire stick to protect him. But an arrow could travel silently and hit either one of them before he would have time to put down his oar. Her father's assessment of the man had obviously been flawed. He was no more than a careless brute. She planned to ignore him, doing only as she was told. Maybe that way he would grow tired of her and leave her alone. With her thoughts.

Which came rushing back like the swift current beneath the birchbark canoe that this "Pole" had either stolen or traded with some of her own people. She judged that a man such as this would be unable to craft such a fine vessel; it was not heavy and ugly like an Iroquois canoe. So he knew her People, then, appreciated their skill and had troubled himself to learn some of their language. But why, why had her father abandoned her to him? She blushed as she remembered suffering penetration under his sweaty, smelly body until he had satisfied himself, then rolled over and snored like a bear in a cave. She knew that what had happened was inevitable, as she had learned all about it long ago and it held no mystery for her. But at least with her own people she would have had a choice of mate from another clan and, if she didn't like him, she could leave and choose another. She should have been free to choose, as was her right! If her mother had been alive, her father wouldn't have dared to trade her like so many sorry animal pelts! Grandmother certainly would have forbidden such an outrage! But the Bear clan mothers were dead, and there was no one to speak on her behalf.

She almost wished the Iroquois had captured her the day of the raid, for her fate could not have been worse. Was she worth no more to her father than a thing, a stick belching fire and smoke which he didn't even know how to use? If Taretande really believed, as he had said, that he had to give her up, even an Odawa would have been better than this creature, with his pale, hairy body, light, impenetrable eyes the colour of river water, and long, unkempt hair. He didn't even know enough to oil and braid his hair like a decent warrior and his smell made her retch. She had expected to feel joy and pleasure at her first mating and, if she were lucky, a sense of deep bonding, like her parents had known. But no, for her it had turned out to be just a selfish, unrequited act, where she felt more like a dog than a human being.

"Ah, Grandmother, another first come and gone, and nothing like what you had described to me. You had been so envious of me, about to experience all the firsts of youth. If only you had known," she thought as the canoe slipped along the green ribbon of water, past an unbroken wall of trees on either side, and the man continued his incessant howling.

"And worst of all, I will never be able to tell you about it and have you console me and tell me what to do. I will never be able to help to set your soul free at the Feast of the Dead, back at our village where your bones await the proper rituals, as I promised, for this man will take me farther away from you. Will Father even be able to ensure that it happens, in his preoccupation with vengeance and this new lack of good judgment? Thank goodness I convinced him to visit the village, before we reached the trading post, or I wouldn't even have had the chance to commune with you there one last time. And I gathered every seed I could find, for a garden. I am glad at least that I don't have to share them with those stupid women back at the camp! It serves them right! And I managed to find my secret talisman, right where I had left it that horrible day of the massacre, before I even knew what pain and suffering were. So far, it has not brought me much fortune, but I will keep it here in my medicine bag, around my neck where HE cannot find it, and it will remind me always of you, Grandmother, and Mother, and Baby Brother."

Yellow Bird began to sob, pressing her lips firmly together, as the tears flowed freely down her face. Her anger for her father's betrayal rose in her throat and turned her saliva to sand. She couldn't help her body from shaking and, on the next upswing of his oar, Paul noticed.

Realizing that she was probably suffering from homesickness, he decided to sing a more soothing song, its tune almost a lullaby.

"Auprès de ma blonde, qu'il fait bon, fait bon, fait bon, auprès de ma blonde, qu'il fait bon dormir..." *Beside my beloved, how nice it is, how nice it is, beside my beloved, how nice it is to sleep...* Ah oui, he thought with a smile, how nice it will be to sleep beside this lovely young girl tonight. He plied his oars with even more vigour, anxious to distance them from the trading post and reach the village far upstream, where he would trade his goods for supplies and head further into the bush to his cabin, to begin a new life, with his... wife! He could hardly believe his luck.

Paul dreamed his memories of their meeting, while Yellow Bird stroked her belly and continued to sing, wondering what had become of her father, and Grey Cloud, and her brother who had been captured by the Iroquois and her sweet cousin, Sunrise, whom she had left behind with the Odawa. Fortunately, she would never know that when her father and his companions left her to head back up the river a band of Iroquois assailed the flotilla, despite their constant vigilance. Taretande had had no time to even raise his bow, let alone load his new musket, before an arrow pierced his chest. Too late, his cry of pain sent a warning to his companions ahead of him in the canoe, for as master steersman, he occupied the last seat. With waning strength, he dropped his oar, reached down and tossed the fire stick into the river, so that his enemy might not profit from it. An Iroquois warrior coming alongside noticed the sudden movement and planted a tomahawk firmly in Taretande's throat before diving to retrieve the weapon. His shrieks of triumph echoed along the wooded shore.

To this day, Yellow Bird had a feeling that something bad had happened. As Paul's canoe sped against the current, as he raced to outpace the sun, she had shuddered with a sudden chill, despite the heat on her back. Turning around, she pressed two fingers to her lips. She sensed danger lurking in the trees. She thought she had heard a warrior's cry. Clambering off the seat, she knelt on the bottom of the canoe, leaned against a bale of furs and scanned both sides of the bank for the remainder of the day, her fingers worrying the talisman in its leather bag around her neck.

When they stopped to make camp for the night, she watched as the man prepared food for them both from his provisions of dried meat and some type of sticky substance which he roasted on a stick over the fire. She was unable to swallow more than cold river water, which served also to bathe her swollen eyes. As soon as he had eagerly made up their bed of spruce boughs and furs next to the tipped up canoe, Yellow Bird burrowed in, curled up and feigned sleep before he could return from banking the fire. She steadfastly ignored his grumbling and muttering and before she knew it, her pretence became reality as her body succumbed to exhaustion.

She smiled now as she remembered how she had deliberately tormented him by withholding her embraces. That had been her only form of revenge. But slowly, due to his kindness and patience, and her overpowering loneliness, she had opened a small space in her heart for him to reside. And at moments like these, when she could sense how much he needed her, she began to feel that he was almost like family. Not a white stranger, not a lover, but at least as close as a cousin. With just each other to rely upon for survival, closeness and cooperation were inevitable.

Now, if she understood correctly, he was planning to move to the white man's village. The prospect filled her with dread. What if the baby caught the white man's disease? What if Paul left her there, as she knew had happened to other women of The People, thrown over for a white woman and left to starve or beg for charity? Their gaunt faces haunted her each time she and Paul returned from the village, where the white women stared and pointed, and her own kind followed her footsteps with sorrowful eyes. The noise, the smells, the clothing, everything was strange and terrifying there. Maybe she should just run away, before spring. But where would she go, how would she survive alone with a new baby? No, she would talk to him: he knew it was a bad decision. She had seen his angry reaction to the Black Robe. She would be extra kind to him and help him to see the wisdom of staying clear of them and their kind, for the safety of their child.

*****

The rough cobblestones punished the soles of Paul's moccasin-shod feet worse than the pebbles on the shore of a lake. A paved street! What next? His nostrils crimped shut to fend off the stench. Sewage and garbage flowed sluggishly in open stone gutters a few feet from the doorways of the stone buildings lining the streets. Even the light spring rain couldn't clear the air. A cart rattled by, splashing his buckskins before he could leap out of the way. Slop hurtled down from an upper storey window, barely missing him. He whipped off the wide-brimmed leather hat that he had just purchased and hastily brushed off droplets of rain mixed with greasy water. His gaze flew upwards to curse at the careless offender. His angry glare was met by the sparkling laughter of a young woman in a white bonnet, leaning out the stone windowsill to wave at him.

"Bonjour, Monsieur! Lucky I missed ya! Maybe I should kiss ya!" she chanted and he couldn't help but laugh out loud. Perhaps it was a good omen. She *had* missed, after all and besides, how long had it been since he had received such an offer from a pretty girl? Come to think of it, never!

He patted his leather jacket where the letter of recommendation had been tucked in the inner breast pocket, sewn in so carefully by his wife. From this day forward, letters, not furs, would be his stock in trade. Taking a deep breath to calm his nerves, he pressed down the iron handle and the door creaked open on its massive hinges. Soundlessly, his moccasins entered the domain of the Seigneur. At that moment, he realized that his next stop would need to be "chez le cordonnier" for a new pair of boots. It would not be seemly for a notaire to tread the cobblestone streets in moccasins.

*****

At that moment, back in the cabin, Yellow Bird grunted, almost screamed, but didn't. Her arms were wrapped tightly around the centre post. She had a knife, a bowl of water and a towel on the table, at the ready. She bit down hard on a piece of leather between her teeth and bore down with each contraction. She knew how babies came into the world. She had witnessed it many times, from earliest childhood. Still, she could not stop the flow of tears that mixed with her sweat and streamed down her face, as she thought of her mother and grandmother, who should have been there to help her. She felt sorry for herself, all alone, with no one to hold her upright, rub her back, sing to her, wipe her brow, catch the newborn and place him in her arms. Nothing but memories of her family, long dead, had sustained her so far, through the lonely hours. Even Paul was away, though she doubted he could have been of much help. He probably would have fainted long before now. Grimacing, she suddenly remembered her mother, a skilled wise woman, warning other women not to close their eyes with the pain. If she should faint, who would ensure the baby's safe passage? No, she knew she must fix on something and be strong. The talisman that she had retrieved before leaving the village was always with her, in a pouch around her neck. She managed to loosen the buckskin tie, took out the brooch and squeezed it, hard, until the pointed end penetrated her palm. Her brown eyes shot open. With a gasp of pain, she dropped the pin to the floor, just as in a gush of fluid and blood her baby slipped out from between her legs. Her pierced hand reached down to retrieve her newborn son.

Chapter Nineteen

Québec, New France, 1650

Two years. Two whole years of scrubbing, cleaning, washing, cooking and pretending to pray. Feigning belief and obedience, for survival's sake. And it had been a successful ruse, just like the first one. The nuns did not suspect that she pitied and despised them. Brides of Christ, bah! They were slaves, no less than she had been. Their God demanded sacrifice, fealty and worship. At least the Madame hadn't required all that! And for what in return? More and more of the same drudgery, with a promise of reward, at the end. When life itself had been worn down to the bone? Well, no more. She would release them from their bonds, whether they wished it or not.

True, the nuns had kindly rescued her, taken her in despite, or maybe because of, her circumstances. Thanks to dear Père Thomas, who might just as easily have betrayed her to the captain and had her shipped back to France in disgrace for her many sins, not the least of which had been donning men's clothes to disguise herself. That alone could have cost her life. Luckily for her, the priest honoured the sanctity of the confessional, when others may have found an excuse to break it and have her clapped in irons, never to leave the ship. Of the many priests she had known in a professional capacity, he was the first she trusted. True, he could not deny the debt he owed her for tending to his needs during the miserable ocean voyage, a debt he had promised to repay. But with priests, one never knew. So she had sighed with relief when he whispered to her, just as they disembarked at Québec to replenish supplies before continuing on to the great island, that he had convinced the captain to allow Tito the cabin boy to accompany him on some errands. She had no idea that he had planned to "help" her, by substituting one prison for another.

As soon as they had stepped off the dock, Père Thomas stopped the first man he encountered and asked where he might find the Ursulines. The man pointed to the Upper Town with the hat he had removed in deference to the priest, affably offering to lead him and his servant to the location of the Convent.

On the way up the steep hill, they were informed in glowing terms of the saintliness of the Mother Superior and founder of the Convent, Marie de l'Incarnation, of how she and three other women had boldly come to Québec eleven years before and miraculously established the Ursuline order, treating the sick and attempting to save the souls of the Savages. A stonemason, he had laboured to erect the three-storey convent on its prominent position at the point of the cape. While he prattled on, she had tugged desperately on Father Thomas' sleeve, trying to pull him back from leading her over this precipice. What was his intent? That she become a nun? Perhaps the long months of sickness had eaten away his reason, as well as his strength, for he leaned heavily for support on their guide while ignoring her head-shaking and silent pleas to stop.

When at last they arrived at the convent doors, Father Thomas blessed the man and sent him on his way. He finally agreed to listen to her protests.

"Yes, I understand that you have no vocation and no money to support your application to the convent, in any case. That is the crux of the problem, for if I abandon you here on your own, you will be forced to fall back into your former life, or starve in the street. Do not ask me again to take you with me to Ville Marie. It is far too dangerous. You heard the captain as well as I: the colony is barely established, the natives are constantly on the attack and the winters are even harsher there, with a constant lack of supplies. Would you rather return to France? No. Then I don't see as you have much choice in the matter."

Once inside, standing in an austere office before the tall, imposing figure of Mother Marie, her knees had almost buckled in fear as Père Thomas begged for her admittance as a servant to the holy Order. The plain, stony face displayed no emotion as he recounted the dedication and skill with which she had nursed him through the trials of his seasickness and assured the Mother Superior that she had not fallen into her life of sin, but rather it had been forced upon her, just as Mary Magdalene...

"Very well, Father. No need to go that far," the woman interrupted, holding up her hand. "I do understand the trials of womanhood, rest assured. Now, my dear, will you swear to serve God to the best of your ability, in whatever capacity may be required, to be chaste, humble and obedient and a helpmate to our Lord, Jesus Christ?

"Yes, well, I will take that nod to be assent. You may be overwhelmed with the opportunity which our Lord has placed in your path. For our part, we are pleased to accept your service, for we are always in dire need of help in our work. Here you will find food, shelter and blessed respite from the demands of the world outside," she said in a surprisingly kind voice as she gestured with her hands to encompass the whole building.

"But the price is your devotion to duty. It may sound hard, but when you see the little native girls, the delights of my heart, you will be utterly transformed into an angel of mercy. Remember, they depend upon us for the salvation of their very souls. We try to teach them to say the catechism, to sing, to sew and to pray, but it is exceedingly difficult for them to adopt our ways. You must persevere and always be kind and gentle in your dealings with our pupils, as you will find we shall be toward you. Perhaps, in time, you will hear your calling, as I did so many years ago. I left my own dear son back in France, so strong was my compulsion to do God's work. In the meantime, thank you, Father, for bringing... Tito? Ah, my dear, you must choose a new name, for your life in New France to begin. And then it is straight into the bath with you, for you stink worse than a pole cat!"

And so, once more, she assumed a new identity, choosing the name "Georgette" in honour of the man she considered her true saviour. If Georges had wept when she left, how many more tears would he cry now, to see her living in these conditions? Far from enlightening, as Mother Marie had suggested, her work was mere drudgery, for she was assigned the lowliest tasks, from emptying chamber pots, to feeding the pigs, to scrubbing the sheets in icy river water. Each morning she awoke stiff and sore, with the words, "Oh God, another day," on her lips. And she found it impossible to be thankful for the food provided; she silently cursed the thin cabbage soup and dry crusts of barley bread the nuns considered adequate sustenance. The local petitioners, professing devotion to the Church while in fact being merely anxious to rid themselves of unwanted daughters, paid the entry fees "in kind" with pigs, butter, and salted eel. But there was never enough food to go around, what with all the "little angels" to feed. At least in the brothel, she had been well fed, she often thought to herself.

Her shelter was not much more of a blessing. In winter, the stone walls seeped with damp, absorbing the icy cold breath of the great river less than half a mile below the convent. Day after day for six long months, the snow fell in heavy clusters, the frost coated the barren trees and fog shrouded the limestone buildings. The sun rose late and set early, and despite the gifts of firewood, the convent was impossible to keep warm. Two interminable seasons she had trudged through the deep, heavy snow from the Lower to the Upper Town on the Sisters' errands. The arrival of spring was almost worse, as the river shuddered and howled for nights on end during the breakup of the monstrous ice sheets tossed asunder by the ocean tides. Then came summer, with its sweltering, humid heat, flies and mosquitoes, to add interest to the hours of cultivating and weeding the kitchen garden. The chores were endless and unrewarding, for despite all the work, the women were able to maintain only the minimum of survival standards in the relative safety of the convent. The threats of disease, famine and the dreaded enemy, the Iroquois, were ever-present. Yet the Sisters, with their religious fervour and conviction in the worth of their mission, remained cheerful. It sickened her. In the brothel, the girls had the good sense to complain about their lot.

"For this, you travelled across the open sea to the New World? You could have been a house servant in France, with a lot fewer chilblains!" she would admonish herself. She constantly reviewed the voyage and the disaster that had brought her to seek refuge onboard ship, disguised as a cabin boy. If the crossing was Purgatory, the life she had landed in was Hell. Purgatory she could accept—she probably deserved it. Looking back, she assured herself that her daring escape and resourcefulness ought to have reaped a greater reward, if there was a God. Surely the priest could have done more for her.

After all, "Tito" had saved his life, she thought as she wrung out the cloth she was using to wash the floors on her hands and knees. She twisted it dry in her red, chapped hands as she recalled the months of unstinting devotion she had paid him in the close quarters below the deck, with only stolen moments topside to release her from his stench. Aching back, sore arms, growling belly, these were nothing compared to the restricted breathing forced upon one by the fetid air swirling like sour cabbage soup below the stairs. However, just as she found later in the convent, there was a trick to avoid being caught looking like you were not working. All cabin boys were targets of abuse, and if seemingly unoccupied, someone would yell at you, while others would kick you or slap you about the head. Worse still, they might grab you by the shirt and that could be disastrous. As often as possible, she would seek out a pile of discarded sailcloth and curled up underneath it, in an effort to disappear.

Ah, yes, a nap, that was a truly guilty pleasure. Just to drift off with the soothing motion of the ship on the waves and sleep in the fresh, salt-sprayed air, free for a while from the smell of shit, vomit and death below deck. Under the heavy, musty cloth, that reprieve was difficult to obtain. Her skin crawled with lice, her teeth hurt, one was loose in fact, her blistered feet burned in her ill-fitting boots, and the bands binding her chest constricted her breathing. Sweat escaped from every pore, drenching her filthy, tattered clothes. Mouth breathing helped and silently chanting a half-remembered song, until at last, the relief of exhausted slumber overwhelmed the discomfort. But if she should dream...

A dark street. Screams, raucous laughter, thunder, lightning, the rain pelting down. Shivering against a stone wall illuminated only by the faint light inside the inn, when the door swung open to admit another customer or toss out an inebriated one. Hoping no one would bother with the crumpled figure hiding in the shadows, until morning at least. Moaning between teeth bolted shut against the pain. A flood of warm liquid, seeping downhill into the gutter. Blood? Too dark to see, but the telltale smell drew the rats, anticipating fresh meat. Swinging a stick to beat them away, as they boldly approached, closer, closer. A momentary lapse, passed out maybe? Waking eye to eye with a huge rat, screaming as it bit the cold end of her nose and tore off with the scrap of flesh. Heart racing, wrenched by a sob, "Tito" would awake from the nightmare that was actually a memory. Then, as now, the rest would come flooding back, though she worked herself into a frenzy of scrubbing the stone floor, endeavouring to wash it away.

"There, there, my child. No need to erase the very patterns from these stones! You mustn't exhaust yourself so from work, Georgette. The Lord himself wouldn't approve. Come to the hall later and dance with the little angels and myself. It will do you good and the children will make you smile," the Mother Superior said warmly, as she passed by.

"I will try to come, Mother, if I get this work done. There is no rest for the wicked, as they say," she responded, keeping her eyes lowered respectfully.

"I don't care for that saying and it certainly does not apply to you, in any case. Come dance with us in one half hour. No excuses." Marie de l'Incarnation placed her hand on the kerchief covering Georgette's hair. Through the material, the blessing radiated calm and forgiveness. Maybe the Mother Superior's sanction alone could erase the past. Two hours of joyful dancing with the Sisters and their charges temporarily lifted her spirits, but as soon as she lay down on her straw pallet, memories once again suppressed sleep. She tossed and turned, weighing her former misery against the prospect of a monotonous future, unable to decide which was worse.

Curling into a fetal position, she relived the cramps and stabbing agony in the gut that had driven her into the street, on the worst night of her life. She remembered stumbling out of the house in search of an alley for refuge, away from prying eyes. Struggling for breath, wincing, pushing, scratching against the cobblestones, breaking every nail, she finally vomited what little food remained in her stomach. Then, in a rush of water and blood, she expelled a mass of sludge that she knew contained a stillborn child. She passed out, for how long she did not know, until she woke up eye to eye with a rat! She didn't dare look at what she had left behind, as she tore into the street, holding her face, covered in her own blood, a rat still clinging to the bottom of her skirt. She kicked it off with the toe of her boot and then stamped on it with her heel as it struggled to right itself. But she was weak; the rat prevailed and scurried off.

She staggered to the back door of the house, where Georges gasped at the sight of her and carried her in his strong, black arms to his tiny bed upstairs in the garret. Hushing her with a finger to his lips as she begged him with her eyes not to tell, he helped her strip off her soiled clothing, poured water into the wash basin and sneaked soundlessly into the hall for a clean linen nightdress, scented with lavender. He pressed a wet rag against her burning forehead and plastered the end of her swollen nose. Feeding her by hand like a baby, with bread soaked in warm milk, he crooned wordlessly, tonelessly, trying to comfort her. Sensing her need, he would assist her to sit on the chamber pot. Each morning of her convalescence, he set out cheese, biscuits and wine on the small table next to the bed, for he had to be downstairs to attend to his duties. He slept next to her on the floor, waking to check on her every few hours, for how many nights? She wasn't sure. But long enough for her to regain her strength and make a decision. She would not go back down.

Georges would help, of that much she was sure. As a deaf-mute manservant, he was perfectly suited to his role in the brothel. Madame relied on him for everything, but especially prized his discretion. The girls knew he was trustworthy, for they too confided in him constantly, speaking to him with words and gestures which they were sure he understood. Bernadette was certain that no one in the house knew she was here, in the attic. They probably assumed her dead. If so, they were right. Bernadette had died in the street. Disfigured by the damage to her nose, they would not hesitate to cast her off anyway. She would not give them that satisfaction. She would choose her own destiny, for once. Her mother had sold her to the Madame, for a few coins and a pound of salt pork. Since then, she had been traded for money, for liquor, for tobacco, for gambling debts, for sport. From now on, she would determine her own worth, or die in the attempt. No one would own her again.

Gesturing to Georges, she asked him to bring her a mirror. At first, he protested, pointing to her nose which he thought she had better not see. She just laughed and showed him the gap where she was missing a front tooth, the pockmarks on her cheeks, and the scar across her forehead where one of the girls had smashed her with a pot. He relented, but it would not be easy to sneak such an item from one of the rooms. If caught stealing, the punishment would be severe: the loss of a hand. Bernadette knew that, of course, but smiled and indicated the collection of small trinkets that graced the window ledge. Inconsequential things that no one would miss: a bead, a clay pipe, a hair clasp, a pin. She thought she even recognized a brass ring that had been given to her by a satisfied, if cheap, customer, which she held up to his face with a raised eyebrow as if to say, "Well?" He just smiled back at her with his gleaming white teeth. Her eyes begged Georges to take the chance, assuring him that she needed the mirror for a very good reason.

Within a day, he produced it for her, whipping it out from behind his back as if he were performing a bit of magic. Greedily taking it without a glance at her reflection, she placed it face down on the bed, then made Georges understand what she needed next: a set of men's clothes. She held up his trousers against herself, to show him that his were far too large for her, but that this is what she needed. His eyes registered bewilderment. She picked up one of his dirty shirts from the floor and slipped it over her head, showing him how it did not fit. She drew a picture in the air of a dress, pointed at her body and then shook her head left and right, to say "no" and held up the trousers once more. Georges shrugged and left the room, securing the door behind him.

While he was gone, she hastily grabbed Georges' straight razor from the washstand, filled the wash basin with water from the jug, tipped the mirror against the wall where she could see the top of her head, and began hacking away at her hair. As the copper ringlets dropped to the floor she felt lighter and lighter, as if she might float away through the tiny window and into the sky. She wished she could burn the hair, to kill the crawling lice, but that would be too risky. The razor swirled around her head until her scalp gleamed back at her in the mirror, except for the spots where she had slipped and drawn blood. She leaned over, rubbed down with soap and poured the remaining water in the jug over her head, spitting out long strands of hair. Gazing in the mirror with a satisfied grin, she was just about to replace the razor on the table when behind her, the door creaked open, making her jump in fright.

Georges gasped and threw both hands in the air, dropping the clothes he had been carrying. Rushing toward her, he reached out to lay his broad hands on her wounded scalp, then glancing down, saw the hair on the floor and began to collect it and place it back on her head, as if he could attach it there. Tears rolled down his cheeks as he caressed the curls, winding them around his index finger and brushing them with his lips.

Angrily, Bernadette tore the hair from his hands and threw it back on the floor, kicking it under the bed with her bare feet. She gestured for him to bring her the clothes, as she shamelessly dropped the nightshirt Georges himself had dressed her in. She quickly donned the loose trousers and baggy shirt he had somehow retrieved from downstairs. Maybe some things left behind in a girl's closet, by one of the regulars. Or maybe some poor bugger would wake up from a drunken stupor to find his clothes missing. Serve him right! But she didn't know, or care. At least they fit well enough, but her breasts were still visible under the light cotton. She needed bindings. She knew what to do, for when the girls had babies, they were immediately bound tightly across the chest, to prevent their milk from coming in, and preserve the beauty of their breasts. Bernadette had helped bind many a crying girl, weeping for the loss of her child. A wet nurse in the country would feed the child, if the decision had been made to keep it alive. If it was a pretty girl babe, the Madame might decide to have it raised, as an investment. More often than not, it would be left in the street, where a passerby might take pity upon it. One way or another, to Madame, the problem was solved.

She took the ragged towel from the bed and showed Georges how she would need strips of cloth, only longer, to wrap around her and flatten her chest. He quickly grasped her meaning, as he too knew the process required, and scurried out of the room, forgetting to shut the door. Up in the attic it was quite safe, but she crossed the room to close it. She wanted to keep any whiffs of cooking odours or sounds of chatter from the other girls from reaching her hideaway. Here, no reminders of life downstairs could touch her and entice her back with the false promise of security.

Georges returned before nightfall with the bindings, an oversized coat and a misshapen cap. He insisted she cover her head, which looked hideous, as he made very clear by sticking his tongue through his perfect teeth. He had found a large pair of worn out boots that she managed to keep on her feet once they were covered in thick woollen socks. Georges took her hand, kissed it and then led her silently down the back stairs into the alley. He handed her a packet of bread and cheese, wrapped in a lace handkerchief. Holding her hand up, he placed the copper ring on the little finger of her right hand, pressed a single coin into her palm, and shooed her off into the dusk, but not before one of his fat tears melted against her cheek.

She knew exactly where she was headed: to the docks. For months now, there had been talk among the customers of an expedition leaving Dieppe for New France, with the intention of establishing a new colony on some island. From what she had overheard, the enterprise was doomed to failure. But three ships had been commissioned by de Maisonneuve and had left in early April. Now, another vessel with fresh supplies and more labourers was set to depart and surely the services of a cabin boy would not be refused. She called herself "Tito," after a young Italian servant the Madame had employed in the brothel to run errands. She liked the jaunty, foreign ring of the name.

Among the sailors and dockhands bustling about the shipyard, finding the ship about to undertake "la folle enterprise" posed no difficulty: everyone agreed on the stupidity of the whole notion. With her disguise, her plain, blemished face and self-effacing air, she easily convinced the first mate, responsible for taking on crew members, that she would be a willing hand, able to cook, serve, scrub, and tend the animals, whatever was necessary. Fortunately for her, the recent miscarriage meant that she should not be troubled by her "monthlies" for the length of the voyage. She had to count on that, otherwise her subterfuge might be discovered. She had convinced herself that whatever awaited her in foreign parts could be no worse, and hopefully better, than her present circumstances. And at least she would be free.

Once onboard, she kept her head down and did as she was told, doing her best to draw no attention to herself. Once, when she was scrubbing the upper deck, with her shirt sleeves rolled up and kneeling on hands and knees, she noticed a sailor scrutinizing her backside. She worried that the curve of her hips might give her away, even under the loose trousers, so she donned the old jacket Georges had given her, claiming to be suffering from the chill of the sea breeze. In fact, she sweltered under the weight of the clothes and the strain of the bindings across her chest. She daren't wash, as there was no privacy to be found. Her body odour grew ripe. She itched from a thousand flea bites. The bristle on her head started to grow back, but she kept it covered with the cap. The scabs from the wounds she had inflicted on her scalp kept breaking open, as she couldn't stop herself from scratching wildly at the lice. Trickles of dried blood clung to the dirty ring around her neck. She blended in easily with the rest of the crew.

When the young priest had shown no sign of improvement in his "mal de mer" after two weeks, the captain had assigned Tito to keep an eye on him. It would be bad luck for the priest to die en route. If he chose to do so once in New France, that would no longer be their concern. In the meantime, however, they would endeavour to keep him alive, so they could not be held accountable by his family or the Church. And that, she thought now, was precisely what she had done, since his safe arrival represented her ticket to independence. He had kept his promise, as far as he was concerned, for she was safely ensconced with the Ursulines, out of trouble and working for the good of the little native girls housed there. How could he understand the suffocation she felt in the stone prison on the hill? Was she not better off than before?

Yet she envied the merchants' wives in the Lower Town, for their lives seemed, if not easier, more sociable at least. She had no desire to marry, but felt isolated, alone and degraded in her position as servant, forced to comply with all the rituals of the Order with none of the camaraderie the Sisters obviously experienced. Despite Mother Superior's example of devotion to the native girls, she was indifferent to their suffering. Her sole focus was escape. She kept herself aloof, as if she had taken a vow of silence, meekly acceding to every request while watching for an opportunity to present itself. The Sisters thought she was wonderful, never bothering to question her history or how she had come to be there. Each girl had her own sad tale, but now, as Mother Superior said, they were all equal in the eyes of God.

On Christmas Eve, during the long, boring mass she was forced to endure, she made a plan. Mother Marie had announced that she would return to France in the spring, to seek more funds for their holy mission. In the meantime, she would leave immediately for the Jesuit monastery, to help draw up a constitution for New France, which they planned to present to the Archbishop of Paris. The Mother Superior's timing could not have been better, as far as "Tito" was concerned, Georgette thought, smiling and coyly crossing herself, before rising to join the other servants exiting the chapel.

Part III

The Village and Vancouver, 1962

Chapter Twenty

Her parents' raised voices seemed even louder from up here. But Jocelyne loved sleeping on the upper bunk. Pauline still had to have a chair pushed against the bed below. Hah! The first night they had installed the bunk beds, the little brat had whined and whined until she got the top bunk. Then, in the middle of the night, bang! She had fallen all the way to the floor! Hah! Served her right! Jocelyne grinned smugly to herself, but she snuggled up tight against the wall, just in case. Imagine falling out... she shuddered.

To block out the sound coming through the thin wall, she thought about what had happened just a few nights before when her cousin Sarah had been allowed to stay over. They planned to share the top bunk. Of course, Jocelyne had chosen the side next to the wall and squeezed up as small as she could, to give Sarah enough room, but soon after everyone was asleep... thud! It was mean to laugh, but it really did look funny when mom had switched on the light, to see her laying on the floor in her pyjamas, hair askew, with that startled look on her face! Then she had started to scream and cry, blubbering that she wanted to go home and would never stay again.

Sure, sure, that's what she had said, but she really didn't mean it, Jocelyne knew. It was great that they could play together now, because they lived so much closer to Mom's brother's family in the village. Jocelyne hadn't felt lonely on the farm, but now that Sarah was nearby, she missed her if a day went by with only Pauline for company. They'd had so many adventures already, tearing through the fields next to the house, running around the haystacks, even finding an old scooter in the ditch. How strange to find a toy like that, a genuine treasure. Who would have left it behind? Oh well, it was theirs now—finders, keepers! They had played with it all day, running up and down the sloping gravel driveway. Jocelyne's heart pounded just thinking about her new best friend. "Lucky, lucky me!" she thought to herself.

And tomorrow was the first day of school! The day when she would finally get to wear her beautiful yellow lace dress and her new hat and those special "saddle" shoes that she had never been allowed to wear, after scuffing her "church" shoes. So much to look forward to, except that Mom and Dad's arguing was keeping her awake. Pauline snored peacefully in the bunk below. Oh well, she was too scared and excited to sleep anyway, so she strained to hear.

Mom's voice: something about Chantale. Chantale had upset everybody by running away. What did she have to go and do that for? Wonder if she took the little red doll shoes in the box under her bed. At least the record with the pretty little girl's picture on it was safe, in a box at the top of Mom's closet. Maybe if Chantale hadn't taken the clown pictures, Grandmère would let me have them. Even though they're crying, they're still nice. What did Chantale call the little tiles they were made from... monsicks? Misaics? Something like that. She would have to remember to ask Grandmère.

"...this damn house—too small to stay in all winter, cold and drafty, with no one to help, and what about the new baby... three kids to look after... way out here, so far from town..." Mother's shouting interrupted her thoughts. Then came Dad's much deeper tone—harder to make out: Chantale something something, money, murmur, murmur and a dog.

Oh yeah, when were they getting the dog? This she really needed to hear. She flattened her ear against the wall. Mom was shouting that she didn't want a goddamn dog (What??!!), "didn't want something else to look after and feed and worry about... enough to worry about without bringing a puppy into the house to clean up after and train... Nicolas not even trained yet. Diapers to wash with only that clunky excuse for a washing machine downstairs." Mom crying. Dad's deep rumble vibrating against the wall, getting softer, slowing down.

"Okay, okay, okay, that's it, don't listen any more. No puppy? No, no, no. Can't be. School, okay, school tomorrow. School, school, school." She rolled over, back to the wall, and started rocking, thumb in her mouth, humming to herself.

"Pretty yellow dress—I get to wear my dress tomorrow! With a crinoline to show off when I spin and spin around. White socks and black and white "saddle" shoes. Saddle. Just like a horse. Why were they called "saddle" shoes? Saddle up, horsie. Just like a horse... Horsie, horsie, Blackie, Black..." Her tuneless song blocked the voices as she rode her horse to sleep.

*****

"Josyleene Gerard. Oh yes, hello, Mrs. Gerard. My goodness, you brought her yourself! Not a bit necessary, you know. Best to let them get started on their own, right from Day One. The more fuss you make, the worse it is. I guess it's your first one to start school, right? That's usually the way. Mom finds it hardest with the first. By the time the last one is ready to go, you can't wait to get them out your hair. You won't be bringin' the next one on the first day, I guarantee you that! So, Joseyleene, is it? Let's call you Josie for short, make it easier on everybody. Well, and don't you look nice in your pretty dress? Perfect for your picture to be taken—we take their pictures on the first day. You won't dress her up like this every day though now, will you? You'll find it's pretty hard for her to stay lookin' so clean and nice around here—it's a pretty rough bunch on the playground. And of course we don't allow hats at school. Mom will take it home and look after it for you, dearie."

"Excuse me, Ma'm, but her name is pronounced Jocelyne Gerar—no "d" at the end and the 'lyne' is said stronger than the 'Joce' part. Her grandmother gave all the kids French names and she's pretty insistent on no nicknames and saying the name the French way. It's not so hard, even I can do it, and it's such a pretty name, I want her to keep it. If the kids start using a nickname, that will be it. I'm sure you understand."

"Oh yes, I know Ma-dame Gerard all right. I taught some of her children, too. I know what she's like about this French.... Hmm, hmm... Of course I have been the teacher in this Grade One classroom for over twenty years, don't ya know? All the children in the village and the countryside start with me." She paused and, with her enormous hand, patted her curly grey hair. "Well, sure, we'll do our best, but I can't promise the kids won't tease her, with such an unusual name. Suzie, Betty, Lucy, those are the names we're mostly used to. The kids don't do French until grade four, just because the government says we have to teach it. No earthly good to anyone out in Western Canada, so's I can tell, but we have to do it so we manage somehow."

"I'm a little worried about her. She's always been at home... " Suzanna's voice came out strained, subdued.

"Nonsense! She'll be just fine. Well, come along, Joceyleene, we line all the children up outside before school starts and then everyone gets settled in a desk. I'll put her right up front, Mrs. Gerard, don't you worry, because she's so small compared to the other children. Let me check, you did say she was six already? My, my, you'll have to eat your spinach, my girl. You can run along now, Mrs. Gerard. Best let her get settled. She'll be just fine. Come, come, now, no tears. Let Mom get along home and she'll see you at four o'clock. You'll have lots of stories to tell her." A firm hand gripped the tiny shoulder and directed the child to a large desk directly in front of the blackboard. The teacher's dress gave off a strong, musty odour that caught in Jocelyne's throat as she was forced down into the desk.

Jocelyne waved weakly at her mother's back as her blue high heels clicked through the door. She sat quietly, staring around the room. Sunlight streamed through the windows that completely covered one wall, illuminating the white alphabet letters printed on green cardboard, pinned above the blackboard. As she waited, she started to name them aloud, hoping the lady would hear her and be impressed with how much she knew: "A, B, C...." The teacher did not look up from her desk, until a bell went off in the hallway and outside.

"Come along," was all she said, prying her huge body from behind the desk and heading through the door. She led her outside where children were forming a ragged line and indicated with her crooked forefinger that Jocelyne was to join them. Reluctantly, she moved forward to insert herself where a tall redheaded girl was elbowing a scrawny boy in the ribs.

"Hey, quit pushing me, jerk."

"Ah, c'mon you snot-nosed crybaby. Shove over."

"Hey watch it, you just pushed the little princess into the dirt. You alright, Miss Priss? Looks like you might have torn your fancy dress. Too bad. Ah, c'mn now, don't start bawlin' and don't you tell. If you say a word, you'll get it double at recess."

"Come along now, boys and girls, line up in order when I call your name, girls in this row, boys over here. Last name first, first name last. You will sit in order of your names and this will be your line up from now on, so remember who is in front and who is behind you."

The class trooped up the stairs two by two and filed into their assigned seats in the wooden desks. Jocelyne found herself not at the front, as promised, but behind a heavy-set girl with blond curls that blocked her view of the board.

"I can't see," Jocelyne called out to no one in particular.

"Joseyleene, we don't shout in the classroom. If you have something to say, raise your hand and I will call on you. Now children, settle down, sit up straight in your desk, hands folded on the top like this, and look at the board. This is my name. Mrs. Hoffentrauder. Now, let's practice how to say it. Together, and..."

Mumble, mumble.

"Well, you'll soon get better at it. Now it's time to learn how to print your name. You will print your name on every paper, so you have to learn how to do it correctly. We'll go in alphabetical order, so you all can learn your alphabet. Let me see, where's my list? Oh yes, you first Suzy. Suzy Atken. Up to the board, Dearie. There you go. Now, hold the chalk in your right hand, look up and I'll point out the letters while you copy. Watch carefully, boys and girls, so you know what to do when it's your turn. Here we go. Capital S... small U..."

With her hands clasped in front of her, Jocelyne's arms began to ache. Stealthily, like she would in church, she moved her hands down to her lap and started to rearrange the frill on her dress, pouting at the tear in the lace. Bending slightly to look beneath the wooden tabletop of her desk, she could glimpse her black and white shoes which she swung back and forth. They didn't touch the floor because the desk was too big for her. Her feet were tingling but it helped to bang them against the inside panel of the desk drawer.

"Joseyleene Ger-**ard**. Stop that noise, right now. Sit up and sit still, like you were told," The teacher's tone had changed from sweetness to venomous in an instant. The rest of the class sat straighter in their seats, until the teacher's back was turned again to face the board. Then several students turned and pointed at her, silently laughing. The broad back in front of her turned around and the girl shook her curls, put her thumbs in her ears, wiggled her fingers and stuck her tongue out. A burst of laughter from the class brought the teacher's stick down on her desk with a crack.

"Class, that's enough. I won't tolerate any nonsense. The next child who disrupts this class will find herself in the corner with the dunce cap on her head, do you hear?" She pointed her stick toward the stool in the corner, then directed her icy stare right at Jocelyne, who ducked to hide behind the girl in front of her.

"Now, where were we? Oh yes, Richard Brown. I know your daddy, he's the garbage man in town, is he not? Right, well, let's make it easier and call you Ricky, shall we? Now come along, R. Straight line, a loooop and then add a little stick. No, that's backwards. Try again. This way."

"Please get it right this time," thought Jocelyne. She longed to go up and help him, but didn't dare ask. The teacher took his hand, covered it with her own, and wrote the R the correct way.

"Come on, no that's the wrong way, again. Can't you see, it's this way, toward me. Well, you can stay in and practice over recess. Next." Jocelyne realized all of a sudden that she hadn't been breathing the whole time Ricky was up at the board. She took in a huge gulp of air, as Ricky returned to his desk and buried his red face in his arms.

The sun climbed higher in the sky and Jocelyne watched the clouds drift past the windows, far away from the school. Golden poplar trees lining the playground trembled in the slight breeze outside. Chalk dust swirled in shafts of light caught in the half open blinds at the top. The smell of the wooden desks and bookcases was comforting, familiar like Grandmaman's house. So many books waited on the shelves! What stories would they tell? When would they get to read? The teacher's voice droned on and on, becoming a sing-song. Jocelyne's mind wandered to the field, where Blackie would be happily munching the long, waving grass. Did somebody remember to give her a sugar lump once in a while, now that Chantale was gone?

"Joseyleene. Are we ready now, Missy, if you've finished your dream? Come on, hop to it, we haven't got all morning. Land sakes, we still have so much work to do!"

Finally. Now she would show the teacher how smart she was. She took the chalk and as the teacher started to slowly pronounce "J" quickly printed her entire name: JOCELYNE MARIE GERARD.

"I could print my name since I was five," she announced proudly, putting the chalk back on the wooden rail and dusting her yellowed fingers. Head held high, she turned to walk back to her seat.

"Good for you. Yes, you know all your upper case letters. But that's not how we write our name, Dearie. We need to start each name with a capital and then all the rest of the letters are lower case. Come back to the board, let's erase that and start again. See, capital J, then small "o." Such a long name for such a little girl. I still think we should call you Josie, but...now what comes next? Let me check my list again. Yes, a 'c.' No, that's too big, erase it and start again..."

Suddenly, a bell rang and Jocelyne jumped, dropping the chalk on the wooden floor where it shattered in pieces. She bent down to gather it up, her ears and cheeks aflame. She heard a few suppressed giggles.

"Recess time, already? Now, now, children, remain in your seats until I dismiss you, row by row. When you show me you are quiet and ready, you may go. Which row will be first? Ah, just leave the bits there on the chalk rail, Joseyleene, and return to your seat. Ricky, remember you stay in with me at recess time. Already have some catching up to do, I see. Ah well, it runs in the family. I remember your brother, Harry, just the same..."

"C'mon, c'mon, last one to the swings is a rotten egg," squealed

Crystal, the chubby girl who sat in front of Jocelyne, whose name had been a long and painful lesson on the board—she had kept getting the "y" and the "s" backwards. But she had finally succeeded and so didn't have to stay in with Ricky at recess time. She grabbed Jocelyne by the hand and pulled her out of the cloakroom and down the stairs to the playground.

"Bet you can't even run in those dumb shoes. Hurry up or all the swings will be gone."

A swing? Crystal yanked the chain holding the swing and tumbled a smaller girl off into the dirt, swung up, plumped her round bottom on the wooden seat and said, "C'mon, Josie, give us a push."

Obediently, Jocelyne stood behind and gently pushed her wide backside, which was as high up as she could reach when the swing approached her. Crystal's light pink skirt flounced up in her face, as the swing cut through the air, but she simply straightened out her bare legs even further, as if her toes could tickle the belly of a cloud in the blue depths, if she just stretched out far enough.

"No, harder, harder! Hurry up or I won't get high enough for an under-duck before the bell goes."

"Under-duck?"

"You'll see. See how I pump with my legs, in, out, in, out. Really high! Now watch, I'm gonna stand up. Wheee! Now you grab underneath when I swing back, hang on tight, then run underneath me, see? Under-duck! Ready, set... no you missed, stupid, c'mon. Watch out. Now here I come back again. Ready... go!

"Ah, you fell, too bad. See, I tol' you ya couldn't run in those clunky shoes. C'mon back an' catch me an' slow me down, so you can have a turn."

"I see London, I see France. I see someone's underpants!"

"Ah, shut up, Jimmy, an' go to hell. Whad'da YOU know anyway? What colour are they then, if you're so smart?"

"They're pink, so there. And I know another smartypants who's not so smart. Right, Josseyleeene?"

"Ha, ha, goes to show what you know! They're white! You leave us alone, ya little ass-wipe, or my big brother will beat the snot outta you, ya hear?" she taunted.

"Look out below, parachute jump!" Crystal yelled, let go of the chains and threw herself into midair, landing on both feet in the grass, well ahead of the wooden swing's return arc. Jocelyne stood open-mouthed at her daring and skill.

"Dammit, there's the bell. Hurry up or we'll be late in the line and then there'll be hell to pay from fatty fatty two by four, couldn't get through the kitchen door," she yelled, laughing as she ran away from Jocelyne, who was trying to catch the wildly twisting swing, so she could have a turn.

After they had been rearranged into their original order once again and all trooped in, the teacher announced it was time to have their picture taken. She had never had a "pitcher takin'," but remembered the faces in the photographs her grandmother had shown her, and grimaced. It was obviously serious business, because the teacher was even more strict, demanding absolute quiet. This time, they had to line up in order of size. Jocelyne was first, Ricky Brown was last. The teacher lead them down a hallway where they stood against a wall and waited. Jocelyne leaned out to look back and find Crystal, who again stuck her tongue out at her from near the back of the line. Jocelyne returned the favour with a grin. The teacher turned and jabbed a bony finger into Jocelyne's shoulder, directing her back against the wall. The class stood silently, fidgeting and shuffling their feet.

Suddenly, a door flew open and a tall man in a black suit came out of a small room. Behind him, Jocelyne could see a strange object on three long, metal legs supporting a small box covered in a black cloth. The child swallowed hard in fear.

"Will it hurt?" she wondered, thinking of the frozen expressions on the faces in the old black and white photographs she had seen. She didn't dare ask.

"So, you're first then, little lady? What a pretty yellow dress! I'll bet that's your Sunday best, special for the first day of school. How nice. Well, c'mon in, sit right up here on this high stool. Whoops, here, let me lift you up. Ahh, you've torn the lace a little bit and your knees look a little scuffed up there, honey. Here, let's wipe your face and hands with a damp towel. Now, put your hands in your lap, sit up very straight... that's it, head up... lovely. I'll go over here under the cloth and take the picture."

His hand held a small round object to the side, as his muffled voice came from under the cloth, "Now, watch the birdie. Smile. Come on, let's see those pearly whites."

Jocelyne couldn't see any bird, in fact, she couldn't see anything with the light that flashed in her eyes, leaving purple spots appearing instantly everywhere. She squinted to make it stop, and when she opened her eyes, noticed that another man, much older, was standing beside the stool. He lifted her off and stooped down to look at her face.

"And who do we have here?" he asked the photographer. The man reached over to the counter for a paper, skimmed along with his finger until he found Jocelyne's name.

"Ahh, you're the young Gerard girl, are you not?" he enquired gently.

"A serious little thing she is, too. She'll look like quite the young lady in this photograph, I'll warrant."

"Well, my dear, I know your grandma very well, and I knew your grandpa, too. All the Gerards, in fact. Hard to believe, the next generation, starting school... Are you having a good day, your first time at school?"

"Yes," she managed a whispered reply.

"You are to say, 'Yes, sir,' next time, all right. That's how you talk to the Principal. I am Mr. Fredrick. Well, this is an important day for you. You will never forget it. I hope you like school?" He waited.

"Yes, Sir Fredrick."

He laughed heartily and said, "Well her Majesty hasn't given me a knighthood yet, but she might have had I remained in Jolly Old England! Instead, I came to this part of the world, and gave up my chance at the peerage forever!" He patted her head and her face flushed to her ears.

"No. 'Yes, sir' or 'Yes, Mr. Fredrick.' Try again. That's better. Now work hard and you will do well. Isn't that so, Mrs. Hoffentrauder?"

"Yes, sir, they have all worked very hard on their lessons this morning."

"Good, jolly good. Well, come along, Miss Gérard, and stand at the back of the line while all your comrades get their pictures taken. Such a nice memento, a photograph of your first day at school. Land sakes', never heard of such a thing in our day, did we, Mrs. Hoffentrauder? Lucky little blighters nowadays is all I can say."

*****

"So, Honey, how was school today? Wasn't it wonderful to start school? What a big girl you are getting to be! I sure missed you around here to help out with Pauline. She was lonesome today without you, too. Tell us all about it. What did you do?"

"Nothing much. I'm soooo hungry. I thought it was never going to be home time and I almost fell asleep on the bus and then I woke up I was sooo scared I'd missed our place. That was close! Mama, teacher says I can't print with you anymore 'cause you don't teach me right. Something about capitals and cases... I don't get it. But those other dumb kids didn't even know how to spell their names. They're a buncha dummies. Wait 'til the teacher finds out I can read. They can't even read their own names! An' guess what else? I made a new friend and her name is Crystal, isn't that a pretty name, and she taught me about doing 'duck-unders' and parachute jumps, have you ever seen them before? It's sooo fun. But I tore my dress just a little bit and it's kinda hard to run in my saddle shoes, but I don't care, I love those saddle shoes, 'specially 'cause I can click on the sidewalk and no one else can do that in their dirty ol' runners. Can I have a peanut butter and jelly samidge and go out to play on the scooter? I'll change into my play clothes first, I promise. Do you think you can fix my dress, so I can wear it next time we go to church?"

*****

The photograph, printed in black and white, arrived in two weeks. If she squinted, Jocelyne could imagine the yellow lace and the little pink roses at the neck. She was proud of her picture and the little identification card that came with it, officially recognizing her as a Grade One student of the county school. With Mr. Sir Fredrick's very own signature! What would she need the card for? The teacher hadn't said, but best keep it in her pencil box, just to be on the safe side.

Suzanna scowled at the photograph. She thought that her daughter's face looked pinched and wan.

"How come you're not smiling, Honey? You'd think you'd have a grin a mile wide on your first day of school! Didn't the photographer say 'Cheese' or something, to get you to smile?" Suzanna asked, as she cut out individual pictures to send to relatives far away.

"Grandmère said you're not s'post to smile in pitchers. You're s'post to look serious and not show your teeth. Did I do it good?"

"Ohhh, that woman!"

Chapter Twenty-one

Chantale melted into her sister's arms. They stood in the bus terminal, holding each other, for a long time, neither saying a word. Danielle petted her sister's hair and murmured, "Ssh, ssh, it's okay, 'sokay, 'sokay," just as she had when Chantale was little. Chantale let her tears flow freely, until she had no more strength to cry, though her body continued shuddering with cold and fatigue. She flopped down on a bench, wiped her eyes on the sleeve of her coat and blew her nose into the tissue her sister offered her. Then she rummaged in her purse for her cigarettes. Finding two left in the pack, she offered one to Danielle. They smoked in silence. The cigarettes were half finished before Danielle spoke.

"God, it's good to see you. It feels strange, seeing someone from home again. It's been so long... How's Ma? Does she ever mention me? The same, yeah. Always the farm, the farm, the farm. It's all she thinks about, all she knows, I guess. But Christ, it's almost 1963! We all need to have a life. Not stuck on that crappy old pig farm... God, her and Dad moved to the other end of the country when they were young! Jesus H. Christ, she will die there and she wants us all to do the same! Not me though, I'm never going back! And Richard—he still there? Creepy little bastard..." She clucked her tongue as she flicked ash off her cigarette with her long fingernail.

"I don't blame you for leaving, not one little bit. It's what I did. I finally got fed up with being Mother's workhorse. Nothing but work, work, and more work! It never ended! And what thanks did I get? Just, 'Do this, and don't forget to do that, and have you done that yet?' So I packed it in! Didn't have a goddamn clue what I was doing, but I headed out here on a wing and a prayer. Wanted to see the coast, live by the seashore. I thought it would be so great to live by the ocean, maybe get to sail in a boat even. Hmmpf. Not much like I imagined, Vancouver." She rolled her eyes, flicked more ash onto the bus terminal floor and coughed into her closed fist.

"Well, I figured you'd need to leave, too, once you grew up. You're younger than I was though, so it makes it tougher, to my mind. I'm glad I can help you, but there's a bit of a problem. See, the guy I live with, Damian, he won't want you there for too long. It's a bit... awkward." She paused and flipped back her long, black hair, took another long drag on her cigarette, then blew the smoke out through her nose.

"There's not much room, but I definitely want to help you out and make sure you're safe. God, you have no idea. You're gonna have to stay on the couch in the living room—we only have one bedroom. It's a really small place. We live near Chinatown. They call it Skid Road, 'cause of all the bums 'on the skids' as they say, but they're pretty harmless and it ain't so bad once you get used to it. Nobody gives me any trouble, anyway, with Damian around. We'll have to find either a basement suite or an apartment with a roommate for you near us, as soon as we can. You won't be able to afford your own place. It costs way too much. Everybody lives with somebody around here, but don't let Ma know! Maman definitely would not approve, and as for the priest!"

Both girls burst out laughing. Chantale impulsively grabbed for her sister's hand. Corded blue veins were visible through the pale white skin. She turned toward Danielle and studied her face for the first time. Lank, stringy hair hanging to her shoulders, dark circles underlining bloodshot brown eyes, high cheekbones jutting out even further as she sucked in the smoke: she looked so much older than her thirty-eight years.

"Wow, she looks so old! So tired and dragged out. Look at her old, baggy clothes. And she's so thin. That's not how I remember Danielle at all! She used to have such beautiful black hair...I wouldn't have known her if she'd passed me in the street at home. Maybe Carol was right, Vancouver is pretty tough," Chantale thought.

Aloud, her voice sounded self-assured. "I don't care. It doesn't matter to me where I stay, as long as I'm not on that goddamn farm or in that one-horse town. I hate it there. I need to get a job right away,

I know. My money is running out. Is there any work at the restaurant you're at? I'll do anything, bus tables, wash dishes, I don't mind. I'll pay my way with you guys, don't worry. I have a little money, but I need to get working."

"Oh yeah, sure, there's lots of low paying jobs, but like I said, it costs a lot to live here. You'll probably have to work two jobs like me, just to get by. The best thing would be to get a job in some small office, answering phones or something. Then you can do that during the day and waitress at night. Save enough money to get a decent place. But let's not talk about that right now. Let's just get you settled in and let the future worry about itself for a while, eh? C'mon, let's go."

They waited outside the bus terminal for the city bus and got off downtown. Danielle kept a brisk pace as they passed barred shop windows and alleyways where figures huddled in the dark.

"C'mon, you have to keep up and look like you know where you are going. This ain't a place to hang around and look like a tourist," she whispered hoarsely and pulled Chantale along beside her. They kept crossing streets to avoid shifty-eyed men leaning against brick buildings. A misty rain started to fall, scenting the air with the smell of wet garbage. Chantale shivered and her teeth chattered audibly.

"Yeah, I can see we're going to need to get you a raincoat. There's no way you can walk around here like that. Unlike at home, here it rains all the time, and it soaks you to the skin. You'll need an umbrella of your own to carry with you. Mine's at home, I forget it half the time. You already look like a drowned rat. You'll soon catch your death in a coat like that. Come on, quick, we'll hop the bus and get you home."

As they ran for the bus shelter, the smell of the pig barn came back to Chantale, and she wanted to retch. A small creature scurried just in front of them as they rounded a dark corner—a cat? Chantale didn't think so. She shuddered, chilled and afraid. The bus was overheated and the stark light brought tears to Chantale's eyes. After careening around corners and jerking to a stop countless times, the bus dropped them off in front of an old building that looked like it had housed offices in the distant past. They climbed a narrow staircase to a landing, proceeded down a dark hallway, past doors with numbers on them, to the last door.

"We have the biggest place, because ours faces the street. It's pretty good—it's got its' own bathroom with a shower, and we have a fridge and stove. So we're pretty lucky. I'll get a key made for you. You have to be careful in this hallway—make sure you're alone when you open the door—otherwise somebody might try to follow you in. If somebody's behind me and I'm by myself, I just keep walking in the hallway until they leave or go inside. The downstairs door is open to the street, so all kinds of crazies try to get in here. We're lucky too because there's a place to do laundry in a room down the hall, but I never go there without Damian. There's always somebody in there tryin' to find a warm place to sleep. Usually harmless, but you never know. Anyway, here's home sweet home!"

Danielle unlocked the door and it opened to a burst of sound and light. Bare bulbs hung from the ceiling, illuminating the kitchen and living room in one open area. A small television set, sporting a broken portable antennae, blared in a corner. A tattered armchair was filled to overflowing with a slumped figure, a beer bottle balanced on a protruding stomach. Danielle called cheerily, "We're here! Chantale, this is Damian."

"Yeah, yeah. Hi. Quiet. I'm watchin' the game." He didn't turn around.

Danielle shrugged her shoulders toward Chantale and motioned for her to drop her duffle bag and sit at the table against the opposite wall. She opened the small refrigerator and pulled out a loaf of white bread, a jar of processed cheese and a round package of bologna. Chantale glanced in and saw that there wasn't much else in the small 'fridge, except about one dozen beer bottles on the lower shelf. Danielle took two, popped them open with an opener sitting on the dish-covered counter, and passed one to Chantale. She made three sandwiches and placed one on the arm of Damian's chair.

The two sisters ate their sandwiches in silence, sipping beer and smoking when they were finished, until the roar of the game was over and the announcer was giving the final score. Damian got up, switched off the television, and sauntered toward the table. He stood behind Chantale, leaned over, deliberately brushing his belly across her head, and kissed Danielle full on the mouth. Then he stepped back, put both hands on Chantale's shoulders and squeezed.

"So, you're the little sister, eh? Nice to meet ya', Sis. Welcome to our humble abode. Not much, but what are you gonna' do? Stay as long as ya like. Here, have another beer. Don't worry, it's on the house!"

Danielle shot him an angry glare, narrowing her dark brown eyes and tossing her greasy hair off her shoulder.

"Hey, what'd I say to get that look? That's what I meant by it... have a beer, put your feet up. God, what do you think? I'd turn away family, for Chris' sake?" He popped open another beer and handed it to Chantale, then placed two more on the table and pulled up a chair beside her.

"So, Sis, tell me about yourself. Chantale, right? That's a weird name. I call your sister Dee Dee, so I'll call you Sissy, eh? That's better. Now, what're your plans? What do you hope to find in this great city of Vancouver?"

"Well, I... I just want to get some work first and get my own place and then I'm going to save money to go back to school. Secretarial school, I was thinking, that'd be the most practical so I'd have a good paying job," she stammered.

"Sounds like a plan to me. But just where are you going to get the dough to go to school? Schoolin' is expensive, you know," he said scornfully, running his fingers through his thick, black hair.

"I've got a little money to get me started. I don't expect you guys to look after me. Just a place to stay until I can find my own apartment."

"Oh sure, sure, we'll help you as much as we can, won't we, Damian? What's family for? My only little sister, the baby of the family," said Danielle anxiously, her voice high and breathy, almost unrecognizable to Chantale.

"C'mon, honey, why don't you take a shower and get ready for bed? You're probably beat. That overnight bus trip is hell, I know. You shower, while I get some blankets to set you up on the couch. Have you got a nightgown? Take it into the bathroom with you, 'cause that's the only place for you to change. Here's a towel." She handed over a thin towel and steered Chantale into the small bathroom, following her inside.

When she had closed the door, Danielle whispered, "Just ignore him, okay. He can be a real pain in the ass. He's down on his luck and hasn't had a job in six months. He doesn't much like depending on me and money's tight right now." Danielle nonchalantly pulled down her pants and used the toilet while continuing to talk.

"That's what's pissing him off. He's getting money from somewhere, too. I'm not sure how and I don't even ask. There's always plenty of beer around here, though, and I'm not the one buying it, so he must be getting some cash somehow. Just humour him and stay out of his way, okay?" Danielle warned as she left, shutting the door behind her.

Chantale flushed the toilet and stood looking at the dirty seat for a moment, then took paper and covered it, as she would in a public washroom, before relieving herself. The room smelled of mould and urine. The sink and mirror were stained with rust, and the cement floor of the shower was slippery with soap residue. Chantale curled her toes tightly but stood under the hot water for a long time, letting it soothe her, until she thought she heard a banging at the door. Quickly, she turned the metal shower taps off, her heart pounding.

"Hey, I'm payin' for that water, you know! Don't be in there all night!"

Her hands shaking, Chantale rubbed herself dry as best she could with the small, rough towel and pulled her flannel nightgown over her head. With effort, she yanked her jeans up her damp legs, underneath her nightgown, feeling uncomfortable about crossing the room in the glare of the lights. She had no robe to cover herself. She wrapped her wet hair in the towel and emerged from the bathroom in her bare feet, then slipped across the room, stooped over to seem as small as possible. The living room area was in shadow, with the one floor lamp shut off. She slid under the blanket Danielle had spread over the couch and curled into a ball, burying her face in the pillow.

She didn't make another sound, but waited until the couple

232

finally left the kitchen after they had finished two more beers each, and smoked several cigarettes, arguing the whole time in subdued but vicious tones. Chantale kept her head covered and tried not to hear what they were saying, though she figured it was about her. Damian had been none too welcoming. Under the blanket, her face burned with shame. At last, Danielle called softly, "Bonne nuit, chérie," as their mother used to do, and closed the door in an adjacent room. Chantale pretended to be asleep. She was so exhausted, she forgot to pull down her jeans and toss them on top of her canvas duffle bag sitting by the lamp, as she had intended to do once Damian was out of the room.

Before long, there came the sound of mattress springs squeaking rhythmically. Chantale let the tears flow freely then, suppressing her sobs into her pillow. Her mother's face appeared before her closed eyes and her chest tightened with remorse. "I just wish you knew the truth, Maman. But you would never listen anyway, so what else could I do but leave? I couldn't take it anymore. But this..." she spoke to her mother, silently. She saw Jocelyne's tiny, pinched face swirling upside down and her head being plunged in the pig trough. Richard's taunting voice resounded in her ears. She shuddered, huddled deeper into the blanket and tried to sweep her mind clean by rocking her body back and forth, back and forth. Despite herself, from old habit, she crossed herself, said a prayer, and started to recite the rosary she knew so well. She drifted into a restless sleep, tossing and turning on the lumpy couch.

Awakened by a noise, Chantale resisted the urge to sit up. She lay perfectly still, barely breathing, her face turned toward the back of the couch, listening. Someone was rustling around at the foot of the couch, by the floor lamp. She heard the zipper on the duffel bag being carefully opened, the scratch of nails on the canvas as things were rearranged inside. Then the zip being slowly drawn closed. The click of the clasp on her purse. Soft clatter of things moving inside the hard shell—lipstick hitting against a compact? Compartments inside the purse zipped quietly opened, closed. Bag placed back down on the floor. Finally, heavy footsteps headed toward the bathroom. Door clicked closed in the dark. A clank as the hard toilet seat hit the porcelain tank. A curse. A fountain of water hitting the water in the bowl. No flush. Then feet stumbling out of the bathroom door. A bump against the coffee table next to the couch. A mumbled, "Goddamit." Another click of a door being softly closed.

Chantale let her held breath out slowly. She pressed her icy hand over her nightgown, against the front pocket of her jeans underneath, where her money was folded in neat bills, organized in five, tens and twenties. She had carried her cash separately during the three day bus ride, in case her purse was stolen. Thank God she had thought of that. Thank God her money was still safe. It was all she had left.

*****

"Not much experience, eh, Honey? Well, youse could start by bussing tables and helping the waiters, and then we'll see... get started slowly. Do a good job and the waiters will share their tips. Youse'll get minimum wage and one meal per eight hour shift. Youse can eat anything on the menu, 'ceptn steak. One coffee break per shift. Uniforms supplied. Always come to work clean and pressed, hair pinned back. How's that sound?" The older woman blew smoke out of her nostrils and tapped her lipstick- stained cigarette against the ashtray with a long, painted fingernail. Her voice was gravelly, from years of smoking and yelling orders at cooks, Chantale imagined.

"Oh, and no smokin' or eatin' out front. Staff have a table in the back. That's the office, see there, through those glass doors, and Mr. Wong works in there. You never need to go in there, for any reason. Any problems you have, come straight to me, hear? Can you start right away?"

Chantale nodded, relieved to have a position at last, after days of walking the streets, being turned down in every office and store, finally resorting to restaurants, and finding no success until now, in this Chinese restaurant at the entrance to Chinatown. Chantale later learned that with a large clientele of non-Asian businessmen during the day, the boss liked to hire some Caucasian workers, though in the evening the waiters were exclusively male and Chinese, brought in directly from Hong Kong by Mr. Wong himself.

"Good. Lucky for me you showed up! I got a big wedding banquet comin' in tonight and one of the girls just called in sick, as usual. She's on the verge of getting' fired, that one. Probably couldn't get a sitter for her kid again. Oh well, her loss is your gain, eh?" Her sideways grin turned into a chuckle, then a cough. Stubbing out her cigarette, she shoved herself up from the table and motioned to Chantale to follow her.

Chantale would soon learn that Louise, "the old dragon" as everyone called her behind her back, was the unofficial boss of the restaurant, the only white person on staff the owner ever spoke to directly. As head waitress, her domain was the front of the restaurant and every decision, from scheduling staff, ordering supplies, booking weddings and Christmas banquets and hiring and firing the non-Chinese staff was hers alone to make. Everything went through Louise. She acted as Mr. Wong's eyes and ears on the staff, a trusted employee since his father had opened the restaurant twenty years before, working her way up from busgirl to head waitress. None of the other staff dared speak to him as she did, or at all. She was especially hard on the female waitresses, who worked during the day. She went home at five o'clock, unless there was a banquet to prepare, so the male waiters were left to the night manager, the owner's cousin, to oversee.

The "boys," whom the owner had sponsored to gain their landed immigrant status in Canada, rarely interacted with Mr. Wong himself. He housed them in rooms above the restaurant. They worked the afternoon and night shifts, and attended school during the day. They owed the boss their opportunity to learn English and the possibility of earning a place to stay in Canada. In turn, they showed him the deepest respect. If they ever had anything to say to him they always spoke barely above a whisper in Chinese, keeping their eyes lowered and bowing deferentially. Chantale later observed this mannerism and found it strange, as if the boys feared the owner might strike them, though he seemed like a quiet man.

As she strode past into the staff service area behind Louise, Chantale felt three sets of dark eyes following her. One young man smoothed his black vest, another straightened his tie, the other ran his hand over his glossy black hair. They all stared right at her until she dropped her gaze to Louise's backside. Chantale was to learn from their critical remarks and their ways of finding every excuse to avoid sharing their tips, how they lorded their status over the other staff, especially the lowly busboys and girls. Among themselves, they laughed and chided and joked, constantly poking and elbowing each other as they moved swiftly up and down the aisles, taking and delivering orders, never missing a beat, rarely making a mistake, always finding someone else to blame if anything went amiss.

Feeling uncomfortable and insecure, even without the blazing eyes on her back, Chantale could only hope she would be up to the job. She had never been a waitress and certainly never been in a Chinese restaurant in her life. Her only experience with eating out was having a milkshake and a doughnut at the Kresge's lunch counter. Families back home never dined out and, in any case, her mother would die before eating in the one Chinese restaurant in town.

"What, no meat, potato, gravy? You call dat food for civilize peoples?" Chantale smiled, thinking what her mother would think of a daughter of hers working for a "Chinaman!" Mon Doux! For herself, she was just happy to know that she would finally be able to earn some money; she didn't care if her boss was purple with green hair, as long as he paid her. She couldn't stand any more of Damian's snide comments about her "sponging" off them. As if he had anything to complain about, since he never seemed to contribute to the household anyway. She wanted to quickly earn enough money to get away from him. Such a creep and totally untrustworthy... almost as bad as Richard! Shuddering, she hurried to keep up with Louise's brisk pace, through the kitchen and down a long set of stairs, into the basement under the restaurant.

"You cold, Honey? I know, it's cold and damp and stinky down here, but it's all we's got for a changing room. Don't be surprised if you see a rat or a mouse every now and then and don't scream your gall darn head off, neither! It upsets the customers to hear screaming coming from the basement. Just tell the head cook, Tom, and he'll set another trap. Here we are, Shangri-La!"

A corridor created by boxes of food led to a small room with a rod along one wall holding a series of uniforms, all the same colour, a putrid yellow. The room also had a filthy toilet with no lid or seat and a sink clogged with stands of long black hair. On the wall above it hung a chipped, smoky mirror. There was no door, just a curtain hanging across the opening.

"This is the staff washroom. Youse can change down here before every shift if you want or you can come in your uniform. Some of the girls just refuse to ride the bus dressed in their uniform, so they change down here. Youse'll see why soon enough, when you lay your clappers on our beautiful outfits. Just make sure old Tom isn't down here, makin' a pretence to set traps, hoping to catch a glimpse... Hmm. Joanne's old uniforms should fit you. She was a big girl too. What a laugh that gal had! Kinda miss her, every once in a while. Went back to Saskatchewan purty damn quick though. Missed her Mama's cookin', don't ya know," she cackled, then choked on her own laughter. She drew a handkerchief from her uniform pocket, spat into it, wiped her nose, and carried on talking, yanking a short dress from a rack above the toilet, sending the metal hanger clattering to the cement floor.

"Here, try this on, Darlin'. Grab a black apron from that big box under the sink. Now a little blank hanky from that box on the shelf to tuck above your left boob and that makes the outfit complete. Georgeous George, huh? The designer doing the renovation picked this god-awful colour to go with the leather upholstery on the chairs. What a genius! Red flocked wallpaper, totally impractical, black lacquer on the booth frames that shows every fingerprint, and pukey-looking furniture, with uniforms to match! Colour reminds me of baby shit! I could'a done a better job with my eyes closed! I liked what we had before, didn't see nothin' wrong with it, but this is s'posed to be more modern, bring in more customers. Hah! But what do I know? Mr. Wong wants it and what Mr. Wong wants, he gets. Youse'll learn that quick enough. If this one don't fit, pick another size. There's plenty here, nobody is exactly stealin' one to wear to the prom! Come back down later and get another dress to take home, so's youse'll always have a clean uniform. Mr. Wong insists on that!" she declared, patting the side of her bouffant orange hairdo. She glanced down at Chantale's feet and clicked her tongue.

"And get some decent shoes, for Cripe's sakes. I can advance you on your paycheque, so's you can get some work shoes. Nurse's shoes are what I always wear. Cost the earth, but they're worth it to save the old dogs. Youse'll be walkin' many miles, now I tell ya. Get ready and hop it upstairs on the double, Honey. There's lots to prep. We wouldn't want to disappoint the lovely bride on her weddin' day, now would we?"

Louise turned around, leaned into the mirror, and picked up a tube of lipstick from the battered shelf. Squinting into the spotty glass, she drew a bright red line on her mouth, then used it as rouge, dotting her cheeks and smearing the colour across her papery skin. Her eyebrows were outlined in dark brown pencil and she licked a finger and smeared it over each one, turning her head from side to side like a bird. A greasy brush collected more of her fine, dyed hair as she fussed with the few curls on her forehead. Chantale guessed that it was probably white, but the red dye had turned it the most wonderful shade of orange she had ever seen. In the mirror, Louise noticed the girl staring at her and that she still wasn't changed.

"C'mon, Darlin'. We don't stand on ceremony 'round here. You ain't got nothin' I never seen before. Leave your clothes hangin' here, but bring your purse upstairs and I'll lock it in the office. C'mon, time's a wastin'," she said with her mouth open, face almost against the glass, checking her teeth and wiping them clean with the same hanky she had used from her pocket to blow her nose. At last she left the bathroom, calling over her shoulder, "See youse upstairs then, shy Suzie!"

The uniform was too tight, the buttons straining across the bust and the back of the dress pulling up across the rear end.

"Oh well, no one will notice me anyhow," Chantale murmured to herself, tying her apron in a lopsided bow behind her back and poking a black swatch of cloth into the breast pocket. She followed the snaking corridor lined with huge cartons, back to the lit stairwell. Just at the bottom of the stairs, her eyes focused on the small rectangle of light coming from the upper floor and she practically ran into a huge metal bucket. Someone was sitting behind it.

"Oh my God! Jeez, you scared me! Almost jumped out of my

skin! I didn't see you sitting there when I first came down. It's so dark down here! Hi. I'm new, my name's Chantale." The young Asian girl didn't answer her, just smiled at her slightly, then lowered her head and plunged her hands back into the large bucket. Chantale didn't stop to watch what she was doing, deciding she'd talk to her later. Anyway, maybe she couldn't speak English. Best get upstairs and get to work as quickly as possible now, she cautioned herself.

The hours from noon, when she had started, to the four o'clock coffee break, flew by. She listened and followed every one of Louise's instructions, spreading white tablecloths, setting the places with all the forks, knives, spoons in the right order (which impressed Louise: "Most gals we get in here don't know a salad fork from a shovel!") and wiping all the glassware to eliminate spots before placing it on the tables.

"You're a good little worker, Hon'. Keep it up and you'll make lots of money in tips." Louise lit up a cigarette as she collapsed into a chair at the head table. Chantale's were in her purse and she would have been too nervous to smoke in front of Louise anyway. She was just delighted to find she could have as much soda as she could drink in fifteen minutes and she gulped down two glasses of cola.

After the break, it was time to bring out the steaming trays of food and place them under heat lamps at the front tables. Chantale's stomach growled as she smelled all the exotic dishes, prepared in ways she hadn't known existed. Mixed vegetables, steamed and crunchy, still retaining their bright colours, bathed in a luminous sauce! Battered chicken breast fried and sliced with onions and almonds. Chicken balls—really? Won ton soup—square white things floating in a broth—what was a "won ton?" Battered shrimp kept warm under a heat lamp—just like the baby chicks at home! She had never even seen a shrimp, let alone eaten one. Heaping mounds of white rice! She had never tasted rice in her life. Chow mein with long, stringy things in it—what was that? The words, the aromas, the presentation, everything was new to her.

She felt faint with hunger and the excitement of the day. But it was far from over. There were three more hours until the end of her shift, when she could have her supper. The motivation of a hot meal at the end of her day, before returning to Danielle's to tell her the news of her success, kept her moving as fast as she could on her tired, swollen feet. Louise was right. She would definitely need better shoes. She'd reminded her of it just before she left her under the charge of the Joey, the head waiter for the evening shift.

"Hey, sleepy head. Get over here. You know how make a miyky shake? I need twee miyk shake, chocorate, vaniya, stlawbahwy, wight away. Den get me fouw sarad in de back, twee srice of pie an' den you cyear ta-boo six. Quick. Many customah waiting. What you name? You new, wwriiight? You *sure* you know how make a miyky shake?"

Chantale nodded and busied herself with the fiercesome looking milkshake machine. She found the ice cream, the flavourings above the freezer, and prepared three metal containers. She shoved each cup hard onto the beaters and turned on the machine from a switch she found on the side. The cups didn't move. The beaters ground in protest. The machine growled. Desperately, she looked up and saw Joey striding quickly down the aisle between the tables to the waiters' station, where they prepared coffee, tea and toast, refilled the soft drink and milk containers and self-served portions of pie, ice cream and condiments for the customers.

"Hey, whata mattah with de machine? Tun off, tun off quicky, quick. Moto on machine buln out! Look, you didna put in any miyk! Dat not miyky shake! Dat ice cweam shake! Why you tink'a dey call it miyky shake? You pletty stupid, huh? I finish dis mysef, if you can't even make a miyky shake. Get pie an' salad, put on countah and den quicky up an' clear ta-boo six. Move. Fastah, fastah, many customah waiting."

Chantale's head whirled for the next three hours, being told every minute to do some other task, double-time. She was stunned by the waiters' speed as they took orders, never writing down a single word, remembering every order perfectly, and making the whole process look effortless. She, on the other hand, kept going in the wrong swinging door with the tubs of dirty dishes, dropping dishes as she cleared the tables, and shaking so much water out of the glasses as she walked to the tables with her tray that there was barely a sip left by the time she got there. Joey kept watching her, shaking his head, folding his arms across his chest and rolling his eyes heavenward. At eight o'clock, her shift was finally over. She threw herself in a chair at the back of the restaurant with relief, almost too tired to eat. But there was Joey, standing next to the small table, to her surprise, taking her order for supper!

"What you wanna eat? Anything fwom menu except steak."

She studied the menu. "Moo goo guy choo; Egg foo yung; Moo goo guy pan..." She ordered the roast beef special, with mashed potatoes and gravy. Her first real meal in two months. It reminded her of home. Joey took his coffee break and sat with her after he brought out her supper. He watched her eat for a moment, before asking, "You come back tomowow? Pletty hald wowk, huh? You make a too many mistake to get tip today, but maybe next time you wowk faw me, you do much a bedder. I tink you understan' soon. No mow ice cweam shake, no mow bwowken dish, okay? You rucky, boss don' charge us each bwowken dish, rikey do most place Chinatow. Odderwise, you owe him money faw wowk today! Ha, ha! I make a funny joke! You taka menru home an weawn it, by heawt. Customah arways aks us whatta mean, even it plinted wight in flont o dey eyes. But my Engrish not so good yet. You come back tomowow, wighty Missy?"

Chantale finished her supper, then stepped as lightly as she could on her swollen feet back through the kitchen and down the stairs. She glanced to see if the young girl was still sitting by the white bucket. Curious as she was to see what the child was doing there, Chantale knew she was too exhausted to stop and chat. The girl was gone, but had left behind another bucket piled to the top with shrimp shells. The smell was like rancid cat food and Chantale hurried away to avoid throwing up her hard-won supper. She yanked another uniform down from the rod, folded it under her arm, and leaned over the sink to splash water on her face, staring at her blue eyes reflected crazily in the cloudy mirror. Digging her purse from behind the uniforms where she had hidden it for safekeeping, she took out a lipstick and tried to make sense of her mouth in the jigsawed reflection.

"Of cawse she come back, Joey," she said aloud, puckering her lips while parroting his accent. He had turned out to be kind of nice to her, in the end. Anyway, "What choice did she have?" From the darkened corridor beyond came the snap of a metal trap. She shuddered, pulled her coat down from its hanger among the uniforms on the rack, and picked her way back through the maze leading to the kitchen stairwell.

She took the stairs two at a time to escape the basement as quickly as possible. Her heart was pounding by the time she reached the landing. She paused to catch her breath, before heading back through the gauntlet of the kitchen. She had been told staff weren't allowed to enter or leave through the main entrance, so she had no option but to squeeze past Tom, the cook with the enormous belly, leaning against the counter near the door. The Chinese cooks hooted at her and Tom slapped her bottom on the way by with a "Nice rump roast there, Girlie." When she had made a comment earlier that day to Patty, one of the other non-Asian waitresses, about the cooks' crude manners and rude remarks she'd already endured, she had been warned to stay in their good graces.

"They're harmless. They just like to tease. It's the only fun they have back there sweating in that hellhole! Don't piss them off or you'll be in real trouble when you start waiting tables. They'll make your life miserable if they don't like you. And remember, it's the cooks that make your tips for you, and they know it. So mind your ps and qs and stay out of arm's reach."

So, trying to ignore her smarting behind and hiding her red face with her hair, she shrugged and said, "See ya," as she pushed open the screen door. Laughter erupted behind her, following her into the dark alley and out to the street, where she wearily made her way to the bus stop.

As the bus rumbled down the streets, all that played in her tired mind, over and over, was the rhyme Suzanna used to chant to her little ones, "To market, to market to buy a fat pig, home again, home again, jiggity-jig. To market, to market to buy a fat hog, home again, home again, jiggety-jog." Home.

Chapter Twenty-two

How she longed for her own space! So she could say goodbye and good riddance to Damian's leering stares and snide remarks.

"Hey, how come you don't have a boyfriend? Bet you're getting' lots of pats on the ass at the restaurant, eh?" Chantale would curl her lips in disgust at his insinuations, but Danielle would smile and agree with him.

"Yeah, you do look great, chérie, now that you have a job and are getting out more. This Vancouver lifestyle seems to agree with you!" Was she naïve or really that stupid?

He would offer to drive her home. "Aren't you a little scared to come home all that way, on the bus, by yourself? Want me to come by and pick you up?"

Then one day, the bathroom door wouldn't lock. Chantale was alone in the flat, so she decided to take a shower. Ahh, to stay in as long as she wanted, with the hot water on full blast and no one to tell her otherwise! Humming away, her ears blocked by foamy shampoo, she revelled in the water streaming over her head. Then, suddenly the water started making a different sound. She drew her body back out of the flow, rubbed the soap from her eyes, yanked the curtain aside and peeked out into the steamy room. Damian was standing at the toilet, relieving himself.

"Hey, this is perfect. Now with only one john, a man can take a piss and enjoy the view. That's why I decided to fix that ol' bathroom door."

"Do you mind? I'm ready to get out now."

"Naah, not at all. Just think of me like I was your brother."

"Get the hell out of here, Damian!" she screamed. "Or when Danielle comes home, I'm telling." Just like old times, she thought, trembling with fear.

"No you won't. You say one word against me and I'll kick you out on your ass, and your dear sister won't back you up, I guarantee it. What's wrong? It's the perfect solution to three people sharing one tiny bathroom and we're all family, right? What's the big deal?"

The result of this incident was no more showers unless Danielle was home and then just a quick splash and out, before anyone could complain, or walk in. She took on extra shifts at the restaurant, to stack away cash and avoid spending time in the apartment. $100, $200, $500...the bank account kept growing. Eating only at the restaurant to avoid being with Damian and constantly announcing, "It won't be long now. Almost ready to move out and leave you guys alone. Thanks again for all your help, but you know, gotta get out, make my own way in the world."

Danielle seemed more bitchy and tired than Chantale had imagined she would be. From a distance, she had admired her sister's bravery and independence, but now Chantale grew to pity her. It seemed she had merely traded one hell for another: slavery to her mother and the pig farm for slavery to Damian, the pig. Even at thirty-eight, her sister was still lovely, with her tall, slim body, long black hair and sparkling brown eyes. Surely, thought Chantale, she could attract someone better than an overweight, out of work bum, ten years her senior? He was already losing his hair, for God's sake! And those teeth and that disgusting goatee! How could she stand to kiss his ugly mouth, let alone...? Why did he have such a hold on her?

Obviously, Danielle, though fluently bilingual in French and English, hadn't learned how to say "no" in either language, Chantale mused, smirking without humour at her own joke. After more than ten years away from home, Danielle still lived from hand to mouth, working two jobs, answering phones in an office by day, hostessing by night in a nearby bar. Meanwhile, her "partner" sat in front of the television drinking beer, or was otherwise occupied at the pool hall. He spent so many hours there that the manager finally offered him a job cleaning the place when it closed at 2:00 a.m. Naturally, he recruited Danielle and Chantale for this duty. So the sisters would go arm in arm down the block at two in the morning, often after finishing their midnight shifts, to empty ashtrays, sweep floors, and wipe down counters.

Chantale took advantage of this time with her sister. When they finished cleaning, around four a.m., Damian generously gave them free-rein to play as much pinball or pool as they liked. Chantale learned the rules of snooker, with Damian leaning over her back, teaching her how to hit the balls. She endured his beery breath on her neck, and the feel of his stomach pushing against her rear end, to learn the game. Soon she could clear the green surface of the table all by herself, methodically and precisely pocketing ball after ball. Sometimes they played until dawn, and then Damian would spring for an early breakfast at a restaurant. Those were the best times. Of course, neither girl ever saw a cent of the money they earned. By moving away, Chantale's days at the pool hall would be over. Danielle would have to do all the work on her own. Danielle begged her younger sister to reconsider moving out.

"Why don't you just stay with me? I'd feel better, knowing you were safe with us." Her gaze quickly scanned the room to see if Damian was within earshot. No, luckily he was in the bathroom.

"It's great having you here. Keeps Damian in line. Notice we are arguing less? I do! And, hell, it's been nice, being together, don't you think? We're like a real family. I never knew how much I missed that, 'til you came," she added softly.

Chantale's hesitant suggestion that she leave Damian was met with silence. Danielle shook her head from side to side, ending further conversation by saying, "I need him. It's tough to survive in this town alone. You'll see, soon enough," she sighed. Chantale looked at her sister's fingers busily picking at her hangnails, tugging at the skin until she bled. Her hand trembled as she lit a cigarette.

"You have no idea what it was like for me, when I came here with nothing, just some idiotic notion of living by the sea. All I knew was that I had to get away from HER! If I stayed one more day, I was afraid I might … well, let's just say, hmmhmm, I couldn't stand her anymore. So phony, coming across to the priest like we were the perfect family when… Do you want to know what really happened to Dad? No, well, I think you should. You're too young to remember."

Chantale's eyes flew back to her sister's face and she frowned.

"Wh, What do you mean? Mom always told me he had a heart attack and died in the machine shed while he was cleaning his gun."

"Oh, is that what she told you? And I suppose Richard never contradicted her? No, he wouldn't. Well, at the time, she had another story for the priest, and a different one for the community. But Richard and I know what really happened, because we found him."

"Found him? What do you mean?"

"This is going to be hard for you to hear, Sweetie, but the truth is... Dad shot himself. Mother made us lie and tell the priest that he had been cleaning his gun and it went off. But we knew that Dad could not have had an accident with his gun. He taught us everything there was to know about gun safety from the time we could walk, for Chrissake. We found him in the machine shed alright, with his brains spattered all over... Oh, Jesus, I am sorry, Sis. You were just a baby at the time. I did hang on and try to help Ma for as long as I could, but I just couldn't."

"But, but why? To hear Mom talk, Dad was a saint! Why would he do that, leave us all?" Chantale's voice broke. Her whole body was shaking in shock and disbelief.

"I don't understand it myself and, of course, I couldn't ever get a straight answer out of Mother. She denied everything. But I have my suspicions. I think the pressure finally got to him. The farm, the expense of the new house and Mother carrying on about needing this and that, and Luc's death, and Ghislain refusing to stay on the farm. It was insane around there at that time. But afterwards, we put on a brave face for the neighbours and no one ever suspected. Henri, the hired hand, helped us a lot, but he finally left, too. There was no money to pay him. Paul was away in Edmonton at school, Richard refused to work the land or help in the house, so that left me and Ma to do everything ourselves, including raising you. You were what, about six when I left, I guess. Well, it just got harder and harder, and I couldn't see anything ever changing, so I just packed a few things and left. Didn't seem worth it to try to explain to Ma. She never understood anyways. Still, I miss her sometimes..." Danielle's voice caught in her throat and tears sparkled in her eyes. Chantale put her arm around her and gently rubbed her bony shoulders.

"It must have been so lonely and hard for you, growing up. Ma was what, forty-something, when you were born? Unbelievable. In some ways, you have to feel sorry for her. So many kids to look after. Like old Mother Hubbard. Starting at a young age and then still looking after babies in middle age. Well, that's being a good Catholic for you. Hell, you might as well have been an only child, with so many years difference in age between you and the rest of us. And Ma getting more and more obsessed with keeping the farm going. I know it drove Richard out of the house, to live in the hired man's shack, just to get away from her."

"Let's not talk about it anymore," Chantale interrupted. "You were telling me what you did when you first got to Vancouver."

"Oh, yeah. Well, I spent a few nights in the bus depot, until I got kicked out. Then I was on the street, looking for shelter. Some guy showed me a place where a bunch of people were sleeping, open bins under a warehouse. I was too scared to sleep there, so I found my own spot, underneath a bridge. Panhandled enough for food and tried to keep clean by using the facilities in gas stations, so I could get a job waiting tables. The last thing I wanted was to get caught for vagrancy. I was twenty-eight, but I thought if I had no address I'd be shipped back home. I was always so scared some pimp would get to me or some guy would crawl into my hiding place and rape me, maybe even kill me. I had to sleep with one eye open all night long." She visibly shuddered, threw her dark head back with a deep breath and continued.

"Then I got a job at a little coffee bar where I met Damian and he took me in. The rest, as they say, is history." She made an exaggerated gesture with her cigarette and added a hollow laugh.

"Now, at least I feel like I have a home. So don't be too hard on him. It's better than being alone in this town. Never did get to spend much time at the seashore, though, did I?"

She blinked through the bangs covering her dark eyes. Then she changed the topic abruptly. "Hey listen, I'm taking you to my doctor to get you on 'The Pill' before you go out on your own. Last thing we need is for you to get knocked up and you never know when Mr. Right will come along. Then it's a little too late to think about it and guys sure as hell never worry, that's for damn sure. It's a lifesaver, I can tell you. I have no intention of getting strapped down with a bunch of brats like Ma did, do you? Can't be too careful. And you make sure to call me anytime if you need anything. After all, what are sisters for?" Danielle squeezed Chantale's arm and reached up to pat her cheek. Chantale responded by leaning over, kissing her sister and clinging to her for a long time.

Chapter Twenty-three

Tuesday. Day two of first grade. No fancy little dresses from now on, her mother said. She would wear a plain, sensible school dress, dark brown so it wouldn't show the dirt.

"And don't run around and fall down and tear holes in it. It'll have to do you until you grow out of it. You make sure to change into your play clothes the minute you get home. You have to keep it clean for the week—I can't keep up with the wash as it is. Now stand still while I put a little whitener on the toes of your shoes. Here, let's pull those pincurls out. Now let me rub your head a minute and all the curls will fall out really nice. There you go, cute as a pixie in your little pixie cut. Grab your lunch bag and hop it down the lane to the bus. You don't want to be late. Give us a kiss and off you go!" Jocelyne hugged her mother hard and nuzzled into her neck.

"Mmm, Mommy smell," she said wistfully, a lump rising in her throat. Then her mother took her by the hand and led her through the door to the steps. She playfully smacked her bottom and then stood waving from the porch, as the bus pulled up at the end of the lane. Jocelyne hurried down the gravel slope, hoping the other kids wouldn't notice her mother waving at her like she was a baby. Please, please don't let them see.

On the way, Jocelyne frantically ran her fingers over her itchy scalp and yanked at the tight curls, trying to straighten her hair. She hated her short hair. She wanted long blond hair like Crystal's with loose, bouncy curls. Her thoughts were spinning as she raced toward the yellow bus.

"Why does Mom have to go and make me keep my hair short like a boy's, with a stupid 'pixie cut?' Who wants to look like a pixie, anyway, whatever that is. Does school mean I'll have to have my hair in pincurls all the time? It's bad enough to have to wear a dress every day! Just 'cause I'm a girl. It's not fair. I never had to wear a dress every day before, only for church. And now the boys will see my panties when I go on the swing for under-ducks. Stupid, stupid teasing boys. Those dumb bobby pins pinch my head all night long and I can't get to sleep. And my hair looks stupid, stupid!" She rubbed her cheek, trying to erase the marks where she had slept on the pins all over her pillow, because she had tossed and turned and torn the scarf off her head.

"Well, I won't let her put my hair in pins tonight and that's that," Jocelyne thought as she raised her foot up high to reach the first step of the bus. Grumpily, with barely a hello to the bus driver, she flopped down into a green leather seat near the front of the bus. Hers was nearly the last stop, so there was not much choice where to sit. She found herself next to Jimmy, who immediately kicked her and soiled her white ankle sock. She poked him with her elbow and pushed her bottom more firmly into the seat as the bus lurched forward. Peeking around his head, she saw her mother still standing on the step, waving goodbye. Fluffy pink slippers, hair in curlers and all! She slid down into the seat. She didn't wave back.

*****

"Well, there she goes," Suzanna sighed, leaning across the wooden rail on the step, blowing a kiss toward the bus. "Off on her second day as a big school girl. What a happy time, to be just starting out! How I envy you, my sweetheart! What I wouldn't give to be young like that again! The things you will learn! Do you know what it means, to have your whole life ahead of you? No, I thought not. Neither did I."

Her thoughts were interrupted by the honking of a flight of Canada geese just overhead. Nothing unusual at this time of year. Flocks and flocks of the huge birds swooped down to the newly harvested grain fields near the house throughout the day. They waddled and picked greedily through the seeds on the ground, squawking and gossiping like ladies in a supermarket. At some mysterious signal, a group would arise as one, sailing up into the blue autumn sky, veeing their way southward. Late into the evening, their leaders' calls drove them on. And no matter how commonplace the sight, anyone standing below automatically looked up, as if in answer. Suzanna rested her back against the rail, supporting her heavy middle with her palms, dropping backwards, to watch them. The rush of their flight buoyed her up, pulling her along with them. They flew so low she felt she could touch their smooth white underbellies. Or grab a set of tail feathers and hitch a ride. She laughed at the sudden image she had of a fat woman in a pink dressing gown, hair curlers and fuzzy slippers, flying through the sky like a kite on the tail of an elegant triangle of geese. None too happy to bear the weight of a pregnant lady, they would probably drop her into the nearest swamp! She giggled as she saw herself landing amid mud and cattails.

"It would be so nice, though," she mused, "to spend the winter somewhere warm, like Florida, or California or..." She took a deep breath and turned her face toward the rising sun. Pink clouds, puffy on the inside, with feathery edges, decorated the sky. "Angel wings" her mother called them. Ah, the sky was full of angels this morning. Magical! A good omen for her little girl. She must take a moment to write it in Jocelyne's keepsake book, which chronicled her life from zero to six. She had been quite diligent in keeping it up so far. For Pauline, well, a few pages were done, baby weight, baptism, first tooth, a lock of baby hair. Nothing on Nicolas yet, though she had recorded his weight, as the doctor insisted she track his growth. How had time passed so quickly? Already married seven years, with a daughter now in school. Three babies and another on the way. And she already twenty-eight years old. The time had whirled by in a blur of diapers, formula, spit up, and constant crying, much of it her own.

Her mother had warned her: "Raisin' kids basically alone ain't no picnic, ma dear. That man's in construction. He'll never be home a single day, now I tell ya, and won't be much help when he is. More'n likely sittin' in the bar with his cronies, from what I can see. You get married, you make your bed, you will lie in it, ma girl, and no mistake. Don't come cryin' to me afterwards. I ain't one to say I told you so, you know. I'm just givin' you a piece of advice. After that, it's up to you. Never could tell you anything, anyways. Headstrong as a mule, always was."

Had she listened? No. So there was no one to blamè but herself. And no where to turn for help. Her mother had been right, and they both knew it, though it was never said out loud. How many times had she silently sworn she would leave? But where would she go?

Sometimes, driving back from town, she could see the outline of the distant Rocky Mountains on the western horizon and she would imagine herself driving, driving to meet them. She could just keep going, until the mountains swallowed her up, leaving behind just a white plume in the wind. When they were staying at the farm, more than once, instead of turning into the driveway, she had gone one, two, three miles down the gravel road. The mountains were calling. She longed to escape.

But how could she leave first one, then two, then three, now four with Paul, or more likely, his mother, God forbid! With tears streaming down her face, she always slowed, reached a path into a farmer's field and turned the car around. She would sit in the Desoto for fifteen, twenty minutes, wipe her face, reapply her makeup and paste on a smile, ready to greet them all back at the farm.

One day, Mme. Gérard came back from her weekly coffee clatch and told them about a woman in the village who had just left her husband and three boys, all under five, a set of twins two years old. Paul and his mother had ranted and raved about it, calling her a wild, irresponsible tramp, and worse. Suzanna had remained quiet. Paul went on about it later that night, in bed. Still, she gave no response. Paul prodded her, saying it was very unlike her not to have an opinion. She had just smiled and shaken her head. He dropped it and was a bit more helpful for the next few days, while he was home.

Yes, he could be very sweet. She thought of her new ring, safely stored away in its blue velvet box in her dresser. Pearls and diamonds in her favourite setting, white gold. Must have cost a fortune. Silly, extravagant, with a new house and a baby on the way, but then, that was a man, and what could you do? She had thought of asking him to take it back so they could buy a new crib instead. She had argued with herself for days and even hesitatingly consulted her mother about it.

"Won't do to hurt a man's pride. He might never buy you anything again. Start off the way you mean to continue, I always say. There'll be plenty of time to be practical, down the road. We'll find you a used crib somewhere, never you fear."

She resigned herself to keeping it and wore it proudly to the bar on Saturday nights. At least it showed he was thinking of her while he was on the road. She still wondered what Chantale had meant, when she'd said he was feeling guilty. What would he have to be guilty about, working out of town, away from his family all week, with his wife expecting a baby? She could be such a bitch! And the way she had acted before they left. Shameful! Who did she think she was? She treated her mother and her brothers like dirt. Paul certainly didn't deserve it—look at how generous he had been to her. He was generous with everybody, always bringing the kids a little something. He could be tender, too.

She smiled to herself, as she opened the screen door with one hand and began unrolling the curlers in her hair with the other, remembering last night, after their argument. What was it about? Oh yes, the damn dog he wanted. For the kids, he said. Hm, hm. Well, he wasn't going to get his way this time and, at last, he had seen her point of view, and made up for it, massaging her aching back and holding her close until he left at 5:30 this morning.

So, off he went again, on the road, leaving her to manage the household. That was her job. His mother had done it, all on her own after her husband had died, as Suzanna had been told, many times. For his part, he earned a paycheck, kept food on the table and a roof over their heads. Really, when all was said and done, he was a good provider. There was always plenty of work in construction and the money was great, if you didn't mind living in a camp somewhere in the bush for weeks on end. It was hard slogging for Paul and she needed to support him and do the best she could, for her kids' sake. At least she wasn't still slinging hash in the one horse Alberta town where Paul had found her, told her she was beautiful, and promised to take her away from it all. And besides, soon there would be a new house, with a huge kitchen and four bedrooms and...

Startled by the ringing of the phone and a subsequent cry from the baby, Suzanna dropped the prickly curlers she had collected in her hand. The rollers scurried wildly down the steps behind her and plastic pins scattered on the landing.

"Damn," she sputtered, yanking the screen door and tripping over the threshold in her oversized slippers. Grabbing the black receiver, she grumbled, "Who in the hell is calling at 8:00 in the morning, waking the baby and…"

"Oh, good morning, Madame Gérard. Oh yes, she's off to school already. A bit cranky getting up so early to catch the bus. Yes, she had a good day yesterday. She looked like a little doll in that dress you got her. Thanks again. Boy, that teacher is really something. What an old battle-axe! Oh, of course, I'm sure she's very good. Seems a bit harsh, that's all. Well, Nicolas is awake and Pauline will be wanting her cereal here in a minute, so I'd better get a move on. Thanks for calling. Oh, any word on Chantale? Well, I hope you hear something soon. Paul called the constable again, yesterday before he left again, to keep them on the ball, as he said. What was that clicking sound? Oh, I get it—somebody's listening in on the party line. Well, mind your own business, whoever you are! Where was I? Oh yes, Paul'll be gone about three weeks this time, but said he'd phone every day to check up on us. Baby's not due for six weeks yet, so he should be back in plenty of time. Well, must run. Nicolas is howling his head off. See you Saturday. Pick you up about ten? 'Bye now."

"Oh brother. Now with nothing to do and nobody to look after except Richard, who's about as talkative as a fish, the old lady will be phoning us twice a day, won't she, baby? Just what we need." Suzanna spoke to Nicolas as she lifted his soaking wet backside out of the crib. Damn plastic pants leaked again. Now all the bedding would have to be changed as well. More goddamn washing. Pauline appeared, trotted over and tugged on the tie of her night dress.

"Ceweal. Me wants Alpha-bets ceweal."

"Sorry, sweetie. Mommy is all out of Alpha-Bits. I'll make you a nice bowl of porridge in just a minute here, as soon as I get Nicolas changed. See, he's all wet."

"No. Alpha-bets, alpha-bets! Pawidge yucky. No pawidge. No,

no, no."

The phone rang again. Now what?

"Pauline, run answer the phone like I showed you. I'm right in the middle of changing Nicolas' diaper and I almost poked him with the pin. Ouch, dammit, poked my finger. Quick, just pick up and say, 'Just a minute, please.' Now that Jocelyne is at school all day, you have to be a big girl and help Mommy."

"Me wants to go skwoool wid Josheely. Me go too. Take me, take me."

"Pauline, don't whine, for pity's sake, you'll give Mommy a headache. Hurry up, or we'll miss the call. It might be Daddy on the phone. You can do it, go on, there's a good girl."

"Mooooommmeeee, it's Graaaaaammmmma."

"Oh my God. What does she want now?" Suzanna muttered under her breath as she hoisted the baby to her hip and hurried into the kitchen.

"Oh, it's you, Mom. Yeah, got her off to school okay. What a morning! I'm not even dressed and it's nine o'clock already. I can see I'm going to have to get into a new routine, what with a lunch to make and Jocelyne to get ready. She makes such a fuss about getting her hair brushed, you'd think I was trying to kill her. Then I no more get her off and the other two start up. What'll I do when the new baby comes? Do you think you could come and stay for a while, to help out? Yes, I know, you have the garden and Dad and everything. Hmm, mmm, yes well, I better go. Everybody around here needs to be fed and I have washing to get on the line today while it's nice out. Yes, I know yesterday was washing day, but what with taking Jocelyne to school and getting her supplies and all, I didn't get to it, so I'm already behind and it's only Tuesday for Cripe's sakes. I'll call you tomorrow. Tell Dad I said hello. 'Bye." She closed the connection by pushing down the buttons on the cradle with her fingers.

"Fine, fine, fine! Don't help out, see if I care. But you just wait 'til you need me next time and see what excuses I come up with," she hissed through gritted teeth, slamming down the receiver. Pauline started and headed straight for her chair. She climbed onto the vinyl seat and sat quietly, peeking at her mother from under her long lashes. Suzanna filled a pot with water at the sink and flung it down on the stove, still holding Nicolas in her arms. Twisting and turning, he kicked her distended belly. With an exasperated sigh, she plunked him roughly into his highchair. He started to whimper. She ignored him, opened the refrigerator door and lifted out a slippery glass bottle of milk, gripping it firmly in her swollen fingers. Supporting her stiff back with one hand, she leaned down and yanked open the heavy pot drawer beneath the stove. She banged another pot onto the range and promptly filled it with half a bottle of milk and a generous portion of golden syrup poured from a tin on the counter.

"Just hold your horses, Pauline! As soon as the water boils, Mommy can get your cereal on. And you, young man, will have to wait a minute until your formula is done and I can sterilize some bottles. Sure, sure, I know what your grandmas would say: 'We raised ten or twenty or maybe a hundred kids out on the bald prairie, with no running water and no washing machine and we milked cows and raised chickens and baked our own bread, all before sun up. And we weren't standin' around in our nightgown and slippers with our hair in curlers at ten o'clock in the morning, either. So there, Missy. Stop your whinin'.' Yes, yes, we've heard it all before. Well, best get my work duds on and get on with washing day. Wait there you two, I'll be right back."

Suzanna turned down the burner on the gas stove and went back into her bedroom. Sitting on her bed, she reached for a pair of wrinkled pedal pushers on her chair but as she leaned over, the smell of urine from the crib overwhelmed her with nausea and she flopped back on her pillow. She rested for a moment until the feeling passed, then sighing, rolled off and gathered up the wet bedding and the diaper. Lifting the lid of the diaper pail, the bleach fumes almost knocked her flat again. She pushed the wet things on top of the soaking cotton mass and hoisted the heavy bucket into the bathroom, where she had to lean it over the toilet to drain some of the water. The tie on her nightdress promptly fell into the toilet and the filthy, pungent water spilled onto the floor.

"Shit," she cursed under her breath. She was only able to empty the bucket by half without spilling all its contents, but it was still very heavy. She managed to swing it back down and drag it to the top of the stairs in the kitchen, leading to the basement where the wringer washing machine awaited her for the day's work. She glanced over to the stove and noticed the steam rising from the pots. She hoped the milk wouldn't boil over before she got back. Cleaning the gas stove was a terrible chore—all spills dripped underneath and wouldn't come off without steel wool and a lot of elbow grease.

"Mommy will just be a minute," she called over her shoulder. "I'll just get this stinky bucket downstairs and we'll have our brekkie, kids. Pauline, go over and talk to your baby brother and keep him occupied. I'll be right up."

She stood the bucket on the top step and grabbed the handrail for balance. The only way to move it was to hump it down, one step at a time. On the third step, she didn't notice that she had set the bucket down on the edge of her oversized, floppy slipper. She went to take the next step with her right foot, lost her balance, pulled the bucket over with her left foot and tumbled to the cement floor, twelve steps below.

Upstairs, the baby cried, and the phone rang.

*****

Danielle had been right about one thing, though. Homesick. Chantale had never thought it would happen to her, since she had been so determined to leave the farm. She had never felt it once while she stayed with Carol. But one night, curled up on Danielle's creaky sofa, she dreamt of her mother, wandering through the house. She saw her sit down at the piano. The porcelain doll on its red velvet cushion turned its head. It opened its mouth and spoke. She woke up with her heart pounding, drenched in sweat.

She started to fear sleep, due to Damian's nocturnal habits and her nightmares when she did drift off. Inevitably, each night she gave in, from pure exhaustion after working in the restaurant all day. Once, she dreamed she was sleeping in her own room, tucked up in her beautiful, white, cozy bed. The lace curtains were blowing in the breeze and the air coming into her room was fresh and light with birdsong. The morning smell of bacon was wafting up the stairs. Then she woke up, her empty stomach rumbling, and she couldn't remember where she was. The sound of someone retching into the toilet in the bathroom reminded her. She gave in to self-pity, crying into her pillow for half an hour, before crawling to her feet to get ready for work.

The next night she found herself in the field, surrounded by wildflowers, searching for Blackie, a sugar lump melting in her hand. The sun warmed her back, the wind gently tousled her hair, a butterfly landed on her arm. A dark shape was approaching, across the plain. Blackie, come on, girl! Here I am. No, not Blackie, a man with black hair and ice blue eyes... no, not a man, a boar, a giant boar, landing on top of her, pushing her down into the grass, entering her body, between her legs. The stench of hot, piggy breath. Blood, there was blood... She suddenly awoke, ice cold and aching with the memory of... Richard, her nightmare. Her hatred for him roiled in her stomach, making her retch. No wonder she was losing weight. She could barely eat or sleep.

That was it. Before her shift began that morning, she ran to the pay phone on the corner. She would call Suzanna. Just to let her know and then maybe she could get some rest... Paul's new telephone number was not hard to get from the operator, as Paul was the only Gérard in the village.

"Pauline, hello Sweetheart! What a big girl, answering the phone all by yourself! Is that Nicolas screaming? Listen, Honey, go get Mommy. I need to speak to Mommy, okay?"

"Mommy faww down. Fawn down stairs. Bye. Bye." The phone receiver dropped with a bang.

What to do? What to do? Call Ma. Come on, come on, quick, pick up the goddamn phone.

"Maman? It's me, c'est moi, Chantale. Oui, oui, I'm fine, fine. Listen, I can't talk now. Get over to Paul's right away. Call an ambulance and get there as quick as you can. Something has happened to Suzanna. Maybe you did just talk to her, but I just called and Pauline said Mommy fell down, Nicolas was screaming and Suzanna couldn't come to the phone. Je sais pas, I just know something's wrong. I'll call you back later. Don't talk any more, Ma. I mean it, go!"

*****

"Today, boys and girls, we must learn to do our opening exercises. These will be done every morning, right after I take attendance. After that, I'll be checking your face and hands and ears for cleanliness. Every day that you pass, you will get a gold star on the class chart. Don't let me have to send you back home because you're too dirty to be at school. Remember, cleanliness is next to Godliness.

"Stand up everyone. Now the first thing we do is sing "God Save the Queen." Here is a picture of our dear Queen, the head of our country." Her long pointer tapped a framed photograph above the blackboard. "Isn't she pretty in her beautiful crown? Now follow along with me while I play the piano. You'll soon learn the words, with practice. Practice makes perfect."

The piano banged away as the class mumbled along with the teacher's boisterous singing. Jocelyne kept her eyes fixed on the lady in the photograph. Her dress and her crown sparkled with jewels, but her enormous eyes stared starkly from her pale white face. Tiny teeth were visible where her lips parted, but not in a smile. The blue eyes reminded Jocelyne of her grandmother's doll. Had the man taking her picture told her, "Watch the birdie?" The teacher's voice interrupted her thoughts.

"Now children, look over here. This is the flag of the Dominion of Canada. The flag of Great Britain, called the Union Jack. We must pledge allegiance to our queen and country every morning. We hold the first two fingers of our right hand to our temple, like so, and we say, 'I salute the flag, the emblem of my country, and to her I pledge my love and loyalty.' Now, repeat after me."

"Teacher...."

"Excuse me, children, but we don't interrupt during the morning exercises. Now, once again, repeat…"

"Teacher…"

"Josie - leene, we raise our hand when we have a question. And we practiced my name yesterday. We don't call out, "Teacher." Now, say my name properly and I will answer your question."

"Mrs. Hoffentreader…"

"Hoffentrauder. Try again."

"Mrs. Hoffentrader, are we supposed to love that queen?"

"Why of course. That's what we pledge, to love our queen and country. She is the head of our country."

"Well, I don't like her. I don't even like her head. She has a pretty crown, but she looks mean. Besides, I never even met her. Why should I say I love her?"

"Don't say such a thing again, Missy. It shows a lack of respect. Oops, no, no, we're not finished yet, Jimmy. Stand up again. Now, let's go on. Time to repeat the Lord's prayer. Bow your head and say each line after me."

Jocelyne glowed with pride, as she didn't have to wait for the teacher to say the words a second time, but kept right up with her through the whole prayer. It was the same prayer she said in church and with her mother every night, and she knew it off by heart. But wait, the teacher was going on, adding different words. It was supposed to end with "Deliver us from evil, Amen." But no, she said something about a kingdom and…

"Josie-leene, I know the Catholics don't say the correct ending, but in school, you will repeat the whole prayer the right way. 'For thine is the kingdom, the power and the glory, forever and ever, amen.' Understood? Very good. You may sit down, boys and girls, and take out your pencils for printing. We will practice your name again."

The day dragged by, broken only by the excitement of recess and lunch hour. Jocelyne was delighting in her newfound friends and their games, as she had spent most of her young life alone or being pestered by her much younger sister. So many new experiences—jacks, skipping ropes, tag, parachute jumps from the swings...

She couldn't tell time, but her mother had shown her on the clock that when the little hand came to the four, it would be home time. All afternoon, she glanced at the clock by the door. Finally, late in the day, it was time for reading. Jocelyne rubbed her hands fondly all over the book she received, admiring the colourful pictures and searching the print for words she recognized. "Easy," she said to herself. "There's 'look,' 'Tommy,' hey, even 'Susan,' just about like Mommy's name." The teacher was going through the sentences one by one, having each child stand and read. Jocelyne counted the number of children ahead of her, put her finger on each sentence as she raced ahead to the sentence she was sure would be hers to read aloud. She began sounding out the letters and practicing silently, so she would be ready when her turn came. There, now it was Crystal. Poor Crystal, she couldn't read at all. Okay, now...

Just as Jocelyne rose from her seat when her name was called, she glanced at the door and saw her grandmother standing there. She swallowed hard. How could it be home time already? She checked the clock again. The little hand was only near the three! And besides, she was supposed to take the bus home. Didn't Grandmère think she was old enough to take the bus?

"Bonjour, Grandmaman!" Jocelyne blurted out. Her grandmother put a finger to her lips, tapped gently on the open door, and waited for the teacher. Frowning, the teacher shut the door so they could speak in the hall. As soon as the class was left alone someone called out, "Bon gour! Bon gour!" and the others took up the chorus.

"Nah, nah, Josie's iiiinnn trouble. Ha, ha!" another child added.

"Am not."

"Are too."

"Am not. Just shut up, why don't you?" Jocelyne screamed, sticking out her tongue.

The door swung open. The teacher swept a stern glance across the classroom and settled her gaze on Jocelyne.

"Joceleene, please go to the cloakroom and get your coat and lunch pail. You're to go with your grandma, now. I'll send you some homework with Jimmy on the bus. Quickly now, off you go. I am so sorry, Ma-dame Gerard. I hope everything will... well. All my best to your family."

Chapter Twenty-four

"What do you mean, Mmmommy lost the bbbabbby? Where did it go? I wanted a new brother! Why didn't the baby come home ffffrom the hospital with you? How could you llllose it, Daddy? How ccan a baby get llost? Go to the hospital and get it back! What's wrong with Mommy? Is she sick? Grandma says she can't get out of bed for a while. You mean she'll sleep all day long? Who will get me ready for school? Who will curl my hair? I don't want Grandma to stay. She's mean and she makes me do stuff and says 'shush' all the time. I want Grandmère. She would cook beans just for me, and and tell me stories and *not* curl my hair. It's not fair!"

*****

"Mrs. Gerard, I hope you are feeling better. I'm sorry to bother you by calling you at home, but I am obliged to let you know that Joceyleene has been having trouble at school. I know things have been disrupted... your mother has been looking after the children for a time, so Joceyleene tells me. Yes, I understand. She hasn't been getting along with the other children, Mrs. Gerard, especially the boys. I've had to send her to the principal's office for fighting at recess time! In Grade One, my goodness! Land sakes alive, she scraps like a pole cat! And one more thing. I think it might help if you don't teach your children to read anymore. I know you mean well, but it causes nothing but problems when it isn't taught properly. I can't keep the children in their groups. Now Jocyleene is too far ahead of her classmates in reading and she's doing nothing but chatting all the time. I declare, that girl could talk the ear off a huntin' dog, Mrs. Gerard. I keep moving her desk to the blackbird row, as a punishment, and once I even had to put her in the corner with the dunce cap. Kicked the wall for half an hour—you must'a seen the marks on the toes of her shoes. Left scuffs on the wall but I made her clean them off, of course. She has to learn how to behave in school. I'm sure I can count on your help to keep her in line. You have enough to contend with, what with... hmm, well, all my best, Mrs. Gerard. I'm sure I won't have to trouble you again. Goodbye now."

*****

"Grandmère, ever since the baby got lost, Mommy has been different. She cries a lot and sometimes when I come home from school she is still in her nightgownd. She hasn't brushed her hair or put her face on like she used to or anything. Sometimes baby Nicolas is dirty too. Smelly as a baby pig. Eueuh! Pourquoi, Grandmaman? Why is she so sad? Doesn't she care about us anymore?"

"Non, non, écoute, chérie, c'est pas ça du tout. Maman is jus' tired an' she need 'er res'."

"But where did the baby go? I worry about it being lost and alone."

"Not to worry. The baby went to heaven, chou-chou, avec Papère."

"Where is heaven? What's it like there?"

"Up in the sky, like I show you be-fore in your petit Catechism book, tu te souviens, wid de angel crowd all aroun' in de pink cloud, so beautiful? Singing an' 'appiness alla de time an' no worry nor prob-lem any more."

"Well then why is Mommy sad? Shouldn't she be happy now if the baby is there with Grandpapa? When do I get to go there?"

"Not any time soon, I 'ope, ma belle. Grandmaman need you 'ere wid me for a while yet. 'Ush up now and step up 'ere an' 'elp me peel da patato. We make a nice supper to 'elp Maman, d'accord?"

Just as Jocelyne was setting the table, Suzanna wandered aimlessly into the room, holding her housecoat closed. Its belt trailed under her feet. Nicolas came toddling behind her, carrying his potty. With a giggle, he pulled down his loose diaper, plopped the empty potty on his head and danced around the room, all the while peeing all over the floor. Everyone laughed at his silly antics.

"You little monkey! Stop laughing everybody! It won't make it any easier to train him to pee in the pot if he thinks he can keep entertaining everybody! What a little card you are! Just like your daddy," laughed Suzanna, as she whisked him up in her arms and carried him off to the bedroom. Grandmaman was busy dishing out the supper, so Jocelyne was given the task of wiping up the floor, but it was worth it to see Mother laugh. It seemed so long since she had heard her musical laughter.

Night came. Grandmaman had left to go back to the farm. Mommy was once again very quiet.

"Mommy, read me a story. How come you never read us bedtime stories anymore?"

"Not tonight, Sweetheart. Mommy's tired," she sighed, as she gave each daughter a peck on the cheek.

"Go to sleep now. Morning comes early and you don't want to be late for your bus."

Soon Jocelyne could hear the squeaking rhythm of the rocking chair, where Suzanna rocked for hours each night, staring out the curtain-less window into the dark. Nicolas whined in his tiny bed next door, in his mother's room. He hated sleeping in a bed, and even chairs put against it wouldn't keep him in. He wanted back in his crib, but that had been freed up for the baby. Sometimes he managed to climb up into it. But if he was too tired, he toddled down the short hallway to the girls' room and snuggled in next to Pauline. Jocelyne could hear his little bare feet now, padding up to their door. But Mommy had closed it firmly, trying to stop Nicolas' midnight wandering. He whimpered and curled up next to the door. Jocelyne climbed down the ladder from the top bunk, let Nicolas in and then found her way through the dark house to the bathroom. She peed and deliberately didn't flush, glad that she could disobey Chantale's rules. She smirked as she shut the bathroom door and headed back down the hall.

"Bonne nuit, little monkey," Jocelyne whispered, chucking Nicolas under the chin affectionately as she pulled the covers up and tucked him in next to Pauline. The squeak, squeak of the rocking chair went on and on, while Jocelyne kept time rocking herself to sleep.

Morning came. Jocelyne splashed cold water on her face, gave a quick brush to her short, straight, brown hair, which she was thankful her mother neglected to curl during the week, shovelled down a bowl of cereal, grabbed her lunch box and flew out the door to meet the bus. No chance even to get a kiss goodbye from Mom, what with Pauline and Nicolas whining to be fed. Jocelyne was glad to set her foot on the bus, eager to get to school and play with the other girls. After school, there was nothing to do. Pauline just wanted to play with dolls. Jocelyne did her best to ignore her, keeping her nose in a book, unless Mom forced her to "keep her sister occupied."

"All right, all right, what do you want to do, Pauline? A tea party? Sure, let's go outside and make mud pies. That will be fun." Lately, Mom hadn't been asking her to watch Pauline as often. She merely bought her more dolls and doll clothes and let her play on the floor at her feet.

The house was so lonely when Daddy was away. It felt empty, especially at night. But every Friday night, he would magically reappear, bearing gifts: roller skates, a double-dutch skipping rope, once even a new bicycle. Then, suddenly, "A pony! Look, Pauline, a pony! Can I ride it to school? Lift me up, Daddy, so I can ride. Look a little saddle and everything! Holy cow, will the kids ever be jealous when they see me ride up to school on a pony! What's his name? I'm going to call him Black Beauty, like the horse in the storybook. Yeah!"

"And just where do you expect to keep a pony, Paul? Tied up behind the garage? Are you crazy? We don't even have a paddock. And how I am supposed to get hay to feed him all week, while you're away? And who is going to clean up his messes?"

In a few days, Black Beauty was gone, to a new home.

"He needs to live on a farm, Jocelyne. We'll come and visit him often, you'll see. We want what's best for Blackie, I mean, Black Beauty, now don't we?"

A few weeks later…

"Goats! Baby goats! What, they're called kids? Just like us, Pauline! What do goats eat? Do they need hay? No, they can live off the grass on our lawn? Holy cow! So, we can just tie them up in the yard and give them water and they'll be fine out there? We'll play with them and train them to do tricks, Pauline. Wait 'til Sarah sees them. They're soooo cute. What will we name them? I know—Tweedledee and Tweedledum, like in *Alice in Wonderland*. Doesn't that suit them fine?"

"What? We can't keep them? Why, Mom? Look how good they're mowing the grass, just like Daddy said they would! I love those goats! I've been giving them water and talking to them every day. It's not fair!"

Then, in springtime…

"Ducks, baby duckies! How sweet! You found them where? Richard found them in the field at the farm? Did they lose their mommy? You mean we can keep them? In the tub? What do baby duckies eat? Pauline, you can't play with them all day while I'm at school. Leave them in the bathtub and shut the door so they can't get out. Remember what Dad said, they'll die if we play with them too much.…"

"Oh no, you see I told you it would happen, but you wouldn't believe me! All dead! Well, we better plan their frooneral. I know a good place out by the shed where we can bury them. The ground is soft, so it will be easy, but we need to find a box…"

Then, just before they were to move into the new house in the village…

"Oh, Daddy! Just what I always wanted—a dog! What do you call him, a Chermin Shipper? What's that mean? And his name is Happy? It's the perfectest name! You got him where? At the auction? He's such a big dog! I really wanted a puppy, but he is so nice and smart. Look, he already knows how to sit up and beg! We will train him to be a guard dog for the new house, won't we? And we will build him a doghouse and everything, so he can live with us for a long, long time, right? I can't wait to tell Crystal I got a dog! Can we bring him to Grandma and Grandpa's tomorrow when we go to town? Grandpa would love to see Happy! What a great name! Well, I guess he'll be okay tied up outside, as long as we leave him food and water. I'll make sure he has lots of dogfood in his bowl for the whole day. I'll miss you, Happy, but we'll be back soon, don't worry."

The day after Happy arrived was Saturday, the best day of the week. As usual, Dad drove them all into town. He said he didn't mind. It gave him a chance to get a shave and a haircut at the barbershop and then unwind with his buddies at the "watering hole." Jocelyne didn't know what that meant, but he was always in such a good mood on the way home, it didn't matter. While Mom and Grandmère and Grandma went shopping, the children would spend the day with Grandpa, at their mother's parents' house in town. They couldn't go to the farm anymore, because Chantale wasn't there to babysit and, of course, Richard couldn't or wouldn't look after kids. It was just as much fun to stay with Grandpa, who would tell them stories, sing them songs, and give them cookies and crackers to eat, as many as they wanted, much to Grandma's chagrin. Every Saturday, when the "womenfolk" came back, Grandma asked Grandpa if he had given them treats, and he innocently replied, "No, of course not!" with a wink in Jocelyne's direction.

It was nearly dark when they dropped Grandmère off at the farm and headed toward the village. Jocelyne was rejoicing in the back seat, rocking back and forth while making up a song, trying to drown out her parents' arguing in the front.

"Hurray, we're almost back home. Happy, Happy, Happy the dog! Happy, he's so happy, he's so special, Haaaappy the dooogg!"

"Jocelyne, quiet down, for pity's sake! Dad can't hear himself think, let alone drive! Paul, really, you should let me drive. Slow down, you're twenty miles over the speed limit." A slap over the back of the seat, aimed at Jocelyne's bare leg. "Not another peep out of you, you hear?"

"Yeah, not another peep. Peep, peep, peep." Dad looked around at her and winked, his green eyes flashing bright against his red cheeks. Jocelyne shared a laugh at their favourite bedtime joke. A horn blared as a car whizzed past.

"Paul!" Suzanna screamed. "Keep your eyes on the goddamn road. For God's sake! That's it—pull over up ahead. I'm driving. You'll get us all killed!"

The car slowed to a stop. The adults got out to change places. Jocelyne exchanged glances with her sister and put her finger to her lips, signing "shh!" Suzanna slammed the door and leaned over muttering, trying to adjust the seat. She lurched the bench seat forward and inadvertently pressed the horn with her elbow. Standing outside, next to the car, Paul jumped and swore. Suzanna looked up in time to see him adjust the front of his trousers, then stumble toward the open car door and slide into the seat.

"Oh, Paul, for Chrissake. It's still light. Think of the girls, if you have no shame yourself. Now shut that goddamn door and let's get going. The ice cream in the trunk will be melted by the time we get home."

After supper, since it was Saturday night, Jocelyne knew her parents would be going out. Her mother wore a different dress every week. Jocelyne couldn't wait to see her prance out of her room, twirling in front of the children in her flouncy skirt and clicking her matching high heels. Tonight, the dress was like a piece of the sky, the same colour as her mother's eyes. Her black hair smelled of flowers as she knelt over to kiss them goodbye. Her pearl and diamond ring sparkled on her hand, set off by her red nail polish.

Dad looked handsome too, in his dark suit, white shirt and shiny shoes. His black hair glistened, slicked back with what Pauline called "Bwillcweem." His cheeks were rosy and his face was soft, smooth and smelled of soap when he rubbed his chin along Jocelyne's neck and said, "Bonne nuit, chérie! Be good for the babysitter now and get a good sleep. We need to be bright eyed and bushy-tailed for church in the morning, n'est-ce pas?"

The babysitter had them in bed even earlier than usual, but it was her parents' arguing when they came home that kept Jocelyne awake most of the night. Tossing, turning, tearing at the Saturday night pin curls in her hair, she finally stuck her thumb in her mouth, covered her head with the pillow and cried herself to sleep.

Before a moment had passed, Dad was flinging back her covers and threatening to pull her from the bunk. Her eyes were welded shut from the tears she had shed and she started to scream. With a laugh, her father tossed an ice cold wet face cloth over her face.

"There, that'll wake you up, Possum. Now shake a leg, you gotta help me get Pauline ready. We're going to let your Mommy and Nicolas sleep, 'faire la grasse matinée,' comme on dit, sleep in like a grand lady, this morning. We gotta meet Grandmère on time, though. You know how she'll fuss if we're late, so get a move on."

"Noooo, I'm so tired, let me sleep, please," Jocelyne wailed. "You and Mommy made so much noise last night I couldn't sleep. Let me stay home like Mommy, today, Daddy, pleeeasse?"

Mother hardly ever went to Church anymore. Once, when Jocelyne had asked her father why, he said Mom needed her rest on Sunday morning, and it was her treat to have some time to herself. Jocelyne hated it, because now she had to get Pauline ready. Mother would curl their hair and lay out their clothes the night before, but it was such a pain to do anything with Pauline. She twisted and fussed the whole time she was being washed, combed and dressed, screaming when the brush went through her fine, knotted hair, whining for her mother. The worst part was, they weren't allowed to eat or drink anything before Mass. Pauline howled for her "ceweal" until Dad gave her smack on the bottom, which left her a sobbing, blubbering mess of twisted clothes with shoes on the wrong feet. When they finally got in the car, they were firmly warned not to talk (or sing) for the whole seven mile ride.

"Daddy has a headache ce matin and needs some peace and quiet," he groaned, turning the key to fire up the Desoto.

Since they had moved from the farm, Grandmère met them at the portico of the Sacred Heart Church in town every Sunday, for ten o'clock Mass. If they were late, she froze her son with cold disapproval for the rest of the morning, even at breakfast. Grandmère kept strict discipline with the girls also.

"*Sit up straight. Follow everyone else as they stand, kneel and sing, even if you don't know what's going on most of the time. It doesn't matter. Behave like a young lady should,*" she would whisper harshly. A bruise on the arm from a sharp backhand, or a wrenched wrist from being pulled back to a sitting position, were reminders not easily forgotten. No leaning on an adult, no crawling into a cozy lap, as Mother had allowed.

The prayers and songs seemed to go on forever. Jocelyne didn't understand a word, but tried to keep up with the adults standing, kneeling and sitting back down. When her stomach growled, she pressed her tiny gloved fist under her rib cage to silence it, then fussed with the lace on her dress and the tops of her socks. Smack. A look, a hiss, "Sit still! Arrête de bouger!"

The priest droned on. The wooden seat was finally warm, but still uncomfortable against the bare flesh under her dress. "Oh well," she told herself, "just look around and think about what we'll have for breakfast. How come Pauline gets to nap? I can tell she's leaning on Grandmère. It's not fair. But so what, she's just a baby, and I'm already a big girl in school, and she's not, so there." She sat up straighter and arranged her wide-brimmed hat, revelling in the feel of the long ribbons flicking along the back of her neck as she turned her head from side to side, until... another slap!

With a quiet sigh, she turned her head to stare at the statue of Mother Mary. She refused to look at the naked figure bleeding on the cross above the altar, but she adored Mary in her hooded blue gown, smiling down so sweetly from her perch. She found if she squinted, she could block out everything else and focus just on her.

One of the children at Catechism lessons had told her that once, someone had seen the statue shedding tears. A miracle. "I wonder if she will cry tears today?" Jocelyne stared at the head, slightly bowed, crowned with a yellow halo, searching for signs of flowing tears. The painted blue eyes looked past the congregation, somewhere beyond the doorway. No, the eyes, the cheeks were dry. "I think they made that up," Jocelyne said under her breath.

The statue had such a peaceful expression about her red lips, what would she be crying for, anyway? Her white hands, so delicate, were pressed together in prayer and you could clearly see the bones of her long, elegant fingers and her perfect fingernails. The hands looked like they might move at any moment. Strangely, her heart was visible right through her dress! It stood out in an angry, bloody stain. A torch burned with a yellow flame in the middle of the red heart shape. Jocelyne reminded herself again to ask her grandmother what it meant, why the lady's heart was bleeding and on fire at the same time, when she looked so happy. It must hurt, to have her heart wide open, burning like a candle! She wondered about it every week and every week, right after Mass, she promptly forgot to ask, in the excitement of racing outside to freedom.

Coloured light streamed through the stained glass windows. Candles flickered in their tiny rainbows of glass in the corner where every week they lit one candle in memory of Grandpapa and another for the "lost" baby. A hymn from the choir drifted down from above. Incense wafted heavily in the air as the priest and the altar boys walked past their pew, chanting. Amen, mm, yes, amen...ouch, another nudge from Grandmère's bony elbow. Smoothing her dress, pretending to be paying attention, Jocelyne peeked up at her father. Sometimes, if she was behaving very well, he would send her a smile with his eyes, and the glow would last the rest of the week, while he was away.

Oops, time to kneel. Almost missed it! Jocelyne stole a look at her father's shadowed face as he knelt down beside her. She knew she wasn't to stare at people as they were praying, but instead busy herself with her own prayers, and beg forgiveness for all her sins. Too bad she could never think of any. That was a sin, too, said Grandmère. Thinking bad thoughts about Pauline, yes, that was probably a sin, but she was such a brat! Just then, she noticed Daddy's face was wet.

What? Was Daddy crying? Real tears? She felt as if she couldn't breathe. She quickly checked the statue of Mary. Was she crying now, too? No. Then Daddy couldn't be crying. She turned back to see him mouth a prayer as his giant hand wiped his eyes with his white handkerchief. Then he placed his forehead on the pew in front of them and left it there, his shoulders shaking, his huge fingers clasping the wood, for what seemed a long time. Jocelyne looked at Grandmère, who glanced at her father's bowed head and then back at her with a stern, warning look as if to say, "Never you mind." She reached over and placed a hand gently on his trembling back.

A bell sounded and, without looking at anyone, her father stood up and followed a line of people to the front of the church. He had never done this in church before. For the first time, Grandmère stayed behind. The priest gave everyone something, one at a time, and spoke to each person. Then Daddy came back with his hands folded in front of him and his head bowed, making the sign of the cross at the end of the pew before kneeling down beside them again to pray some more.

Then, suddenly, Mass was over. Her father reached over to put on his wide-brimmed hat, steered the girls by the shoulders out onto the sunlit portico, lit a cigarette and cheerily greeted everyone they met. As if it had never happened. As if just a few moments before, he hadn't been crying, in front of everybody. Strange. He said a warm goodbye to the priest with a handshake, then drove Grandmère and the girls back to the village for breakfast in the café, whistling to the car radio and chatting the whole way.

Such a treat, to have breakfast "out" on Sundays. It almost made the ravenous hunger worthwhile, waiting for the platters of food to magically appear from the kitchen. They always sat in a booth rather than on the rotating stools at the counter, where the girls could be safely ensconced in each corner. Perched on their knees, they bounced on the red vinyl seats, while Dad ordered coffee and lit another cigarette. When Grandmère returned from the washroom, she gestured to the children to sit properly as the waitress passed out menus to each adult. Jocelyne peered over her father's shoulder, leaning on his arm, until he finally passed her the menu.

"What'll ya have there this mornin', Sunshine?" the waitress asked cheerily. Jocelyne, not realizing she was being addressed, remained hidden behind the broad vinyl cover.

"She'll have..." Paul started.

"No, Daddy. I can read it. Yes, please, I will have two pancakes, bacon and sausages, with toast and peanut butter for dessert."

"Just bring the usual, Maggie, with two plates so's I can split it up for the girls. They'll never eat that much. Mornin' there, Bill. How's

Mr. Thompson doing this bright Sunday morning? Quite the crowd in here last night, eh? By God, the hotel trade, that's the business to be in. Sure as hell beats workin' for a livin'!"

"Nooooo, Daddy. I don't want to share with Pauline. I want my own plate! I can eat it all, you'll see. I'm starving! Pleeeeaassse!" Jocelyne interrupted.

Paul groaned and rubbed his hand across his forehead. She heard her grandmother gasp and saw her arm reach across the table. She knew she had spoken out of turn and was about to get a smack.

But Mr. Thompson caught Grandmère's hand, clasped it in both his own and said, "Ah, you are looking lovely this morning, as usual, Madame Gerard. Such a beautiful hat!"

Then with a wink at the waitress, he leaned over toward the girls and added, "Don't you worry, little Missy, Maggie will fix you up a plate just right. 'Course you're hungry, why heck, it's almost lunchtime. And your little sister there looks like she has quite the appetite on her, too. A plate of pancakes for them both is just the ticket, I'd say. We'll make sure you're as full as a tick before you leave here this mornin'. Here, Maggie, let's get Mr. Gerard some more coffee. More for you, Madame?"

While they waited for their breakfast, Jocelyne was allowed to pick any song she wanted from the jukebox selector right at their table. Dad would slide one shiny dime to her, and she would remain occupied until the plates arrived, flipping the cards in the machine by the shiny tabs at the top of the plastic container. There were at least twenty cards, with about ten titles on each, arranged by song title from A to Z. "Which one, which one? Go with one you know, or just take a guess?" Sweet agony. She couldn't ask. She had been firmly told that the adults wouldn't read the titles for her. She had to read them herself. Turning the cards back and forth , sometimes one at a time, sometimes a few at once, she struggled through as many titles as she could, trying to make the perfect choice. It was fun to watch the cards fall, forward and back inside the plastic box. "I wonder if I can flip them all at once," she mused to herself. Then suddenly, "Quick, quick, here comes Maggie with the plates. Oh look, I get my own plate... hurray! Okay, here goes!"

She had to put her money in the slot and press the right buttons (E14, or A10, or M3....) before they started their meal, or her song might not play before they left. She also was careful not to press the wrong letter and number together. You never knew what you might get if you made a mistake! Once she had selected a cowboy song that Dad happened to know and he had sung along and it was just...awful!

Just one song. Only one dime from Daddy. What would it be like to have a quarter? But no, better not think about that. One is enough, but it makes it so hard! Once, she had secretly hidden her dime for the collection plate in her gloved hand, saving it for the jukebox. When her second song went on, and Jocelyne announced proudly that it was a surprise for everybody, Daddy had asked her where the money had come from. The sting of the spanking she got afterward, and the lack of jukebox music for the next two Sundays, reminded her never to try that trick again.

"Isn't Mr. Thompson nice, Daddy?" Jocelyne watched carefully as the tall, elegant figure smoothly moved up and down the aisles, stopping at every table. "He looks so nice in his suit. You should get a blue suit like that, too. Mmmmppf, these pancakes are nummy yummy! See, I *can* eat the whole plate! Pass the syrup, s'il vous plaît, Grandmaman."

Sunday morning. Perfect. Except just one thing was different today. She would have to remember to ask what the priest gave Daddy up at the front of the church, that made him so happy, after he was so sad. But not right now. This was not the right time. Yes! This is it! This was her song!

"Listen, Daddy. This is how it goes: 'She loves you, yeah, yeah, yeah...' I know all the words off by heart! All the girls are practicing at recess. I can sing it all by myself! I'll sing it for you in the car on the way home!"

Chapter Twenty-five

The golden fall leaves wove a blanket to protect the ground from the coming winter snow. By October, the school day started and ended in a cool walk down the block, against a brisk wind. The deep blue summer sky chose to wear grey clouds more often than not. Now that they had moved into the village, Jocelyne missed the cozy, bumpy, noisy bus ride every morning and afternoon. That and recess had been the highlight of her days. Jocelyne found that the time from nine o'clock to noon, followed by one-thirty to four could pass easily and dreamily if she did exactly as she was told. After being placed in the corner or the "dumb" row with "the crows" a few times, she had learned to remain still and silent in class. She'd twirl her finger in the hole in the top of the desk and wait, wait, wait to be called upon. She had asked her mother what the hole was for and been told it was for something called an inkwell that held ink for writing with a pen. Foolishly, she had then asked Teacher when they would get their ink.

"As if I could give bottles of ink to you lot! What a sight that would be! No, you young'uns will be writing with pencils for a looong time to come. Besides, we don't even use ink anymore, thank Heavens! In Grade Four, you'll learn to write with a ballpoint pen."

"But then why are the holes still there, in all the desktops?"

"Joceeleene, cease with all your endless questions and get back to your printing, girl!"

So down her head went again. As long as Teacher's back was turned or she was out in the hall you could get away with wriggling in your desk, to alleviate "numb bum" and poking or making faces at the child in front or behind. But must be careful. Musn't get caught. Teacher said there were a few things you had to learn in Grade One, to show you were ready for Grade Two: to sit in a desk: hands clasped in front, back straight, feet crossed, pencil and eraser ready; to wait your turn: stand in line, arms to your sides; to walk down the hall properly: third tile from the wall, in a straight line, on the right hand side, no running, no pushing; to ask a question: raise your hand and wait to be called upon. But there were no more questions. Just answers. Give the correct answer when Teacher said your name. Otherwise, keep quiet. Run your finger around the rough edges of the empty inkwell hole and daydream, with an ear cocked, just in case. Best not to upset Teacher. She might call home or send a note and that would upset Mother again. Stand up, sit down, copy this, repeat that. No less, no more.

Jocelyne used to look forward to the bus ride at the end of the day. Nose in a book, she could block out voices, Jimmy's taunting, the bang-bang-bang of his boot against the back of her seat. She would munch on an apple saved from lunch, kick off her boots and warm her toes on the metal heater underneath the windows. If it was really cold outside, she drew pictures in the frosting on the glass, hearts, flowers, initials. The engine's rumble thrilled through her spine and the warm currents of air and the buzz of children's voices lulled her into a comfortable daze. When the bus stopped in front of her house, she would stumble down the aisle and the two steps to the folding bus door half-asleep, mumbling a polite goodbye to the bus driver. Then she would run down the lane to her front door as if a wolf were after her, hitting the bottom step out of breath, fling the door open wide and shout, "Mom, I'm home. Can I have a samwidge?"

Then, as now, her mother was always home when Jocelyne arrived after school, and since they had moved to the village, she was there when she came home for lunch. Jocelyne's face still burned with shame when she remembered her first day of going home for lunch. She had left at the recess bell, amazed at how fast the morning had slipped by. Suzanna had been startled to see her at the door at ten thirty and sent her back to school with a note. She couldn't walk her back, since she couldn't leave Pauline or Nicolas. So Jocelyne had been forced to face the taunts of the other children and the sympathetic smile of her teacher alone.

Suzanna rarely went into the village stores or anywhere else. She stayed in the house, minding Pauline and Nicolas, doing the chores, according to the common housewife's regimen: Monday, wash clothes; Tuesday, iron; Wednesday, mend and tidy; Thursday, bake bread; Friday, scrub floors. Saturday was the day reserved for shopping in town, including buying clothes as well as all the groceries for the week. The weekly menu was set, so the list was not complicated: Sunday, roast beef or pork; Monday, leftovers; Tuesday, pork chops; Wednesday, chicken; Thursday, leftovers; Friday, fish; Saturday, macaroni and cheese. Buying enough provisions to last the week was challenging, though, and they usually ran out of milk, bread and eggs mid-week. That meant packing up all the children and making the short drive two miles into the village, when they had rented the house. Now that they lived close by, Jocelyne could run the errands.

Suzanna railed against the village stores. "Produce: not fresh; meat: too expensive; canned goods: no selection." Paul urged her to support the local businesses and get to know the other housewives, even before they moved to the new house. HE thought she would enjoy the company. She stubbornly refused. "Those old biddies, who stand around in the store or meet for tea and do nothing but gossip about what they hear on the partyline? Not on your nelly! I hate the village! I don't want to move there, even if it is a new house! Why can't we live in town? At least then I could be closer to my mother!"

The nine hundred people in the village knew everything about each other and everything that happened for a radius of ten miles. From the highway, a three hundred-sixty degree vista of prairie was punctuated by only two landmarks: a tall green water tower and a single grain elevator. The grain elevator waited to unload its cargo next to the railroad tracks, not far from the abandoned train station. The passenger train between Edmonton and Calgary no longer even designated this place a whistlestop. The school, one church and all the local commerce lined the one paved street, cutting in from the highway and leading back to it in less than a mile. Down Main Street, services were provided by two grocery stores, one hardware store, the bank, the post office, a machine shop, a gas station and one dry goods "variety" shop. In less than ten minutes, a child could run from one end of the street to the other. A car would be back on the highway within five minutes. But most travellers didn't bother to leave the main highway and passed the village by unnoticed. The few businesses struggled to survive, depending more for their income on the wealthy farmers on the outskirts than the blue collar workers clustered together on the prairie. With the exception of a few school teachers, the policeman and the garbage collector, the households were more or less supported by construction and oilfield workers, truck drivers and labourers. Like Jocelyne's father, the men worked far away, often for months at a time, leaving their families home in the village. Housing was cheap. Expenses were few.

For adult entertainment, there was the bar in the one hotel right off the highway. Every Saturday night men in suits and ties, their pockets brimming with cash, crammed the noisy, smoky room, eager to quench their enormous thirst. Mr. Thompson, the hotel owner, circulated, flashing his smile and gold jewellery. The diamond rings on both pinkies left an impression on his customers' hands as he crushed them with his firm handshake. He greeted them all by name. Every weekend the bar was occupied to capacity. When the bar was closed, at midnight on weeknights and on Sundays, according to Alberta law, socializing continued at Mr. Thompson's café. Coffee: ten cents a cup, refills, five cents, served hot and strong all day. Especially on Sundays. Special customers were given refills "on the house" if Mr. Thompson happened to walk by. He could afford to be generous.

Other business owners in the village were not so prosperous. "Greene's Grocery" had been in the same family for years. The mother, father and their two girls lived above the store. Children at school secretly envied the Greene's daughters. Instead of living in a tiny bungalow, as they did, Valerie and Tammy's home was a spacious apartment overlooking the main street. Not to mention that they seemed to have free access to the candy counter, for they doled out an endless supply of treats to their chosen friends at recess time.

"Imagine, having a store with everything you want, right below your bedroom, where you could go and get pop and candy any time of the night or day!" the children marvelled.

Well-loved, respected members of the community, who went to the local Protestant church on Sundays, Mr. and Mrs. Greene didn't fraternize with their customers, but quietly offered credit when they knew it was needed. The wooden-framed building, with its high, old-fashioned whitewashed storefront, had not changed in over fifty years. Anything could be found in its spacious aisles or stacked on the hardwood floor, from fresh farm eggs to fashion magazines to firecrackers. Most people in the village stopped by once a day, to pick up a few groceries along with the latest morsels of news from anyone who happened to be there. It wasn't hard to keep tabs on everyone's business.

Just down the street, on the same side, separated only by an abandoned hotel, was the Greene's only competition. The other store was much smaller, in a plain, modern block brick building with a fluorescent sign advertising "Lee's Convenience Store." The last owner had gone bankrupt and disappeared in the middle of the night. Then, to the surprise of everyone, the store had been taken over by a Chinese family. Promptly labelled "the Chink store," it was shunned by adult shoppers except after hours and on Sundays, when the Greenes, quite rightly, closed down. In fact, one of the main reasons the villagers avoided the store was the smell. The family of five lived in crowded quarters at the back of the store, and the sour odour of their cooking oil, garlic and fish permeated everything. The meat and potatoes crowd in the village made up all sorts of stories about what the Lees ate, including the neighbourhood cats.

But the one advantage for the village children was that, unlike Mr. Greene, Mr. Lee traded pop bottles for frozen ice cream treats, so they bravely gathered around the glass doors after school or on Saturdays, daring one another to go in. They would make a show of holding their noses, taking deep breaths, breathing through their mouths, and then venture inside. The store was always in semi-darkness, for the only light came in through the glass front doors and a few dim light bulbs. The children would quickly make their trade and pour back out into the sunshine, rubbing their eyes, giggling and screaming. All the way down the wooden sidewalk, one direction leading to their homes or the other heading back to school, they chanted, "Chinky, chinky Chinaman, sitting on a fence. Tryin' to make a dollar outta fifteen cents."

Sometimes, if Mr. Lee had been disturbed at his dinner, the

door of their back room suite would be ajar and a shaft of light would illuminate one of the aisles of dusty canned goods. The children would curiously peer in, catching a glimpse of Mrs. Lee feeding a baby in a highchair. No one knew how many children they really had. Only little Shelley was in school and she never said a word. The children reported on what they had spied and speculated about what they were eating, in the back room. The taunts and the mocking continued when the children came back to the playground after their noon hour excursion to buy candy. Shelley played with her skipping rope or threw a ball against the wall, pretending not to hear. If anyone took pity on her and asked her to play, she shook her head silently and ran in the opposite direction.

Jocelyne was not allowed to go to the store and buy candy at lunchtime, but once they moved into the village, her mother said she was old enough to run and get milk and bread when they ran out. It would save her getting dressed and going to the trouble of putting her "face" on.

"Mom, do you want me to go the Greene's store or the Chink store?"

"What did you say?"

"The Chink store—you know, the other store down the street."

"What did you call it? Where did you learn that name?"

"At school. That's what all the kids say. They have this little song too, that goes…"

"Never mind, never mind. Oh that goddamn school! Those horrible, ill-mannered little brats! Never, never let me hear you use that language again. You are not to repeat that song or use that name again. Do you understand? It's not nice, but those little savages wouldn't know any better. God, what a place to have to bring up kids. Now, here's the list. Go to Greene's—it's closer, and tell them to put it on the account."

For her efforts, she was allowed to buy ten cents worth of candy from the bins on the counter. At two or three for a penny, it took quite some time to decide. One day, while Mrs. Greene was busy finding the items on the list and Jocelyne was contemplating the choices she would make, Mr. Greene suddenly looked down at her, through the half-glasses perched on the end of his nose, and called out, "C'mere, Mother. Will you look at this child's eyes? All the time you'se a been comin' in here, I never noticed them so well before. Must be the sun shinin' in at the window, catchin' 'em just right in the light today. Did you ever see such eyes in your life? Not green, not blue, what colour'd you call that, Mother? Hazel? Now you don't say. Are they like your mom's? No. Like your dad's then? No. Well, you have beautiful eyes and that's a fact. Very unusual. Puts me in mind of that song, 'Jeepers, Creepers, where'd you get those peepers? Jeepers, Creepers, where'd you get those eyes?'" He threw back his head and sang out of tune at the top of his lungs. Jocelyne laughed, astonished.

"And they're even prettier when you smile. Now, how 'bout a caramel for the sweetest little gal in town? Have you finished with the order there, Mother? Let's tally it all up."

"Mr. Greene, can I please ask you a question?" Jocelyne stood on tiptoe and peeked over the counter, whispering even though there were no other customers in the store.

"Why sure, what can I do for you, now, there, Hazel?" he answered with a laugh at his new nickname for her.

Jocelyne hesitated for a moment, then burst out with, "The other day, there was a whole bunch of ladies in here, buying a lot of food and saying there was going to be another war. They said we have to get ready because there might not be any food so they were buying all these cans to put in their basement. But my mom didn't buy food for our basement yet so we might not have any. The other day there were planes that went over the school really loud. It even shook the windows. We been doing something called 'Duck and Cover' at school. It's not like a under-duck. It's where you go under your desk and hide in case there's a war. Do you think…"

"Whoa, whoa, hang on there, Hazel! Slow down and take a breath. Why, that's the most I've ever heard anyone say in one go, let alone someone your size! You musta' been bottlin' those words up for a spell. It's been worryin' you, I can tell. Well, I don't really know how to explain it to you, but they say that President Kennedy down in the U.S. of A. is thinkin' of shootin' off some kinda missiles down in

Cuba and that might cause a war. But I don't see as it's anything for us folks up here in Canada to be all fired up about. Why, we're so far north, they probably think we live in igloos!" Mr. Greene exclaimed and Jocelyne giggled.

"The ole U. S. of A. ain't gonna pay us no mind, Honey. Why, they ain't given us a second thought, I'll warrant," he assured her.

"But hey, if it makes them ol' gals feel better to have twenty cases o' mushroom soup stocked up in their basement, why, who'm I to argue? Just money in my pocket, I say. So much the better for Mrs. Greene and me. Them missiles ain't gonna make it all the way up here to our little ol' prairie town, even if they do shoot them off! But mum's the word, okey-dokey?" he said under his breath, looking around with a gleam in his eye as if to see if anyone else was listening.

"I got a big special comin' up on tomato soup next week!" he said, holding his hand against his wrinkled face to cover his words.

"Okey-dokey, Mr. Greene. I get it now. I'll be sure and tell my mom. Thanks!" Jocelyne shouted cheerily as she swung open the door with one hand and stepped out onto the sunny front steps. Arms wrapped around the brown paper grocery bag, she skipped down the tree-lined gravel streets, anxious to get home. Kicking dry brown leaves and delighting in the crunching sound they made underfoot (like Nicolas eating his cereal!), she chanted a song she had just learned in music class.

"*Bobby Shaftoe's gone to sea, silver buckles on his knee, he'll come back and marry me, little Bobby Shaftoe*! I love that song! I have to remember to sing it for Daddy when he gets home. *Little Bobby Shaaaaftoe!*" Her voice sailed into the crisp breeze.

"Just wait 'til Mom finds out there isn't going to be a war, after all. Mr. Greene said so, and he should know, he's got every newspaper in the world in that store. Holy cow, forgot to get my candy. Oh well," she shrugged, bouncing up the wooden steps to her back door. She set the brown paper bag down on the steps, flung open the screen door, then leaned against the heavy inner door to tumble inside.

"Mom, Mom," she shouted. "Guess what Mr. Greene says?"

Chapter Twenty-six

"Surprise." The word stood out amongst all the familiar ones on the page. The Grade One Reader glittered with a word she could not yet read. The teacher had sounded it out: "sur—pri—ze." A ringing, happy sound—like "hurray" or "I'm home!" A warm thrill raced down Jocelyne's spine as she stared at the picture. A family gathered in a sunny garden blooming with flowers, under an apple tree. Imagine, apples growing on a tree right in your own yard! Tommy knelt in the grass with Spot the dog. A feast awaited the family, spread out on a picnic table covered with a red and white checkered cloth. Susan, her beautiful blonde hair spilling across her pink dress, was opening a brightly wrapped present, amidst balloons and a cake with candles.

"Surprise, Susan! It's your birthday!" said Mother. She smiled, leaning forward with the cake.

"Surprise, Susan," said Mother. "A birthday cake for you!"

Father's outstretched hand offered Susan a tiny plate.

"Happy birthday, Susan," said Father. His bright smile beamed upon the family gathered around him. The sun shone out of the page and into Jocelyne's eyes. Surprise, surprise, surprise.

Far away, the teacher's voice was saying, "Wait, children. We're all on page five. That's right. Everybody point to the first word. Now, it's Ricky's turn to read. Come on, Ricky. Stand up and try now, there's a good boy. Follow along with your finger, boys and girls. Good, good, that's it. Everyone stay together."

"Surprise!" Jocelyne read under her breath. "Quick, turn the page to find out what happens next. Oh no, look, someone lost a balloon." There could never be enough words, enough stories, enough books.

"Look, Tommy, look!" Susan pointed at the sky. A red balloon is floating up, up, up. Where will it go? Who will find it?

"Joceyleene Gerard, please stand. No, you are on the wrong page, as usual. Follow along just for once, can't you? Now start. No, too fast. Take your time. There's no use rushing so's not to understand anything."

The class giggled. Jocelyne's face turned the same colour of the balloon in the picture, and she wished she could float up, up...

The hours between nine and four passed in a blur of worksheets and rituals, always the same. The only break came during the daily practice of "duck and cover." A warning siren went off every noon hour in the center of the village as a "test," planes whizzed low over the school, setting the windows a-rattle. The threats of war on the radio disturbed Jocelyne's nights, but also gave her one consolation: maybe one night a plane would bomb the school and blow it up! She put herself to sleep with her fantasies of what might happen to the stark brick building and all who "lived" there.

"Look, Tommy, look up! See Mrs. H. See Mrs. H. go. Up, up, up! Surprise! Oh, look! A piano! Down, down, down. See the piano fall. Oh no, look out, Mrs. H.! Run, Spot, run! Surprise, Mrs. H. Surprise!" Giggling and sucking her thumb, she would rock in her bed until she drifted off.

One cold November day, Jocelyne arrived home to find her mother in front of the television set, crying. She was standing in the kitchen at the ironing board, holding the iron in mid-air, tears streaming down her pale cheeks. Nicolas crawled at his mother's feet, pulling clothes from the basket and throwing them on the floor.

"What is it, Mommy? What's wrong?" Jocelyne asked, trembling.

"*The president has been shot. President Kennedy is dead,*" a deep voice resounded within the black and white screen.

"Who's that, Mommy? Do we know him? Why are you so sad? What's going to happen?"

"No, no, we don't know him. He's the President of the United States. He's a very important man. He was shot in a car, with his wife right beside him. It's terrible, terrible! I don't know what will happen now. What's this world coming to, when the President can get shot like that, right in the open? Poor Mrs. Kennedy, what a shock for her!" Suzanna's voice shook as she spoke into the air, without looking at Jocelyne.

Her mother sobbed as she continued to stare at the images flashing on the television. There was no after school snack. Jocelyne silently took Pauline's hand and led her out to the porch. She pulled a set of jacks from her school bag and they played for a while, until Pauline dropped the little pink ball down the steps and it disappeared between the slats of wood. They went back inside. The television was still on, but Suzanna was in the bedroom down the hall. Nicolas had burrowed into the pile of clothes on the floor and fallen asleep. Jocelyne slid a chair across the kitchen to reach the counter, so she could make peanut butter sandwiches for herself and her sister. Climbing onto the counter, she retrieved two glasses from the cupboard, then awkwardly poured them each a glass of milk from the cold, slippery bottle she had managed to lift out of the refrigerator. In the fading evening light, they ate and watched the moving shades of grey on the television screen.

"Look, there's the man in the car, smiling and waving. That's his wife. Isn't she pretty? Now he's ffffalling down. That's 'cause he got shot. Like Uncle Richard shot the dog when he was run over, 'member? With a gun. In the hhhhead. He's dead now, I guess. He's the principal of the Nited States. That's what happened to make Mommy ccccry. He's 'spost to ddddoo something very 'portant, but inssssttead, now he's ssshot, so he's dead and he ccccaaann't do it no more. I wisht he didn't get ssshot like that, to make Mommy cry ssso much."

After that night, though, her mother seemed happier. Jocelyne thought of it as a switch going on, like turning on the television. Her mother started talking and laughing again. She came back from the faraway place where she had been for such a long time.

"The principal of the Nited States must'a been very special," she thought, "'cause when he got shot it made Mommy so sad, and at the frooneral on t.v., when the little boy saluted, she cried so hard I thought she couldn't breathe. But then after, she was like Mommy again. A very 'portant person, that's for sure. Holy cow, I wonder what he did that was so 'portant? I know, I'll ask Mr. Greene. He knows everything."

Chapter Twenty-seven

Death. There it was. The answer. Why hadn't she thought of it before? Now the thought repeated over and over in her head, giving her a place to focus her attention. Too bad it hadn't happened during the miscarriage. So much pain. Could have been over so quickly. Just to go to sleep. No more diapers to wash, meals to make, floors to scrub. No more arguments about money, about drinking, about other women, about sex, about family, about…anything and everything. That would end it. Finally, once and for all. What a perfect answer. A bottle of the sleeping pills the doctor had given her. The whole bottle. In one go. It would only take a minute.

She'd put it off until tomorrow. Or the next day. But the thoughts gave her power. She got things ready. Prepared the meals. Cleaned the house. Went through her things and decided who would get what. Not much to leave behind anyway. Dresses, shoes, hats—who would want those? And her jewellery. That was a laugh! A bunch of cheap rhinestone earrings and necklaces she had accumulated over the years, an ugly old silver brooch from Paul's mother, and her diamond and pearl cocktail ring. Well, those two things might be worth something someday. She wrapped them in tissue and wrote Jocelyne's name on the package. Just before closing the lid, she casually tossed her wedding band on the top.

Then she spent time with the kids. Really noticed them for the first time in ages. Bought them toys and played with them for a whole rainy Saturday, making tents out of blankets in the living room and cuddling inside, telling them stories like she had in the old days, before… She stayed home all day. So what if they had no food in the house. It was too exhausting anyway. Paul could do it himself! Let him look after the kids and see what it was like, since he thought it was so easy. Then maybe he'd understand why she got so bitchy and tired.

Why hadn't she listened to Evelyne, her best friend at the old restaurant? Almost ten years ago now.

"Listen, Sugar Pie. You could have your pick of men. When was the last time you looked in a mirror? Why, you're prettier than that actress, what's her name, Liz Taylor. Thick black hair with natural curl, damn you, that skin of yours, like milk it is, high cheekbones with a little mole in just the right spot, settin' off those baby blues. What's she got that you ain't got, I ask you? Well, yeah, a bigger bust maybe. You are a bit skinny, I'll grant you that. But nothin' that a few years of the good life wouldn't cure. Why don't you cut outta this one horse town and head for Hollywood, or at least the big city, get yourself somebody with some prospects? Paul, why, he's a nice enough fella an' all, but he ain't exactly marriage material. I know his type! For God's sakes, he was doggin' after me, before you come along. I let him know where the bus gets off, never fear! "

Or Dad?

"The last thing you should do in the world is to marry that man! Don't do it, Suzanna. Don't get married. That man, he's no good for you. I want my little girl to be happy. He will never make you happy, you mark my words. He's brash, self-centred and loud: a big talker but a slow walker. You know what I mean by that, don't you? C'mon, Sweetheart, it's not too late to change your mind. Here now, I know how to make my gal smile."

Lifting his banjo down from its hook on the wall, he plucked away and in a fake Southern accent, sang with all his heart: "*Well, it rained all night, the day I left, the weather, it was dry. Sun so hot, I froze to death, Suzanna don't you cry. Oh, Suzanna! Now don't you cry for me. For I come from Alabamy, with a banjo on my knee.*" Sure enough, he brought on her usual fit of laughter. She could still see him, sashaying around the kitchen in his misshapen wool sweater and his battered felt fedora. With his grizzled, care-worn face and his shabby work clothes, no one would suspect that he had once been a renowned entertainer at county fairs far and wide. In later years, only his children and grandchildren would delight in his musical talents. His legacy to his daughter included an ability to play the piano by ear, and her name.

"Crazy, mixed-up song made about as much sense as my life

ended up making. Should'a known better than to name me after a goofy song like that," she laughed mirthlessly to herself. "Nobody ever got it right except him and Ma, anyhow. My kids are not going to suffer like that. They're gonna keep their names and insist they be pronounced right. In school, it was always "Suze" or "Susan" and with Paul's clan, "Suzanne." Pronounced in French, like that would make me feel special. Part of the family. But then they go speak French all the time, leaving me out, to just sit there, like a piece of furniture. Paul doesn't even try to make them include me. Well, from now on they can call me "Suzanna." I'll make sure she knows it, too, the next time I'm at the farm! How dare they change my name?"

Slam! She hit the brakes on that train of thought. How had it gotten away from her again?

"I'm done, and that's final!" she stated emphatically, aloud, to make it official. The children playing on the floor were startled and looked up at her with puzzled faces. She put her finger to her lips, shook her head and motioned for them to go back under their tent.

Another route opened in her mind. What about divorce? She threw up the customary roadblocks. Not an option. As a Catholic, Paul would never agree to it. If she tried to leave, he would hunt her down. How far would she get, with no skills, no money, nowhere to turn? How would she pay a lawyer? And even if she did succeed, what would it mean? Poverty for her and her kids, as she worked long hours as a waitress in some greasy spoon. Who would look after them then? She might lose them altogether.

It would be nice to see them grow up, though. Go to school, get good jobs, buy nice cars, give her grandchildren. What might Jocelyne become, with her quick mind and vivid imagination? Pauline, always moving in time to the music on the radio: a singer or a dancer like her grandpa, for sure. And Nico, that little clown, he was sure to be a comedian... Now look—she was doing it again! Crazy. That's what it was. She had finally gone crazy. Stuck here in this damn house alone week in, week out, with no one to talk to but the four walls and the kids, it was bound to happen. Her thoughts ran in endless circles.

Where was she? Oh yes. Death. Final. Complete. No coming back. So tired. She rocked in her chair, humming to herself, while the children giggled and squirmed in their tent.

"Suzanna, don't you cry." Tears streamed down her smooth, white cheeks.

"I'm trapped. Only one way out. They'd be better off without me anyway. Poor kids. Their mother is useless, worn out. At twenty-nine!" She held her breath to suppress her sobs. A deep sigh and again her mind reeled forward.

Such great kids! Everyone said so. Paul's mother would take care of them, anyway. It wouldn't be so bad. She'd already raised six and somehow still had energy to spare. She was so iron-willed and capable. Such a decisive, efficient person. Her house was always clean, dinner always ready no matter what else was going on. She made everything, even bread, from scratch. Her whites always whitest, ironing always done. Housework, too. How did she do it? And she had managed a whole farm! But, she had such strong hands, like a man's. Stirring a pot, knitting a sweater or making a pie, it all seemed equally easy for the big-boned, vital woman, even at her advanced age. Suzanna gazed down at her tiny hands, limp and idle in her lap. So pale, fine-boned and delicate.

"Maybe I just wasn't cut out to be a mother," she muttered. Rocking and thinking. Thinking and rocking in time with her thoughts.

"I needed someone to look after me, not the other way around. That's what Dad saw in me."

Back then, blinded by...dreams...she hadn't given a thought to children, and what that would mean. She had dismissed her mother's advice, given in such bitter tones, warning her about the terrors of sex, the threat of pregnancy, the agony of childbirth. Suzanna had laughed it off dismissively, as if the woman didn't know what she was talking about. What a little fool she was, just as Mother had said, though she would never admit it to her now. She hadn't a clue that there would be never-ending work, always the same, dull chores, and children constantly wanting...something....always underfoot, making noise...

"Let's pretend that you're a fairy princess and you didn't know it.

Nicolas, you be the king. I'll be the mean old witch, AAAAAHHHH!"
Jocelyne, as usual, was directing the children's play on the floor.
When she screamed, Pauline and Nicolas giggled and kicked their feet
in the air, almost tugging the blankets off the chairs. Despite herself,
Suzanna smiled.

"Ha! What did you imagine, Suzanna, in your fairy tale world?"
she asked herself, digging her nails into the upholstered arms of the
chair, surprised at the viciousness of the question. Almost sounded
like…Mother?

"Fine clothes, a big house, nice car. That's what impressed you,
isn't it? That's what you thought he meant, when he said he'd give you
everything." The voice pestered her, an annoying fly in her ear.

"Yes, to be honest, yes," she roared back in her mind. "My God,
that farm—riches beyond anything I'd ever known. When I came
from nothing, nothing, do you hear? Scrounging for every penny,
slaving my fingers to the bone in that restaurant, with no hope of ever
having anything decent. Stupid me, I thought that we'd live better.
Paul always had pockets full of money, showering me with gifts. He
made huge money in construction and, with no expenses, living at his
Mother's, of course he had money to burn. With Mme. Gérard still
waiting on him hand and foot when he came home from the road,
what did he have to worry about? Never had to do a thing for himself!
But could I see that? No! His little princess, he'd called me. Well,
Paul, your fancy diamond ring is now hidden at the back of my drawer
and can stay there, for all I care. What good is it, when it doesn't pay
the bills? But then, Paul you don't pay them half the time either, do
you? Showing off, as usual, in front of your mother, trying to prove
to her that you're such a success. Little do you know, she sees right
through you."

"Ummhmm, some princess I am, all right!" her mind droned
on. "Imprisoned in this half-finished castle and left to rot, while you
gallivant all over the goddamn country! Must be nice! And who wants
to make a bet that your castle will never be finished either, Buddy,
when you never do a day's work on it when you ARE home. The bar
and your buddies look better than a hammer and nail, I guess. Just
like Dad said about you, 'A big talker, but a slow walker.' Good at

starting things, not so great at finishing them. Why, why couldn't I see that back then?"

With annoyance, she brushed the imaginary fly away from her ear, flicking back the loose black curls against her neck.

"I should cut off this goddamn hair. Too much work anyway," she mumbled. "Cut it short and start wearing a wig, like Paul's mother. Much more, how you say…efficace, as she would say, efficient! Yes, Madame Gérard, ever efficient. Incredible, that woman, just incredible."

Despite her feelings of inadequacy around Paul's mother, Suzanna had learned to admire her while they stayed at the farm. Mme. Gérard worked constantly and seemed to take so much pride in a clean house, a starched shirt, a delicious meal. Why? The stoic old woman had no patience for anyone who claimed to be tired or sad. There wasn't time for it, she had explained to her daughter-in-law. After surviving the Depression, the death of her son and her husband, and on and on, she had learned that you had to "simply get on wit' work, ma chère, an' try not to tink about it. God, he 'ave a plan, an' he know bes', you'll see. 'E will solve it da way 'e sees fit, an' we mu' accept 'is Will. We mus' 'ave fait' in somtink, for what else is dere, odder dan dat?"

After the miscarriage, though, she had been such a help. Suzanna's own mother had stayed all of three days. Then Mme. Gérard took over. A pillar of strength. She had fed the children, cleaned the house, held Suzanna's hand while she cried. She had told her to cry it all out. After one week, though, she bustled in one morning, threw open the curtains and declared briskly, "Bon, dat's e-nough lay about. Up you get now, get dress an' see to Nicolas. Il a besoin de sa maman. 'E an' de girl, dey need dere Maman. I stay an' 'elp a few more day, den I mus' get back to my hown 'ousework or my place, she turn into de pigsty! My Richard, 'e can clean out de pig barn, but 'e not too good to keep up a 'ouse. Chantale non plus, come to dat, even if she was 'ome, which she is not."

Okay then. She had tried. But she felt as if her feet were slipping on clay, every time she climbed the hill. She knew Mme. Gérard would never approve of her self-pity. Neither would her own mother.

There was nowhere to turn. She had to "get on wid it."

"...now don't you cry for me..."

The kids loved Mme. Gérard and loved the farm. They'd be happy there.

"Yes, that's it," she whispered, shaking her head decisively. "Let Paul's mother raise them!" She'd leave a note, saying that was her wish. It would be the right thing for the kids and, besides, she needs something to keep her busy, to stop worrying about Chantale, who had abandoned her poor mother. Didn't she care that the poor old lady was sick with worry? How could she be so heartless? Of course, she didn't understand what a mother went through.

But surely Chantale would come home again soon, tail between her legs, as Paul said. Then she would be around to help with the kids. Despite her bitchiness, Suzanna knew Chantale really cared about them; she had witnessed her gentle manner when she thought no one was watching. And thank God she had called the day of the miscarriage, out of the blue like that! It seemed that she was a decent person, except in the presence of her mother and Richard.

If his family wouldn't help, well, Paul would just have to deal with reality, for once in his life. Suzanna left the rocking chair and joined the children on the floor, pulling a blanket over her head. So tired. Just lie here for a little while, just for a few minutes, before getting supper ready. What to make? Oh, bacon and eggs, yes, that would be good enough.

Suddenly, she heard the kitchen door being slammed against the rubber stopper. She peeked out from under the tent blanket. Paul's huge frame filled the doorway. She didn't move, but waited for him to come in. His clothes were soaking wet. Shaking himself like a dog he called Suzanna's name as he tramped across the kitchen floor in his muddy cowboy boots. She rolled her eyes in annoyance. How many times had she told him to take his boots off at the back door? Not as if he ever had to wash the goddamn floors and get the black marks off! Now that they had linoleum, he could at least try to keep it clean. She cursed under her breath.

The children stayed hidden, giggling softly, planning to jump out and surprise their father. Jocelyne put a finger to her lips, warning Nicolas to keep quiet.

"Surprise!" Jocelyne and Pauline chorused, throwing back the blankets.

"Mother's dead," Paul announced.

Part IV

Nouvelle France, 1650

Chapter Twenty-eight

Québec, December 31, 1650

"Au feu! Au feu! Au secours! Au secours!"

One of the sisters had managed to race up the smoke-filled stairwells to the belfry and frantically sound the alarm. Fortunately, almost all the residents of the Ursuline Convent were in the chapel for Matins, the early morning service. The servants gathered in the kitchen, breaking their fast before starting their daily chores, quickly evacuated the building after checking the dormitories for any stray child who might have stayed abed and become disoriented in the smoke. The nun who had rung the bell, finding the way back down impassable, turned to the window, shattered the single pane of glass with her shoe, and jumped safely into a snowbank, three storeys below. The townsfolk summoned by the alarm, congratulated her on her quick thinking and bravery, while they helplessly watched the flames consume all but the convent's stone exterior. They could do nothing but join the Sisters in their lament for the loss of Mother Superior's precious books, her letters and exquisite embroideries and all their supplies! Christian charity demanded that the townspeople bundle every survivor in a blanket and billet them in their own homes. At least God had seen to it that not a single nun, servant or student had been killed in the fire. But what would dear Mother Marie do when she returned to find the Convent a devastated ruin?

Georgette did not know, or care. She had successfully accomplished her mission, with no loss of life and a hero's welcome in the cozy home of prominent notary, Paul Gérard. Perhaps now she would gain the freedom she desired. The Sisters and their charges would be better off out of the confines of that stifling Convent, they would soon discover. Let the native girls return to their own people and those deluded French nuns, bound and determined to "enlighten" them, go back to France and save themselves. She, for one, intended to cut a new life out of whole cloth, this time.

*****

"Oh non, Monsieur, you misunderstand, if you will pardon my saying so. I am not a 'réligieuse,' but only one of their humble servants, serving God by caring for their needs day and night. It must be that God awoke me from my sleep to smell the smoke and, as soon as I did, I ran for the tower to sound the alarm. How could I think only of myself, with so many lives at stake? It was not bravery but necessity that made me jump through the window, and I trusted in our Lord and Saviour to break my fall. For once, the deep snow was not a curse but a blessing, n'est-ce pas?" Georgette laughed brightly.

"Mmm, please thank your wife for her kindness. This hot soup is delicious. I wish I could speak to her in her own language. Mère Marie is learning the Huron tongue and teaching it to some of the students, but of course, I have not had that privilege. Perhaps while I am here, I will pick up some rudiments, which will then help me in my encounters with the sweet little ones at the Convent when I return," she said before taking another spoonful of the soup, a thick, satisfying broth of ham hocks and dried split peas. She sat for a moment, warming her face, smiling into the steam rising from the bowl. A delightful shudder ran down her spine as her body responded to the heat from the food and the blazing fireplace. The weight of the woollen blanket on her shoulders strengthened her resolve.

"Oh and please let me assure you that I will earn my keep! I see you have a young son and another, may it please God, on the way. Your lovely wife, Solange, you say? Such a pretty name, she does indeed resemble an angel on this earth! Well, surely she could use my help. She looks tired and a bit sad, if you will excuse my boldness, Monsieur. She is probably lonely and missing her kinfolk. Believe me, I sympathize. I am a hard worker and will pitch right in to lighten her load, at no cost to yourself except my room and board. Who knows how long it will take to rebuild the Convent and in the meantime I

300

am not one to depend on charity. Would that be acceptable to you, Monsieur?"

*****

Who was this stranger he had brought into the house now? Always someone, coming and going, in, out, in, out, the door always open, the cooking pot always empty and the eau-de-vie flowing like water downstream. His business he said: "documents" to verify, "transactions" to sign, "letters" to write. What did it all mean besides a constant influx of noisy, backslapping, arguing men tramping into the house in their filthy boots? And the continuous shouts of: "Solange! Woman! Get this man something to eat. Never let it be said that a man went away hungry from my table, by God!" That much French she had quickly learned to understand, even back when they had lived in their cabin in the woods. For the rest, it was no more than the chatter of squawking ravens in the trees, as she quietly occupied herself with her own thoughts, her chores and the delights of caring for her son. Her only joy.

But in spite of her obedience, hard work and patience with his occasional outbursts of violence, she must have displeased him, for it seemed he had decided to bring another woman to live with them. A white woman. An ugly white woman, with a pockmarked face and only half a nose! Did it mean he planned to discard her? So many white men routinely abandoned their native wives upon moving to this stone village, Kébec. Her only friend, Taïranronk, principal chief and orator of the few remaining members of the Huron tribe, had explained to her that the Black Robes frowned upon the intermarriage of the French and The People. So he had counselled her to accept the water ritual for both her and her son, to let herself be called by a foreign name rather than Yellow Bird, the beautiful name Grandmother had given her according to custom, and to learn their ways of eating, dressing and behaving in public. For survival. Most of the girls of their whole tribe who had not been killed or captured by the Iroquois were now sheltered in the huge stone longhouse on the hill, with nowhere else to go. The warriors were dead or living rough in the woods, with no homeland to call their own. Only the kindness of the tall white Mother on the hill had kept their children and many of the adults from starvation, crouched in their huts next to the Hotel-Dieu and the Ursuline Convent. "Do what you must to fit in," he had advised. She thought she had done her best. Then why was this woman here?

The smell of smoke hung heavy on the stranger, she had come in half-frozen and barefoot so she obviously needed help, and she smiled widely at Yellow Bird, revealing her missing front tooth. But not the truth behind her eyes. The dog growled and glared at her with his tail between his legs, even when she reached out her hand to pet him. Petit Paul clung to his mother and howled in fear when the woman approached. Nevertheless, Paul directed Yellow Bird to make up a bed for her next to Paul's crib in the room beside theirs. He seemed anxious to explain, through pleading words, gestures, and even taking her outside to show her the billowing smoke hanging in the air above the hill, that they must help the woman. Fine, she had no choice but to comply with her husband's wishes, but she would not leave her son alone in a room with any stranger, let alone this one. She took him to their own bed by telling Paul in her own language that the boy wasn't feeling well and needed his mother near him.

"D'accord, Solange, but please, you must try to speak French! Georgette, perhaps that is another way you can be of service to us, by teaching my wife to communicate in our language. I swear, she is just stubborn and refuses to learn, for she is not stupid by any means. Maybe you will have more patience with her than I do! After all, we have been together for nearly three years and she barely speaks a word."

"Oh, oui, bien sur! Of course, it would be my pleasure, Monsieur. And the little one, too, he must speak his father's tongue, to grow up strong and prosperous in New France, like Papa. N'est-ce pas, mon petit chou?" she said, clucking her tongue in the boy's face, which he quickly turned to hide against his mother's breast.

"Yes, it is obvious he is not feeling well. I too am exhausted from my misadventure. Thank you again so much, from the bottom of my heart, for taking me in, and once I have rested, you may be sure I will repay your kindness in every way I can. God Bless you and your lovely wife for your kindness. Bonne nuit, until tomorrow. I can't believe that it will be New Year's Day. The start of a whole new life for all of us, n'est-ce pas?"

*****

Speech delivered by Chief Taïraronk to Mère Marie de l'Incarnation and the Ursuline Sisters, January, 1651, upon the presentation of two porcelain necklaces, last remaining treasure of the Huron tribe, as an offering toward the rebuilding of the Ursuline Convent:

"You see before you, sainted sisters, naught but poor cadavers, all that remains of a nation that was once flourishing, yet exists no more. In the homeland of the Huron people, we have been devoured and ravaged to the bone by wars and famine. We cadavers stand upright only because you support us. You bear witness to the extremity of misery to which we are reduced. Look at us from all sides and ask yourselves if we should not justifiably spill torrents of tears for our sorrows.

Alas, this terrible accident that has befallen you will also renew all our misfortunes and the flow of tears that had only just begun to subside. To see this beautiful house of Jesus burn, to find this house of charity reduced to ashes, to know that the fire did not respect the holy sisters who inhabited it, forces us to relive the memory of the inferno which destroyed our homeland. Does this fire follow us everywhere? Let us cry together, dear sisters, as we share this misery."

Relations des Jésuites, 1651

*****

Contract between Paul Gérard, his wife, Solange, and Georgette Lapierre, of the parish Beauport de Québec:

The said Georgette Tessier promises to serve her master and mistress according to their wishes, in a forthright and honest manner, for a period of four years, whereby the said sieur Gérard

and his wife agree to pay thirty pounds per year, as well as to provide clothing and living expenses, as they do each so solemnly swear.

Signed at Québec the afternoon of July 17th, 1651: Paul Gérard, Georgette Tessier

Witnessed by: Richard Thibault, Notary

Chapter Twenty-nine

Québec, 1669

"C'est ça, Madame! That's it, you have him now! You see, there is not a horse alive that you cannot conquer! This magnificent stallion will do wonders for your stable! Soon you will be supplying horses to the Seigneur himself, for all of New France!" the trader shouted enthusiastically, all the while admiring the skill and grace of the woman prancing about the ring on the pale horse. Her svelte figure and shiny black hair only added to his pleasure in watching her move as one with the powerful animal.

She boldly rode astride, without a saddle, guiding the horse's movements with a light touch of the reins on his neck and the subtle pressure of her knees against his massive white sides. She wore buckskin breeches, gloves and moccasins she had made herself, exclusively for riding, as she was not permitted to dress like a native anywhere else. Of course, this clothing was perfectly suited to her passion for training horses, which surprisingly, her husband allowed. She seemed fearless, so different from the women in town, with their simpering ways, not to mention his own domineering wife.

By God, but Gérard was a lucky man! To have a woman like this, who had given him ten children, still so young, beautiful and fertile. And what's more: quiet! For she rarely spoke except to praise a horse or one of her children. He had heard tell that Paul had brought her out of the woods when he had been a "coureur de bois," back in the old days. A chief's daughter, no less. Well, that's what they all said about their "country wives," didn't they? But who could blame him for keeping such a lovely mistress, with that copper skin and eyes like a hunted doe? And on top of that, the bastard was rich, with lands granted to him by the Seigneur, a beautiful home, a barn, livestock, a plum position as notaire generating constant income, a servant (not much to look at, that one, but still...)! What more could a man ask for? Too bad he didn't have a touch of humility to go along with all his good fortune, the arrogant ass! Oh well, at least the old man wouldn't stint at buying his wife another horse, if she wanted it. He rubbed his hands together at the prospect of making a bargain in his favor.

*****

"So, does it make you happy, sweetheart? He is an outstanding animal and will no doubt serve us well, yes, but I want to see you smile. It's always been nearly impossible to tell what you are feeling, what is going on behind those black eyes of yours. Even after twenty years together, I can't say I know you. You could have at least made an effort to become a proper French wife. But no, you kept to your ways, not to say I don't admire them, but it makes it hard for me to live, with one foot in either world. I had to sacrifice, too, you know, to give up my freedom, for the sake of our family. A home, ten children, land, horses...you have more than most women will have in a lifetime. Yet still you seem to resent me, after all I have done. And since Gaetan died, you have become more silent that ever. Et Chris, you would think I had married a cloistered nun!" Paul slapped his hand against his thigh before taking another swig of the liquor in his mug.

"Ah well, at least you have been no trouble. Not like you, hein, Georgette? With your bewitching wiles! How fortunate for you that you did not remain in France, where they would have burned you at the stake as a sorceress and a heretic. Especially had word got out about the many ways you know to please a man. Where did you learn your tricks, anyway? I'll wager my mother didn't even know so much and she was a professional, that one! A courtesan, so called, in the court of King Louis himself! Did I ever tell you that? I see by that admiring look on your face that I have. Well, I'm not too proud to admit it, nor to say that I am the son of a French nobleman, no more than a cast-off bastard, in truth, but of noble blood nonetheless! And I haven't done so badly for myself, have I? Thanks to the old bitch and her generous legacy. Never gave me so much as a sideways glance when I was a boy, so why shouldn't I prosper from the fruits of her labour, so to speak? Made me a "notaire" so she did and now they all have to come begging to old Paul to bear witness to their official documents. Who would have guessed that a bastard like me could rise so high in the world? As you can testify, pussycat, your master can rise higher than most men! Get that pretty ass over here, wench! Sit on my lap and tell Papa you love him!" he shouted, grabbing the woman by the apron strings as she leaned over to stoke the fire.

"Yes, of course, Monsieur, just as soon as I have finished preparing the meal for nine children, yourself and your sweet wife. There might be a moment to spare, once I have eaten the leftovers, washed the dishes, swept the hearth and readied the children for bed. I will be sure to make hardening your cock my first priority, after that!" Georgette rolled her eyes and sketched an exaggerated courtesy.

"Listen, you sassy bitch, don't let your head outgrow your hat size! I could cancel your contract anytime, for your lack of obedience to your master. So don't push me too far and watch your mouth around my children, too!"

"Oh leave off with your empty threats. You know what would happen if you ever kicked me out and I were to tell dear Father Thomas of your doings behind closed doors, let alone to let the Seigneur know of some of your so-called deals. Besides, what would you do without me?" she scoffed, pinching his florid cheek and finishing her point with a light tap. Paul savagely grasped her forearm and twisted her around until she fell into his lap.

"Don't tempt your fate. Remember what I said about what happens to heretics like yourself. And look what you have done, upsetting your mistress with your crude talk. Just shut your trap and get back to work. I will deal with you later," he said as he pushed her away with a boot to the backside.

"There, there, my love, my little Yellow Bird, don't cry. Does it at least please you when I call you by your Algonquin name? I know how you hate conflict in the house. This whore is not worthy of your tears. You go off to bed now and rest, after your big day with your new horse. Imagine, taking on an unknown stallion in your condition! I am not convinced that you should be riding at all, with another babe so close on the way, but I never could control your actions, so why try now? Have you thought of a name, par exemple? For the horse, I mean, not the baby! Seems like a wild one to me—I know, 'Sauvage!' Wouldn't that be fitting?"

*****

"Come on now, Madame, push, just once more, you must push. Almost there, almost there...please, try again. Georgette, fetch her another mug of water and add even more whiskey to it this time."

"Oh for pity's sake, for mercy's sake, stop! She has laboured for thirty-six hours. The baby is breech. It will not come out of its own accord. You know your duty, now stop being such a coward and do it! Get the knife and cut, or I will do it myself. I can't bear to see her suffer so. I wouldn't leave a dog to endure such pain, let alone my dear mistress of twenty years! Solange, Solange, can you hear me? C'est Georgette, tu sais, ton amie. I have always been your sincere friend. I love you so much, for you are the kindest, gentlest, most patient woman I have ever known. That bastard Paul doesn't deserve such a wife! If God doesn't punish him for this, I will. I tried so hard to keep him away from you. I hope you understand, pleasuring him means nothing to me and it is easily done. It is for your sake—ten children, it is enough! And you becoming thinner and more fragile with each one. Listen to me now and try to comprehend. Christ, I wish I had troubled to learn more of your language, for I am never sure how much French you really... Solange, we must remove the baby from your womb, or both of you will die. Here drink this. C'est de l'eau, de l'eau de vie...the water of life. Let's pray that for once it is actually true. Yes, you must swallow it. Don't shake your head and seal you lips, for I will simply force it down your throat. It will ease your pain, I promise, and when it is over, I will sew you back together again, good as new, and you will be up on your horse in no time, with a new babe strapped to your back. To hell with the priests and their edicts to save the child at the cost of the mother! I will not let you go!" Georgette's tirade broke on a sob.

"Georgette, ça suffit. That is enough," Solange whispered

308

hoarsely. "Je comprends, je comprends tout. Of course, I understand... everything. And I thank you with all my heart for all you have done for me and my children. Years of hard work, with no home or children of your own to show for it. And putting up with Paul, that alone would try the patience of a saint, and we are not that, neither you nor I!" She attempted a smile.

"I have always hated him for taking me from my father, but now I see, it was probably for the best. I resented my father, too, for bartering me away like so many trade goods, to an unknown white man. But Father was only trying to protect me. Maybe he had a vision of the future of our people. And Paul is not such a bad man. He is just a lost little boy, who has spent his whole life looking for his mother. She never cared for him as a mother should. He always praised me as a good mother. Who will raise this child, I wonder?

"Please don't cry. I have never seen you weep and now is not the time to start." Her head lolled to the side as she gritted her teeth on another contraction. When it was over, she begged for water, just water please. Georgette propped her up on the pillows, bathed her brow in cool water and put the mug to her lips. She drank greedily, gave a soft moan as she tried to sit up, then gave up and merely turned her head to one side to look at Georgette.

"Do not be sad, for I dreamed of this many years ago, and for The People, dreams always come to pass. Grandmother did not know what the dream meant; neither of us had ever seen or heard of a horse, but I saw my white stallion way back then. I was riding him and suddenly he was cut to ribbons by a wire, and I fell and was drowning in blood..." her voice drifted off and her eyes closed. Then, with a deep breath, she spoke again. Georgette could not believe the torrent of articulate words spilling from Solange's lips, as if she had unstopped a bottle that had been corked for twenty years.

"Please, save my child. Do not worry about me. It is time for me to join my Grandmother, my mother and father at last. How I have longed to see them again. We are back in my village and I am in the garden in the sun, tending to the three sisters: corn, squash and beans. I am digging with my stick and yes, Grandmother, I am not being so lazy and I am bending my back to weed the plants properly.

What's this? Something shiny sticking out of the dirt..." Solange reached out her hand to clutch at Georgette's arm. Her voice lost its dreamy quality and became urgent and clear.

"Georgette, quickly, you must fetch my medicine bag. Over there, in the bottom of my cedar trunk. Dig around, it is hidden deep in the corner! Ah, that's it. Untie the cord and hand it to me. Here, you see? Look. I found this in the garden at my village, the day of the raid that killed my mother, my grandmother, almost all my kin. It is some kind of jewelry, a brooch I think you call it. Very old and not made by my people, that much I know. The time I spent hiding it probably saved my life. I went back for it later when my father and I returned to the ruins of our village. It seems to possess a protective spirit. I have held it in my hands through the labour of each of my babies, but this time, ahhh, I forgot. How could I forget? You must give it to my eldest daughter, Marie-Neige. Please? Tell her the story and make sure she keeps it safe." She closed the pin around Georgette's hand, who jumped as the sharp clasp pricked her palm.

"Oh forgive me! You have to be careful, it has a stinger! I used to think it was alive, for it stung me each time I held it. Maybe that is just its way of protecting itself! It drew my blood and made me stronger, just like the warriors used to cut and burn themselves to build their endurance to suffering. Hah, I just realized that. I so wanted to be a warrior when I was a child and here I became one, after all." Georgette was stunned to hear her mistress laugh. Where had this strong, light-hearted spirit come from? The pain must be affecting her mind, she concluded, as she dipped the cloth to bathe her mistress' forehead once more.

"Ah, ma petite Marie-Neige. My little snow angel. And Soleil, my sunshine, and Fleur, my flower, and Jacinthe, my lovely hyacinth. Paul let me name all the girls and I followed our ways and chose something from nature. It was not exactly right, since the grandmother names the child, but in our case, that was not possible. Please, Georgette, if this is a girl, act as her grandmother and give her a beautiful name, of a wild thing that cannot be tamed. Take care of my baby for me, I beg you, as a sister. Don't abandon my children!"

"Hush, hush, do not trouble yourself. Your children are my

children, don't you know that? No more carrying on. Come now, drink up and it will all be over soon. We will have you back on that horse of yours in no time... God, I beg you, not for my sake, but for this sweet woman, please save her, please, please, I will be good from now on, if you will only..."

Part V

Vancouver and The Village
1963 - 1973

Chapter Thirty

Vancouver, 1963

"Education, Chantow. You come backa skoo' wif me—I help you wif mat', you herp me wif my Engrish. We make a team and den we get troo skoo' togedder. You wannna wait on a ta-boo arraa you rife? Rike Rouise? She nice, but you smawt. Plletty, too. Me, I study to be enginee-ah. I buiwd blidge an' highway. I not come Canada to wait on ta-boo, what you tink? No! I come to get a de-kree, become enginee-ah."

"That's great for you, Joey, but I have nobody to support me. How can I pay rent, bills and afford school, too? It's just too hard. What about you, Stevie? What are you going to do when you finish school?"

"Be waiter."

"A waiter! Let me get this straight. You go to school all day and work here at night, just to keep being a waiter!"

"I will be waiter who knows more."

Chantale was taken aback. All the waiters were going to school, studying to become doctors, lawyers, engineers. They were already in their late twenties, early thirties, their English was not fluent, and they still had years of studying ahead of them. That didn't seem to matter. Each knew what he wanted to accomplish. Now that she was one of their number, among the wait staff, and she had shown she could keep pace with them through the busy evening shifts, they told her about their dreams and their plans, in snatched conversations over coffee or dinner breaks. She learned about their hard lives in Hong Kong. Subsisting in the apartments above the restaurant, they worked day and night, to earn enough money to send home to their family and pay for schooling in Canada. Every step was another rung on the tall ladder they were climbing. They were grateful for the chance Mr. Wong had given them, sponsoring them to come to Canada to work for him.

Mr. Wong had given her a chance, too. She shuddered when she remembered back to just a few short months ago, when, still a busgirl, she might just as easily have been fired. Everyone told her that any other boss would have blamed it on her and used any excuse not to cause a scene...

At first, she wasn't sure it was happening. Then she felt it again. The man's hand was definitely going up her leg, toward the inside of her thigh. She stood frozen, unable to move, unable to breathe. The tips of his fingers climbed higher. All the while, he kept talking to the three other men at the table. Chantale's feet were glued to the floor. She was too shocked and afraid to speak. The water glasses on her tray began to shake and water spilled onto the table. Joey came up beside her and was about to reprimand her, when he looked at her face. She cast her eyes down. Joey's dark eyes followed and saw what was happening. He took her by the arm and led her roughly away from the table.

"You comma here now, Missy Chantow," he said gruffly.

He escorted her to the staff table near the back of the restaurant and headed for Mr. Wong's office. Chantale trembled as she lit a cigarette. Her mind raced through all the possibilities. Maybe they would think it was her fault, that she had done something to deserve it. Maybe they would fire her. Where would she get another job? What if they kicked her out right now? They might not give her a chance to explain. What a living nightmare, made worse by the fact that, as luck would have it, Damian was sitting in the restaurant. He had been hanging around all night, making her uncomfortable, expecting her to keep refilling his coffee. She had been upset enough, wondering what he might say in front of her co-workers or other customers, to embarrass her. Imagine the shame of being let go in front of him. And he would be all sympathetic and...

"Get out. No, all of you just get out my restaurant and don't ever come back. No bill. Just get out. I don't want your money. You don't touch my staff! Get out or I call the police."

My God. She had never seen Mr. Wong angry. His round face was red and his tiny black eyes were blazing as he shouted and pointed toward the door. Chantale had hardly ever heard him speak. All instructions were given to the staff through Louise. He would appear, impeccably dressed in a suit, white shirt and tie, late in the afternoons, gaze around, nod, then close himself behind the office doors. He might stroll out to the front desk to chat with some regular customers once or twice during the course of the evening. By eight or nine o'clock, after a brief visit to the kitchen, speaking in Chinese to the cooks, he was gone. His cousin Charlie was in charge until midnight, supervising the takeout orders and cashing out the till. Mr. Wong remained aloof from the day-to-day running of the restaurant and all but a few favoured staff.

Now the entire restaurant was hushed as the men scrambled to their feet and pushed each other through the glass doors. The Chinese waiters and busboys exchanged open-mouthed stares of disbelief. Mr. Wong had thrown customers out of the restaurant—in front of other customers! Chantale hid her face in her crossed arms resting on the table and sobbed. She wanted to die of shame. Hot tears poured down her burning cheeks. She could hardly raise her head when he approached the table.

"You all right, Miss? That man and his kind won't bother you again. This is a respectable place, not a place for scum like that. I throw them out and they can never come into this restaurant again. I guarantee it. My staff deserve respect. It's okay now, it not your fault. You just doing your job. You want some supper? Joey, you get her anything she want from the menu. Even steak. Listen, you have a steak, you feel better. I guarantee it." Mr. Wong was speaking to her like a real person! How embarrassing, she thought. I will never live this down with the other staff. How will I go on working here, with everyone looking at me and thinking about it? Everyone knowing that Mr. Wong had intervened on my behalf and thrown customers out of the place! Feeling sorry for me! Oh my God.

"Hey, can I help? Listen, I saw what happened. I really appreciate that you threw that bum outta here! How dare he lay hands on my little sister-in-law! You obviously take good care of your people. She's some lucky to have a boss like you. Put'ter there, pal." Damian had appeared beside the staff table, stepped in front of Joey and thrust his hand toward Mr. Wong.

"That's right, Chantale, those bums deserved what they got. Hey listen, why don't you eat a good meal and, if your boss here will let you go early, why, I'll drive you home. I think she's too upset to do any more good tonight, don't you, sir? It's just lucky I was here. I was just waitin' for her big sister to get off work, so I thought I'd check in and see how Sissy here was doin'. Lucky break, huh?"

Chantale was so overcome with shock at all that had happened that she couldn't protest. She simply nodded her head and picked at the steaming plate of food that Joey placed in front of her while Damian kept up his chatter across the table. A busgirl brought her coat from the basement and placed it around her shoulders. Chantale numbly followed Damian out of the restaurant to his rusty old Pontiac parked in front. She pulled her short, fake fur coat around her and shivered in the cold rain, as Damian opened the passenger door.

"Wonder why he's being so nice?" The question floated into her mind, but she let it evaporate as she threw her exhausted body onto the sagging seat. She reached into her handbag for her cigarette pack. Damian leaned over to push in the lighter, unnecessarily brushing her knee with his hand as he did so. Chantale unconsciously moved her legs to face forward and nervously flicked her cigarette between icy fingers while she waited for the lighter. The car motor squeaked, squealed and finally sputtered to life.

"Course I can't say as I blame the man. Not that he wasn't an asshole to do that to you right there in the restaurant. But he'd prob'ly had a few too many and couldn't resist those sweet gams and that cute little ass. By God, when you first came to live with us you was fat as a seal and not much to look at, but you've slimmed down real nice and developed some luscious curves on ya. Look like a nice little package, even in that ugly ol' uniform that don't fit you proper. Tell that cheap Chinaman to get you a decent-sized outfit for God's sake. Looks like you're wearin' a potato sack tied up in the middle."

Chantale wasn't listening. She had learned not to take anything Damian said seriously. She tried to appreciate the fact that she hadn't had to catch the bus in the dark for once and let his mindless chatter flow over her like the smoke from her cigarette. She stared out the window at the rain. Vancouver rain. Dirty, cold, never-ending.

"Course you know your sister, she's frigid. Always complainin' about being too tired. Or a headache. Christ, she gives ME a headache. A man has needs, you know. She's startin' to drink too much, too. Drinks 'til she passes out at night, for Chrissake. I really don't even know why I hang around. Now, I wonder if you..."

Chantale started to register what Damian was saying, noting the change in his voice. Softer and faster. Her heart started to pound as she reached over to the ashtray to stamp out her cigarette. Covering the movement with her purse, she gripped the door handle in her right hand. Damian grabbed at her left arm.

"Hey, why don't you come and sit closer over here, now. You've had an awful fright from that creep and could use a cuddle from your good ol' big brother D, don't you think, Sissy?"

"Look, I'll just get out here. It's close enough to walk from here. You go pick up Danielle. Thanks, see ya!" Her voice cracked as she shouted the words, much louder than necessary. She wrenched her arm free of Damian's grip as he slowed for a red light, opened the door and jumped out into the street while the car was still moving. Both feet landed in a deep puddle on the curb. She didn't even close the car door, but ran down the street in the opposite direction. Turning back, she saw the car turn the corner and stop. The car door slammed and the tires spewed a fountain of water as Damian sped off. Exhaling with relief, she spun around and headed back toward the lights.

"*Now I'm really screwed,*" she sighed miserably. One of the only good things about where she lived was that the city bus picked her up right in front of the restaurant and dropped her almost directly in front of the door on the street. That way she didn't have to be in the dangerous neighbourhood alone at night. Now she faced a long walk in unfamiliar territory.

People stood in groups smoking and talking in front of bright store windows, sheltering themselves from the weather under the awnings. Even if she heard a few comments and whistles, she could brush them off and still feel safe. Nothing would happen out here on the main thoroughfare. But as she turned the corner toward her street, the area was less illuminated. In shadowy stairwells or alleyways, individuals huddled in layers of clothes or tattered blankets. Chantale couldn't make out their gender and didn't try. She didn't run, but kept to a brisk walk. Almost there. Good. Eyes front, keep focused. Just two more corners, then home free. Like the old chant from her playground days: "Ollie, ollie, oxenfree!" Where the heck did that come from?

All of a sudden, the street was quiet and she felt someone behind her. Following, maybe? Footsteps, getting closer. She turned around to look and saw a figure dart out of the middle of the sidewalk to the shadows beside a nearby building. She started to walk faster. The footsteps kept pace. Still walking briskly, she rummaged blindly through her purse for her key, gripped it tightly in her fingers, point out, as Danielle had taught her.

"And never show fear! Just walk right down the street like you own it, but if they get too close, knee 'em in the nuts!"

Despite the warning, Chantale broke into a run. The steps kept pace behind her as her mind raced ahead to the plate glass door on the street that gave access to the upper floor of the storefront where she now lived. It had no lock, so she flung it wide and tore up the stairs two at a time, bent double, almost on her knees, her nose against the musty old carpet in the hall. Hands shaking, she turned the key in the lock, leaned against the door and then quietly clicked it shut. She could only hope her pursuer hadn't seen which room she had entered. She kept the light off, barely breathing in the dark. "Silently now," she told herself. "Jam the chrome chair against the door. Slip the chain into place. There." She fumbled in the half-light from the skylight for the old butcher knife on the table and pushed the blade silently into the door jamb. Heart in mouth, holding back her sobs of fear, she waited. He could still break down the weak door, if he wanted to. No heavier than a bedroom door, with a useless push-lock handle. She'd already opened it with a bobby pin once, when she'd locked her keys inside. Her pursuer was now roaming the hallway, yelling incoherently, banging on all the doors. The handle on her door was turning...

Suddenly, one of the motorcycle gang members from down the hall flung open his door, thundered down the hallway and hollered, "Get out, ya damn bum!" A body slammed against the wall in several places before reaching the landing. Then came another series of thumps on the stairs. Then she heard a few muttered curses as her unknown saviour trudged back up the stairs and stumbled back down the hallway.

"Thank God for those guys," she thought, not for the first time. Who would have believed that she would be glad that a biker gang lived down the hall? Better than security guards. They knew the neighbourhood and helped her willingly whenever she dared to ask. They had given her tips on survival in the city, such as the knife in the door jamb trick, and warned her not to come into the building if she were being followed, but to turn in somewhere else so the person wouldn't know where she lived. Good idea. Too bad it didn't work when you were scared.

She decided against sticking her head out into the hallway now to say thank you. No point in getting too friendly. She wasn't sure of their motives in helping her. Didn't pay to trust anybody.

Flinging herself onto her mattress, she kicked her shoes into the air, rolled over and wrapped her arms around herself, not bothering to take off her coat. She awoke an hour later, her arms stiff and aching from the constriction of the thick sleeves of her jacket. Her bladder was full to bursting. "Maybe it would be safe now to go to the bathroom for a pee."

She threw her clothes on the floor, then pulled an old flannel nightgown over her head and yanked her jeans on underneath. She never wanted to be caught in the hall wearing just a nightgown. She grabbed a clean towel from the chair next to the couch, which served as her clothes rack. She longed for a hot shower to wash memory from her mind. She tiptoed down the hall past two closed doors, knocked, then entered the bathroom, locking the flimsy door behind her. Looking down at the filthy sink with a sigh, she reached for the cleanser that she had purchased for the communal bathroom. Before using the bathroom, she was compelled to thoroughly disinfect it, no matter the urgent calling of her bladder. Chantale kept the place livable for herself. Cheap rent equalled necessary precautions. Tired beyond thinking, she turned on the shower and stood under the hot water, letting it mix with her tears, hopeful that at this hour, no one would interrupt her to use the toilet. No such luck.

"Yeah, yeah, okay, I'm comin'."

Hair wrapped in a towel, head down, she didn't look at whoever stood at the door waiting for her to come out. Back on her mattress, she leaned over to check the time on her little alarm clock, before switching off the lamp next to her bed. Two a.m. Hours and hours before daylight. Shit. At home, all she had wanted to do was sleep. Here, she could barely get two to three solid hours of rest, before, wide awake, she would toss and turn until the morning sun filtered in from the dirty skylight above the couch. As soon as her head hit the pillow, her mind became a carousel of words, images, and fears.

Now, she replayed the trauma of the evening over and over again. The man at the table, Joey's worried face, Mr. Wong shouting, Damian's leering stare, the car lurching away in the dark, footsteps pounding up the stairs behind her, the door handle turning... Stop, stop. Whirling, swimming, drowning... She sat up, hoping to silence the noise in her head.

"What am I doing here? What am I doing? This place is so horrible, a shithole, a goddamn stinking..." She wailed into her pillow, squeezing it against her chest and rocking back and forth. "But where can I go? What can I do? Go home, go back. No, please God. Can't even tell Danielle... she would hate me, blame me. Men! Such pigs! Worse than pigs! Danielle is crazy to stay with that bastard. He's killing her and she doesn't even see it. But what's the alternative? Maybe if we lived together, just the two of us, we could get a better place."

Bang! A door slammed down the hall and she started. She got up and started to pace the room. Mother, came the sudden thought. Why did she always come back to her mind, when she had tried so hard to erase her? She thought of her still keeping up the house back home, the cooking, the routines of the farm, living her dream of family pride, dynasty, heritage. It was always "de bes" with her—the best clothes, the best food, the best house, the best car... Yes, "pure laine" all right. So fucking pure. The best French Canadian stock.

But what about when your children needed you? To see them for who they really were? To help them? Tell the truth for once, Mother, she longed to scream. But it was no use. She couldn't even begin to explain why she had left, when she had called back to check on Suzanna. Maman had just sobbed into the phone, plaguing her with guilt, begging her to come home.

How could her mother begin to tell the truth, when she had such a giant lie to protect? Suicide was a mortal sin, undeserving of a Catholic burial. Everyone knew that. Yet Papa had had his funeral in the church, the priest had sung the mass, Maman had probably worn her best black dress and a new hat. Chantale vaguely remembered the neighbours offering sympathy, asking questions. Maman had pretended she didn't understand—suddenly she couldn't speak English anymore. She "forgot" the truth and never confessed it, even to her own children. To protect them?

Secrets. Is that what made her feel so old, at nineteen? Was it the weight of secrets, or was it fear? Would telling her mother of Richard's sexual abuse have made her feel light, cleansed and free? Like confession was supposed to, but never did? She had tried to open up a few times, but, too ashamed and afraid of the consequences, she had moved far away, hoping to escape. But it was all happening again. It must be her fault, otherwise, why would it keep happening? The man in the restaurant, Damian... ugh, she shuddered and her teeth chattered uncontrollably. Hate coiled in her stomach like a worm. She tasted the sweet metallic taste of bile in her mouth. Breathe, bite it down, swallow, it'll pass, like always, she assured herself.

Should she tell Danielle the truth about Damian? Would she believe her? Or would she also close her eyes, like Maman, and pretend? Make do, make up, make over, make like it never happened? Should it just be another secret? What difference would it make, in the end?

The agonizing questions kept whirling, sending her spinning back to flop on the mattress, exhausted. At last, just before dawn, she slept.

When she showed up at the restaurant for her two o'clock shift, all the staff, including the Chinese boys, were attentive and kind. Just as she had feared. They smiled and solicitously offered her coffee and even a piece of Mr. Gee's special homemade banana cream pie, which staff were supposed to pay for. Though it was her favourite, she could hardly swallow. Then Louise beckoned her into Mr. Wong's tiny office.

"I heard what happened last night, Honey. Don't youse worry about it. Happens all the time in this business to pretty young things like yourself. Now, now, let's not see those eyes rollin'. Youse as pretty as a pitcher, and young too, which I was once, hard as it is to believe, I know. Why I remember...well, never mind." Louise grinned her infectious, crooked smile and with a flourish, took a stick of celery out of her uniform pocket. She chewed away noisily, picking the occasional green string from between her teeth with her long, painted fingernails.

"Gave up cigarettes for celery, Honeypie, an' I ain't lookin' back. Puffed on two packs a day, but my kids've forced me to quit," she had answered Chantale's curious question.

"It's a sure-fire cure for anything: losing weight, smoking, nail biting, you name it! Even cleans your teeth while you're at it. You oughta try it!" she said, fishing in her pocket for another piece of lint-covered, limp celery and offering it to Chantale, who shook her head, gesturing lamely at her lit cigarette. Louise's jaw worked thoughtfully like a camel's for a few moments, before she continued.

"Lucky for you, them kinda goin's on hardly ever happen here. This is one of *the* finest restaurants in Chinatown and Mr. Wong intends to keep it that way. Gets really riled if the staff is mishandled by customers. He just won't tolerate it. That's one of the best things about him—reason why I've worked here for nearly twenty years. Most bosses would have found some excuse to fire you! That just ain't right, in my book, and our Mr. Wong, why, he don't say much, but he knows what's what, an' that's a fact."

Louise handed her a brown paper package that had been sitting on the desk.

"Here, he insisted you have two brand new uniforms. Should fit you a lot better. And we think you're ready to start waitin' on tables. What do you think about that, eh? You're our best busgirl and that's why you get so much of the boys' tip money, but you'll make a lot more waitressing. And if ever you're worried about a table, why, you just see me or Joey and we'll handle it. They wouldn't dare lay hands on an old dragon like me!" She laughed and Chantale joined in.

"There now, 'atta girl. Nice to see that pretty smile. Dry your eyes with that ugly black hanky in your pocket, at least it will do some good for once! C'mon, let's not waste any more time and get started! You have plenty to learn, Honeypie!" Chantale rushed to follow Louise's long strides back down the aisle to the swinging kitchen door.

"Number Four, hold the onions, mayo on the side," she hollered in her brassy voice, as she burst into the kitchen through the swinging doors.

"Now, the first thing to remember is not to take any guff from these cooks here. Keep 'em in line, or they'll walk all over ya! Ain't that so, Terry, you mean ol' cuss?"

Chantale couldn't help grinning every time she remembered how Louise had simply erased the humiliating incident from everyone's mind by promoting her and keeping her busy. Now, after Joey's admonishments, she started wondering: could she really do it, finish school? All on her own. Then try for a better job?

Maybe. After all, she was managing to look after herself. At last, she had a place of her own. No luxuries like a window, a bathroom or even a sink. A walk-up one room flat above a store front. But $55.00 a month and close to the restaurant. The landlady knew Mr. Wong and therefore had given her a "good deal, Missy, faw Missa Wong's girl." A furnished room she had been assured—"furniture" consisting of a dirty mattress on the floor, a broken store carousel to hang her clothes, a couch with more springs than cushion, a card table and one wooden chair. The only light filtered through a filthy skylight, in the centre of the room and one bare light bulb. The bathroom down the hall was equipped with a tub so black with grime it was not fit to wash a pig and a sputtering shower. Home. All hers, away from Damian and Danielle.

Even at this, I'm still better off than Danielle, she told herself. With her need for a man, any man, to make her feel secure, she had ended up looking after Damian. After six years of not seeing each other, keeping contact only by the surreptitious cards and letters Danielle had always sent through a friend, there was suddenly a vast gulf between the two sisters. Chantale moved out amid cold glares from Damian that also infected Danielle and now they lived two bus transfers apart. Neither had a phone. Sometimes Chantale thought to use the restaurant office phone during the day shift to call her sister at work, but when she did, their conversations were brief and strained, with Danielle always making an excuse to cut the call short. Chantale suspected that Damian had become abusive again. She sounded distant and unhappy, but obviously didn't want advice from her little sister. After a while, they lost touch.

And what about Suzanna? So beautiful and young when she first came to the farm, with her whole life ahead of her. Now she was stuck in that squalid village with three snot-nosed brats and that useless Paul, unable to look after himself let alone a wife and three kids. It occurred to her that the miscarriage had been a blessing in disguise for Suzanna. She resisted the urge to cross herself for her sinful thought. The poor woman would have to look after all of them forever. Neither woman had the future Chantale envisioned for herself. But what was?

Chantale talked over the idea of returning to school with her best friend at the restaurant, Sherry Lynn, the only other non-Asian female waitress. They sat together at the staff table, smoking and folding paper napkins into swans for the dining room tables. During the slow hour before supper, or anytime there was a lull, the girls rushed to re-stock the banquet napkin supply. It was a chance to get off their feet and relax, and worse, if they didn't keep up the appearance of being busy, they would be assigned to any number of less pleasant jobs, including cleaning toilets, washing walls and scrubbing the booths with bleach. Mr. Wong did not permit idleness and Louise and Joey made sure the staff earned their keep.

"We all end up as waitresses, in the end," Chantale lamented. "My mother waited on my Dad, till he... died. Then she waited on my brother. My sister and sisters-in-law wait on their... men. As soon as you get hooked up with a man, that's it. You spend your life catering to him, and then your kids. What's the difference between that and working here? Jeez, you don't even get tips!"

"Yeah, but think of the alternative, working in a place like this, 'til you're old and worn out like Louise? Look at me, I got a kid to raise now, on my own, and I would just love to meet some rich sugar daddy to look after me. That's what I'm waiting for, you know like that song: *Someday, my prince will come!* By God, it should'a happened by now. I kissed so many frogs, I should be able to croak!"

Both girls burst out laughing, then covered their faces with half-folded napkins. Luckily, Joey was in the back with the cooks and Louise was on the phone, placing a supply order. It wouldn't do to appear to be enjoying themselves. Chantale lowered her eyes and snorted once more. Sherry kicked her in the shins under the table. Then her chatter rolled on.

"It's different for 'the boys,' you know. For them, it's just make a plan, work hard and it'll happen. Sure, they have to slave for Wong for the next ten years. But what other responsibilities have they got? And it's a helluva lot better than where they came from, as far as I know. But ever notice how none of the Chinese girls even get a sniff at waiting on tables? They stay well hidden in the back, doing the dirty work until they become 'marriageable.' Then, they disappear. You watch. And we're just here to appeal to the older Asian men, don't kid yourself. Ever notice how they're our best tippers? Mr. Wong won't allow no hanky-panky, as you well know, but he's one smart businessman. Blond, blue-eyed, buxom beauties like ourselves, keeps 'em comin' in for the view!" Assuming a serious air, Sherry blew smoke through her nostrils as she ran her red fingernails through her bleached hair, spreading it across her shoulders. Chantale exploded with laughter and received another kick.

Chantale had never registered that any of the Chinese females on staff were simply busgirls, dishwashers, or assistants setting up banquets. They never dealt directly with customers. She had assumed it was because they couldn't speak English. Now, she began to wonder. The head chef's own daughter was relegated to the basement, peeling shrimp.

327

Chantale felt sorry for Annie. As far as she could tell, Chantale was the only person on the staff who ever bothered to speak to the child, for child she was, not more than fourteen years old. Annie always smiled when Chantale said hello as she came back from changing in the washroom. The thin, black haired girl sat on a stool, leaning over her buckets after school on weekdays and all day Saturday and Sunday. Her small fingers deftly tore the hard shells off the slimy grey shrimp. Her hands, plunged in the icy water for hours, were raw and red, nicked by tiny tears in the skin from the rough-edged shells. The smell from the buckets of discarded shells would have made a cat retch. The space was dark. The only light came from a bare bulb hung at the foot of the stairwell. Boxes stacked everywhere created shadows where rats and mice could hide. Every so often, a trap would snap. Otherwise, only faint sounds drifted downstairs from the kitchen above: the bang of a dropped pot, a loud curse, a sprinkling of laughter.

One day, Chantale's curiosity and pity got the best of her. She dared to ask the child, "Don't you mind, being down here alone all the time?"

"No, why would I?" Annie responded in a quiet but cheerful tone. "I help my family. It's quiet. No one tells me what to do or bothers me. I'm not on my feet all day like you. I think about things. Time goes really fast. I'm always surprised when Dad comes down to say it's time to go home."

"What do you think about?" Chantale wondered.

"I don't know, just things. It's okay."

Still, Chantale refused to eat the battered shrimp piled under the heat lamps. They reminded her of the baby chicks they used to raise at the farm. Besides, she knew what they cost to prepare. She couldn't bring herself to try even one, until the night Joey teasingly popped one into her mouth. It melted like honey. After that, she could barely resist sneaking a shrimp or two from the trays while waiting for her orders to come up, careful not to get caught. Shrimp, like steak, were strictly off the menu for staff.

The other "girls," as they were called, worked long, hard hours, kept their heads low, never made eye contact with the customers, and spoke only when addressed, shaking their clipped, poker-straight black hair. They smiled sweetly and did as they were told. Chantale could tell by their tone, even in Chinese, that the "boys" spoke to them even more harshly than they had addressed her when she had started. The girls took their abuse without complaint. The "boys" didn't treat the white female staff this way. They either treated them with deference, as with Louise, and surprisingly, Chantale, or ignored them completely. Chantale could never understand why they were so talkative with her. It never occurred to her that she was the youngest non-Asian female on the staff and therefore possessed an exotic appeal to the male waiters, who vied for her attention.

"The boys" were favoured above all. They dominated the night-shift, when the most money was to be made, in tips from wealthy Asian businessmen. Their skill of pleasing the customers in their own language was highly prized and they kept all the cash left on the table, except if they deigned to give a small stipend to the busgirls. Sherry-Lynn had caused Chantale to start observing the dynamic between the males and females more closely and suddenly her own situation somewhat diminished in comparison.

Even the boss' daughters had to "work" in the restaurant on weekends, hostessing, answering phones for takeout orders, and setting up banquets before the customers arrived. Mr. Wong brought one or two of his daughters in with him every day and took them home each evening, but he never spoke to them while they were on duty. Like his staff, they were kept at a distance. The five girls had no more time for fun than any of the staff in the restaurant, but they laughed and joked more freely than the other Asian girls did. It was their only social life. With their teasing, they made themselves part of the group, though they never donned the staff uniform. In this way, the boss kept them apart. Their place was clear, and "the boys" treated them with superficial politeness. Most of the staff did the same, but Chantale soon befriended little Alice, the youngest daughter, just thirteen. Chantale was curious as to why such a well-to-do family had their children working. Not for money, surely! What would they need it for? According to Joey, they lived in a mansion in the swankiest part of the city.

Alice explained matter-of-factly that her father wanted his children to understand the value of money and to learn the meaning of hard work. In addition, they were to keep up with their studies, maintain excellent marks, study a musical instrument and help out at home.

"We must finish university, marry a chosen Chinese suitor, then bring honour to the family by bearing many Canadian sons. My little brother, Johnny, will take over the restaurant business when he grows up. We must support our family, respect our elder who know better." The child recited as if she had memorized the words by heart.

"You are never allowed to go to a party or to a movie? What, you can't even take the bus downtown? Have you been out of the city?" At every suggestion, Alice wagged her coal black hair across her face, brown almond eyes open wide, giggling behind her hand.

"What does your mother say?"

"My mother?" Alice furrowed her narrow brow. "She not say too much."

"Don't you ever feel, you know, kind of frustrated, that you can't do what you want?"

"What we want? What do we want? If I or my sisters ever asked to do such things, Father would disown and disinherit us, Chantowel! We lucky, safe at home."

"Ah, yes, well, that does make a difference. So you are happy, then?" Alice's bright smile and snapping black eyes gave the answer.

"Hey, you want to hear a funny joke? This one really funny, seriously. Knock, knock..."

Chantale was intrigued, humbled, even jealous of the lovely, nurtured daughters. But when she thought of Annie's restricted life and compared it to her own hard-won freedom, she felt pity. Her sympathy was wasted on Mr. Wong's girls however. Four of the five daughters would not give the time of day to such a shameful excuse for a daughter. They were appalled by her story of leaving home, which somehow had become common knowledge. Only Alice accepted her, endlessly questioning her about the farm. Her curiosity reminded

Chantale of Jocelyne. The child marvelled that anyone would want to leave the countryside, where there were animals and space to run and, especially, horses! She had sighed with envy when Chantale, with tears in her eyes, had described her horse, Blackie, and spoken of riding through the open fields and spoiling the horse with sugar lumps.

"Your family must be so worry about you. Even your horsie miss you, I imagine. Why would you come here, all alone, to work in Father's restaurant, so far from home?" the child wondered.

"Education," was the only answer Chantale could give.

Chapter Thirty-one

The Village, Central Alberta, 1967

Jocelyne's stutter appeared in Grade Five, when she was eleven. For most of that school year, she didn't speak unless called upon by the teacher.

"Frenchy, Catholic, little princess, thinks she's better'n the rest of us. Wattcha readin', Josie? Whatsa' matter, cat got your tongue?"

"Nah, she's a cat herself. Ever seen eyes that colour before, 'cept on a cat? And she scratches like a cat when she gets mad too, so be careful. She'll scratch your eyes out!"

"That's why she ain't got no friends an' she's readin' all the time. Sssshe cccaaan't ttttallk."

"Well, why don't ya read up on somethin' useful, like how to play baseball? How to hit, for cryin' out loud! Did ya see her tryin' to hit that ball yesterday—swung and missed every one! Good thing she gets a 'walk' once in a while. Sure couldn't run to first base in those dumb clunky shoes! Whyncha get a pair of runners like the rest of us?"

"Ah, she couldn't get far wearin' that frou-frou dress, anyhow. Hey, didn't your mom figure out that girls can wear pants to school now? Whatcha wanna keep showin' up in those stupid dresses for? They're not even in style. Where'd they come from, the Army and Navy?"

"Yeah, I bet that's all her momma can afford these days. They live in that big, fancy house, but my Momma saw a truck pull up there the other day and take a load of furniture out! Not putting it in, taking it back. To the store. Hauled out a table, chairs, a piano, even the television set. Momma said it took 'em more'n an hour to get it all. Momma says they're called the "repo men" and they come to the house with a sheriff and take stuff if you don't pay. Hey, Josie, did that sheriff have a gun? That'd be neat. I wish I would'a seen them."

"Hey, maybe your drunken ol' man shoulda called him out into the street for a gunfight. Just like on television, you know? Oh yeah, I forgot, you don't have a television no more!'

"Ha! Ha! That's pretty funny, Tommy. You crack me up! C'mon, let's leave her alone and play ball!"

Heidi. The Bobbsey Twins. The Secret Garden. Read, read, read, read.

*****

"Girls, when you say your prayers tonight, I want you to pray for snow."

"Sssnow? Wwwhy? I dddin't know you liked sssssnow sssoo much, Mmmom."

"Yes, snow. If we get snow, then Daddy will get work in the city, either hauling it away or grading the streets. But if we don't get snow, I'm afraid there won't be any Christmas this year."

"Nno Chris..Christmas? Hhhow can that be? Can't Santa's sleigh cccome, even if there's no sssnow?"

"Santa can't afford to buy presents, if there is no snow. So pray, pray hard. And make sure to say all your blessings for everybody. Jocelyne, you say your prayers with Pauline, while I go tuck in Nicolas."

"Nnnnow I lay me dddown to sssleep, I pppray the Lllord mmmy soul to keep. If I ssshould die before I wake, I ppray the lord my sssoul to tttake. God Bless Mommy, Dddaddy, Nicolas, Grandpa and Grandma, Grandpère et Grandmère in heaven, our lllittle baby in heaven, and Pauline and Happy the dog, and…oh yeah, me. And ppplease God ssend us ssnow for Christmas. Amen."

That night, as on so many nights, she dreamed she was back in her grandmother's house on the farm. There was a warm fire in the parlour and she was laying on the couch. The old pendulum clock was ticking softly in the background. Grandmère was rubbing her legs with liniment and telling her a story. She couldn't make out what she was saying. It was like a soft humming in her ears. Then suddenly she was above her body, floating through the house, visiting every room. The beds were all made upstairs. As usual, the rooms were impeccably tidy. The leather-bound books gleamed in the bookcase under the upstairs hall window. She longed to stop and open each one, for she knew how to read them now, but for some reason she had to hurry. The oak banister shone like polished brown glass, swirling down to the swinging doors into the kitchen, where the table was laden with food that smelled so enticing. But the chairs were empty. Jocelyne called, "Grandmère, Grandmère, where are you? Dinner is ready!" She was sobbing, desperate to find her. The spinning wheel whirled, the piano played, the rocking chair on the verandah rocked. All by themselves. She cried out, "Grandmère!" and woke with a start.

Her pillow was damp with tears. Her stomach grumbled with hunger, as the smell of cooking bacon drifted to her nose. Morning? Was she at Grandmère's house? Quick, get up and run downstairs! Grandmère will be there waiting at the kitchen stove, with a hug and a spoonful of beans! Then…she remembered and thought, no, just lie still for a little longer and wait. Mom will call soon enough.

She breathed deeply and tried to recapture the scent of Grandmère that had been so strong in her dream: liniment, cinnamon, lavender talcum powder, and what else? There was nothing that smelled exactly like Grandmère's house and it was gone forever. Bulldozed to the ground.

The sights and sounds of that horrible day came flooding back and suddenly she felt as though she were drowning in tears. Before her eyes, a huge yellow machine belched out black smoke, revving forward and back, forward and back, as it tore into the kitchen walls with one giant whack of the bucket. It carelessly trampled Grandmère's roses as it bit into another side and cracked off the verandah's supporting beams. From the driveway where Richard and the children leaned against the DeSoto to watch, they could see the white siding buckle and feel the house shudder. In no time, the edges of the building had been crushed and folded in on themselves, until all that remained was the tall roof, leaning at a sickening angle with the second floor windows turned sideways. Crack! One more blow and the house split in half and tumbled in a heap of dust and flying glass.

Nicolas cheered and clapped his hands. "Hurray for Daddy!" he cried. Uncle Richard encouraged him, swinging him to his shoulders so he could get a better view. Pauline jumped up and down, shouting, "More! More!" Jocelyne stood speechless, tears streaming down her face. She turned and opened the car door, and waited alone.

After what seemed like hours, her father turned off the machine and came to join them. His face was black and streaked with sweat. He flung off his cap, exposing a white line across his forehead. Fanning his face with his hat, he deftly pushed his cigarette package up from his breast pocket with one hand, then jammed his hat back on, peak backwards, so he could light up. With one more swipe of his brow, he poked his arm into the open back seat window of the car, reaching for a bottle of beer from the carton on the floor.

"Hey, ma girl. Wattcha doin' back there? It's stinkin' hot in this car, even with the window open! You tired? Not half as tired as your ol' man, I can tell you that. Well, Richard, whaddya think? Fast enough for ya?"

"I guess! I never thought she'd come down so quick. Did you see that roof just snap like firewood? That's what she was all right, a fire trap. I'm surprised we were never burned alive in our beds. Needed all new electrical, new plumbing, a new roof. Why, the cost would'a crippled us."

Jocelyne had remembered something. She stole out of the backseat and now tugged on Richard's sleeve.

"Where's Grandmère's pppitchers?" she asked softly.

"Pitchers? I didn't find no pitchers. Although with all those antiques to sell off, who knows what all went. Some things I just tossed in boxes and it went in the auction as lots. Didn't have time to sort through all that old crap."

"Nnno, I mean the pitchers that were in the drawer in Grandmère's parlour. Ssshe made me pppromise to look after them, bbbut I ddidn't know..."

"Oh, you mean those old pictures? The old photograph albums

336

and stuff? Oh yeah, I just took the whole drawer full and threw it on the bonfire. Didn't think as anybody'd want it. Whadcha want that ol' junk for anyways? Just a buncha old people, don't mean nothin' to any of us."

"Wwhere did you have the fire, Uncle Rrrichard?"

"Oh, over there somewheres. In the open field down by the barn. As I was sayin', Paul, we'll put up a new house for half the price, one o' them real modern jobs, prefabricated, with aluminum siding. Won't take long and then if the goddamn county will agree, we'll sell off the land in sections, make a killing."

"Sssell? Ssell the farm, is that true? What will happen to the pppigs and the ccats and the ddogs?" Jocelyne cried, tugging on her father's sweaty shirt-tail, hanging loose at the top of his pants.

"Jocelyne, stop interrupting for Chrissake! Go back and sit in the car, or run and play." With a swipe of his hand, Paul brushed her away.

She fled down the sloping driveway to the weed-infested space between the barn and the machine shed. Out of habit, she prepared to avoid the mean, barking dogs tied to the bunkhouse. But the bunkhouse and the dogs were gone. For that, at least, she was thankful. She wandered through the open space until she came upon a deep pile of black ashes.

"What all did he burn?" she wondered. Searching around, she found a length of rusty wire and poked through the charred remains of the photograph albums. Grey ash rose in a cloud and the sharp scent of cold, wet smoke filled her lungs. She didn't care. She kept clawing through the sodden mess, until she saw the glint of a tiny white triangle. One of Papère's arrowheads! She reached down to gingerly retrieve her treasure with the tips of her fingers. Clutching it in one hand, she continued scraping, but could not find the dinosaur tooth.

"Prob'ly burnt up," she sighed glumly. Suddenly, an image appeared in her mind, of Grandmère's body lying on the floor in the parlour, Richard stepping over her, tugging open the heavy bureau drawer and carrying it out of the house, making a fire, watching the black and white people curl up and disappear in smoke. A chill ran down her spine as she turned away from the ash pile.

"Might as well go and say goodbye to those smelly old pigs," she muttered. "I wonder if they missed me?" she thought with a smirk on her face.

As she approached the barn, she sniffed the air and noticed right away: the overpowering pig smell was gone. The barn door was ajar so she could easily slip inside. The stalls were barren, cleaned out down to the cement floor. No cats prowled on the window sills. Instead, light barely filtered through the panes of glass, filmed with dust and cobwebs. The wood panelled chop bin stood empty but for some powdered remains rounding off the corners. A mouse boldly peeked through the slats, then scurried across the wide central aisle and wriggled through a knothole to the pens outside. Jocelyne shrugged, then retreated backwards through the door, scraping her skin on the metal latch. Unnoticed, a line of blood trickled down her arm.

She climbed up on the wooden fence that had once enclosed the hogs outdoors. The pen was still deep in straw and muck and here the sour odour of pig urine lingered, but it was dead on the wind. From her vantage point, miles of abandoned fields stretched into the distance. Grey clouds gathering on the horizon threatened rain. Jocelyne scanned the view, even though she knew the horse was gone. Blackie had been sold before Grandmère died. When Chantale left, there was no one to ride or care for him. Richard had decided that "the old hayburner" had outlived her usefulness. Did Richard remember to tell Blackie's new owners to bring her sugar cubes and apples, like she and Chantale had always done?

"I'll bet Richard never even told them what to do. He wouldn't care," Jocelyne grumbled, jumping back to the ground. She kicked dust and gravel all the way back up the driveway to her old hiding place under the pine trees' musty green canopy. Picking up a broken, knobbly branch, she drew aimlessly in the light, needly sand. She wasn't aware that she was drawing faces, then rubbing them out, and starting again. When her father finally called, her shorts and tee-shirt were covered in dust, her hands were black with soot and her dirty face was streaked with tears. Seemingly startled by her appearance, he brushed her off briskly with the flat of his dirty palms, opened the car door and motioned for her to get in. They were ready to leave.

She collapsed on the seat beside Pauline and started to rock and hum, lifting her legs one at a time to peel her sweaty skin from the plastic seat covers. Paul turned the key in the ignition and reached over to push in the cigarette lighter. He was just about to shift the car into reverse, his hand on the chrome stick shift above the wheel, when Richard thrust his hand through the open window on Jocelyne's side.

"Hang on there a minute, Paul. Hey, Squirt, I got something for you. I thought since you and Ma were always goin' to church together, you might wanna keep this. No earthly good to me and we wouldn't likely get more'n fifty cents for it at auction."

As he spoke, he poured a string of beads onto the vinyl seat between Jocelyne's legs. The sound was like water from the old pump filling an empty metal bucket. Jocelyne started and Richard laughed as the heavy gold cross at the end of the rosary landed, cold and heavy, in her lap. Then he squeezed her bare thigh and left his hand there while he reached further in to ruffle Pauline's hair and smack Nicolas playfully on the back of the head, as he bounced against the front seat.

Jocelyne lifted her arms from her sides and awkwardly pushed the hand aside while she collected the rosary. She noticed a ring on his little finger, Grandmère's emerald ring from Papère, the one that she had always worn around her neck. She suddenly envisioned him unfastening the gold chain while Grandmère lay dead or dying on the parlour floor, in front of the oak cabinet. She didn't know if this was how it had happened, but she shuddered as she put the rosary around her neck, clutching the cross in one hand. With the thumb and forefinger of the other, she traced the amethysts and pearls, as she had seen Grandmère do so many times in church while she had muttered her prayers. Jocelyne had no idea what to say. A sob caught in her throat. Tears spurted from her eyes.

"Perfect, I knew you'd like it. Well, Paul, good job today. Things are lookin' up. This'll be our very own Centennial Project, how 'bout that! A new era! Salut!" Richard shouted, banging the roof of the car twice to send them on their way.

"Listen, Honey," Paul said, as he slowly pulled out of the drive and lit his cigarette. "I know it's sad to see Grandma's house come down. It's hard on me, too. Imagine, I grew up in that house. So many memories. Maybe I shouldn'a brought you all out, but I thought it would be nice for once for you to see your old dad in action."

"Yeah, it was great, Daddy! Can I come next time?" Nicolas exclaimed, bouncing on the seat beside his father, clinging to his bulky arm.

"We'll see, little man. Anyways, Jocelyne, we had to tear it down. We had no choice. There's no one in the family who can afford to maintain it and no one wants to live out here anymore. We need to sell up and split the profits. Lord knows our family could use the money."

Jocelyne refused to listen. She put one finger in each ear and kept humming and rocking. Over and over in her mind she chanted, "I hate you. I hate you." She meant it for Paul. But even more for Richard and his dogs and his pigs and those mean cats. She was glad at least none of them had a place to live anymore. Served them right! Wonder where Richard lives now, anyway. Still, it was nice of him to give her the rosary. At least she had something from Grandmère, even if the "pitchers" were gone and she had promised to look after them. She remembered the arrowhead and checked her shorts' pocket again, to make sure it was there.

Now, lying in bed awaiting her mother's call, Jocelyne's mind blossomed with questions: Who told Richard he could have Grandmère's ring? Why had he burned all Grandmère's papers and photographs, without even asking anybody? Where were all Grandmère's fancy books from upstairs? Why did he call tearing down Grandmère's house a "Centennial Project," when at school they had said that a project to celebrate Canada's one hundredth birthday was s'posed to be something good and special, not something horrible? Like Daddy said, the new baby on the way was his "Centennial Project," every time he patted Mom's swollen stomach....even though Mom always swatted him and said that was a disgusting thing to say... anyways, it means building something, not wrecking something! Where was Blackie now? How had Richard gotten rid of all the cats?

Prob'ly shot them, or drowned them and left them under the trees to rot, or...

"Jocelyne Marie Gérard! Get out of that bed right now! You'll be late for school. Get a move on! Were you readin' with a flashlight all night again, so you're too tired to get up and help out around here in the morning? I swear, I'm gonna burn those damn books of yours! Hurry up, it's eight-thirty already!"

Chapter Thirty-two

The Village, 1970

"It is the season of perfect works, of hard, tough, ripe twigs, not of tender buds and leaves. The leaves have made their wood...able to survive the cold. It is only the perennial that you see, the iron age of the year."
    Henry David Thoreau
    Journal, November 25, 1850

"She was not beautiful, but she carried herself as though she were." Jocelyne repeated this line to herself, mouthing each word slowly, over and over. She had come across the line on Saturday night in a romantic novel, one of the many strewn all over the house where she babysat each week. She had been startled to come across such a powerful line in a book which she would normally consider "trash." She always read them to amuse herself and help her to stay awake until the early morning hours when Mrs. C. would finally return home. Besides, the books provided her only source of sex education. At thirteen, she was starting to think about boys as more than an annoyance, but she didn't dare broach the subject to anyone, least of all her mother. So, she guiltily devoured the racy paperbacks while she waited for the car to finally drive up, making sure to put them back just as the key was turning in the lock.

These words from last night's book had impressed her and stayed in her mind through Sunday and Monday. Was it possible to "make" yourself beautiful? Even if you were ugly? Hmm...Could you make boys believe you were beautiful, by the way you "carried yourself?" What did "carried herself" mean? The way she walked, the way she held her head? I should practice, walk around with a pile of books on my head, like Hayley Mills did on television. Holding her nose in the air, she held her arms out from her sides, raised herself to her toes and tried to prance down the gravel path.

"I'm Hayley and I don't have to speak to anybody if I don't feel like it. I can do whatever I want!"

She stumbled, almost fell. The November wind took the opportunity to huddle under her short jacket, stealing warmth. She shivered, regained her balance and pulled her jacket down fiercely, scolding herself for her imaginings. No, ugly was ugly and no amount of wishing or dreaming would change it. That's why they were called "romance" novels, stupid—no connection with reality. What could you do with freckles and big teeth and frizzy brown hair? No amount of wishing would make you grow as tall as everyone else, or change your eyesight so you didn't need to wear hideous glasses. Remember what Grandpa used to say, "If wishes were horses, beggars would ride." You're a beggar, you are. Does that mean you'll get a horse? Not bloody likely, she scoffed to herself. You'll never be mistaken for beautiful, either.

To escape further thought, she broke into a run. She was so light that the wind seemed to carry her along and within seconds she had reached the corner lot enclosed by hedges and tall trees. Up and over the sloping lawn, then down along the windowless side of the house, where she brought herself to a stop by lightly throwing her weight against the fence. She knew she hadn't been seen. No one ever looked out the front windows during the day. Only at night were the curtains drawn open, when her mother sat alone in the dark, rocking, staring out at the empty street, scarcely illuminated by a single street lamp. Then, there was no chance of anyone seeing into the house. The lights would be off everywhere but in the children's bedrooms, and besides, nobody walked the streets of the village at night. Why would they? There was no place to go, nothing to do after dark.

She passed through the wooden gate and slowly slid to the ground against the cement wall of the house, huddling into the corner out of the wind. Only the worn seat of her blue jeans separated her bottom from the cold, unyielding ground. Instantly, she felt the frost seeping into her bones, but she merely tried to pull her jacket beneath her, and brought her knees up to her chin. She didn't want to go in.

Hungry, dreary little sparrows flitted through the barren lilac hedge next to the fence, picking at paper wrappers and seeds and chattering amongst themselves. The gray, cloudy sky threatened snow. The wind kept up its pathetic, aggravating whine. Her bare fingers ached with cold. She curled them tighter in the pockets of her jacket. She knew she wouldn't be able to take it much longer. The time would come, soon enough.

Thoreau was stupid, came the sudden thought. She'd been reading his journal, in a book she'd borrowed from the library, along with *War and Peace* and *To Kill A Mockingbird*. Something about rugged beauty, Nature revealing her enduring strength in November. What a dope! November was so ugly, without colour, light, sound…

"Jocelyne! Jocelyne Marie Gérard!"

Except for that one. That was to be expected, whatever the season. It scarred the hours of stolen freedom in the spring, summer and fall, and sealed her winter prison. She didn't move, except to again cover her ears with numb hands, sticking a finger into each. She knew that after a "damn that girl," the door would slam and she would have a few more moments to herself.

The slam of the door was swallowed by the wind, while Jocelyne stiffly pulled herself to her feet. She stood for a moment, waiting. Then, after rubbing her backside as best she could with her forearms, she turned to close the gate behind her. She hurried across the yard, eyes never straying from the back door and the kitchen windows as she moved in the opposite direction. She wouldn't go in yet. She would check on her dogs first. Arriving at their little house, she opened the door, stooped, and went in.

It really wasn't a doghouse, but a playhouse her father had ordered when the new house was being built, so many years ago now. He had wanted it as a place for the kids to play in the back yard. The exterior matched that of the big house right down to the blue shutters trimming the windows. Inside, it was equipped with a little wooden bench and a cupboard attached to one wall, as well as a handmade table and chair set. A solid little palace, built by Dad's carpenter, who had no kids of his own to spoil. Besides, Mr. T. liked Paul's kids, especially Jocelyne. When it was finished, he had even presented her with a china dish set for the miniature kitchen, glowing with pride at her delight in every aspect of her very own playhouse. She smiled, remembering his kind eyes.

Now, she was too big to play here anymore. At school, she was painfully aware of how small she was in comparison to her eighth grade classmates, but still, she was too big for the playhouse. It had long ago become the haven of the dogs, which her mother refused to have in the house. None of the other children in the family cared about it anyway. But it had been Jocelyne's special place, her school, her library. She had cleaned it every spring, stocked the shelves, peopled it with dolls, slept in it, lived in it for every moment of freedom she was allowed. Now it belonged to her father's female dachshund, Peanuts, and her puppies—puppies that were supposed to be sold for profit, in another one of his money-making schemes.

The last time Peanuts had whelped, he'd ended up giving all the dogs away. "Oh yeah, Joe, they're a fine animal, a great family pet. The best you can buy. I know, most folks around here just get a mutt from any old farm and that's that. But once you have a fine, pure-bred dog like this one, you'll never go back. Yeah, I know, it's a bit steep, but there's my cost for the bitch, then the breedin' fees and the expense of raisin' the pups. Nothin' good ever came for free, you know. Here, just take the one home, I know the wife and kids will just fall in love with him. Don't worry about payin' me right away, I know you're good for it. Pay me when you can. C'mon, sit right down here and have a drink to seal the bargain."

Same old story. Same that had happened with the fine antiques he had brought in from Québec. His mother's estate had given him the idea, when he found that a lifetime of collecting "junk" had commanded quite a price from the antique auctioneer from the city. What he hadn't considered was the cost of the shipping, the fact that most wood from out East would not survive the harsh, dry Alberta winters, or that the people in the village could neither appreciate nor afford a two hundred year old table. Hand-me-downs and make-do were good enough for them. Another bright idea down the drain.

Like the one about shipping in pure maple syrup from Québec, which also ended up in the whiskey exchange, as the villagers couldn't tell it from corn syrup.

But, ever hopeful, her father had the dog bred again, and then promptly left for "up North" to work in the Yellowknife mines for the whole winter. He wouldn't be home until spring. So it had become her job to look after the puppies. Another responsibility.

She couldn't begrudge them, though, especially not now, as she snuggled a soft warm puppy under her jacket. With her free hand, she gathered the blankets around the remaining puppies and covered the mother, who gratefully licked her palm. It was terribly cold in the little house, colder than it was outside, except for the small circle of warmth under the heat lamp. Jocelyne could see her breath in its rosy glow. Suddenly, she caught her breath, the puppy sucking greedily at her finger, as screams of her name exploded all around her. It would not be a good night to again try to persuade her mother to allow the dogs into the house for the winter. It would not be a good night.

She raised the puppy to her neck, holding his warmth against her aching throat. Tenderly, she placed him back among the others, covered them all with the blanket, jumping only slightly as the door outside slammed for the second time. She rested both hands on the mother dog's smooth head and soothingly whispered to her in the sudden silence. At last, having calmed her own emotions, she was able to get up and step outside. She latched the door to the doghouse carefully behind her and then turned to race to the back steps. Although the distance was short, she arrived at the door flushed and breathless, just as she had intended. Without hesitation, she stamped noisily into the kitchen.

The heat in the room rushed towards her and set her chilled flesh alight. Fire raged in her legs, hands, cheeks and ears, but she didn't show the slightest sign of discomfort. She appeared casual, while struggling to loosen her zipper with fingertips that couldn't feel the tab. Finally, the flat of her thumb and index finger served the purpose and she managed to unzip her coat and hang it on a peg behind the door. She pushed one running shoe off from the heel in the usual manner, but it was going to be painful to remove the other with a numb stockinged foot.

"How many times do you have to be told not to take your shoes off like that? You're so damn lazy! You don't seem to realize or care what it costs to put those goddamn shoes on your bloody feet! Break the backs down, see if I care. You won't get another pair until next fall. You can damn well wear them till they fall off. Bend your lazy back and untie that shoe and take it off properly. And don't leave them right in the doorway for everybody to trip over, like you usually do. Where in the hell have you been? It's almost five o'clock! The school bell rings at four—it doesn't take an hour to walk home, that's for sure. It takes *five* goddamn minutes, for Chrissake! You know you're supposed to get home right after school! Out gallivanting, I suppose. You better not have been sittin' out there with those dogs all this time. Always shirking your responsibilities, just like your father."

"I...I had to stay after ssschool, Mom," Jocelyne interrupted at this point to stop the course of criticism which had found its familiar path and now would flow on indefinitely.

"You better not be in trouble at school again, or I'll knock what little sense you have..."

"No, no, I'm not," Jocelyne put in quickly, adding an innocent smile. The lies fell effortlessly from her lips and she listened to them herself with a modicum of interest. She could never understand how it came so easily to her, to make up stories, on the spur of the moment, in self-defense. It was like magic, making her heart race with fear and hope that she would sound believable. She always seemed to succeed, for neither her teachers nor her parents ever accused her of lying. Which she did, all the time. Sometimes for pleasure, mostly, out of necessity.

"The teacher asked me to stay after school, to, to help her with some things for the Christmas play—she wants to start early this year. And she's going to help me with my part, too, so I don't start stuttering again, like I did last year."

"Well, you just tell her you can't stay after school to do no stupid-ass fooling around for those childish plays. You tell her you have responsibilities at home. You hear me? If it can't get done in school hours, then you just won't be in on it, that's all there is to it. Now get in there and see to your brother while I get supper on. Look at the time! Everything's behind now, because of you..."

The ranting went on and on, following Jocelyne as she hurried from the room, down the hall to her parents' bedroom. She turned the doorknob fiercely and threw the door against the wire stopper, setting it off. Immediately, she stooped and reached around to silence its reverberations in her hands. Then she softly closed the door behind her.

Sitting on the bed, she rubbed her numb toes and stared blankly at the form in the crib. Her mind was dark. Deliberately, with a sigh, she raised herself up from the bed and shuffled over to the crib. Leaning against the bars for support, she looked down. She didn't feel her face shape itself into a scowl. She simply stared at the still figure under the blankets, avoiding the face. She stared down until her eyes filled with warm tears, like a relieving bath that somehow gave her strength.

"Don't forget his medicine. And hurry up, he should have had it half an hour ago. Get a move on, supper'll be ready soon. Nicolas and Pauline are hungry."

Even through the closed door, the voice was piercing. Jocelyne shut her eyes, holding back for just a moment. Then, she reached to lift the blankets and check the diaper. Wet, as she had expected. Efficiently, she picked him up, with one arm at his neck and one at his knees. Despite his size, he was heavy. Dead weight. But her arms were strong with practice and she manoeuvred his rigid body to lay facing her without difficulty. Her hands expertly removed and replaced his diaper, without altering his permanent fetal position. She didn't have to think. The actions were automatic. For the past four years she had been caring for her brother. And, for some reason, lately, her mother had given up the daily warnings, shouted from kitchen, "Don't you twist him, you hear? If he goes into convulsions once more on account'a you, I'll send you into convulsions, you hear?" Jocelyne was left responsible for the night routines for her brother, Luke, with no interruptions or advice.

Her brother was a baby. He would always be a baby. His body

would never grow, never move. But his head, his head was her six year-old brother. And he would stare, straight ahead, with their mother's beautiful blue eyes. And never make a sound.

She avoided those eyes now as she pushed the thumb and forefinger of her left hand against either side of his jaw, in order to force open his mouth. Just like Blackie. Chantale had shown her that when you wanted to put the bit in her mouth, you had to find the right spot on the jaw, and pop, it would open, just for a moment. Then you had to be quick, slipping the bit in before she could chomp down and spit it out. Same with Luke. Though it was awkward, she used a spoon to push his pill between his teeth and almost down his throat. Once she had pushed it in with her thumb. Her left hand had lost its grip on his jaw and she hadn't been quick enough. He had closed his teeth. It had been a long time before she had stopped screaming. And before her mother and father had stopped screaming.

"What do you expect, letting a kid look after him? He belongs in an institution, for Chrissakes. You can't do it all and it's not fair to put this on the other kids. Just how long do you think this can go on? You know the doctors said he can't live long—why do you want to torture yourself, me, the kids, and him? Just let him go, please, Suzanna, Suz, hear some sense, for God's sake."

"It's all your fault in the first place! I didn't want another one. But oh no, you had to try for another son. Your goddamn dynasty, carrying on the famous Gérard name! Who gives a shit about your goddamn name! And then there's the almighty church, with its rules. To hell with them! Are we still back in the dark ages? Let the goddamn Pope come and live my life for five minutes and then we'll see what he has to say." Her voice rose to a shriek that seemed to shake the walls between the girls' and their parents' bedrooms.

"Well, you wanted a son, you got one," she went on in a darker tone. "God's been good to you. Now look after him and the rest of us, too! And don't pawn him off to an institution, just to make it easier to look your goddamn drunken friends in the eye. Who cares what they think? I don't give a shit what anyone in this stinkin' hellhole thinks!" Pausing for breath, her voice broke, drowning in tears.

"What do they know about anything—nothing but a bunch of

welfare bums and alcoholics anyway. I won't put my son into a home and that's all there is to it! We made our bed, now we can goddamn well lie in it, and make the best of it, like my mother used to say. It won't hurt Jocelyne to learn to look after her brother. It's good practice for her. She'll have to face motherhood herself someday. Might as well learn early. I wish I had. At least then I would've known what I was in for." She stopped abruptly. Nothing but quiet sobbing came through the walls. Jocelyne and Pauline curled up in their twin beds, each facing a different direction, hands over their ears, and rocked themselves to sleep.

Since then, her father hadn't interfered in any of the decisions about the family. He said less and less, when he did come home. Sat in his chair, watched the hockey game, read the paper. He came in quietly on Fridays, empty-handed—no more pockets filled with treasures—left early Saturday morning and came home early Sunday morning. He didn't wake the kids up for Mass anymore. No more church, or Sunday breakfasts in the café. Not since Grandmère had died. A beer was never far from his reach. Then he left, off on the road Monday morning, with hardly a word the whole weekend. Her father's coldness burned like fire in Jocelyne's stomach. She tried harder to do everything right, so he might notice and praise her. No more mistakes, at school or at home. One mistake and everything fell apart. Really bad things happened.

She lifted the spoon towards Luke's mouth. It clattered against his teeth and suddenly he clamped down, hard. She pushed against his jaw with her fingers until the knuckles turned white, but the mouth wouldn't open. She let go of the metal handle and fought against the jaw with both hands. His mouth gaped for an instant. The bowl of the spoon slipped down his throat. His teeth gripped it near the end of the handle. He started to gag. If he lost his breath, a convulsion would rapidly follow, and she knew it.

She wanted to scream, to cry to her mother for help. Instead, she was frozen with terror. Without thinking, she grabbed the end of the spoon and tried desperately to wrench it from his mouth. His face was turning a sickening shade of blue. Savagely, she grasped his face between her hands and squeezed. His mouth opened just enough for her to whisk out the spoon. She held it in a clenched fist, gasping for breath, as she watched her brother's face. It showed no sign of their struggle but the horrible colour of his skin and his streaming eyes. Something was still wrong. He was wheezing.

"The pill must be stuck," Jocelyne realized. She threw down the spoon and bent to lift his heavy body out of the crib. She would have to slap his back to dislodge it, before he choked to death. She slipped an arm under his emaciated legs, supporting his heavy head with her other arm. His raven hair—their mother's hair—lay soft, thick and straight on his wide forehead. His neck was warm though his tiny limbs were ice cold. His skin was flawless, not covered in brown freckles, like Jocelyne's. She looked at his eyes, as beautiful as their mother's, ice-blue, trimmed with long, dark lashes. They seemed to be full of tears, though Jocelyne knew this was only a reaction. He couldn't cry. She wondered if he even felt fear, anger, pain? She was overcome with sadness and with a feeling she didn't know was pity, mixed with fury. Love and hate at the same time—a painful feeling that twisted like a knife in her heart. The heavy form in her arms shook with spasms as if to some unnatural rhythm. She heard the tongue writhing, the breath straining for passage, the teeth grinding involuntarily. Still she hesitated. Wouldn't it be for the best if...

"It will be over—soon..." she assured him softly, waiting, looking into the baby blue eyes. They seemed to answer.

The door had opened but Jocelyne didn't notice. In a sudden, swift movement she firmly held her baby brother high and thumped his tiny back. The choke he made could not be released through his bolted mouth, but she knew the pill had gone down. His body was still wracked with convulsions as she replaced it carefully in the crib and covered him with the blanket. She reached blindly to the table for the cloth that sat ready next to a bowl of water. She splashed the burning face. Holding it there with one hand, she stretched out to retrieve a bottle of medicine from the collection on the table. This would be all that she could do. If the convulsions didn't stop, he would have to go to the hospital, again. Jocelyne's hand trembled as she dropped the bottle on the blankets and hunted blindly on the table for the spoon, while her eyes anxiously watched her brother.

Then she remembered that she had dropped the spoon on the floor. As she leaned down, she glimpsed the open door, and looked up. A sob escaped her.

"I'm... I'm sorry, Mom. He... he... the pill got stuck..."

Her mother stood leaning against the headboard, staring blankly at the crib. She turned her beautiful blue eyes to her daughter. Jocelyne watched them fill with tears. Suzanna reached down, placed a cool hand on her daughter's pale, freckled cheek and didn't say a word.

Chapter Thirty-three

The Village, 1973

"A cheque? For…two hundred dollars! Yup, it's made out to you all right. But from Mrs. Christiansen? What did you do for her, to earn that much money?"

"Babysitting, Mr. Greene."

"Well, lands' sakes, how much do you charge, Hazel? Why at the going rate of fifty cents an hour, a dollar after midnight, that my girls get, you would've had to practically live there! Still, I've heard that Mrs. C. does go out a lot… Hmm, well, never mind. In any case, Hazel, I normally don't cash cheques, you see, and especially not from…well, how do I know she has the money in the bank to cover it? Does your mother know you have this cheque? It's an awful lot of money and Mrs. Greene would kill me if it came back NSF. NSF? That means "not sufficient funds." Wouldn't surprise me a bit. You should insist on cash next time, Sweetie," he cautioned gently, looking directly into the young girl's eyes.

" It just don't pay to trust people like…well, like… her. Believe me, I know from experience and frankly, her reputation ain't the best. So that's how she's been lookin' after her two little girls, every time Chester is out of town, eh. Figures. Well, it won't take him long to put two and two together, once he sees this money drawn on his account. If there is one. Tut, tut. Now, come on, don't start those pretty eyes to cryin'. I know you didn't know no better. It ain't your fault, for Pete's sake." He hesitated, removing his reading glasses to make a show of polishing them on his cotton apron.

Placing them back on the tip of his nose, he cleared his throat as he said decisively, "All right, I'll do it for you, just this once. Not as if I don't know where she lives and can't track her down if it don't go through."

He punched zero sale on the ornate metal cash register, hauled on the handle, then stood back as the till popped open with a "ding!"

"I know," he chuckled brightly. "I'll just add it to her account, if it don't clear, and, by gum, she won't get any more groceries from me 'til it's paid in full. That'd sure frost her! I can see that she's been runnin' up a tab with you, too. You gotta change your policy on that from now on. Strictly cash on the barrelhead!"

The old man slammed the flat of his hand down on the counter and then laughed at how he'd made Jocelyne jump. Peering at her over the rims of his half-glasses, he continued. "You need to be a lot tougher with people, Hazel. My word, even some of your oldest friends, your best customers, wind up not payin' at the end of the month, and I got bills to pay, too. How they expect me to run a business...Hmm, well, at any rate, I'm sure our Mrs. C. wouldn't want Chester to get wind of her stiffin' me. Not his old buddy George. She mighta gotten away with stiffin' you, though, Hazel. You just gotta be more careful, in the future. But mum's the word, got it? Next thing you know, I'll be puttin' up a sign sayin' 'Greene's Bank of Canada,' 'stead of 'Greene's Grocery.' And then what'd Mrs. G. do with all this fresh fruit?"

He counted out her cash in twenties and tens.

"Here's your cash and a caramel, for your business. Mind you be careful with all that money, you hear? Don't spend it all in one place!"

His voice was lost in the jingling of the bell as the glass door swung shut.

*****

It was still dark. The words of the Beatles' song played in her mind as she stepped through the door: *"She's leaving home...."* But she wasn't doing it for the same reasons as the girl they sang about: for fun! Far from it.

Money! Finally enough! She patted the wad of bills in her front jeans' pocket and bent her tiny frame almost in half. Jeans, tee shirts, sweaters, her diary, a few of her favorite forty-fives, an extra pair of shoes, socks, underwear, everything she thought she might need was crammed into the Army and Navy backpack she'd kept hidden under her bed for months. An old woolen blanket was strapped to the top, wrapped in a raincoat. She would have to walk to the highway. Only a few blocks away, but the weight of the backpack made for slow progress and she didn't want to be caught by the sunrise. She shivered in the chill pre-dawn air. A few stars still twinkled in the soft blue sky and the sun tipped the easterly clouds with pink and gold. Hurry! Hurry! Walk faster!

The Greyhound bus did not stop in the village, so she'd have to thumb a ride. There would be plenty of trucks on the road at this time of the morning and some kind-hearted old trucker would surely stop and give her a ride the seven miles to town. She'd done it lots of times, though her mother didn't know it. Just to escape for a few hours. She'd been lucky so far. A truck driver always seemed to take pity on her, pull over and wait for her to climb way up onto the seat. First, without fail, he would admonish her for hitchhiking by herself, then start to cheerily chat away, maybe even share his coffee before dropping her in town or back on the highway near the outskirts of the village with a warning never to take rides from strangers again. This time was different. A one way trip. As soon as she got to town, she'd buy a bus ticket for...

"Should'a practiced walking with a pack on my back. What a dummy! What if I have to go a long ways before a ride comes along? Gotta get outta town, before anyone sees." She spoke aloud to herself, but soon stopped, breathless. Stumbling along, she tried to quicken her pace. For her it was a question of life or death. If she didn't go, she knew someone would die. She couldn't hold on anymore. She had barely lasted the winter. There was no question, something bad was going to happen if she stayed. She had left a note, saying not to worry, that she would be okay and not to look for her.

A ragged sob escaped her throat and tears started to stream down her cheeks, as she recalled kissing Pauline's forehead this morning while she slept. They didn't get along, but she still felt sorry, leaving her sister alone to deal with their mother. Would she have to take over "the chores" now? Probably not. But Mom would be furious and she would have to take it out on somebody. Nicolas and Luke had each had their farewell hugs and kisses the night before. Luke, of course, couldn't respond to her tearful goodbye but Nicolas had tried to squirm out of her embrace and tickled her until she let go.

"What's with you, Sis?"

They wouldn't understand. Not now. Maybe never. The Beatles' song replayed in her head as she opened the stranger's car door:

".... *Bye, bye.*"

Chapter Thirty-four

"Dr. Gerard, you have a call on Line One. A man claiming to be your brother. Says his name is Paul. I wasn't aware you had a brother. He's on hold. Do you wish to take the call? Your next appointment is waiting."

Paul. My God, what the hell could he want? How did he get this number? Must be some family crisis. The last time she'd talked to him, she'd been the one to call and let him know about Danielle's death from a heroin overdose. He'd shown little sympathy for their sister, Danielle, who'd died alone, desperate and depressed after her common-law husband, Damian, had left her. Chantale had made all the arrangements alone, but thought her family should know. Just in case they wanted to acknowledge their sister's passing with flowers, a card, or something.

That's when she'd found out about their mother's estate and that he and both her other brothers were doing their best to have the girls cut off from their due inheritance. No will had ever been found so they thought it would be easy to prove that by running away from their home in Alberta and maintaining no contact with the family whatsoever, she and Danielle had abandoned all claim to any proceeds from the sale of their parents' farm. Paul's wrath poured through the phone like poison into her ear, as he accused her of bringing on their mother's heart attack by abandoning her. That one act had literally broken their mother's heart, he had hollered. She had worried herself sick over the sixteen year old and never recovered, even when she had found out that her daughter was alive and living in Vancouver, with Danielle. As far as he was concerned, his sisters were both written off a long time ago. In response, Chantale had sworn she would never speak to him again, but he'd be hearing from her solicitor. He'd said, fine, keep it that way, and slammed the receiver in her ear. And that had been the end of it. Not a word, except legal wrangling back and forth, with no settlement still in sight. What in God's name could be going on, to make him swallow his pride and call her now?

"Paul? What's going on? How'd you find me? Oh yeah, I guess through the lawyers. Well, we haven't spoken in, what, ten years? Must be serious, for you to call me. Are Suzanna and the kids all right?"

"Well, I'm grasping at straws, here, but I thought I'd try you, and anyways, let you know, just in case... Jocelyne is missing. She hasn't called you, has she? We have a cross-Canada search on for her, but so far, no luck, and it's been two weeks. We're still hoping she'll see some sense and come home, but the longer it goes on, the more likely it is that something terrible has happened to her. That's what the cops say, anyway. They haven't got a goddamned clue." His voice was strained and he seemed to be babbling. Chantale wondered if he was drunk. But Jocelyne had run away from home? It couldn't be.

"Oh my God, you can't be serious. No, I haven't heard from anyone from home for years. I wish I could help. Jocelyne was such a great kid. Smart as a whip, too. What happened? How'd she go missing?"

"You tell me. You're the psychologist, Dr. Gérard. Boy, must be nice to be a big city doctor now and have somebody answering your phone. Anyways, you have personal experience in this area, n'est-ce pas? What do you think? What makes the girls in this family run away from home? That makes, let me think, three now, for Chrissakes!"

"No, Paul, *you* tell *me*. I had my own reasons, good ones, I can assure you. But I was lucky, I worked hard and I made it on my own. Danielle—well, there's a different story. Anyway, she wasn't a child when she left. She was a grown woman, ready to make her own decisions. I would hate to think what might happen to a young kid like Jocelyne these days. The streets are lined with hippies out here, bumming around, taking drugs. Jocelyne was amazingly bright, as far as I remember. What's been going on at home? What's been happening at school? Who are her friends? Does she take drugs? There are a million reasons, but there's always an explanation. Believe me."

"Yeah, well I can't figure it out. I don't know what goes on in that head of hers. Got suspended from school for a while, lipping off a teacher. Since then she's always locked in her room, listening to that damn hippy racket of hers. I don't see many kids hanging around. The kids never bring friends home, what with…well, we give them the best home we can. It ain't no picnic for any of us, with a handicapped child to look after. Her mother needs her help. She should'a thought of that. Poor Suzanna is run ragged as it is. Now she has this to contend with, caaalisse de Christ! The kid has no money, that I know of, nowhere to go, and she's only sixteen!" he raged, forcing Chantale to hold the receiver away from her ear. She waited for silence from the other end before she attempted to speak.

"Paul, listen, if I hear anything from her, I'll let you know. I hope she does find me, because I could help. Danielle helped me or I don't know what would have become of me. I'd do anything for Jocelyne, you need to know that." He didn't seem to hear, but kept ranting right through her words.

"What's she gonna do, lie on her back to make money, just to feed herself? Get hooked up with some pimp and become a little whore? I thought we'd taught her better than that, tabarnak! I give my kids a good house to live in, good food, they have whatever they need, and this is all the damn thanks I get. Goddamn it, I don't know what to think anymore!" he shrieked, desperation in his voice. Chantale remembered how emotional he always was, and despite how cruelly he had treated her since their mother's death, she pitied him. An unexpected rush of love for the big brother he had once been to her washed over her. She was moved to ease his pain.

"Paul, Paul, just listen a minute. I'm not surprised the police don't have a clue. There are thousands of kids on the road. It's still the thing for kids to do, to hit the highway come summertime. Even though it's '73, there are plenty of old hippies looking to discover Woodstock or live in a commune and save the world. And the young kids just don't realize that the 'Flower Generation' is over. The roadsides are lined with them, from Hope all the way to Vancouver. You just have to see it to believe it. How they get anyone to stop and give them a ride is beyond me. I sure as hell wouldn't stop to pick any of them up. Filthy for one thing and might pull a knife or a gun on you, for another. Hmmm, hmm, sorry, Paul, mais c'est vrai, I mean, it's true. Jeez, I don't know where that old French slipped out from. Wow, I guess it's still there after all this time. Anyway, if she's hitchhiking, there's no way the police will find her, at least over the summer. They'd have to stop every ten feet and question every group of kids and I can't see them doing that."

Paul's response was to snort in her ear.

"Well, we've had nothing to go on, not a word to let us know whether she's dead or alive. We have no idea where she was headed. Just like someone else I know! What the hell's the point o' bringin' kids into this world, anyway, if they're gonna treat you like dirt the minute they're half-grown? I almost hope she is suffering—make her appreciate what she's got for once. Her poor mother. She's at her wit's end, but she won't say a word. You're lucky you don't have kids. You don't know what it's like. By the way, you married yet? Guess not, you still have our name, though you'd probably be one of these new women's libbers and keep yours anyway. That's why I thought she might look you up. She knows you live in Vancouver." His voice came across cold and flat now.

Chantale tried not to be annoyed at the comment about her marital status. Keeping her tone even, she replied, "Jeez, I hope she doesn't make for here. It's worse now than when I came, ten years ago. A lot more dangerous, at least it seems that way to me, since I don't live downtown anymore. Send me a recent photo of her, will you? By express mail. I haven't seen her since she was, what, six years old? About to start school anyway. I wouldn't recognize her if I walked by her on the street and she wouldn't know me either. I've changed quite a lot in ten years. I'll go down to the police station here and see what I can do. It's a real hellhole down there—God forbid she should wind up in East Hastings or in the parks downtown, where the kids all seem to congregate these days. The city's even set up sprinklers, to keep them from lounging on the lawns. It could be tough to find her, if she's down there already, but I promise you I will look. I really hope she calls you soon. Please, let me know, and call me if there is anything more I can do."

With a mumbled, "Okay, thanks then," Paul hung up and, with

a trembling hand, Chantale dropped the receiver into its cradle. Shaking her head, she rose from her padded leather chair and stood to look out the window. Memories she had worked hard to suppress came rising to her throat. Tasting bile, she began to cough, just as the intercom sounded again.

"Dr. Gerard? Are you able to see Miss Stephenson now? She's been waiting for half an hour."

"Yes, yes, Marion, send her in. Do I have any other appointments after lunch? Okay, well, do your best to call the two clients and cancel for the rest of today and tomorrow also. There is a family emergency I have to deal with. I will give Miss Stephenson her half hour and then I'll be leaving the office until Monday at the earliest."

Chapter Thirty-five

"C'mon, Honey, whaddyou say your name was? Oh yeah, Josie-leene. You gotta try a hit, Josie. It's the good stuff. Not mixed with any shit. You ain't never been high 'less you've been on acid. The colours, the images, man, it's wild. Like nothin' you ever seen before. And don't worry, we're all here to take care of you, if you get into the wrong head space and start havin' a bad trip. We won't let anythin' bad happen."

Jocelyne waited in stunned silence while the two boys and the girl took her arms, grabbed her hands and then gently lifted her backpack off her shoulders. All three were dressed in loose, ragged clothes. Their bell-bottomed pants dragged on the ground under their feet. Their cotton shirts had once been colourful but were faded and torn. The two or three inch heels of their scuffed boots made them seem taller and even thinner than they actually were. They all had shoulder-length hair. One guy wore a bandanna around his forehead so that his curly red locks encircled his head like a flaming bush. The other let his thin greasy blond hair trail down his back from a straight part down the middle. Both young men had scruffy, sparse beards. The girl had plaited her thick, black hair into two braids, held tightly in place by a beaded headband. Cheap, heavy rings adorned each of her fingers on both hands. It was hard for Jocelyne to tell if they were teenagers or already young adults, except that their wan faces were dotted with fresh, red pimples. Their brief smiles slid quickly sideways and their dull eyes easily lost focus on any given point. But to Jocelyne, they had seemed to sincerely want to help her, when they had found her lost and alone, in front of the bus depot.

"Yeah, sure, why not? How about later? Oh, sure, I trust you guys. It was really nice of you to bring me here for the night. I guess I looked a little dumb out there on the sidewalk. A real goober.

Vancouver is so… humongous, I just didn't know where to start. Holy cow… I mean, Christ, I'm lucky you're giving me a place to stay. I spent all my money on the bus ticket out here from Alberta. But as soon as I find my aunt then I'll be all set. Anyways, it's cool that people can just come and go from 'The House,' and nobody bugs them or asks them for anything. Why's it called 'The House' anyways?" Jocelyne asked.

"'Cause it's where it's all happenin', man. If it ain't happenin' here, it ain't fuckin' happenin', you dig?" the blonde man answered, spitting on the sidewalk for emphasis.

"Jeez, good thing you took me in off the street, 'cause I have nowhere else, until I find my aunt, like I said. There sure are a lot of people stayin' here."

"Oh yeah, lots of people from The House come back and forth all the time. We don't keep tabs on anyone's business. See, East Van's the only place to get the good heroin, man. But I ain't getting' you on that. You stay away from that shit. It'll fuck with your mind," the red-haired guy warned in a serious tone, pointing to a corner of the room, empty but for a dilapidated couch and a few broken chairs. Two people huddled together under a torn blanket.

"You just check out Tanya and John over there, shootin' up. Some guy came in a while ago, askin' to store some dope here, for safe keeping, and he gave them some in exchange. They were sure joyous, man, 'cause they ain't had money for food for the last few days, and now they won't be needin' to eat for a while. They'd just puke it all up anyhow, if they did eat." When Jocelyne shuddered he added, "Don't worry about them, man. They'll be out of it for a while, so they won't even notice you're here." One of the guys opened the door and yanked her back outside by her sleeve, forcing her to leave her pack behind on the floor.

"That's the thing, there's no food, so we better get outta here and scare us up some munchies. I'm starved. Soon's they're high, they'll be fuckin' like rabbits right here on the floor, anyway. It'd be kinda embarrassin' for a innocent young thing like yourself," he snorted with what was supposed to be a laugh. The black haired girl rolled her eyes as she flipped one of her braids over her shoulder.

"We'll come back and crash later, long's the narks don't bust the place in the meantime, which has been known to happen. Gotta keep an eye out for trouble in this neighbourhood," he said, raising his round wire-rimmed sunglasses off his nose while he looked around. Then, with a hop, he raised his booted foot, and high-kicked an empty pop can off the sidewalk into the street. Catching a glimpse of Jocelyne, he added, "Hey, don't worry, kid, we'll keep you safely hid from whatever it is you're runnin' from. Take you under our wing, so's to speak. Let's hit for downtown, guys."

The blonde put his arm around the other girl's waist, while the redhead draped his arm possessively across Jocelyne's shoulder and led her down the street.

"You're kinda a cute little thing, now ain't ya? Kinda... unusual lookin'. Let me see, yeah, you do have nice eyes behind those funny specs you're wearing. You sure you're sixteen like you told us? You look a lot younger than that. We don't hang with no jailbait, now do we, Chad? We party, but we don't want noooo trouble! No way, man. Here now, you just open your sweet sixteen lips for this, and then you'll be flyin' high!" He showed her a small bit of paper with a dot in the centre.

"Seems harmless enough. Is it like candy?" Jocelyne asked, puzzled.

"Yeah, man, that's it, the best candy you ever tasted. Droppin' acid is the coolest high. Way better'n smoke-dope, when you can get it. I hit it lucky today. That's right, Sugar, put it on your tongue, there ya go," he cooed like he was talking to a baby, as he stuck his finger with the paper on it into her mouth. Then he put the same finger into his own mouth, rolled his eyes and sighed dreamily.

"Yum. Sweet as candy, don't mind if I say so myself! Hey, guys, let's go to the bar. I'll buy us all a burger or somethin'. I got some cash leftover from the deal I did today. There's a great band playing. They play *Yes* and the *Doobie Brothers*—great vibes, man. We'll have a wild time! Here, little sweet sixteen, comb your hair over your eyes, pocket those funny specs and throw on these dark glasses. There, you'll pass. They never bother checkin' us for I.D. anyway. They know our crowd and we bring in lotsa business for 'em. C'mon, let's go in. Kid, you just

367

act natural."

"Here ya'll go. Beers all around. And a toast to our new little pal, Josie. You're bound to be thirsty after your long trip from…where'd you say you was from again? Oh yeah, I remember, Dog Shit, Alberta! Here's to good ol' Dog Shit, population three thousand minus one!" The redhead shouted, raising his glass and gesturing for Jocelyne to do the same. Everyone at the table, including people who had joined them when they came in, howled with laughter, above the deafening electric guitar solo rattling the speakers on the stage. Jocelyne could barely see them for the cigarette smoke burning her eyes. She squinted to focus through the hazy veil, but her vision would not clear, and it didn't help that she wasn't wearing her glasses. Maybe that was why everything seemed to be moving, even the food and the glasses on the table. Sounds blurred into a single hum in her ears. Were they talking about her?

"No, Derek, that wasn't it! It was Shithole, Alberta. A one horse town if ever there was one. Even the horse is tryin' to get out! Ha! Ha!"

"Good one, Chad. Hey, so, whatcha think there, little girl? Is this a good trip or what? Are you diggin' it yet?" Derek stuck his face into hers and waved his hands in front of her eyes. Jocelyne could see nothing but a wave of colour.

"C'mon guys, I think we should get outta here. This kid needs a quieter space to trip. Let's blow this joint before she's too far gone."

"What're you catchin' now, Babe? Cherries on the trees? Rainbow clouds, what? Me, I got neon lights, flashing Joe's Bar and Grill, Joe's Bar and Grill, over and over in the sky. Ain't that wild? Look, see the lights up there, all different colours. Groovy, man."

"Hey, Derek, grab her before she falls into the street," the black-haired girl shouted, reaching for Jocelyne's hand as a car raced by and splashed them all with water from the gutter.

"Great, now she's bawlin' so hard she's gonna puke. Hold her head up so she doesn't choke! Ahh for fuck's sake, this is a bitch, man. Listen, Honey, don't worry, you'll come down, in a day or so. Might have a few flashbacks after that, this is some pretty strong shit… half a one prob'ly would'a been enough for her, Derek, you fuckin' asshole. Sorry about that, Sweetie Pie, a bit more than we figured on, for your first time."

The blonde flicked his lighter off and on, off and on, peering into Jocelyne's eyes.

"I hope she don't crash. Man, her pupils are really dilated. That'd give us some serious shit to deal with, man. She can't handle it. A country bumpkin, we landed, for certain, man. Shoulda left her at the station where we found her."

"Ah shut up, Chad. You're bringing me down. She'll be fine, don't worry about it, man," Derek mumbled into Jocelyne's hair as he supported her against a lamp post. Jocelyne held onto the cold metal with both arms and threw up beer and hamburger into the street, until her stomach was empty.

"S'okay, s'okay, you just got the dry heaves now. Hang on, I'm holdin' you. All gone. Wish we had some water to give her. We'll get some as soon as we get back to The House. Come on, we're almost there, and then you can lie down, although that does sometimes make it worse. Better if you can sit up and enjoy the trip, Babe," Derek muttered, half-carrying her along as he stumbled over his pant legs slopping through the water on the sidewalk. A car suddenly swerved and splashed them again.

"You did that on purpose, you fuckin' asshole," he screamed and shook his fist at the car as it sped away into what Jocelyne saw as snakes of light weaving through the darkness.

"Listen, kid, don't cry anymore, for Chrissakes. That'll bring everybody down an' send us all on a really bad trip. Just relax and you'll be fine," the girl reassured her in a whiny voice as she walked with her arm around Jocelyne's waist.

"Careful now, here, hold your head up or you'll do a face plant into the sidewalk. Fuckin' I could kick your ass, Derek, for doin' this to the kid and puttin' it on us to talk her down. That's all we needed. There now, 'kay, that's it, let your mind fly free, let go of everything in your mind and it'll be fun, like a roller coaster, you know, like at the carnival."

"Yeah, whatever you do, don't think o' nothin' serious, man, or your fuckin' head will hit rock bottom and just explode. Nitroglycerin, man. Just stay up in the clouds, Babe. It ain't every day you see a pink sky with cherries hangin' from the trees, is it? So groovy, you lucky girl. This is good stuff, so don't waste the ride. Here we are, c'mn, watch the steps. Don't trip. Hah, that's funny, don't trip when you're on a trip. Fuckin' hilarious, man. That's it, take one step, two steps... up we go. C'mn and help me get her upstairs, Chad."

"I wanna go home. I wanna go home. I need my mother. My mother needs me. I gotta get home. Help me get home, pleeeease," Jocelyne whined as they pushed her onto a bed.

Her head rolled back and forth on a stained pillow, sending her mind reeling downward into a vortex of swirling colours. Her teeth chattered from the chill of her damp clothes. Derek covered her with a coat he retrieved from the floor. She curled into a fetal position and pressed her arms against her aching stomach. There were no sheets. The sour smell of the musty mattress combined with the stench of her own vomit-covered clothing made her gag. She started to heave again, leaning over the bed to spit on the black bugs crawling all over the floor. She didn't know if they were really there or not. A separate part of her knew that it was as bad, either way. Trembling with cold and fear, she let her swimming head drop back onto the pillow. The room was illuminated only by the light of a street lamp, filtering in through a dark window. She felt the urge to escape and tried to sit up, looking for a door. Just as she made out the rectangular shape of the closed door, she watched it cover with vines and become a grave, complete with a headstone at the top. Trapped. With no strength left to cry out, she whimpered "home."

"You are home, Honey, now, remember? We're here now, at The House and we're a family. We take care o' one another and don't let nobody suffer from no bad trips or negative vibes. C'mon, you know you can't go back to Shithole, Alberta or wherever you come from, otherwise you wouldn'a left in the first place. Right? So, just lie right back here with me, and let ol' Derek take care o' you. Here, let's just slip those tight jeans off, so's you can breathe. Atta girl. Hey, what's this? You been holding out on us, Babe. You got a wad of dough in here big enough to plug a john—a shitload of cash! Leastways enough to keep us in grub and dope for about a month. Sweet Jesus, we *were* lucky to find you! Wait'll I tell Chad! Hang on a sec, think about this, man. Would he tell us, if he hit the jackpot? I think not. Naah. We'll just keep this our little secret, eh, between you an' me, right, Sweetheart?"

Jocelyne turned in the direction of a sound. Someone was speaking. Whose voice?

"Daddy, is that you? Daddy, I'll come home. Just make it stop. Make the spinning stop and the colours stop and I'll be good from now on, I promise I will."

"Sure, you will, Honey. Now you just relax, this won't hurt but for a minute. Always hurts a bit, the first time. An' you bein' such a sweet, young thing, I'm sure you never done it before now. After this, we're on the road to tomorrow, Baby, just you and me."

Chapter Thirty-six

"Yes, this is she. Dr. Gerard speaking. Yes, Chantale is my first name. Excuse me? Jocelyne? Jocelyne, is that you? Oh my God. Okay, okay. Calm down, now. I can't understand what you're saying if you keep crying. Take a deep breath. There. That's better. Just explain everything to me and don't worry. I'll help you. Where are you? Your dad called me weeks ago to say you were missing and he thought you might have come out here, so I did some searching but came up empty-handed. Then when I didn't hear anything more, I just assumed you had made it back home. Didn't expect Paul to do me the courtesy of a phone call. So you are here, in Vancouver? Where? Okay, okay, yes, I'll be right down to get you. Look, you probably won't recognize me. God, I was only sixteen when you last saw me. I used to be fat, remember?" She laughed weakly, trying to lighten the girl's mood. The small voice on the end of the phone sounded desperate.

"Anyway, it's just pouring outside, so I'll be wearing a white raincoat and, and, hey, I'll put on my big, floppy black hat, and then you'll be able to pick me out of the crowd. The bus terminal is really busy, so stand right in front of Gate Number One, okay? What do you look like? You've probably changed too, since you were six or so last time I saw you! Oh, oh, okay, I'm sure I'll find you. Wait for me and don't move. It'll take me at least an hour to get there, through this rain and traffic."

Chantale threw on her coat and hat, wrenched her purse out of her filing cabinet and flew through the office, shouting back to her secretary, "Cancel my appointments for the afternoon and all day tomorrow. I'll be back on Monday. Family emergency. Yes, again. Sorry, gotta go."

"Great. Just great," she muttered to herself, peering through the streaming rain on her windscreen that the wipers couldn't keep clear even at top speed. She struggled to see as she approached the crowded Lions Gate Bridge in order to head downtown. She was cursing more than the weather, the traffic and the detestable trip to City Centre. Paul would have a fit when he found out. How could she tell him, when Jocelyne obviously didn't want him to know where she was? What was she going to do with her? Not much room at her tiny apartment and only a single bed. She would have to sleep on the couch for the night. Oh well, cross that bridge when she came to it, she thought sardonically, as she slowed to a crawl behind the fifty or so cars ahead of her on the slippery bridge deck.

The painfully slow pace gave her time to think and wonder. What in the hell had happened to little Jocelyne? She'd have thought a child of Suzanna's would know better, than to wind up in a big city like Vancouver, all by herself in this day and age, with so many freaks and bums on the streets. What they were hoping to find, Nirvana maybe with peace and love and flowers in their hair? It didn't exist. Instead, they quickly became mired in the seedy underground of the big city. As Danielle had told her sister so long ago, life at the oceanside was hard and cold without lots of money behind you.

But Chantale had believed she had no other choice than to leave home, and she'd had a plan, counting on the fact that Danielle was established in the city and could help her. As awful as that reality had turned out, at least it had given her a start. The kid was just lucky she'd found her long lost Auntie Chantale, for she'd had no guarantee that she still lived in Vancouver. She could have moved to Timbuktu for all she knew—no one back home had heard from her in ten years! God knows what might have happened then! In fact, come to think of it, where had she been all this time, since Paul's frantic phone call? She had already been missing two weeks then, for Chrissakes! She'd sounded so distressed on the phone...

Chantale frowned, remembering some of her own close calls in the dangerous days when she had lived downtown with Danielle and then on her own. Being followed through the streets, accosted by men on the way home and even in the restaurant where she had worked. Jesus, she'd been lucky to survive. Then again, she'd had no choice.

She had to escape... her mother, the farm, and especially Richard, the brother who had preyed on her physically and mentally since she was a small child. Unconsciously, she gripped the wheel tighter, gritting her teeth. Suddenly, more than rain was blurring her view out of the windscreen, as she hastily brushed tears from her face before taking a deep breath to regain her customary control.

What the hell had forced Jocelyn to run away? Paul, well, he was Paul, not Richard. Nothing like him. Lazy and useless, yes, selfish, too, but well-meaning in his clumsy way, always spoiling the kids with something. She couldn't believe he would harm them. That's not how he'd come across on the phone. He'd sounded scared. And Suzanna, well, she was so sweet-tempered, helpful and kind, a really good mother, as Chantale remembered her. Though Paul had hinted that she had changed a lot, especially since they'd had a handicapped child. She hadn't known anything about it.

"Wonder what the handicap is, exactly. Too bad Suzanna hadn't called me. I might have been able to help. But then, she wouldn't know that either, she thought as she drummed her fingers on the wheel in time with the rain pelting the hood of the car. Hell, look how the years had altered her, both physically and mentally. Sometimes, she barely recognized herself anymore, on the rare moments she reflected on the broke and broken girl who had arrived in Vancouver ten years ago. She vigorously shook her head to dispel the memories overwhelming her senses. Mustn't go back down that road, especially now. Why did the past have to come rushing back into her life just when she thought she'd buried it once and for all and had finally found someone to love?

She had recognized him by his scent. Leather, soap, and his own indefinable musk. Well, she'd been really attracted to him, when they'd met at a colleague's house, a few weeks ago. His warm brown eyes, twinkling with every joke told at the table, the olive skin, the dark, curly hair, high cheekbones, lean, firm body under the crisp, white shirt. But, when he'd asked her to dance when they were all out at a club on a Saturday night, and he had held her close, in those brief five minutes, she'd inhaled the smell of his neck, his shoulder, his hair, and she knew he belonged to her. As parents connect to their baby by drinking its scent, so she was aware of his kinship, deep inside, in a place no one had ever touched, that she hadn't even known had existed until that moment. She could taste him in her mouth, through the pores of her bare arms wrapped around his neck. A brief brush on the lips, a murmured, "Thanks for the dance, Chantale," in his rich, husky voice, confirmed it. Oh yes, he was hers all right. If he didn't already know it, he would. She would make sure of that. More than anything she had ever wanted, she wanted him for her own. Colin. What a beautiful name.

There hadn't been others. To her, men represented everything she hated about her past: constraint, trauma, abuse, both physical and emotional. She stubbornly chose independence: women's liberation had long been her creed, as Paul had so rightly accused on the phone. She couldn't help smiling to herself when she thought of how Paul might react to her now. If she walked right into the farmhouse, would he even recognize his chubby little sister as the tall, elegantly dressed woman in a business suit, with two degrees to her name? No thanks to him or any of the rest of her family, she thought bitterly. She glanced in the rear-view mirror to check the traffic behind her and noticed with disappointment that the frown-line between her eyebrows had reappeared. Over the past few weeks, it had seemed less noticeable.

"Shit," she swore aloud, flipping her curled blond hair behind her shoulder as she leaned closer to the mirror in order to smooth her forehead with the index finger of her right hand. Suddenly, a horn startled her and she hit the brakes, only inches from the car ahead. Heart pounding, she shakily re-gripped the wheel and shook her head to dispel the memories. But soon, the stop and go traffic, the warmth of the car, the radio softly playing jazz and the rhythm of the windshield wipers, hypnotized her into replaying the movie of her life in her mind. Jocelyne's arrival on the scene had revived her memories like a brush stroke of water on an old oil painting.

Her personal freedom had been hard-won, from leaving home at sixteen with only the clothes on her back, to working her way through high school, college and finally university. After two years in college, paid for by waitressing, she had been forced to find work to save more money to continue her studies. Fortunately, she had quickly been hired by an accounting firm, with the official-sounding title: "accounting technician." In fact, she was an entry-level clerk. But on the first day, when her boss, Mr. MacIntosh, the chief partner in the firm, had stood her in front of the windows in their offices on the top floor of the skyscraper and said, "You'll enjoy this. Best view in the city from here: look, the harbour, the mountains, absolutely beautiful," her heart had leapt to her throat and she felt as though she was actually going to make her own way in the world. How surprised Mother would have been, she gloated to herself.

But it was the first and last time she took in the sight of the bay from her exalted vantage point. After a short training period, she found herself responsible for everything from distributing payrolls for various companies, to preparing the preliminary figures for financial statements, to researching for audits, to typing the accountants' letters using a Dictaphone. She willingly did whatever was asked, striving to learn quickly. The company had taken a risk in hiring her with no experience or specific financial training, so she was eager to prove her worth.

There was a lot to learn, but she paid close attention to instructions and didn't have to be told twice. She became known as a quick study, a survival skill she had acquired in the restaurant: listen, watch, pay attention, anticipate, and don't make stupid mistakes. Joey, for one, had never let her live down her "ice cweam shake." Soon, six months had gone by and a raise had appeared on her pay cheque. Then, another six months, then two years. Time passed at an amazing pace, marked by the routine procedures of the monthly payroll, the employee payroll summaries due in February, the frenzy of work before taxes were due at the end of April, then a short break before financial statements were due again for the clients.

Good salary, nice people—after all her sacrifices to get this far, it should have been perfect. She stashed away as much money as she could and calculated that soon, she would be able to resume her university studies, even if only parttime. But one aspect of her job really bothered her. No matter how busy she was, how tight her time-line to send out payroll cheques or finish a letter, she had to stop her work twice daily, to serve coffee. Precisely, at ten a.m. and three p.m., she was required to make the tour of the entire floor, remembering how all the accountants liked their coffee, and serving them with a friendly hello and a smile. Mr. MacIntosh had specifically requested the smile, with a twinkle in his eye.

At first, she hadn't minded, much. "Comes with the territory of 'new gal on the block,' I suppose," she had told herself. Despite her experience as a waitress, it made her nervous to walk into the expansive, lavishly furnished offices of each accountant, sometimes in front of several exclusively male clients. If they teased her, or made any remark to her at all, she would blush to the tips of her ears, and her hands would tremble as she handed out the coffee, asking whether they needed cream and sugar . The plastic cups in their silly re-usable holders were easily tipped, but this was the boss' idea of saving money in washing up. So she had to carry a cloth with her and constantly clean up spills, while she profusely apologized. This seemed to delight them all the more. She soon learned to ignore their comments, place the coffee cups down firmly on a clean surface, away from any papers, and keep moving from office to office. She tried to be as efficient and unobtrusive as possible so she could hurry back to her desk.

Only one person refused her service: Barb, the sole female student, studying to become an accountant. Barb barely ever spoke to anyone, but the first thing she said to Chantale when she had appeared at her door with her tray was, "You don't need to bring me coffee, for God's sake. I'm quite capable of getting it myself, if I want it." Chantale admired Barb, but was a little threatened by her, too. Her persona seemed austere, with her short hair, dark, makeup free complexion, floor-length skirts and leather boots. Sometimes she even defied company policy and wore pantsuits. Chantale decided to adopt Barb's style, especially the long skirts as opposed to the bright miniskirts which she had previously worn, oblivious to her powers of attraction. Her coffee duties made her realize how the short skirts exposed her long legs to the gaze of the men in the office.

The female office manager, Mary, who was always dressed impeccably in expensive, flowing dresses, with matching high-heeled shoes, assured Chantale that Barb would never be promoted in the accounting world, dressed in those "get-ups." Intelligence didn't enter into it, according to Mary. It was a matter of being offered opportunities. Covered up like that, almost invisible in her dark colours, why, she would never even be noticed, and the men would climb to the top over her unsuspecting head! Her career was doomed before it started. If only she would listen to reason. Mary had tried to clue her in, but had received a frozen glare for her efforts, and decided to "let her stew in her own juice." She didn't seem to want to take advantage of being a woman and yet she didn't fit in with the men. Didn't smoke. Didn't drink coffee. All that education and still she didn't comprehend what it took for a female to get ahead in the business world! How naïve!

Chantale vacillated between agreeing with Mary that conformity was the price of success and admiring Barb for her individuality and courage. Sometimes she felt proud of the trim figure she had attained and longed to show it off with a short skirt and plunging neckline. Other times, she resented the expectations that men seemed to have for women to be objects of beauty. She wanted to get ahead on the power of her mind, damn it!

When Chantale complained about her coffee duty, Mary explained that the idea had originated with the senior partner—to save time on coffee breaks and needless chit-chat in the coffee room. Ever mindful of the pennies, with strict adherence to the "time is money" rule, Mr. MacIntosh prided himself on his shrewd Scottish business sense. Every moment of an employee's workday was "billable" time. Not that the practice of coffee delivery stopped each person from talking to Chantale for at least five minutes as she served their beverage and collected dirty cups. Including time spent making the coffee and cleaning up, it took a full hour to complete each round. As part of Chantale's salary, she thought it was a needlessly expensive routine.

She strongly suspected that the chief had another motive. Each time she came in to his office, he stopped whatever he was doing and looked her up and down. She knew that he was appreciating the view. Waitressing had given her strong, shapely legs, and an ability to tell when she was being "scoped out," as she called it. The skirt was a requirement—company dress code: no pants for the female employees; business suits and ties required for the men. When she began to adopt the "midi" style, he had passed a remark that he didn't think much of these new granny dresses. She had just smiled and said, "Well, that's the fashion now, sir." If there were clients in his office, he would make a fuss of her, gushing all over about what a great "gal" she was, thanking her profusely for the coffee as if it were a special occasion that she should bring it in—"what service!"— rather than a daily ritual. Really, she was losing all respect for the man, as she whined to Mary.

"It's 1968, not 1950, for goodness sake! Hasn't anyone around here ever heard of women's lib? Why are we still keeping up with this archaic ritual? It's not right that I have to stop what I'm doing and chase around delivering coffee to everybody else. It would do them good to get up and get it themselves, anyway," she complained.

"Doesn't Mr. M. realize how much time it takes me to do this every day? What if we just stopped? How long do you think it would take him to notice? And what would he do about it anyway? Do you think he would fire me over it? I'm getting praised by the other accountants for all my work, so I bet he wouldn't dare. Why should I have to break up my day, fall behind, just to serve coffee? They keep piling on the responsibilities, but I'm still just an underling in their eyes, as long as I keep this up," Chantale declared.

Mary smiled and agreed, but having worked in the office for many years, she was hesitant to make the change. So, one day, Chantale just went ahead and stopped, on her own, without authority from anyone. Coffee time came and went and she just kept working. A few people called Mary to enquire. She put the calls through to Chantale, who stated that coffee was available in the staff room.

At ten o'clock the next morning, Chantale received a phone call at her desk. It was the chief, enquiring about his coffee. When she said she was not delivering coffee anymore, he asked her to come into his office.

"What's going on, Chant-elle? Is there a problem? Are you unhappy with your work here?"

"No," she answered, swallowing hard. " I just find that the delivering of coffee is taking up too much of my day. Do you realize what it's costing you in my time, to do this?"

She went on to explain the time, the waste of coffee often left untouched on the employees' desks, the work that was not getting finished in the meantime... everything in terms of the cost to the practice. Accounting terms. Not a word about the demeaning nature of the task in her eyes.

The next day, at precisely ten o'clock, Chantale was called into the chief's office again.

"I've thought about what you said, discussed it with the partners, too. Actually, it makes perfect sense. I don't know why we didn't see it before. Just habit, I guess. We're still kind of old-fashioned around here. Conservative, you might say. But I have to admit, it's nice to have such a pleasant interruption twice a day from such a pretty girl. Hmmm, hmmm," he paused and looked down at his hands, then shuffled some papers on his desk as if he was searching for something.

"However, I have to agree with you that the cost is becoming prohibitive," he continued in an authoritative tone. "I will issue a memo to all the employees to that effect immediately. The one thing I will ask you, though, is if you won't mind bringing coffee in when we have clients in the offices. It makes for a nice touch. No? You mean, no you won't or no, you don't mind? Good. No, wait, just hang on a minute, there's something else I want to talk to you about."

Chantale turned back. "Uh, oh...here it comes," she thought.

"I've been making some inquiries about you. Talking to the staff. The partners and I, we've come to a decision."

"Wait for it... wait for it... oh well, that's what you get for being such a know-it-all," were the thoughts racing through her mind.

"We'd like to offer you an opportunity to move up in the company—become an accountant if you want to. We'll support you fully, pay your tuition and books, and you can go to school full-time and work here during your time off. All we ask is that you commit to staying here for at least two years after you graduate. No running off to get married or have children. But that's a long way in the future. It'll take you at least four years to start with, then there's the articling to be done... Well, what do you say? You look a little pale. Take some time to think about it. Let me know when you've made your decision. No hurry, except if you want to get started this fall. That will be all. Thanks, Chant-elle.

"Oh, by the way, you wouldn't consider bringing me a coffee now, would you? Just for old times' sake? Don't look so shocked—I'm just kidding! Off you go, back to work! And no more lallygagging around the coffee pot!"

Chantale grinned to herself at the vision of the old man with his shock of silver-grey hair, smiling mischievously at her. His male chauvinism was the product of his environment, she realized now, and his expression of tangible support had given her the confidence to thank him for his offer but gracefully decline and return to university to pursue an arts degree. Mr. MacIntosh had expressed both his encouragement and disappointment, while Mary had said she was downright foolish to decline such an opportunity. But she knew that accounting would never satisfy her.

At university, she had tentatively enrolled in a psychology course, curious to see if it could answer some of her questions. She had ended up pursuing a doctorate specializing in childhood sexual abuse. Once her healing had begun, she had felt compelled to save others from tragedy, while giving meaning to her personal trauma. It was truly a gift, her colleagues said, the way kids opened up to her; she often made headway where others had failed to break through a child's protective shell of silence. She was constantly amazed that even strangers would confess to her, for no apparent reason. Everyone had a story they were willing to share, from the clerk at the post office telling her at full volume about her hot flashes and did she know any remedy for it, mistaking her for a physician because of the "doctor" in front of her name, to the TV repairman recounting the tale of his wife's fourteen hour labour, to the waitress in the local restaurant admitting that the marks on her arms were caused by her violent boyfriend. And so the most reticent child would finally break down and admit to Dr. Gerard, that yes, the neighbour or her uncle, brother or father had touched her "down there."

Oh yes, a gift, that had been bought at a very high price, she would answer, in her head, never revealing her own secret. She had become a psychologist to save children from pedophiles like her brother. The powerlessness, the shame, the self-loathing, anger and fear she had grown up experiencing made her empathetic and fiercely determined to help. She never felt that she had chosen her work. It had chosen her. Small victories lent her strength and renewed her dedication to carry on, but the worst cases, like those where the child had been sexually abused since infancy, devastated her to the point of collapse. She took her work personally. It became her mission. Exhaustion left little energy for a social life.

Outside the office, she remained aloof. She spoke quietly, attended only obligatory social gatherings, and trusted very few people, male or female. Her close friends set her up for dates with Tom, Dick or Harry. She would return home alone, even more disillusioned. Loser. User. Abuser. She labelled them all. She cannily assessed every male who displayed an interest in her, suspecting their motives, for they couldn't really want her for herself. What were they really after? What games would she have to play to satisfy them, as she had seen so many women do? No, she wanted to remain free of encumbrances. Unchained from the fetters of men's desires. In the professional realm, there was no choice but to engage with men, oftentimes terrible, disturbed men. She readily took on the battles, but otherwise, she steered clear, just like Barb had, she now realized. Suddenly, she wondered what Barb had suffered, all those years ago, a lone female working in a man's world, where the expectation was that she would either fail, or give up after a few years and get married and have children. She wished she had taken the time to get to know Barb better. For unconsciously, she had followed in her footsteps. A cold bitch, as some had labelled them both.

Now, she literally glowed with happiness. Infatuation had never happened to her before. When she thought of Colin, she couldn't breathe. When she saw him, her heart pounded in her throat, leaving her speechless and numb with longing. Somehow, they were connected, by a thin, invisible wire that she envisioned as a thread of gold. She wondered if he sensed it, too. She was sure that if she just spent enough time in his presence, he would turn around and see her, recognize her by her eyes, as she had known him, by his smell. He had to, because there weren't a thousand out there. Maybe just one man for her. A woman could wait an entire lifetime, and never find him. The old saw, "You have to kiss a lot of frogs to find your prince," did not apply to her, as she had never been willing to play that game. But what if he...

"Chantale, Chantale, you were saying?" her thoughts drifted back to their first dinner date.

"Chantale, such a lovely name. French? Of course. Sounds like the chime of a bell in the wind... Please, go on. You were telling me about your home. So you were raised on a farm in Alberta? Wow, I would never have guessed. You seem so... sophisticated. The city must agree with you. Me, too. I came from a small town on Vancouver Island and I'd never go back. Vancouver has so much to offer, the ocean, skiing, great parks, restaurants... It's the best! Tell me more about your work. It must be really tough but rewarding, I'll bet. What first drew you to psychology?"

Oh my God. Her name sounded so sweet on his lips. He had really listened, interested in what she had to say and fascinated by her career. Not treating her as if her work was a hobby that she could easily give up for marriage and children. Although for the first time, those ideas came to mind as possibilities, notions she had never considered before, had even denigrated to her colleagues: "Not for me, the chains of matrimony and child rearing!"

When she had met Colin, her life had opened up. He had allowed their intimate relationship to develop slowly. A hopeless romantic, his gifts of flowers, jewelry, tickets to the opera, cards sent to her home and to her office, convinced her that he was not going to run, even after she told him some of the least upsetting details of her past, which might have shocked others. In fact, when he had sent a bouquet of twenty-one red roses to her office the raised eyebrows and teasing comments of the staff made her blush with embarrassment, but also pleasure. She had never been the subject of such admiration before and she didn't quite know how to react to it. Only lately had she begun to let down her guard and allow her deepest feelings to emerge. Her happy smile at the office was a welcome change which her secretary Marion never ceased to comment upon.

Just the night before, she and Colin had made love for the first time. She still felt as if she could taste his being, in every pore of her skin. Somehow, his fingertips were imposed over her own, holding the steering wheel and guiding her through the driving rain. As she had lain beside him, describing the sensations of warmth and safety he had given her, he'd merely smiled and stroked her hair. His silence assured her that he had no expectations of her, that she was enough. And she had never been enough for anyone before, least of all herself. She had been single-mindedly driven to prove herself worthy, to rise above the denigrating abuse she had suffered at the hands of her brother, and the naïve blindness of her mother, who refused to recognize any truth which might damage the so-called reputation of the family. Alone, she had been forced to rebuild herself from the ground up.

Yet even with two university degrees, honors and accolades and her own thriving practice, she had not found solace. Happiness always shimmered somewhere out on the horizon—she believed that she could see it, hovering just at the edge of the ocean, when she walked along the sea wall in Stanley Park. Perhaps if she worked harder, became a psychiatrist, travelled, bought a nicer car, moved... she would get there. Every day, she would weigh her options and come up with some more daring plan, challenging herself to do more, to be more. Her heart would race and she would fight down her anxiety by running or exercising herself to exhaustion. With her heart pounding to the rhythm of her feet, she could find some measure of calm, until the next attack.

But now her heart leapt merely at the sight of Colin's car pulling up in front of her apartment building. Then this had to happen! Out of nowhere, a stick thrust into the spokes of her wheels, sending her wagon careening downhill. What was she supposed to do with a homeless teenager? The thought brought back memories of her own flight from home and the anguish of those days in Danielle's flat, with Damian. To this day, the man's name made her shudder with revulsion.

But what might have become of her, if Danielle hadn't been there for support, however minimal? She would have ended up on the street, like the waifs she passed by every day on the way to her office!

Willing to help strangers then, but not a member of your own family who might disrupt your plans, eh? the voice in her head berated her soundly. Guilt washed over her, as it so often did. She thought of this familiar feeling as "Catholic" guilt, ingrained early and impossible to ignore. How dare she feel resentful of her niece's intrusion into her life?

"Never mind, never mind, you'll figure something out," she repeated over and over to the slap of the windshield wipers, until at last she pulled the car into the brightly lit bus depot parking lot.

Opening the car door and stepping her high heeled shoe straight into a deep puddle, she sighed and thought, "Let's just see that she is safe. That's the main thing. Safe is all that matters." Hunching her shoulders against the deluge, not bothering to grab her umbrella, she raced toward the double glass doors. Pulling the huge handle, she shook her head in bewilderment, with no idea how she was supposed to find sixteen year-old Jocelyne in the crowded terminal. Her eyes were blinded by the memory of a six year-old running through sun-drenched fields with Blackie the horse, back home on the farm in Alberta.

Chapter Thirty-seven

"Pregnant? How, well, of course I know how, I mean, are you sure? When? I mean, did you know before you left home? You mean to tell me that isn't even why you left? Oh, dear. I am so, so sorry that happened to you. I just wish you had found me the moment you... well, never mind, you're safe now. This is my area of expertise. I know just what to do, who to call, where to go. Don't worry, I'll help you. It's okay, go ahead and cry. That's just what you need. Let it out, let it all out."

Later, after she'd had a hot bath and ravenously eaten a mound of leftover spaghetti, Jocelyne curled up on the couch under a warm blanket and told Chantale everything that had happened to her since arriving in Vancouver, three months ago. Despite her years of training and experience, Chantale trembled with rage. This was different. Her own flesh and blood!

"The bastard! You were literally a prisoner! He took all your money, so you couldn't get away?"

"Yeah, well, he thought he got everything, but luckily I had stashed some stuff in my backpack, and he didn't bother to look through it. Look, he didn't get this! Thank God!" Jocelyne extruded a long, glistening necklace from the folds of a sock. Necklace, no...! Chantale caught her breath in wonder.

"Grandmère's rosary, remember? Richard gave it to me, the bum! He burnt up or sold or killed everything else when she died! Believe me because I know, I was there! I cried so hard the day he and Dad smashed down her beautiful house. They didn't even care! But I still have this and I always believed what Grandmère told me, that my guardian angel would keep me safe. Remember that picture in Dad's old room, of the angel with the pink wings? I loved that picture! I wish Richard would have given me that but oh no... Anyways, here

I am, safe and sound! Thanks to her and this, and you, of course!" Jocelyne exclaimed, tossing the amethyst and pearl beaded chain into the air and catching it by the gold crucifix. Chantale shook her head. The child was obviously still in shock.

"So you were locked up, drugged and continually raped for months? Did they feed you at least? How did you manage to escape? Well, thank God that girl finally took pity on you and helped you. But listen, we have to call the police. Those creeps need to be charged with assault, kidnapping, drug possession, the works. Next, we'll get you to a doctor. I can arrange an abortion really quickly, based on what happened, but time is running out. First thing tomorrow..." Chantale assumed a professional tone. Jocelyne interrupted her.

"Thank you so much, Chantale. I knew you would help me. When I was little, I admired you so much. I always wondered why you got us sent away from Grandmère's, but I still loved you. I always kept the record you gave me, you know, the one with the picture of the little blonde girl on it, holding the puppy? I was sure surprised when I found it in my things after we left the farm. Mom thought I might have taken it from you, but I didn't and I knew you had snuck it into my bag. That is, I figured it out after I found out you had left home...I couldn't bring it with me, but it's still in my room. You don't remember? Well, I have it," she exclaimed, pointing to her chest and shaking her soft brown curls. Then she took a deep breath and continued.

"Yeah, I sure would like to see a doctor. That's what I've been dreaming about for weeks, every time I was straight enough to think. I've been feeling so sick. I'd just throw up and lose what little I did have to eat, every morning and night. But as for an abortion, no, that's not what I want. I could never do that. You were raised Catholic same as me, by Grandmère. Listen, I want to have the baby and look after it myself. I know how. I've been caring for my baby brother Luke since he was born and he's a handful, believe me. Please, please don't tell Mom and Dad. I can do it. I'll get a job and..."

"Wait a minute, wait a minute. Okay, okay, slow down. Take a deep breath. Step one is to call the police and get these bastards arrested. Step two is to get you to a doctor. As for... the rest... we'll get it all sorted out. You just tuck up, and go to sleep. You're safe now."

Chapter Thirty-eight

Vancouver, 1974

What could possibly be taking so long? Jocelyne had gone into labour thirty-six hours ago. She was still in the delivery room and there had been no word from the doctor for hours. The nurses just kept reassuring her that this was normal with a first baby.

"Christ," Chantale admonished herself, slapping her thigh with an open hand as she paced the hospital waiting room. "I should never have agreed to keep this a secret from Suzanna. It's not right! It's her daughter and her grandchild, after all."

For the first time, she understood how her own mother must have worried, all those years ago. Back then, she had rejoiced in making her suffer as part of what she'd thought of as just retribution for her sins of ignorance and false pride. Now, as she waited anxiously for her niece to safely deliver a child, guilt washed over her like a tidal wave.

Although, after what Jocelyne had revealed about her life at home, Chantale had felt so badly for her that she'd allowed objectivity to fly out the window. A fatal mistake for a professional. Even worse for a family member. Colin, now her fiancé, had tried to dissuade her from the secrecy, begging her to shed responsibility for her niece and her unborn child. But Jocelyne had been insistent and Chantale had argued that they could not force her to return home. In her state, the consequences of losing her and putting the baby at risk trumped her duty to her brother and sister-in-law. She agreed to tell them, no matter what Jocelyne said, as soon as the baby was born. At that point, surely she would see the sense in going home, hopefully after her parents had convinced her to give up the baby for adoption. In the meantime, they did everything to support her through the pregnancy, and Jocelyne anticipated the birth with excitement.

"I have to have keep my baby, Auntie. It needs me. And besides, I've been looking after a baby for half my life, since Luke was born. Mom made me do everything for him and you know he still needs the same care as a newborn, if not more. I'll be a great mother, you'll see. I love babies! Won't it be fun for you too, to have a little baby to love? We'll be a family! I can hardly wait!"

Fun? Right. The child was... well, a child. What could you expect? And what in the hell was taking so long? Something must be wrong!

In a fit of nervous energy, Chantale strode all the way back to Jocelyne's room. She fussed with a flower arrangement, tidied magazines on the side table, smoothed the bedspread. Reaching to fold the coverlet back, she noticed the gold cross of her mother's rosary jutting out from underneath the pillow.

"Silly girl, shouldn't leave something this valuable here!" she muttered to herself, yanking it hastily out with the intention of securing it in her purse. But as she held it in her hands, it seemed comforting. She wrapped it around her wrist as she returned to the corridor. Back in the waiting room, she puffed on one cigarette after another. She hadn't smoked in six years. At first her lungs had protested, seizing into a brutal cough. Now she sucked the smoke deeper into her lungs, to relieve her nerves. When she wasn't smoking, she was chewing her nails, biting them down to the quick, until Colin joined her after work, and held her hands.

She reminisced with him about the months she had cared for Jocelyne in her tiny apartment, looking after her, as she had promised, just until the baby came. Jocelyne had expected that afterward, they would have to find her a place of her own, and get her on Social Assistance. Chantale admitted to herself that it would be lonely without Jocelyne, until she and Colin were married. She had been surprised to find that despite the cramped quarters, she enjoyed having a roommate. For the first time since she had left home, she celebrated Christmas, buying presents and decorating the apartment. She even prepared the traditional French Canadian Christmas Eve meal of tourtière, which she had to look up in a recipe book, as she had never taken an interest in helping her mother make the time-honored meat pies. She felt proud of the warmth she had managed to create by recapturing some of the fondest memories of her own childhood Christmas rituals. She admitted to herself that some of the Québécois rituals which her mother had insisted upon had some merit, after all.

They had spent a magical Christmas season together and, as soon as January came, it was time to begin planning for the spring wedding. Her niece was the only family member she had to share her excitement about her future with Colin and, since she had few friends, she was thankful for the camaraderie. Like sisters, the two young women fussed over the details of invitations, dresses, and flowers. Chantale wished Danielle were alive to celebrate with her. There was no one to represent her parents, but Jocelyne would be the maid of honour.

"Some maid, huh? Long as you don't expect me to wear white. Oh yeah, it's the bride that has to wear white, that's right. Well, I'm okay, then," she had joked.

"Anyways, tell me more about why you want to marry this guy. He's kinda ...homely, isn't he?"

"Homely! What... oh, very funny! I'll have you know that Colin is the handsomest, sweetest, kindest, most generous, wonderful..."

"All right, all right, I didn't ask for his resumé! So what *exactly* do you like about him? He's just a whatchacallit? Graphic artist? Doesn't sound like a great prospect to me!" she had said, crossing her arms across her chest and frowning, before bursting out laughing at her aunt's hurt expression.

Chantale experienced a closeness she had never shared with anyone in her family before, not even Danielle. She happily spoiled her niece with visits to the best restaurants and shopping sprees "for the baby." Colin treated them to outings, delighting in the teenager's enthusiasm for the attractions of the city: the aquarium, Gastown, Grouse Mountain, the harbour, the museums. He found himself enchanted at her delight in the most everyday things, that he had come to take for granted, from the size of the old growth Douglas firs in Stanley Park to the breathtaking sight of the Pacific ocean from the shore, accessible right in the city. He and Chantale rekindled their love for Vancouver through this small-town girl's eyes, finding themselves continually smiling at each other as she made yet another discovery.

"What I still can't get over are the roses! We don't have flowers anywhere like this at home except in expensive flower shops, and yet here they grow like weeds right in the hedgerows. I just *love* them, especially the yellow ones! They don't even look real! They're so perfectly formed, they look plastic. To me, they just shout 'pure joy!' And the smell—heaven on earth! I wish I could eat them up!" Jocelyne exclaimed as they strolled the residential streets on the way back to the apartment, after an afternoon in Stanley Park.

"Yeah, well, just be careful. You should know better by now, since you almost inhaled a bee up your nose last week! Look before you sniff!" Colin teased, as she plunged her round face into yet another blowsy yellow blossom.

In the evenings, after Jocelyne was soundly tucked up on the fold-out couch they had purchased for the living room, Chantale and Colin would sip coffee in the tiny galley kitchen, and relive the details of their days like new parents.

"Man, that girl could talk the ear off a hound dog, as my old dad used to say," Colin would laugh and shake his head. But Chantale knew he enjoyed Jocelyne's ceaseless chatter. Colin's gentle, easygoing manner with her niece deepened Chantale's conviction that she had found the right mate. For Chantale, it was as if Jocelyne held a mirror reflecting the future, illuminating the possibility of a family life she had only dreamed about, never experienced. Due to the house guest, their lovemaking on her single bed behind the bedroom door became silent and even more tender, until in the early morning hours, Colin would head for home, to wash and change for work. The three of them seemed to be afloat together on a wave of happiness.

"Do you know something? I haven't had so much fun since I was a little girl. You're always laughing when Colin's around. That's a good sign, if you ask me. Did you ever hear my mom laugh? I didn't, not for a long, long time. Just for an example: Dad loved to watch Ed Sullivan on Sunday nights, in the wintertime when he wasn't away working and he'd sit in his chair and holler at her to come and enjoy the comedians or the jugglers or the high wire act with us, but she never would. She'd bang the pots and dishes after supper, then run up and downstairs from the washer and dryer, changing the sheets on all the beds, making a big deal out of getting us our bath and clothes ready for school the next day. But if Dad left to go on the road, then back she would head for her rocking chair or to her bed, leaving everything for me to do when I got home from school. She was usually still in her nightgown or some sloppy housedress when I got home. Sometimes she'd stay in bed all day and I didn't dare wake her up or she'd scream at me. Then I'd have to do everything for Nico and Pauline, too, as well as Luke. I didn't have time for friends, wasn't allowed to have anyone over anyways. It's funny how you say I talk a lot. I do now, but when I was back at school, I got so shy that I couldn't talk at all, and started stuttering when anyone did speak to me. So the kids thought I was weird and started teasing me. Then I started hitting them or kicking them or screaming at them to get them to leave me alone and I would get suspended and sent home. For more washing floors, cooking, ironing Dad's huge shirts big enough to fit an elephant, not to mention changing Luke's diapers, giving him medicine, which was the worst..."

Jocelyne paused to inhale a deep breath, for with the baby growing she found it harder to keep talking without coming up for air. She had also developed the unconscious habit of rubbing her stomach with both hands as she spoke. It seemed to comfort her and make her even more chatty, if that was possible. Chantale smiled inwardly at the momentary gap in the story, remembering the doll called "Chatty Kathy" that used to "talk" after the cord in its back was pulled.

"When Grandpa was alive...did you ever meet Mom's Dad? No? Well, he could make her laugh! He would sing the funniest songs—he was American. He used to be an entertainer, she said, in carnival shows. I still remember him singing: *Camptown Races; Froggy Come A'Courtin'; Clementine; Oh Suzanna.* Do you know that one, with the nonsense words?" she asked, looking at Chantale quizzically. When her aunt shook her head, she didn't hesitate for a moment.

"*Rained all night, the day I left, the weather it was dry, Sun so hot, I froze to death,*

Suzanna don't you cry! Oh Suzanna, now don't you cry for me, For I come from Alabamy with a banjo on my knee!" she belted out at full volume until she lost her breath and burst into laughter at her own exuberance.

"No? It's funny, huh? That one was his favorite—he said he named Mom after it. Anyways, the way he would carry on, he'd have us all in stitches, dancing around the kitchen doing the Charleston and that crazy move holding his knees with his hands crossed, that made his legs look like rubber! He was so funny! It was great the way he could give Mom the giggles. Then we'd all start and we could hardly stop! I wish he hadn't died." Rub, rub, rub.

"Nico, now he could break her up, too! Too bad you only knew him when he was a sickly baby. HE grew out of it. Maybe you'll get the chance to meet him someday. He's amazing. He can sit in front of the television, memorize a whole comedy show, and then repeat the skits back word for word, with the right accents and gestures and everything. He killed us! We'd laugh 'til we cried. Yup, Mom still laughs at Nico, even when he gets into trouble. Once he was playing in the car and backed it down the alley, crashing into Grandpa's garage door! Dad was furious that he had scratched his precious blue Desoto, but no one could stay mad at Nico for long. Another time he and a neighbour kid blew up the kid's parents' garage, yup, blew the walls right down flat. He didn't even get punished—I guess everyone was just glad they weren't killed! But anyways, he can tease his way out of anything, the little devil. I think I miss him the most." Rub, rub, rub, as tears fell onto her distended stomach.

"Yeah, you're right come to think of it. I never heard my mom laugh too often either. I guess they both had a lot on their minds. I'm only just beginning to realize how much responsibility my mother had..."

"Well, I'm going to make sure my child has fun with me and hears me laugh. What's the use in being so serious all the time? It's boring and life shouldn't be boring, don't you agree?"

Listening to her, Chantale dreaded the thought of her niece becoming a mother, at only seventeen.

"My God, she's just a child herself. And despite her 'experience,' she's totally naïve!" she had moaned to Colin, too afraid of alienating Jocelyne to berate her to her face. But one day, driving back from a doctor's appointment, she dared to broach a subject that held her worst fear.

"What about the drugs you took, or were forced to take, Jocelyne? And who knows what those guys were on! It could turn out really badly. You already know what it is to care for a handicapped child. You have to be realistic. Please fill in the papers for adoption, just in case. It would be better for the baby, believe me on this, please, Sweetie. There are lots of really good couples out there, just dying to have a child to love. I am so worried...."

But Jocelyne stubbornly insisted she could look after the baby no matter what. She refused to be persuaded, so Chantale bit her tongue and nervously counted the days until the baby was due. Secretly, between her and Colin, she planned to call Suzanna as soon as the baby was born, and fly her out to Vancouver. Hopefully her own mother could resolve the situation and convince Jocelyne to return home, without the baby. If that didn't work, Chantale had another plan. She would see that Jocelyne got back into school as soon as possible, by covering the babysitting costs and her tuition. That would pose no problem for her. She had plenty of money. She would be happy to help her niece finish her education and get established. It seemed a way to make up for...other things. Besides, more than family, they were best friends now. She had no intention of telling Jocelyne this however. She held the idea close to her heart, as a last resort.

Near the end of the pregnancy, Chantale had rushed Jocelyne to the hospital, in premature labour. Jocelyne finally faced the truth about the drugs, all the drugs, so many drugs, she couldn't remember. She would wake up from nightmares screaming, then refuse to take her medication when the nurse came around. She lived in terror that her baby would be helpless and disabled, like her little brother. Chantale begged her to call Suzanna. She refused. Scared as she was, she clung to Chantale's hand and made her promise not to tell.

"No matter what happens, don't tell. Don't burden Mom with any more. She's been through enough. More than she can take. I realize that now. I got myself into this mess and I have to get myself out of it. I'll be fine, you'll see. Just like you, Chantale. You made it and so will I. I'm lucky, I've got you here. So lucky, I can't believe it. The baby and I are both lucky. We have our very own guardian angel. I'll tell Mom and Dad later, promise, when we're all settled and then they won't be able to do anything about it. But not yet, pleeease! They'd make me go home and that would be disastrous!"

Against her better judgement, Chantale promised, though the seriousness of Jocelyne's health concerns terrified her. Now there was more than just the baby to consider. Paul would kill her if he knew what was happening, she admitted to Colin. Then one night the doctor decided to stop suppressing the labour, as the fetus' heart rate was registering distress. Hard labour came on immediately. Chantale had stayed with her and held her hand until they had wheeled her away. At one point, between contractions, Jocelyne had asked her, out of the blue, "Did you ever read *Little Women*?"

"Why no, I wasn't a big reader when I was a kid. I was more interested in doing crafts, riding horses... Then when I left home, there wasn't much time..."

"Oh yeah, I remember, you did "paint by numbers" and stuff. Well, I read all the time. That's all there was to do in that shitty, one horse town. I read every book I had at least twice, *Little Women* more times than I can count. It was my favourite book. Anyways, it's about four sisters and the youngest one, Beth, gets sick and just before she dies she says, "I always knew I wouldn't live very long. I am not talented, or smart or pretty like the rest of you, and I could never see myself getting older." Jocelyne quoted dramatically, bringing her arms across her chest. She let out a strained laugh.

"Too bad I'm not good at acting, like Nicolas. Anyways, I could really understand what she meant. Mostly I wanted to be like Jo, the sister who was smart and capable and became a famous writer and her life turned out perfectly, but whenever I felt sorry for myself, I wanted to be Beth, and make my family sorry that I was dead. I'd lie awake at night and imagine my funeral, what flowers I would have, which songs, who would be there. So many times at home, I wanted to die. I hated my life so much, I would just wish I wouldn't wake up in the morning. Then I'd feel guilty, because Luke had it worse and it wasn't his fault he was born that way. I used to want to go back to church, just to confess how horrible I was, but by then Dad had stopped going and Grandmère was dead..." she sobbed. Chantale wiped her brow and tipped her head forward to give her water through a straw.

Jocelyne shook her head no, and continued, "Then I made up my mind to be brave, like Jo in the book. Set off on my own for the big city. I could get a job at a newspaper and become a famous writer like she did. That was my dream, anyway. That fairy tale turned into a nightmare, 'cause here I am bringing a baby into this world. Jo would never have gotten herself into such a mess. Now, I want to live for my baby, but... Oh, my God, here it comes again. Can't they get me something for the pain?" she shrieked, squeezing Chantale's hand so hard she thought the bones might snap. But she didn't let go.

At the time, Chantale had dismissed the girl's chatter as the ravings of labour. The nurses had warned her that a woman in labour could spout all sorts of nonsense, some of it not very pretty. Suddenly, the words rang in her ears as she watched a doctor approach her, wearing a look that instantly chilled her to the core.

"Miss Gerard? You brought in the young Miss Gerard?"

"Yes, yes, what is it? How is she? What's taking so long? I've been waiting here for hours and no one would give me any word."

"I'm sorry, Miss. She didn't make it. We did everything we could. Your niece... I'm truly sorry. She's gone. We couldn't revive her from the anesthetic, after the emergency C-section. She died of heart failure. We did everything we could, under the circumstances."

The doctor grasped her arm as Chantale collapsed and led her to a chair. Colin rushed to the nurse's station to ask for water. Somehow she managed to sputter out a question.

"Her baby? Yes, of course, of course. She had a fine little girl, weighing four pounds, eleven ounces. She has been placed in an incubator in neonatal intensive care. We believe she is about six weeks premature, but other than that, she actually looks good. Her heart rate is now stabilized. We are providing her with oxygen and will feed her through a tube until she develops the reflex to suck a bottle. We are very optimistic that the baby will live, with constant monitoring and support over the next few weeks. Tell me, are there any other next of kin to be notified? Are you the young lady's legal guardian? What was her religious affiliation? We have a priest and a pastor, right here in the hospital, on call, if you wish. We need you to fill out some papers. I'm so sorry, Miss. I know this is a shock. Come this way, please. The nurse will help you."

Chapter Thirty-nine

Chantale accompanied Jocelyne's body on the one hour flight back to Alberta. The baby remained at the hospital, in intensive care. Colin would stay behind and keep watch, informing her of any changes when he called her each night. Paul and Suzanna met Chantale at the Edmonton airport. After days of agonizing over what to say, she had no chance to even open her mouth. Paul's broad, ruddy face was a map of pain and bitterness. He waved away Chantale's extended hand. His eyes were even greener for being bloodshot and he turned them on her with such a forceful look of hate that she reeled backwards.

"You'll pay for this, you bitch. How dare you, how dare you…I still can't believe that you knew, you had her the whole time and you never even told us!" he hollered at full volume, despite the fact that people in the waiting area turned to stare. Ignoring them as much as Suzanna's pats on the arm to hush him, he went on shouting.

"The whole time, while her mother and I suffered in agony thinking she was dead or kidnapped or God knows what! The great Dr. Gérard. Some head-shrinker you turned out to be! Maybe you need your own head examined, ever think of that? Ever think what a parent goes through when something like this happens? And then, to have the audacity to offer to pay for the funeral! Don't you think I can pay for my own child's funeral? But you'll pay all right. I'll sue you for everything you've got, for all the pain and suffering you caused us. You had no right, no right…" His voice weakened, then cracked and he dropped his bald head into his hands, while the tears rolled down his cheeks.

Suzanna took his hand. Chantale tried to hide her shock at how much the couple had aged in the past ten years. Her eyes filled with tears as Suzanna tried to reason with Paul, using the same arguments Chantale had provided when she had made the terrible phone call.

"Don't, Paul. That's enough," she interjected quietly. "Chantale only did what she thought was best. Maybe if she had told us, Jocelyne would only have run away again. She would have been so ashamed to be pregnant...I can't imagine what she went through. Chantale kept her safe and looked after her for us. It's not her fault that our daughter was there in the first place. She was going to send for us, as soon as the baby was born, for us all to be reconciled, isn't that right, Chantale? But...it never worked out that way."

Suzanna reached out her other hand to clutch at Chantale. She seemed too weak to stand without support. Chantale gripped her tightly by the arm, choking back her own tears of grief and remorse. Like their mother, Paul had a gift for directing the poison arrow of guilt right to the heart. As usual, Suzanna saw the truth clearly, but it didn't make it any easier. Chantale sent her a watery smile, trying to mask her pity for the woman she had so envied, when she had been an overweight, pimply-faced teenager. Now black hair shot through with white hung limply on Suzanna's narrow shoulders. Her blue eyes had lost their sparkle. She constantly closed her eyes as she spoke to avoid meeting anyone's gaze. The colour of her green raincoat didn't suit her and seemed to engulf her small frame. The bones of her face jutted out from her transparent skin. A web of blue veins showed through on either temple where her hair was white. Her vanity still went so far as to try to cover the loose skin on her neck with a silk scarf, but she wore a simple white blouse and black, polyester pants that dragged under her low-heeled shoes. Her cheeks glowed as they once did, but from exhaustion rather than vitality. Chantale struggled for words to express her sorrow at causing her more grief. Suzanna just shook her head and put a finger to her lips, then pointed to the exit sign, blazing red in the distance.

Chantale and Suzanna organized the small family funeral. Paul simply could not cope. He ignored everyone and everything but his bottle of rye whiskey. Duty left the women little time for thought or recriminations. They had to make all the arrangements with the priest, the funeral home, the caterers, the florist. Chantale made most of the decisions, including filling the church with yellow roses, and requesting one of Jocelyne's favourite songs, *Both Sides, Now* by Joni Mitchell, to be played during the service. Suzanna seemed surprised, but just shrugged her shoulders, quietly agreeing to everything Chantale suggested. They even had to find the strength to shop for mourning clothes for themselves and the two children, Nicolas and Pauline: dark suits, gloves and hats with veils. Chantale couldn't believe that old Mr. Jacques' shop was still in business, but he greeted them at the door, stooped and grey-haired.

"Ah yes, what a tragedy. I read the notice in the paper. I remember your mother, Mme. Gérard so well, my dear. One of my best customers. Such an honourable lady." Chantale held her eyes straight ahead to avoid rolling them, as Suzanna nodded in agreement. If only they knew what a deceiver she had been, she thought. But she was not about to disillusion them now. She simply smiled as Mr. Jacques continued in his croaky voice.

"And the little one with the bright green eyes, so like her grandmother, and pretty, of course, like her mother," he sketched a slight old-fashioned bow to Suzanna as he turned to direct her to the counter.

"Please, please, let me do all I can to help. Here we have a nice black hat, with a veil, and black gloves in this cabinet, for you ladies and the young miss. A suit for the young man, too? Such a handsome boy, reminds me of his father at that age. Yes, that will not be a problem. So sad, so sad."

There was no question of an open casket for the funeral. At the prayer vigil, Paul had fainted into the arms of the funeral director, at the sight of the little pinched face and the tiny folded white hands reposing in the silk-lined box. Nicolas had screamed and run from the room and Pauline had sobbed and blubbered to the point of vomiting. Suzanna had stared down at the body, gripping the sides of the casket, wracked with silent sobs. Chantale had focused her gaze on Jocelyne's lips, wishing now that the sweet voice would come pouring forth in a fountain of excited chatter, sorry that she had ever teased her for talking too much. Her eyes were dry and from somewhere she heard her mother telling her that she had cried all her tears already. She realized that a desert of desolation was almost worse than an ocean of pain.

Chantale dreaded meeting her other brothers at the funeral,

but felt she had to go, for Suzanna's sake more than anything. The legal wranglings her siblings had put her through over their mother's estate seemed so meaningless now, but she could not swallow the bitterness that welled in her throat each time she thought of her stolen childhood. Determined to be civil to Ghislain at least, she nervously hugged him, though he had not even recognized her until Suzanna brought her forward with the children to greet him.

"Wow, you look so...tall and...different. But I guess it is, Jeez, ten, twelve years since I saw you last. You were what, sixteen, when you left home, and I was long gone by then myself. Well, you've changed and that's a fact. I would have passed you right by on the street! Your hair is a different colour now, is that it? And you've lost a lot of weight. My chubby little sister has grown into a stunner! Who would have guessed?" Ghislain exclaimed. Despite herself, Chantale blushed to the tips of her ears at his crude attempt at a compliment, inwardly cursing once again this old reflexive response. She thought she had conquered it.

Ghislain introduced her to his new wife, young and pretty, dressed inappropriately in a short, colourful dress and high-heeled shoes. Chantale was politely enquiring about his grown daughters from his first marriage when suddenly someone came up from behind and smacked her on the bottom. Her back immediately tightened as she whirled around to face Richard.

"Hey, little sis! Long time no see!" A stranger might have thought it a friendly tone, but to Chantale it rang hollow as his cold, unsmiling eyes appraised her up and down.

"Wow, the big city life don't seem to have done you no harm. You're lookin' mighty fine, there, in your fancy striped suit. It's Dr. Gérard, ain't it, now, so Paul tells me? Well, who would've guessed all those years playin' doctor would have paid off in spades! Shame your doctorin' skills couldn't save our little Squirt, though now, ain't it? God, I'm gonna miss that kid. A ray o' sunshine in a dull ol' bachelor's life. Now little chubby cheeks here is all alone," he blubbered, jutting his palm forward to tap Pauline's cheek.

Chantale stepped in front and dashed his hand away, startling the thirteen-year-old, who looked up at them quizzically and let out a weak simper. Richard laughed out loud as he rubbed his hand on the front of his jacket.

"Still, Josie never should'a run away from home, now should she, and this wouldn'a happened. Never tell what can happen out there nowadays. I couldn't believe it when she did the same damn fool thing as you. Damn cryin' shame, though. I hear you're gonna tie the knot soon, Sis. How 'bout a kiss for your big brother, for ol' times sake?" His voice was edged with malice as he leaned forward and grabbed her by both arms. Suzanna frowned, raising an eyebrow to gesture to Chantale to follow as she hurried the children away into the church.

"Take your hands off me, you bastard," Chantale hissed under her breath, trying to avoid attention. Richard's phony smile slid off his face into an arrogant sneer. Chantale wanted to walk away, but she couldn't let the opportunity pass to slap him with the words she had silently rehearsed for years.

"Don't you speak to me or come near me again, or I'll charge you with assault. Better late than never. If you think settling Ma's estate without a will was ugly, just watch me. I'm not a medical doctor, I'm a psychologist, for your goddamn information, and not your puppet anymore. And I know exactly what to do with scum like you. In fact, it's my specialty. Nothing would give me more pleasure than to see you rot in jail, but this is not the time or the place to bring up the past. But if you think I have forgotten, you've got another think coming. Don't ever kid yourself: blood is **not** thicker than water. Then finally Paul might quit accusing me of killing Mother by running away. He would know the truth of why I left and you would never see his kids again. Step out of my way, you pig, and I'm warning you, keep your hands off Suzanna's kids. My hatred for you will never die!" She would have spit in his face, but her mouth had filled with sand. She could not even swallow. With a final, withering glare, she turned on her heel and followed Suzanna down the aisle, joining her and Paul in the front pew.

Trembling with a rage she had long suppressed, she blindly felt in her purse for her mother's amethyst and pearl rosary. She clutched it in her icy hands throughout the service. Attending Mass was a practice she had given up long ago. She had forgotten all of the prayers but one, so she fingered each bead as she silently repeated, "Hail Mary, full of Grace, have mercy on us. Hail Mary, full of Grace, grant us Peace. May your guardian angel protect you, Jocelyne, now and forevermore."

The casket floated before her eyes like a tiny, lonely boat, draped in a cascade of yellow roses. Paul knelt down beside her, accepting her hand when she placed it over his and unashamedly drenching them both in tears. Suzanna remained seated in the pew, hands clasped on her lap, staring straight ahead, expressionless beneath her veil. During the Joni Mitchell song, Chantale glanced over and saw her twisting a handkerchief. She almost regretted suggesting the song as her sister-in-law dropped her head and her shoulders heaved while the tape of Joni crooned. Chantale felt her heart crack in two. "So there really is such a thing as heartbreak," came the unbidden thought.

When the priest and the altar boys led the procession out, Suzanna took Nicolas and Pauline by the hand and followed the casket. Chantale supported Paul's bulk against her shoulder as best she could, for his knees seemed about to buckle at every step.

Even days later, there still remained details to be worked out. The adults barely noticed Pauline and Nicolas, who wandered aimlessly through the house. Mealtimes came and went, sometimes marked with sandwiches and coffee, more often ignored. The two children fended for themselves, filling up on cereal and toast. Luke had been sent to an institution for full-time care, shortly after Jocelyne had left home.

"That's great, Suzanna. Shut the barn door after the horses have got out. If only you had listened to me. But oh no, you knew best. Then you wonder where your daughter got it from, that damn stubborn streak," Paul had said to himself. Aloud he had assured her, "It's for the best. You just can't do it all on your own, without... Nico and Pauline need you. I...need you, too," he had tearfully admitted. Chantale also wondered silently why Suzanna had insisted on caring for their severely handicapped child at home. With three other children and a husband either out of town or in the bar, it was an impossible task. And the price had been...well, Suzanna knew the cost.

Now, Paul sat alone in the living room, supporting his whiskey glass in one hand, a cigarette in the other, staring blankly at whatever was on television. Since his outburst at the airport, he was silent unless he was drunk. When alcohol set his anger free, he blamed Suzanna for keeping Luke at home, overburdening their daughter to the point of running away. He blamed Chantale for Jocelyne's loss. He blamed the "goddamn hippies" for getting his daughter hooked on drugs. When sober, he would not speak to either of the women and flatly refused to be involved in decisions about the baby. He had scoffed when Suzanna had called her his grandchild and asked him to suggest a name.

"Call the little bastard Jigsaw for all I care. Took that many pieces to put it together. If I had thought that a child of mine would become a drug addict and a whore, I would have drowned her at birth!"

Chantale was appalled at his unrelenting anger at Jocelyne. She knew it stemmed from his own guilt but this, added to his cold-hearted dismissal of the innocent baby, led her to a conclusion. She called Colin for support, before suggesting it to Suzanna.

"Suzanna, please let me take her. You have enough to deal with, with two kids and Paul... and for me, for us, it will be a blessing. I have already talked it over with Colin and he agrees. He's a wonderful man, Suzanna. He'll be a great father. He and I both became very attached to Jocelyne. We feel in our hearts that we would love to raise her daughter as our own."

"But she's our grandchild. And I feel... responsible. Besides, you are a career woman. How will you manage? You don't know the first thing about raising a child. Is it really fair to put this on your... Colin... before you are even married? Instant family? I don't think so!"

"Look, it's not exactly as if we are spring chickens. I'm twenty-nine, Colin is thirty. How many kids did you have by this age? Sure, we weren't planning to have a family right away, but that's what happens sometimes. What does any new mother know, come to that? Like all new parents, we'll learn. I'll give up my full-time practice and organize child care. Besides, she may need care that is best provided in a big city hospital. We don't know yet, how she will do once she is out of the incubator. Colin is in love with her already. He spends every moment he can with her at the hospital. We both want to adopt Jocelyne's baby, legally, Suzanna. But there is one family tradition I'd like to maintain. She still doesn't have a name. Ma insisted on naming all the grandchildren. I think she did pretty well with your kids. Well, as grandmother, now it's your turn. What do you say?"

"Well, let's see. Oh, I know. Jacqueline... yes, after Jacqueline Kennedy. It's a French name, so that would satisfy your mother, God bless her, but at least it's easy to say in English. I don't even know the French way to pronounce it, but it's pretty. Jocelyne always complained that nobody could pronounce her name properly, even me. Maybe especially me. Nobody but her precious Grandmère could say her name with just the right accent. Well, even if the kids at school shorten it down to Jackie, it's still a pretty name. I always wanted to be just like her, you know, Mrs. Onasis it is now...beautiful, elegant, rich. It's perfect, don't you think? You pick the second name though. After all, she's your daughter now," she said softly. Her voice caught in her throat and she lay her head down on the kitchen table and sobbed, while Chantale petted the salt and pepper hair, and let her own tears fall silently on the cold, arborite surface.

"I just had a thought," Suzanna mumbled from between her crossed arms. She sat up and brushed her hair away from her damp face. Standing, she wiped her cheeks with the tissue she kept rolled in the sleeve of her blouse. With a ragged catch in her breath, she headed down the hall toward her bedroom, motioning for Chantale to follow.

"You will need to have her baptized. That would have been so important to your mother. I still have Jocelyne's christening gown in my cedar chest. I kept it in case...well, anyway, it's very pretty. This trunk is so damn full, I'm sure it's right at the bottom. Look, here's Jocelyne's dress from her first day of school. You should have that, too. And the little blue and white sailor dress she wore when she was four.... I guess I just didn't see..."

The muffled voice from within the trunk caught in a sob.

"I think I'll keep that. Ah, see, here it is," she declared in a somewhat triumphant tone as she pulled a small tissue-wrapped package from the chest. She sat back cross-legged on the floor and opened it.

"The ivory lace is beautiful, like a wedding dress. And there is a silk shawl to go with it, to wrap the baby in afterward. Look at the cute little bonnet, too. I had forgotten about that. Your mother bought it for her, of course, at Mr. Jacques' store." Suzanna smiled weakly as she fondled the lace and spoke warmly, in a voice from far away.

"Where else?" Chantale grinned, with a slight eye-roll. "Only 'de bes' o de bes' for my grandchild!' I can hear it now." Perched on the edge of the bed, she ran a hand back and forth across the worn ridges of the blue chenille bedspread.

"Exactly. I didn't have much say in the matter, being a heathen. But I didn't mind. In fact, I found the whole ceremony quite beautiful and it is great to have everyone fussing over and admiring your baby, even if only for one day. Of course, we followed the same ritual with all the kids. Your mother always put on a fine tea afterwards, with a special christening cake. Maybe you were old enough to remember? Well, I am sure you were there. Oh and there is the gold cross your mother gave her, too, to put on the baby after the christening. It's in my jewelry box." Handing the package to Chantale, she closed the lid on the cedar chest at the end of her bed, and stood up to face the mirrored dresser behind her. Brushing away dust, she opened a padded, two-tiered pink box. A tiny ballerina popped up and a music box tune began to play. She stopped the dancer with a wrench on the figurine, crushing the fluffy pink dress. The tune continued for a moment, then pinged note by note, to a stop.

"The chain only fits a baby and I never bothered to get a longer one so Jocelyne could wear it. I thought she would just lose it at school and it is twenty-four carat gold, so I put it away, for safekeeping. That was really smart, wasn't it?" The bitterness in her tone had returned.

"I haven't looked in here for years. I never wear jewelry anymore. What's the point? I know it's in here somewhere… ouch, what the hell? Dammit, that brooch pin is sharp! Which one is it? Oh yeah, that thing your mother gave me." Suzanna sucked on her right index finger as she extracted a brooch from the box with her left hand.

"Here, you keep this, too. Your mother said it is very old. I never wore it, of course. You should have it appraised. Maybe it's worth something. She said it's been in the family for years though, so maybe you want to pass it down, too. Here, we'll wrap it in the tissue from the dress. It drew blood, look. Ah, there's the cross, on the top tray. If all else fails, look where it is supposed to be. It's so tiny I couldn't see it; I'd imagined it bigger than it actually is. Hiding there under my pearl ring. You want that, too? No, I didn't think so. Hideous thing—wish I could sell it, but who would buy it? Oh, and look, here's a little snapshot of Jocelyne on her first day of school, in that yellow dress. You should take that, too. We'll go through the photo albums later and you can choose some pictures to take with you, for the baby. Don't know why that picture is in here, all by itself. I must have put it in here that very day and forgotten all about it," she mused to herself. Tears began to slip again from her deep-set blue eyes.

She slammed the jewelry box shut, avoiding eye contact with the face in the huge mirror directly in front of her. She whirled around and quickly handed the cross, the brooch and the picture to Chantale, keeping her gaze on her bleeding finger. Her tone and demeanor became matter-of-fact. Her back stiffened and her shoulders stooped as though she had put on a heavy coat. Her fair skin and high cheekbones seemed suddenly cold and sharp. She brusquely bumped into Chantale's knee as she headed for the door without a backward glance.

"There you go. All set. You go pack while I get dinner on. I'd better disinfect and bandage this cut, and then start cooking before the old bear starts to roar that he needs his dinner. It's getting late."

*****

Suzanna quietly shut her bedroom door. She didn't bother to turn on the lights but collapsed, fully dressed, on the bed. Her body felt weightless, as if she were made of straw and rags, like the dolls her mother used to make on the farm. From behind the door the television blared in the living room, where Paul roared with laughter over some inane comedy. She grabbed a pillow and covered her head to block the sound. He was well into his cups and wouldn't come to bed before midnight, by which time she would be either fast asleep or pretending to be.

Under the pillow, she allowed her tears to flow freely. If she sobbed, Pauline and Chantale in the room next door would not hear her. Chantale, sleeping in Jocelyne's twin bed. Where was her little girl sleeping? In the ground.

The horror of it had only begun to sink in. At first, the shock and the necessity of attending to the funeral details had distracted her thoughts. But today, with Chantale presenting the necessity of dealing with the baby, her grandchild, it had struck her in the face, full force. God, what a mess she had made.

Jocelyne, Jocelyne. For months, almost a year, she had pronounced her name with a curse, so angry and distraught that she had run away. Many times, she assumed her daughter was dead. Many times, she had wished it were so. She wondered if she had killed her child with her thoughts. No, she knew better. She had found a stack of Jocelyne's diaries hidden in her closet. She hadn't even known the child kept a diary, had been doing so for years. School exercise books full of questions with no answers. Why was Luke born handicapped? Why were Mommy and Daddy fighting? Why was Mommy so angry all the time? Why, why, why?

Suzanna tossed her head back and forth under the pillow and mouthed the question aloud. Why?

Stop it. Stop it. Stop it. She heard her mother's stern voice as if she were in the room, though she had been dead for five years.

When I said, "You made your bed, now lie in it," what did I mean? I meant you always had a choice. You decided to get married. That meant having children. You have three of them still and Paul, and now a grandchild. It may not seem like it at the time, but you are constantly making decisions that affect your future, and the future of your children, so make the best of it. It's up to you, no one else.

Suddenly the pillow felt heavy across her face. She decided to get up and run a steaming hot bath.

Part VI

Vancouver, 1979

Chapter Forty

Finally, after five years of marriage, Chantale had gathered the courage to consider having a child of her own. Colin had been patient, letting her bide her time, giving her the space she needed. Besides, they were busy with Jacqueline. As a baby, chronic infections kept one or the other parent constantly occupied with her care until her immune system matured. Otherwise, though small for her age, she was a normal child, bubbly, bouncy and bright. Her curly red hair, pale freckled skin and snapping green eyes attracted plenty of attention. Chantale liked to think that all she had inherited from her unknown biological father was her beautiful hair, for no one else in the family had its colour or natural curl. Eerily, although she had never known her biological mother, Jacqueline resembled her, with her chatty nature and open curiosity about everything. She had started to talk at ten months of age and it seemed she never stopped except on the rare moments when she actually slept. And like Jocelyne, there was often something strangely insightful in her words.

One day, when she was only three, they had been in the grocery store and from her seat in the shopping cart, Jacqueline leaned out and reached toward a huge bouquet of yellow roses in the floral department. A chill ran down Chantale's spine as the child asked if they were "wallies," her word for "flowers." When she answered "roses," Jacqueline declared, "Daddy should buy you some of dose woses!"

Without hesitation, Chantale leaned down to rub noses with her daughter and said, "You're my rose."

Jacqueline had giggled and forgotten about the flowers, quickly turning to some other distraction. But Chantale sensed Jocelyne's presence in that instant and smiled with a renewed sense of peace and purpose. Even rational-minded Colin had to admit that there was something spooky about the incident. Maybe it was just a coincidence, but then again...

Wherever they went, people gravitated to the child and made a fuss of her hair, her bright eyes, her precocious chatter. Chantale and Colin had their hands full keeping their charming, outgoing daughter from becoming a spoiled prima donna. They were eager to have her start kindergarten, where the world would no longer center upon her. But between themselves, they revelled in her every milestone. Only they knew what she had really overcome and how much she meant to them.

"We haven't done such a bad job, have we partner, for a couple of over-educated nincompoops?" Chantale chuckled with Colin.

Now she thought she was finally ready to become pregnant and add to her family. At thirty-three, her biological clock was ticking louder and louder in her head. She had started to obsess about it, waking each morning to the refrain, "I must have a baby. Must have a baby." She would stand in the shower and cry hot tears, hoping Colin would think her eyes were red and swollen from the water. She knew his concern for her would upset him, so she tried to keep her internal struggle to herself.

She was so afraid. Maman had always flaunted the family heritage to anyone and everyone, whether they wanted to listen or not. For Chantale though, thoughts of her background seized her with anger, shame and disappointment, even after all this time. What about the mental and physical disorders that might be passed down, as with Paul's child? Or the horrible proclivities of Richard? And what about suicidal tendencies, since she knew her own father had committed suicide, though Maman had successfully covered it up. That ran in families, too, it was well known, as did alcoholism and drug addiction, to which both Danielle and Paul had been prey. And then there were her own issues to contend with... was it fair to bring a child into the world, with such a legacy and all the things that could go wrong?

Colin did his best to reassure her.

"It's bizarre, but I still recall an episode from *All in the Family* where the son-in-law called 'Meathead' by Archie Bunker, you remember, was feeling the same way about having children, due to the Vietnam War and all the violence in the world. And someone, I can't remember who, said to him, 'But what if your child is the one who develops a cure for cancer, or comes up with an idea for world peace? Do you really believe that your not having a child is going to make the world a better place? What if you are depriving the world of the next Schweitzer or Einstein? Or just a really decent human being?' That wasn't it exactly, but it was along those lines, and it always stuck with me, for some reason. In some ways, I think it's harder for our generation, because we make a conscious choice and we know so much more about medical issues. In the old days, you had to accept children, come what may. Not that I'd want us to go back to that, for I'm sure some of them weren't exactly wanted, as ours will be. But I still think that raising a child is one of the most hopeful, positive things you do for the future. Look at our little Jacqueline. Do you wish she weren't here? Of course not! The past is the past, Chantale. We will create our own legacy. Is it fair to rob us of that chance to make things better and bring a sister or brother into the world for Jacqueline?"

His arguments were convincing, but her nightmares erupted again. One night, she dreamed she was on the staircase at home, heading down, while someone at the bottom of the stairs started up. She thought it was her mother and called, "Maman, Maman, est-ce que tu peux me voir? Can you see me?" The form approached. The hair, the shape of the face, surely it was Mother. The mouth was moving but she couldn't hear the words. The roaring of an engine drowned out all sounds. She looked past the staircase and saw that the house was in rubble. All that remained was the oak staircase from the old farmhouse. The person was near enough to touch now. She reached out her arms in welcome and saw... her own face, only wrinkled and old! She screamed and tore herself free of the embrace. Instantly, she was at the bottom of the stairs, in the basement of the restaurant where she had worked as a teenager, when she had first left home. Annie, the young girl who had peeled and cleaned the shrimp, was kneeling over something. The only light came shafting down from the kitchen above the stairwell. Leaning over Annie's shoulder, she could make out a circle and strange markings traced in the dust on the cement floor. Smiling at her warmly, Annie invited her by a gesture of her bleeding, icy hands, to play a game with her.

"You throw down a pebble and, depending where it lands, it tells your future. Come on, I've already gone. Your turn now." The rock dropped on the cement at the same time as a rat trap snapped in a dark corner. Suddenly, the stone turned into a baby crawling across the circle. It turned its head to look at her and let out a cry. The sound woke her with a start. Her heart pounding, she sat up and looked around as though the crying had come from somewhere in the room. Colin snored peacefully beside her. Shakily, she eased out of the bed to avoid waking him, and walked down the hall to Jacqueline's room. After tucking her in, she got a drink of water, crawled back under the warm covers and spooned Colin's back, in a futile attempt to return to sleep.

The dream enveloped her in a sticky cocoon for days afterwards and kept her awake at night. Once again, there were monsters lurking in the dark, creaking open her bedroom door and sneaking into her bed. Anxiety plagued her. "What if...? What if...?" She had tried so hard to erase her memories and bitterness, by focussing on curing the pain in others. Just when she thought the monster was licked, once again it reared its ugly head.

"Doctor, heal thyself. Never truer words were spoken," she told herself one day. But how, after all this time, with Mother dead and no one to turn to? She decided to call Suzanna.

"Hi there. Are you and Paul still planning to come out this summer? Jacqueline would love to see her grandparents again, you know. Yes, I know it's far. Maybe we can get out there sometime. How are Nicolas and Pauline? It must be strange to have them both grown and ready to move out. Pauline is what, twenty now, and Nicolas is turning eighteen? By the way, just to put my mind at ease, you always followed my advice about Richard, didn't you? You believed what I told you and kept the kids away from him...Oh, he's moved to Jamaica? Good place for him. If the inheritance that he stole from me and Danielle got him out of Canada, then it was worth every cent. Still, I wish I could warn someone there about him. Maybe I should have pressed charges after all, but I just couldn't go through with it. I know what it takes to get a conviction and I needed to keep my head clear for my patients, and Colin, and Jacqueline…so, I'll have to hope that fate will catch up with him." She sighed and waited for Suzanna to respond. When she didn't, she filled the awkward silence on the line.

"How are things with Luke? Still the same? It's amazing, he has such a strong heart. Yes, that would be for the best in my opinion, too, but he will go in his own good time, I guess. And Paul? Yes, it's very difficult. You are so good and brave to stand by him, in spite of everything. You're the best, Suzanna. Depression, alcoholism, drug addiction… what the hell else runs in this family? In fact, that's actually why I'm calling. This is awkward, and I've never asked you before, but Colin and I are thinking of having a child and I was wondering…"

As far as Suzanna knew, there were no other cases like Luke's on her side, and Paul had never mentioned anything about it. Still, Chantale could not rest and no one close by could answer her questions. Paul lived in his own world, pretending the past had never happened, Ghislain displayed nothing but contempt for their family history, and Richard…well, he was, thankfully, long gone. She made up her mind to research her genealogy, first hand. Return to the source. Colin thought a trip to Québec would do her a world of good. In an unusually civil telephone conversation, Paul was able to recall the first names of some of their relatives, and locate the village where her mother and father had been born, on a map. She spent months brushing up on her French at community college. When spring came, she and her daughter would make the long trip across Canada by train. She had never seen more than two provinces in the vast country and the four day, three night journey would be a wonderful adventure for Jacqueline.

They passed the daylight hours in the observation car, spellbound by the beauty and grandeur of the landscape. The first night, cuddled together in their berth, Jacqueline fell asleep as soon as her red curls hit the pillow, exhausted from the excitement. But the next night, after the porter had closed the drapes of their berth, she bounced up and down on the bunk squealing, "Tell me a story, tell me a story, Mommy," until Chantale feared the other passengers might complain.

Foolishly, she had packed their storybooks in the luggage stored under the seat for the night. She clicked on the tiny lamp near the window and fished under her pillow. Since Jocelyne's death, she had adopted the habit of sleeping with the rosary. Hoping to distract Jacqueline, she held it by the crucifix and waved the shiny pearls and amethysts before her eyes.

"Look at this, Honey. This belonged to your great-grandmaman. Here, let's count the beads together, en français. Un, a pearl for Jocelyne, you remember, she's your first Mommy. She was sweet and sparkly, just like you. Let's say a prayer for her. God bless Jocelyne. Deux. Next, an amethyst for me. God bless Mommy. Next, who's next? Grandpa and Grandma, right, God bless Grandpa et Grandma. Trois, quatre. Now who? My mommy? Sure. Quatre. God bless... Great Grandmaman. She would have been so happy to meet you. You have her green eyes. She did a train trip like this a long, long time ago. She used to tell me about it. I wish I could remember...Back then, I just didn't pay attention. Now...no, we aren't going to visit her, but we may see some people who knew her. We're going to try to find the place where she grew up. It seems to me she said there were beautiful apple trees and a pasture right down to the river... It's all right, I'm not crying. Mommy is just tired. Come on, count with me and we'll both fall asleep. Cinq, six, sept..."

Chapter Forty-one

The moment they arrived in their hotel room in Québec City, Chantale hurried to heft the massive telephone book from the desk drawer. Gérard. Dozens of them! Her family name had been unique in the small directory of central Alberta. She'd laughed to herself when they had emerged from the train station and the first thing she had seen was the name plastered at the base and the summit of a high-rise under construction. Apparently, a Gérard operated one of the most successful construction companies in Québec. "Well, at least some of them have risen high in the world!" she'd commented sardonically under her breath. She had expected to see a few entries in the book, but not this many! Which ones were related to her? Probably all of them! Where to start? Even the first names Paul had given her were repeated over and over in the list, or there were just initials. She could never contact them all and, in her halting French, she was afraid to try even one random phone call.

"They would probably just hang up anyway," she rationalized to herself.

All right, that would never work. Plan B. Her mother had often told her about her father Emile's youngest sister, who'd been "sacrificed" to a nunnery when there'd been too many girls in his family, so long ago. Maman had bragged about Sister Mary Joseph, the saint of the family. By now the poor woman would have been cooped up in the same convent for almost fifty years. A chill snaked down Chantale's spine, as she remembered how, desperate to escape Richard's abuse, she had begged her mother to put her in a convent, when she turned twelve. Her mother had actually investigated the possibility, believing perhaps that her daughter had actually been called by God, or maybe just hoping that a stint in the convent would straighten her out. At the time, Chantale had been genuinely

421

disappointed that they were no longer accepting residents, just day students, as the door slammed on another escape route away from Richard.

"Thank God for that. Maybe He really was watching over me! If I had known then what I know now, how my life would turn out..." she thought, as Colin's dear face flashed into her mind and she tucked Jacqueline into bed beside her.

"Well, it shouldn't be too hard to find Soeur Marie-Joseph. There can't be that many nuns of her vintage still around. Check it out tomorrow," she resolved, as she drifted off to sleep.

By visiting the tourist information centre for a map and a discussion with a guide, she discovered that the convent was still there, in Maman's et Papa's hometown, in La Beauce County. She rented a car and drove with her daughter, into the charming Québec countryside, where time seemed to have stood still. They passed roadside shrines to the Virgin Mary, houses built of stone, a church with a spire in every village, and tractors travelling at a snail's pace down the winding roads. In surprise, Chantale pointed out a man plowing one of the long strips of land with a horse. Jacqueline just sucked her thumb and watched the scenery whiz past the car window.

"Are we there yet? I'm hungry," she whined.

"Soon, my angel."

*****

"Ah, oui. She is wid' us since she is a young girl of, maybe tirteen, fourteen year old, even before my time," the Mother Superior assured her upon her inquiry at the door. With a smile, she took Chantale by the hand and directed her into a spacious, wood-panelled office. The springs on the old armchair creaked as Chantale took a seat before the wide oak desk occupying the very center of the room. The wall behind was lined with leather-bound books, reminding Chantale of the small library her mother had kept in the upstairs hallway. Wrapping her arms around Jacqueline on her lap, she tried to overcome her nervousness in the presence of the imposing figure, surrounded by the icons of the Church: a beautifully carved crucifix on the wall behind the desk, a statue of Mary in one corner, a white Bible resting on a stand in the other, next to a miniature altar complete with a set of coloured glass votive candles. Dr. Gérard was suddenly a child again, being reprimanded by the Sisters at the convent where she had taken piano lessons, for not practicing. She could almost feel the sting of the ruler on her wrists. She tried to focus on what the Mother Superior was telling her, which was hard to take in.

"Too bad you not come before now. She miss 'er family so much. Nobody ever come to see 'er anymore, especially since she get older. A cousin use to stop by, even invite 'er to 'is 'ouse, but den, ben, she gets older an' a bit more difficult to manage an' den, well, 'e stop to come. I call 'im when she pass away, but 'e never come to pick up 'er ting, even. I 'ave 'is number 'ere, you might want to look 'im up, since you do la recherche on your family." The smooth white hand flipped through a Rolodex next to the black telephone, took a gold pen from its holder and printed the number on convent letterhead. With a wistful sigh, the old woman handed the paper across her desk.

"It 'tis interesting dat you should be researching your ancêtres. As a matter of fac', your Aunt was, 'ow you say, obsedée, obsess wit' family history. She spend year after year, all 'er free time, looking up on 'er family tree. She 'ad it trace back to de 1600s, when your great, great, great grandpère come firs' to dis country. Un des premiers arrivés. One of the original settler, she was prout to say, aldough pride is a sin, of course," the woman added with a sparkle in her eye.

"She kep' it 'tup, right until she die, an' when nobody came, we put all 'er paper togeder in a box. We figure, well, somebody might come sometime an' want to collect 'er ting. You see, 'ere's 'er cross an' 'er rosary. We inter' 'er with 'er ring, of course. Dere are also many letter from 'er sister-in-law, your Maman, n'est-ce pas? She was so sad when we got de news about your Maman. De las' connection wid 'er dear brudder, Emile." Shaking her head, she reached in the box.

She rose and came around to stand in front of Chantale, as she carefully unfolded a faded paper and smoothed it out on her desk. When completely flat, it covered the surface like a map. Dates, names and precise, connecting lines swam before Chantale's eyes, all perfectly drawn in brown ink in a calligraphic hand. Chantale's face registered her amazement, but she was unable to utter a sound.

"Dere it 'tis, your complete family tree, all trace out dere, so nice, you see, voyez-vous? Magnifique, n'est-ce pas? We tot it 'twas an incredible achievement, so many hour of recherche. For 'er, she say, it 'twas 'er legacy to 'er family. Once she retire from teaching, she 'ad more free time to work on it, an' she never give up, 'til de day she died. I believe she tol' me she sent a copy out Wes', to your Maman. She never show it to you?" The gleaming eyes seemed to see into Chantale's heart as she shook her head side to side and swallowed. The woman leaned over, brushing the grey fabric of her habit against Chantale's bare arm. Smiling, she gently patted Jacqueline's curly head, then continued.

"It 'twas 'er life's work. Always did her bes', Soeur Marie-Joseph. She was a saint, for shore. Never break 'er vows. Dedicate 'er whole life to God and teaching, right up to de en'. Well, if you'll jus' sign for de paper, I'll give you de 'ole box right now. Almos' four year since she pass away. Strange, we tot, but oh well, you young people, you so busy. Please, come an' join us for dinner wid your liddle one. So nice for us to 'ave de visitor from out Wes' on behalf of Soeur Marie-Joseph! An' you want de chance to see 'ow 'Matante' live 'er life, Jacqueline, hein? What a nice French name for such a sweet liddle girl. Matante, she receive a special commendation from de Pope, vous savez, on 'er fiftiet' anniversaire? You didn't know? Oh, it cause great excitement. We 'ave a special ceremony for 'er an' everytink. She was so prout. Too bad no family to come an' celebrate wid 'er." With another heavy sigh, the nun turned toward the door and showed Chantale and her daughter out to the hallway. She locked the door behind her.

In her floor-length grey robe, the woman seemed to glide above the spotless tiled floors as she toured them first past the library, next into the austere classrooms where Marie-Joseph had first gone to school as a girl, then served as a teacher for more than thirty years. She showed them the large, bright dormitory where the majority of the nuns still maintained common quarters. Finally, they were led up a winding staircase to a narrow corridor lined with wooden doors.

Reaching for her keys from a clip around her waist, Mother Superior unlocked a door, flicked a switch and gestured for them to enter a tiny room.

Inside was a single bed, without sheets, a narrow, free-standing wardrobe, two rows of shelves, a desk, a lamp and two wooden chairs. Nothing but a crucifix decorated the bare white walls. The room smelled musty and dank. Making a sour face, Jacqueline put her fingers to her nose and pinched. Chantale gently reached down to move her hand away from her face and held it tightly. Mother Superior pulled a cord to draw the metal blinds, showing them how the window afforded a view of the lovely courtyard below, with its fountain and tall trees.

"Soeur Marie-Joseph, she love dis room, because de bird come to 'er window sill, over 'ere, voyez-vous, an' she feed dem 'er bread cruses, morning an' evening. She say she could imagine dear Saint Francois d'Assiz, at dat time, an' say 'er private prayer. De room is still empty, we don't 'ave so many resident nowadays. 'Ere she pass 'er time, on 'er recherche an' drawing, when 'er duty was finish."

Chantale did her best to prevent her face and voice from betraying pity for the lonely life she imagined had ended in this room.

"You mean, this is where she lived when she retired? She lived here for what, about ten years?"

"Ah yes, she 'ave a room of 'er hown at las', but of course she is still part of de communauté, an' she come to Mass twice a day an' eat wid us, downstair, until well, near de en', a sister 'ad to bring 'er supper... by de way, you mus' be very hungry, n'est-ce pas, ma petite? Les go back down an' meet everyone in de salon de dîner."

By the time they had entered the huge hall, lined up for service at a metal cafeteria counter, been introduced to the whole assembly as dear Soeur Marie-Joseph's long, lost relatives from Alberta, and stood for a series of prayers which included blessings for the Gérard family, the steam had disappeared from the hot dishes on their tray. The meal consisted of thin cabbage soup, freshly baked brown buns, steamed fish and vegetables. The convent still conformed to the old tradition of fish on Friday. Chantale realized that little would have changed over the course of her aunt's fifty years here. In a way, there must have been some comfort in that. Maybe she was happy here, after all.

"You young people forget about de ol'ways an' de ol' folks. Tant pis. Such a shame. Dat's what I say to your cousin de las' time 'e come. I 'ope you can get in touch wid 'im, yourself." The Mother Superior clucked her tongue as she handed Chantale the box of Soeur Marie-Joseph's effects.

"C'est bien dommage, too bad you never knew 'er. A saint on dis eart', we always say, an' such a gifted teacher in de couvent school. Lucky, you can read 'er paper an' fine out all sort of interesting fact an' ting about your family. You might even want to go an' fine where dey is register an' bury. It tis not so difficult, an' all de information is der. It's surprising, but dey kep' very good record in Québec in dose time. Dey did le recensement, de census, for tax, vous savez, for de King of France, and den later, for de English gouvernement. For you, it is probably all dere in writing by Soeur Marie-Joseph. 'Oo knows what you might fine out? A blessing an' a gif' from 'Matante,' n'est-ce pas? I am glad it t'will go to some one 'oo show an interest in histoire. Dat's what she would 'ave want, al-so. Well, c'est un grand plaisir, meeteen' you, an your chil'. Such a good liddle girl! Si mignone! Une petite poupée en porcelaine. She remind me of a little porcelaine doll, wid 'er leedle roun' face an' 'er lovely red curls. A shame Soeur Marie-Joseph never meet...she would 'ave love...ah, well, de intention of God de Fadder in 'eaven are unknown to us 'ere on eart'. Au revoir. God bless you bot'."

Chapter Forty-two

"Oui, Allo? Pierre Gérard? Vous ne me connaissez pas, mais je suis votre cousine, Chantale Gérard, de l'Alberta. J'ai reçu votre numéro de..." In her halting, rusty French, Chantale explained to her unknown cousin how she had obtained his number, that she was researching family history and was hoping to meet him. She did not reveal the fact that the Mother Superior had given her the box of Soeur Marie-Joseph's effects, nor that she was in possession of the entire family tree that the nun had painstakingly drawn out by hand. It seemed he had abandoned the old woman at the end of her life. Chantale wanted to judge for herself whether he could be trusted.

"Yes, I used to visit her regularly, bring her treats, take her on outings, even to my home, which is the old homestead where she and your father grew up," Pierre explained over coffee on the outside café terrasse of her hotel. His English being more fluent than Chantale's French, they conversed with ease.

"But it became more and more difficult. She was so... fanatical! You couldn't have a conversation with her anymore without feeling guilty about some sin of commission or omission. I'm not that much of a believer myself... we don't have time for church anyway. For my wife and I, with our young family, it got to be too much, having her at the farm. She went on and on about what we needed to do with our children to ensure the family legacy. It was damned annoying, I can tell you, to have a woman who had never had any children of her own, advising us on what we should and shouldn't do. I felt sorry for her, too though, but by the end, she barely knew me and only reprimanded me for not coming to see her, even if I had been there the week before. For me, it's a long trip into town, and with the farm to take care of, I just couldn't keep it up anymore. I did it for Maman's sake in any event, that was her sister, your Auntie Louise on your

427

dad's side, but after she went, it all seemed so... pointless. Maudit, c'est chaud icitte!"

Removing his felt cap to wipe his brow, he summoned the waitress and asked to be moved to a table with a parasol. He also ordered a beer, although it was only ten o'clock in the morning. Something in his voice and gestures reminded Chantale of... Paul. Lighting a cigarette, he continued in a brighter tone.

"So, this is your first time in Québec? What do you think of it? I have never been out West, so I can't even compare the two."

"Oh, it wouldn't be worth it to try. The whole ambiance is completely different. Somehow, it's strange, I seem to feel a deep affinity for Québec, especially Québec City. C'est tellement beau! It's so beautiful and it's been wonderful to visit all the sights we only read about in school—the Plains of Abraham, les Chutes Montmerency where the English snuck up in the night and ambushed the French... I could go on and on. I was shocked that the fate of an entire nation was decided on a field as small as the Plains of Abraham and when I learned the battle lasted only twenty minutes, well, it's almost unreal. What if it had been decided the other way, and the French had won? It would have changed everything. Fate is so strange, n'est-ce pas?" She brushed her bangs off her damp forehead. The humid heat was sweltering even in the early morning and Chantale gingerly peeled her cotton blouse away from her skin before she nervously went on.

"Being here, I can finally understand how homesick Maman always felt. I know I will miss it, too, when I have to go home, and I wasn't even born here. It seems familiar in a way I can't explain. I've never even been to Québec before, but I have fallen in love with it. Maybe it's because everyone is speaking French and I grew up in French... I don't know. Jacqueline will sure miss the soft ice cream swirled with maple syrup, won't you, chérie?" Chantale laughed, leaned over and gently rubbed the child's round cheek.

"Oui, c'est délicieux, n'est-ce pas? Say, would you and your daughter like to visit the farm, see the old patrimoine?" Pierre suddenly offered.

"I could drive you all along the Beauce valley, show you where our ancestors came from, even the church and the cimitière where they are buried, in the village. Matante did some research there at one time, if I recall. The church is right next to my parents' house—my mother was constantly running to the priest for advice about every little decision. Drove my father and me crazy. My father was a butcher in town. They're both gone now. The farm, of course, comes down on my mother's side. As it turned out, with three of the brothers killed in the wars, and the others moving out West, the land passed down to me. A blessing and a curse," he said, shaking his head as he paused for a long pull on his mug of beer. He stubbed out his cigarette, pushed the pack up from his breast pocket with his thumb and shook them toward Chantale. She declined.

"No, I gave up smoking when... well, trying to have a family and all, you know..." she confided lamely, surprised at herself for feeling the need to make an excuse. But it seemed everyone in Québec smoked, so there had to be a reason why she refused, and she didn't want to seem impolite.

Pierre just shrugged, lit up and puffed for a few moments in silence.

"It's beautiful, pretty as a postcard, you'll see. But damned hard to make a living off such a small piece of land. Luckily, my wife is a teacher and could supplement our income, but we'll never be rich, that's for sure. I doubt that my children will want to stay on. Life is moving faster nowadays and the city offers so much more for them. I don't want to deny them the opportunities, as I was denied. I wasn't given a choice. How could I let three hundred years of history pass through our fingers? That was drummed into my head. But eventually, it will come to that. So you see, 'les maudits Anglais' will always win, one way or another. Some politicians are trying to save the language and rescue what's left of our culture, bah! Me, I don't have time to think about that. I just need some goddamn money, or there'll be nothing left to save. And those who talk of separation from Canada, ils sont fous! A pipe dream, that's all it is. It'll never happen, that's it, that's all," Pierre declared, crossing his hands in the air in a gesture of finality. Then he stood up, ground out his final cigarette, and took Chantale's hand in his firm grip.

"In any case, I'm so glad you called me. My wife and daughters will be delighted to meet you and practice their English! You can see all the old family photographs, take some with you if you like, I don't want them cluttering the house anymore! You'll get to see the farmstead and the village, maybe meet some of the other relatives. I'll pick you up here at the hotel tomorrow morning and my wife and I will be pleased to invite you to spend the evening at our home. Then I could bring you back to your hotel the following day, so you can finish your sightseeing in the city. How does that sound?"

"Like a dream come true," Chantale smiled, as she too rose to shake Pierre's hand. Impulsively, she gave him the traditional bisous on either cheek, and he embraced her in return with a warm hug.

After more sightseeing in the city during the afternoon, Chantale returned to the hotel, arranged for room service for the evening meal and excitedly packed an overnight bag. She called the registration desk to leave her cousin's number with the concierge, in case Colin needed to reach her. Then, patiently, she completed the bedtime routines with Jacqueline: bath, storytime, cuddles. But as soon as the child had fallen asleep, she retrieved the box from the corner of the closet where she had stowed it the day before. Sitting on the floor next to the standing lamp, she began to spread the contents onto the narrow space between the wall and the beds. A jet rosary, simple and plain. A wooden cross. A worn Bible. A leather bookmark inscribed in gold with a prayer. The fiftieth anniversary certificate, also embossed with gold, signed by the Pope. A fountain pen and an inkwell. The sum total of sixty-four years of life. Well, in the convent, what more would she have needed? Or desired?

Chantale lifted out a thick stack of paper, bound with a red ribbon. She almost lost her grip and quickly grasped both ends, to prevent the sheets from falling out of order. Flipping through, she found that the writing consisted of notes, dates, names, places.

"This must be the basis for the family tree," she thought, as she tentatively withdrew the document from the box. She stood and carefully unfolded the fine, creased paper on the only available table. The tiny stand allowed her to see only a section of the document at a time, but she slowly inched it across the surface as she searched through the names and dates.

Unbelievable. There it was, all here, laid out in perfect, symmetrical patterns. Papa's father and mother. Maman et Papa. There was their wedding date, 1928. Maman must have been so proud. Funny, Matante must have sent the copy after Chantale had left home. She'd never heard about it. Paul certainly had never mentioned it. Not that he talked much about anything to anybody anymore. She doubted he'd even be interested. But she sure as hell was. Now, with this and some research through medical records in Québec City and Montréal, it should be easy enough to set her mind at ease concerning the family's genetic history. Then she could make her decision about having a child of her own.

She scanned through the names in the most recent entries. Full name, date and place of birth for both husband, wife and children. Papa et Maman: Emile-Etienne Gérard, né 1893, Marie-Eve De LaSalle, née 1900, mariés 1920. Emile-Etienne, décédé 1949. Pauvre Papa. Did his sister even know the truth of how he died? Not likely. If it hadn't been for Danielle, Chantale would never have found out. Mother never would have revealed the truth, to any of them. Why, why did he do it? With his youngest child only three years old? She couldn't even remember him. He had committed the most terrible sin, damned himself to Hell forever, in the Church's eyes. As a devout Catholic, he would have known that. Even worse, he had left his wife and children behind. Chantale Elyse, née 1946. Just a little girl, with no father. Was it because of her birth? Had he hated his life so much? Questions that could not be answered. Had her father's death affected her life? Certainly. Could anything be changed? Certainly not.

There she was, last in the column headed by Paul, 1922, followed by Ghislain, 1924, Danielle, 1926, Richard, 1928, Luc, 1930, deceased 1937. And in a line drawn from Paul, Suzanne (spelt the French way, of course), née 1935. All four of their children's names and birth dates. Even their Luke, spelt Luc. Ghislain, only his first wife's name recorded, with their three children. Yes, there was her newfound cousin Pierre, his wife and their four daughters. A huge map to the past, neatly drawn, by hand, in chronological order. Pages and pages, going further and further back. Successive name changes with marriages through the generations: DuBois, Gagnon, Grenier...1928—Raymond et Catherine. 1906—Denis et Line. 1885—Etienne et Chantale. 1829. 1798. Flip, flip. 1719. 1697. 1650. At least thirteen generations.

"This must have taken...ages. No wonder the Mother Superior said it was Marie-Joseph's life's work. It would have taken most of a lifetime...But why? What motivated her to do it? Maman said her family gave her away, like a gift, to the Church, at fourteen. Too many 'worthless' daughters, not enough money for a dowry to marry her off and, according to Ma, not a face or figure that could attract a man without a substantial incentive. You'd think she would have hated them, not..."

Chantale didn't realize she was speaking aloud, until Jacqueline stirred restlessly and kicked her covers off. Despite the fan in the room, it was still muggy and stifling, and the windows didn't open. She slid quietly across the carpet in her bare feet, to tuck her daughter in again, then flopped down in the chair next to the table. Rubbing the bridge of her nose, she contemplated opening the mini-bar, even though she never drank alcohol. All those unknown people, their meeting, pairing, leaving, dying, had somehow led to the little girl snoring blissfully in this hotel room, in her ancestral city, thousands of miles from the city where she had been born. The other side of the country. Might as well be the other side of the moon, everything was so different here!

She continued to skim through the names, after searching for her own family's names. All that seemed to matter was the beginning and the end. If it hadn't been for the medical history, the other names would not even have been of passing interest to her. What did all those names mean to anyone now? Were their lives significant in some way, other than their place as a branch on this tree?

The paper draped over the table like a cloth suddenly fluttered, though she had turned the fan away from the table to prevent the documents from blowing about. Despite the heat, a shudder ran the length of her spine. "Someone walked on your grave," her mother would have said. With trembling hands, she shifted the paper to the bottom right hand corner to find the inscription of the originator of all the subsequent lines:

"Jean-Paul Gérard: Né vers 1620, à Luçon, Poitou, France. Notaire royale, se marie à Québec en 1649 à Solange, et en 1670 à Georgette Tessier. Il mourût des suites de la petite vérole. Sa femme, Solange était décédée depuis 1669. Georgette, née Tessier, était décédée depuis le 25 Septembre 1690. Le 25 juin, 1700 par moy soussigné Prêtre à Beauport, Québec au cimetière du dit lieu a été enterré cy devant notaire au dit lieu décédé le Jour precédent, âgé d'environ quatre-vingt ans après avoir vécu dans la foy catholique et après avoir reçu les derniers sacrements. Presens Richard Thibaut, habitant du dit Beauport lequel a déclaré ne savoir signer de ce enquis et plusieurs autres." The notes had been copied in the original old French, from what seemed to be a death certificate. For Chantale, it proved a challenge to decipher. Maybe, after all, she would have to ask Pierre for help.

She could pick out the age the patriarch had died—eighty, the priest estimated, for he died in 1700. Christ, he was a long-lived old bugger, for those times! Died of "petite variole," smallpox? She shuddered when she noticed that his second name was Paul. A common name, but...kind of spooky that it had come down the generations. In the squared line attached to him, representing his first wife, appeared only the name Solange. No last name, no date of birth, no place of birth. Solange, what? Solange, who? A surname for all the others, but not for her.

"Elle fût baptisée le 3 septembre 1648. Mariée vers l'âge de 14 ans, elle meurt le 5 septembre, 1669, à l'âge d'environ 35 ans."

Married at fourteen? Not so unusual, for the times, but why was she baptized and married in the same year? Could that be a mistake? Hmm. Only one explanation, in those days, if she remembered her history lessons. So much for "pure laine," eh, Maman? "Dyed in the wool" French, right from France, Maman, from the best families, as you were always so proud to state to anyone who would listen? So, that's why you never mentioned it. Papa was descended from Paul and Solange. Pauvre "Solange." Her real name was probably "Running Cloud" or "Red Sky at Sunset." Surely something beautiful in her own language. At least "Sol ange" meant literally "earth angel" in French.

She decided to examine the sheafs of note paper, to find out more information about Solange. It was easy to follow her aunt's clear, calligraphic hand.

Paul et Solange eurent dix enfants dont un seule est mort en bas âge, Gaetan. L'aîné, Paul, se consacra à Dieu dans la patrise. Il fut l'un des premiers prêtres nés en sol canadien...." Here it went on to describe all the accomplishments of their eldest child, one of the first priests born on Canadian soil, the parishes he served, the churches he built and how he was buried in the sanctuary of one of the churches. The other children barely merited a mention.

Les autres, six filles et trois garçons, fondèrent un foyer. Christian, un de ses descendants, adopte le surnom ' Lamoureux.'" "Adopted" a different surname. Why? How did she ever figure all this out, with so many different surnames to decipher?

Good Lord, he'd had ten children. No wonder the poor woman died at thirty-three. And the old bugger didn't wait long to remarry, either. Well, not with ten children to look after! His second wife even died before him—he outlasted them both! Wonder what the women died of—that wasn't recorded either.

"*Character of the* Vallières:

Spirit of adventure of the Normans. Voyageurs, labourers, soldiers. Religious vocations: Brothers, Sisters, Priests, Franciscans. Also doctors, accountants, farmers, industrialists, mechanics, university professors. Voilà ce que le sang des Vallières *a deposé dans nos veines. Avons-nous le droit d'en être fiers? Souhait: Que les générations à venir continuent à la montée. Un souhait ardent: Que les generations à venir continuent à s'inscrire pour le bien des familles glorieuses dont nous descendons.*"

So many "ardent wishes" Matante had added to her life's work. Wishes that no one had ever heard, or even known about, until now. Who did she intend to share them with? Pierre? Her obsession with religion and heritage had driven him crazy, creating a wedge between them that ultimately isolated her from her last connection with family. How ironic.

"*We are descended from a glorious family. This is what the blood of our ancestors has deposited in our veins! Don't we have the right to be proud?...An ardent wish: that the following generations may continue to add to its glory.*"

How blind, how naïve you were, Auntie, in your cloistered world, Chantale thought, shaking her head. Poor Auntie. So alone, clinging to the only dream you had, of family, heritage, pride. I'm glad it made you happy to believe so. I see it quite differently, from where I stand today. Where did you document the abusers, drunks, and drug addicts? What about that blood in our veins? That's the legacy I fear most.

Wait a minute, check the name again. "Vallières." That wasn't on Papa's side! She flipped through to the last page.

"Note: A partir de la neuvième genération, nous avons du sang des 'Vallières' dans nos veines, à cause de notre Mère, Marie Vallières. Normalement, il aurait fallu continuer la généologie avec un de ses frères. Mais j'ai decidé de poursuivre la descendance de notre Mère."

Wow. Good for you, Auntie, researching the history of your mother, against the rules of genealogy, tracing it back to the ninth generation. This is the side of the family you were bragging about— your mother's side! How interesting. Why would a nun, who had so unfailingly followed rules all her life, according to all accounts, break with tradition? Then again, why not?

Chantale gently slipped the red ribbon around the papers and replaced them in the box. It was getting late and Pierre would be there early to pick them up. Just one more thing to check, before bed. Ah, here you are, Auntie, There's your line, from Marie Vallières and Louis Gérard. Sister of: Geneviève, Louis, Philippe, Emile, Jeanne, Sophie, François, Roland, Stephane, Luc, Marguerite. Angeline. So that was your real name, Angeline, before you took your vows. Little Angel, in English. Why did the Church make you change it, when it suited you so well?

A lump rose to Chantale's throat. She spread her hands across her face and massaged her temples in circular motions. Tears flooded her eyes, unexpectedly. She couldn't understand why she felt like crying. She reached for the jet rosary in the bottom of the box. Maybe it was superstition, but Matante's efforts warranted a prayer of thanksgiving.

Guardian angel, Matante Angeline. Maman always told me I had a guardian angel. Who would have guessed it would be you? We never even met! Merci, thank you so much, for giving me all I needed, and more. I honour your life and your work. Especially, thank you for finding Solange. She deserved to be found. Little Jacqueline will know about her great-great-great grandmother from so many generations long ago, a native woman who was the true founder of our family. Though she will never ever know about her biological father, she will be told that she has a right to be proud, as she is descended from a race of strong people. The first inhabitants of Canada, just as you always said Maman. "De bes, always des bes." "Pure laine: Dyed in the wool." We are indeed.

*****

"And this is where your great-grandfather was born, chérie. This land has been in our family for over three hundred years, part of the very first Seigneurie in Canada, can you imagine? No, you can't, I'm sure!" Pierre chuckled deep in his throat as he drew Jacqueline by the hand down the tree-lined path. He responded to Chantale's puzzled expression, answering her unspoken question, as they continued to walk under the huge maples.

"A 'Seigneurie' is the name for the lands that were under the supervision of a Seigneur, something like the governor of a region, back in the day. You didn't learn about it in school? Don't they teach Canadian history way out in the West? Well, no matter. The Seigneur was appointed by the Governor, who was under the rule of the Intendant, who represented the King. Imagine, all that hierarchical structure. There were so many rules and regulations, seems almost as bad as today, n'est-ce pas? Anyway, this area was the first Seigneurie in New France, and this land was granted to our ancestors by the Seigneur, Tanan, if I remember rightly. All the land was divided into long strips, so everyone would have equal access to the river. Smart and, of course, vital in those days, with no decent roads and no sewage systems! Old Tanan, he didn't seem to have much control over his territory, though. The inhabitants were supposed to do work for him, give him part of their crops and especially swear fealty to him. Poor bastard waited nine years, they still wouldn't do it. Outright refused. A proud family story, heh, heh! That's the nature of us Gérards. Bull headed. Ever notice that?" he chortled again.

"Look at the old house, still standing after three centuries. Not too bad, hein?"

The stone building straddled a small rise, overlooking an apple orchard. Huge chimneys seemed to squeeze either end in place. Dormer windows stood out like eyes from the slate roof. The inevitable white painted gallery or verandah, a common feature on all French-Canadian homes, enclosed the entire structure. Baskets of flowers hanging from the protruding roof swayed gently in the slight breeze rising from the river. Swinging chairs attached under the eaves at the front of the house provided an open view of the land and the river far below. Chantale gasped as a wave of nostalgia overtook her. This was the "dream house" her mother had built on the farm in Alberta, a replica of a typical French-Canadian farmhouse. Now it was crushed to dust, buried under one of the monster homes on the sub-divided land. Her parents' homestead seemed to reappear before her eyes, until they were blinded by tears. She tried to cover her emotion from Pierre, by brushing the tears from her face with the back of her hand, as though distractedly wafting away a fly. How proud her own mother would have been of Pierre, for maintaining his ancestral home in all its glory. This realization came crashing in on her with a strength that physically made her stumble and nearly fall. Pierre reached over and grasped her elbow.

"It's this maudite chaleur, the damn heat, my dear. And this is nothing. It can hit ninety degrees in the summertime, and with the humidity, c'est l'enfer! It can be hell! We'll go inside where it is nice and cool and you can have a glass of fresh lemonade."

Chantale nodded mutely in agreement. For it was true that even after two weeks in Québec, she had not adapted to the climate. By comparison, Vancouver, refreshed by ocean breezes, was dry as a desert! Distracted by the sweat snaking down her back and sides under her white cotton blouse, waving a fly from her forehead, she hadn't noticed that Jacqueline was anxiously tugging on Pierre's shirt.

"What's that sound?" the child asked, turning her head from side to side, bouncing her curls. She pointed to a dark triangle perched on the tip of a pine tree next to the house.

"That? Why that's nothing but a little boy robin, singing his heart out to attract a wife. It's spring, after all. Don't you have robins in Vancouver?"

"Well, we live right in the city center, in an apartment, so this is all very new to her. I guess, no, she wouldn't have seen...We just go to the park and there are so many other distractions there," Chantale stumbled lamely over her excuse.

"It's bootiful," Jacqueline muttered, her eyes never leaving the treetop. She plumped herself down on the gravel path, bare legs, dress shoes, white dress and all, to listen. Chantale was grateful for the chance to pause and drink in more of the beauty surrounding them.

"Mommy, is this our house?" Jacqueline asked suddenly.

Chantale, startled from her reverie, shot an embarrassed glance at Pierre, who merely smiled at her and shrugged his shoulders.

"No, Darling, but it is exactly like the house I used to live in when I was your age. How strange that you should ask that question."

Past a deep grove of trees, the river sliced through the narrow strips of farmland, separated by white, wooden fences, a silver ribbon, glistening in the sun. The apple trees, in full bloom, posed like wedding bouquets of pink and white. Bees wrestled busily within the ecstacy of flowers in the garden, setting the moist, warm currents of air alight with the thrum of beating wings. Pollen and perfume swirled in a golden cloud, enveloping them in a heady mist as they made their way to the front steps. The lady of the house obviously took great pride in her flowers, for the arrangements were exquisite in their height, variety and colours. Yet, as they made their way to the porch, stepping nearer to the manicured edge of the flower bed, Chantale noticed a dandelion stubbornly peeping its yellow head from the purple alyssum. She smiled to herself. No matter how carefully one tended the garden, there was always a weed. The Richards of this world, Chantale mused, as she bent down and plucked the blossom and leaves from the stem. Even if she had wanted to, she would not have been able to remove the dandelion roots without a trowel. Weeds stubbornly held their ground. She handed the flower to Jacqueline.

The child looked at her mother with her sparkling green eyes and smiled at the bright yellow pompom. Chantale thought, not for the first time, how perfectly her grandmother's eyes suited the child's golden red hair, which was uniquely her own.

"Wally, Mommy! I love wallies! Thank you! Is dis a 'wose?'"

"No, Sweetheart. It is a dandelion, from the French words 'dent de lion.' See how the leaves resemble a big lion's teeth? Raaahhh! It's gonna get you!" she roared, tickling her daughter's ear with the leaves. Then she tossed the weed onto the gravel path, brushing the dirt from her hands.

Epilogue

Vancouver, 2010

"Hey, check this out. What do you suppose it is?" Jacqueline asked her sister, selecting yet another piece of jewelry from her mother's collection.

"It looks like some kind of brooch. Really old. It almost looks Celtic. I don't remember seeing it before. I wouldn't have thought it was Mom's style at all."

"Let's see. No, me neither. But when we were kids and used to play with her jewelry, we were more interested in the long necklaces and the flashy earrings. I'm amazed, when I think about it, that she would let us paw through all her stuff. I mean, it's just junk, but it must have been valuable to her at some point, or she wouldn't have had it in the first place. Remember how we used to dump everything out on the bed, then sort through and try on each piece, mixing and matching the earrings, bracelets and necklaces, checking ourselves out in this very mirror, pretending we were little princesses?"

Suzanne held a pair of dangly earrings to her ears, sucked in her cheeks and staged an elegant pose with one hand upturned in the air. Jacqueline assumed her customary childhood place next to her much taller sister and flipped a long strand of white plastic beads, circa 1960, over her head. Tying the necklace into a knot, she twirled it in a circle in front of her as she pursed her lips in an exaggerated kiss aimed at her reflection. Placing two fingers to her lips, she pretended to puff a cigarette and blew an imaginary smoke ring, before turning to Suzanne to exclaim, in a highly affected foreign accent, "Ve are shtill zo beeoootiful, daaalink! It must be our vonderful blood!"

They both burst out laughing. Then, for a wistful moment, each woman silently studied her own face in the glass, as if searching for the little girls that had once been there, playing dress-up in their mother's room. Jacqueline's gaze found a face that still looked impish, despite her twenty-five years. Freckles were scattered across the small straight nose, the cheeks retained their round rosiness, and the teeth gleamed white and strong with each peal of laughter, pouring like clear water from her full lips.

Suzanne glanced down at her sister's head and thought how perfectly Jackie's flaming red hair set off her pale complexion and deep-set emerald eyes. As usual, she had to repress her jealousy, for her own hair was mousy blond and her eyes were a nondescript shade of brown. She discounted the fact that petite Jacqueline envied her sibling's height and slim figure. As she compared their reflections, she remembered how often people had made the thoughtless remark, "It's so weird that you two are sisters. You don't look anything alike!" In her typical style, Jacqueline made a joke of it, and officially dubbed them "The Weirdsly Sisters" in a dramatic ceremony, complete with mop handles acting as swords. Then she would answer any queries about their background in that hilarious accent, saying they came from "Transyl-wania," descendants of an old and distinguished family of "vampeeres, daaalink!" The curious would be immediately distracted; the nosey, disarmed. It worked every time.

Of course, they knew they weren't sisters, but actually second cousins. They understood their genealogy well, despite its complexity: their mother, Chantale, and her husband, Colin, had adopted Jacqueline when Jocelyne, Chantale's niece, had died giving birth. When Jacqueline turned six, Suzanne was born. But their family history was no one else's business, Chantale insisted. The girls had grown up as siblings, with Chantale and Colin as Mom and Dad, and Suzanna and Paul as Grandma and Grandpa, though they were really the grandparents of Jacqueline, and Suzanne's great-aunt and uncle.

Suzanne sighed wistfully as she caught sight of a colour photograph of her grandmother and her mother, unframed, propped against the mirror. It had been taken about ten years previously, judging by the car in the picture. Even as an older woman, Suzanna had been strikingly beautiful.

"Pity I didn't inherit some of her looks, as well as her name. Still, it's kind of cool that Mom named me after her sister-in-law. I've always liked my name," Suzanne mused, not for the first time.

She picked up the photograph and tucked it surreptitiously in her back pocket, as she turned around. Jacqueline noticed that Suzanne had taken the photograph without asking her if she wanted it, but she just shrugged, equally ignoring her self-pitying remark. She placed the necklace among the other baubles strewn on the bed, as Suzanne continued to extract items from the jewelry box.

"This ugly old box covered with shells brought us such joy, didn't it?" she said softly. "Where do you suppose Mom picked up something so hideous—at a garage sale? So simple and cheap, but it kept us occupied for hours at a time. She always let us play in here, even though we would mess up her lipstick and eye shadows. Can you imagine us letting kids touch our jewelry or our makeup? At the price of it now? We wouldn't dream of it! But Mom was always relaxed about stuff like that and she loved to see us..." Her voice broke as she traced the tiny shells with her fingers.

"Would you mind if I kept the box, Jackie? It will remind me of all the fun we used to have."

"No, of course not, Suze. You take it. If anyone else found this old jewelry box, they would toss it in the dumpster in a heartbeat, but look what it means to us! I'll take some of the 'sparklies,' for the same reason. Hell, I might even be able to wear them out to dinner. It seems these old rhinestones are coming back into style. In fact, I'll pin this brooch on my jacket right now. It's kind of neat. Maybe I'll take it down to my friend at the jewelry store and have her try to find out more about it. Probably just another trinket, but it's worth a try. Maybe it's worth something," she mumbled into her turtleneck sweater, struggling to close the heavy silver clasp.

"Ouch, dammit! That pin is really sharp. I'll have to get that replaced, for sure!" She sucked on her bleeding thumb, then she raised her head and brushed the unruly red curls out of her eyes as she studied the pin in the mirror. She patted it once and tugged at it lightly, to make sure it was fastened to the material, just as she noticed her sister sorting through a shoebox full of letters they had found in one of the dresser drawers.

"Jeez, it's so tough going through Mom's stuff, isn't it? Some people just end up hiring someone to come in and take everything away for charity or to the dump. They can't handle the emotional stress. I'm so glad you are here. I don't think I could have done it on my own, if you hadn't been able to stay to help me. Thank God your boss gave you extra time off, before you have to fly back to Texas... Christ sakes, it's so unfair, Dad just passed away last year, and now Mom! I guess she just couldn't live without him. But she was only sixty-four and Dad, just sixty-six. That's nothing today—people are living to a hundred years old. It's not fair for us to be orphans so young...oh God, Jackie, sorry, but you know what I mean!" Suzanne gasped, clapping a hand across her mouth. Jacqueline just smiled.

"Yeah, in reality, I always was an orphan, but Mom and Dad were the only parents I ever knew. What a messed up family tree! We couldn't have explained it to anyone if we had wanted to. How could I tell people that my "real" mother had died in childbirth, at sixteen, and I never even knew who my father was? Mom told me that Grandma named *me* because her own daughter didn't live long enough to give me a name. So Mom asked her to name me and she chose Jacqueline, after Jacqueline Kennedy, her idol. Mom liked it, since it has a French ring to it, so it kept that tradition going, you know, with Grandpa and Mom's side being French Canadian. And then Mom told us all that stuff she found out about us having Native blood as well. Wow, Sis, we really are the Weirdslys, in more ways than one!" She placed her head on Suzanne's shoulder and squeezed her arm.

"Ain't it the truth? Thank God at least we still have each other," Suzanne sighed.

A tear slid down her cheek. Jacqueline reached across to brush it away with the back of her hand, and then lovingly tucked a strand of straight, blond hair behind her sister's ear. Leaning over to give her a peck on the cheek, she admonished her gently, "There, now, don't you start crying again, or you'll get me going and then we'll bawl all afternoon! C'mon, gimme a hug! That's better. We should take a break and have a cup of tea. Oh yeah, what are we going to do with all these old letters and papers? Man, this is going to take hours to go through. Wouldn't it be cool to find her and Dad's love letters? I'll bet she had secrets we don't even know about."

•drawing by Jeremy Mayne

Author's Note: Artist's Rendering, Typical Viking Brooch, 1000
B.C.E.

A very simple garment pin, found at L'Anse aux Meadows,
Newfoundland, Canada, helped to prove that Vikings explored
North America 500 years before Columbus, establishing settlements
and carrying on trade with the native peoples. Artifacts have
been found on Baffin Island and as far south as Maine, USA. It
is possible that the Norse travelled through Algonquin territory.
According to the ancient Vinland sagas, Freydis, daughter of Eric
the Red, visited the New World twice, and gave birth to a son at
Vinland, which may have been L'Anse aux Meadows. Whether or not
she lost a brooch is pure speculation.